Keepsake

BY THE AUTHOR OF

THE GREEN BOUGH

Keepsake

ANN RITNER

PEOPLES BOOK CLUB, CHICAGO

COPYRIGHT, 1952, BY
ANN RITNER

PRINTED IN THE
UNITED STATES OF AMERICA

This is a special edition published exclusively for the members of the PEOPLES BOOK CLUB, P. O. Box 6570A, Chicago 80, Illinois, and 228 Bloor Street West, Toronto 5, Ontario, Canada. It was originally published by J. B. Lippincott Company.

Library of Congress Catalog card number: 52-5100

Keepsake

Chapter 1

CATHY AWOKE BEFORE she was ready, nagged into consciousness by the quivery nerves—butterflies in her stomach—which attacked her when any unusual event, no matter how small, was about to take place. It was barely daylight; nobody else in the household would be awake, and she knew from experience that time dragged interminably when one was trying to push it forward, dragged uphill and then skidded downhill without rhyme or reason, so that suddenly the climax not only had been reached but passed and one was left in exactly the same state as before, except that now you were looking backward instead of forward.

She lay quite still in bed, staring up at the canopy over her head. The big bedroom began to take shape around her; the mahogany wardrobe and highboys on the opposite wall became pieces of furniture instead of ghostly forms in the gloom. There was a brisk little fire burning on her hearth; one of the housemaids must have replenished it without waking her.

She forced herself to lie motionless because if she let herself get too excited she would be sick at her stomach—it was one of her several crosses that the seat of her emotions appeared to reside unreliably in her stomach. She sighed; she wondered if she would ever conquer this unromantic weakness; if she did not, she thought, she would have to give up all idea of a gay and adventuresome life. One could not imagine the heroine of a book being sick at her stomach.

Today she had a bona-fide cause for excitement; it was the day when her Aunt Helena and Cousin Lisa were to arrive from Paris for their yearly visit to Keepsake. Cathy never had been to Paris

7

but Lisa made the trip so often that she pretended to be bored by it. Cathy, lying with her arms pressed rigidly against her sides, tried to imagine herself in Lisa's place.

First there was the going aboard a great steamship—did one take a steamship from Paris? No, from Cherbourg, Cathy thought; she skipped over that part because her knowledge of geography was lamentably hazy. But she could see the steamship coming into New York harbor very vividly, where it would be met by Cathy's father who, because he was a very great and important man, was forced to divide his time between New York and Arizona, where Keepsake was situated. Gold mines in Arizona evidently had a certain connection with affairs in the East, even the government, for Cathy's father was called quite often to Washington where he visited with Congressmen and other important officials. He even went to the White House to see the President occasionally—but here Cathy's imagination bogged down completely. When she tried to picture the President she could see only a photograph of Abraham Lincoln, the President who had freed the slaves, whose gaunt sad face did not resemble President McKinley's face at all. President Abraham Lincoln had written a beautiful letter, immortalized in an English book and in Cathy's mind forever, beginning: "May this assuage your grief." If one had a grief, Cathy thought, Mr. Lincoln's beautiful letter would surely assuage it. President McKinley's letters began: "Dear Sir"; Cathy had glanced through several of them and found them wanting.

Cathy shed a few tears now of self-pity; she would have given anything she owned at this moment to be Lisa, just for a few hours. She could see Lisa, seated between Aunt Helena and Michael Brett, Cathy's father, being driven up Fifth Avenue to the New York house to rest for a few days before continuing the rest of the trip, which was considered tiresome and wearing by sophisticated travelers. Cathy herself would have enjoyed it.

Cathy could just remember the house in New York where she had been born; it had been years since she had been there. It was not really open now; Cathy saw it sheeted and shuttered as it had been in her last glimpse of it. Michael Brett preferred it to a hotel when he was in New York; he lived with one servant on the ground floor. For Aunt Helena and Lisa other rooms would be aired and dusted, even though Aunt Helena would protest, insisting that it would be easier to go to a hotel. Her father would not hear of that; his ideas of hospitality were as expansive as all his others; he himself would see to it that rooms were made ready, servants hired, flowers ordered. And so for the two or three days that Aunt Helena and Lisa were in New York he would provide entertainment: shopping trips, dinner parties, seats at the theatre.

Cathy had one consolation: it was Aunt Helena who would take part in these festivities and not Lisa. Lisa, for all her airs, would be left behind. Aunt Helena, though she was young and pretty and gay, had very strict ideas of what a young girl could or could not do, far stricter than those of Theresa, who was Helena's older sister and Cathy's mother. Theresa had been too long outside the fashionable world, she sometimes said, to know what was expected of one inside it. She merely smiled when Helena, who was usually so languid, became animated on the subject. "But one cannot simply ignore everything," Helena would say, putting her hands to her head. She could not have been in earnest, for a few seconds later she would be talking of something else and laughing. Helena adored Theresa, and Theresa adored Helena, but more quietly.

The trip across country would be made in Michael Brett's private car, and it would be made behind drawn shades because the flat western country over which they were forced to travel gave Aunt Helena a headache. What a bore, Cathy thought falsely; her spirits began correspondingly to rise as she pictured Lisa's boredom.

Cathy sprang out of bed and in her long voluminous white cambric nightgown went to the open window and hung out, letting the fresh April morning bathe her face. She was not as innocent as she looked. She knew by now that Keepsake, on whose sprawling wings and outbuildings she gazed down, and her father, whom she loved more than anybody in the world, were regarded with awe by almost everybody who came in contact with them. They were both big, splendid, unique, overpowering. Guests reacted to both in almost exactly the same way; they exclaimed, flattered, gradually grew a little quiet and subdued. Cathy enjoyed this; she had some of her father's love for making an impression, but she knew that her enjoyment was not particularly laudable. Randy, her younger brother, never showed off; he, like their mother, simply ignored anything which intruded into his quiet busy private life. Cathy, however, was not so self-sufficient. To defend herself she had developed a flair for imitating a certain type of guest who came to Keepsake; the kind who said, "What is it, Aladdin's palace?" "More likely Brett's Folly?" "Must have cost millions." "So it did, they say, millions." "But in heaven's name, why, way out here in this wilderness?"

Cathy despised such people as her father did, but in her secret heart she envied them a little bit too because they seemed so sure of themselves. They were easily imitated. Both her father and Randy encouraged her imitations by laughing at her; even Theresa laughed, though she sometimes shook her head cautioningly. Theresa's cautions were always well founded; sooner or later Cathy, carried away by her own brilliance, was reduced to sackcloth and ashes by the retaliating performance of her stomach. Miserable and retching, Cathy had to give up all idea of becoming a great actress.

The cool and quiet of the morning dissipated these turbulent reflections. Directly below Cathy's window was a small courtyard, brick-paved. A few doves were cooing and twittering about a rainspout. Below, clustered about the outlet of the rainspout, was a family of quail. The mother quail led her brood in a formal and disciplined line to the water while the father at a little distance kept watch. All of them were confident, happy, the little lanterns on their foreheads bobbing high-spiritedly; they had no fear of the sleek black cat who lay upon the low wall beside them watching them. The cat would not be quick enough to catch all of them and they were too well organized for him to catch one of them; they knew it and the cat knew it. They drank happily, uttering their little cries, and the cat made no movement.

On either side of the courtyard stretched the side wings of the house, the guest and service wings, upon whose tiled roofs Cathy could look down since her room on the fourth floor of the main wing of the house was a story higher than either of the others. Beyond the courtyard were gardens, stretching to the low hills which rimmed the plateau; stables and servants' cottages were barely glimpsed on the left; on the right were the beginnings of the low hills with ravines gashed in their sides where scrubby transplanted olive trees and vineyards were interspersed with native live oak and manzanita.

Far beyond, in the distance, was the outline of a larger mountain range; there were five of them within view of the house. The most beautiful were the Cresta Blancas which the house faced. By stretching far out, to the extreme peril of life and limb, she could see into the service courtyard where the day was beginning. Servants were coming and going there, entering the house to build fires in fireplaces against the cool southwestern early morning, hosing the courtyards and terraces, going to and returning from their breakfasts. On another day Cathy could have put on riding clothes and gone for an early morning ride; today she felt lazy and disinclined for activity. She remained where she was, yawning and stretching now and then as the sun reached out and touched her, keeping very quiet from habit because Randy was sick, and though his room no longer adjoined hers she remembered that after one of his bad nights he sometimes was able to fall asleep toward daylight.

Stacey brought her her early morning thick black coffee, a custom which like many others had been brought to Keepsake from New Orleans. Cathy's mother and Aunt Helena had been born in New Orleans and grown up there; her father, too, once had lived in New Orleans, though he had not belonged to New Orleans aristocracy. He had belonged to one of the brash northern families who had settled in New Orleans after the War Between the States, but he had courted Theresa Durand and married her.

Cathy often sighed because this romantic upheaval had taken place, necessarily, before she was born. She had never seen her New Orleans grandfather, who had died a few years ago; but Lisa, who managed somehow to be everywhere and see everything, had seen him. Lisa said he had died with a curse on his lips, but Cathy knew Lisa well enough not to take too much stock in that. Aunt Helena's version of him as an ill, bitter, sad old man was probably more accurate. But he never had sent for Theresa nor answered her letters, and so Theresa never had returned to her home in New Orleans.

Stacey put the tray with coffee on a table, scolding all the while at finding Cathy hanging over the windowsill, half in and half out, in a way which offended Stacey from the point of view both of propriety and of personal safety. Receiving no immediate response Stacey burst into a torrent of reproach in a voice as thick and soft and black as the coffee itself, sticking out her lower lip ominously, rumbling like a thundercloud: "You get right in heah, you heah me? What kind of bringing up people going to think you have, perched out there like a monkey? . . ."

"Who is going to see me?" Cathy asked practically; she pulled in her head to look at Stacey, neat and white-turbaned.

"You fall down there on those bricks in your nightgown with your father who he is and you'll find out who is going to see you," Stacey said.

Cathy looked down at the brick pavement in the courtyard below. She pictured herself lying there, cold and white and dead, a little squashed perhaps. Would she be looking up or down, she wondered? It would be sad but horrid, four stories, ugh! She turned from the window and made a running jump into the middle of her bed, pulling the covers high about her neck and wriggling herself into a comfortable position of safety. Stacey was not to be mollified; she went on scolding as she went about the room straightening it. Cathy sipped her coffee; she changed the subject tactfully by asking: "Have you seen Randy this morning?"

"Course I've seen him."

"How is he?"

Stacey's face melted into sentimental sweetness when she spoke of her darling. "Better, bless God. Much better. And good, always good. Not worrying people to death hanging out of windows. Not acting like a savage. He's sitting up; he's going to have breakfast. Do you want yours here or are you going to get up?"

"I'm going to get up." Cathy swung slender legs out of bed and waited for Stacey, who would have been hurt if she had not, to thrust her feet into slippers. Stacey grumbled; she was getting too old to bend down, she said; that Amanda could take a lot off her mother's shoulders if she could be trusted. "I can manage without anybody perfectly well," Cathy said, but Stacey laughed scoffingly; she said she certainly would hate to see the sight Cathy would look without anybody to see to her.

To prove her point she would not allow Cathy to draw her own bath. She preceded Cathy into the long narrow bathroom which had been partitioned off from the bedroom itself, for Keepsake had been built before the days of extensive plumbing. Now each bedroom had its bathroom built into it in some way; Cathy's was built along a side wall behind curtained double French doors.

Stacey, who had skewered Cathy's soft dark hair to the top of her head, stood back finally. "You'd best come out now," she said.

Cathy, to maintain her independence a few minutes longer, lay back in the tub and splashed water over herself, but her heart was not in it.

She asked, "Is Philip still here?" Philip Langley was a young doctor and friend of the family; he had spent the night in Randy's dressing-room as he often did when Randy had a bad attack.

"He's having his breakfast. You'd better be getting out of that tub if you want some yourself."

"There's no hurry. Aunt Helena and Lisa won't be here for hours."

She and Randy and their mother had been going to drive into

Magoon to meet the train. It would have been like a party, with lunch at El Capitan, which was not very grand perhaps by Lisa's standards but which was better than nothing. But now that Randy was sick, of course the plans would have to be changed.

Stacey said, "There's hurry for me. I've got something to do besides stand here all day."

"Oh, go on, then. Send Amanda."

"Now you listen to me, Catherine Brett . . ."

"Oh, all right," Cathy said. She knew she was being disagreeable, taking out her disappointment at the upset of the day's plans on Stacey. To ask forgiveness she threw her arms about Stacey in a damp hug as she stepped from the tub. Stacey, muttering, relented enough to plant a forgiving kiss on Cathy's cheek. She had to stretch upward to do so though Cathy was not very tall, was never, it seemed, going to be very tall, for she had stopped growing in one way though not in others. Certain developments were becoming reassuringly prominent; Cathy surveyed them proudly in the long mirror before Stacey threw a towel over her. Stacey too took unabashed pride in those protuberances in private. "Yes, you're getting might proud-bosomed," she acknowledged, adding rather ambiguously, "For better or worse, women got to have them: there's no way out of that." She held Cathy's underclothes and petticoats for her and brushed her hair, and then she went out of the room leaving Cathy to finish by herself.

Philip was still breakfasting in the small dining room. He looked up as Cathy came in; he looked tired and a little quarrelsome. He said, "Good morning, your royal highness," sarcastically, and watched her while she filled her plate from the sideboard.

Sam brought her hot coffee. Sam was Stacey's cousin by marriage; nearly all the house servants at Keepsake were related to each other. "You'd better eat more than that," Sam said, treating her as a child, as everyone did. He put a chop on her plate.

"Remember your sensitive stomach," Philip warned her. Cathy's feelings were hurt; Philip's teasing often hurt her feelings lately, though she tried to pretend it did not. She pushed the plate back haughtily; Sam, ignoring her, put it into place again. "Eat it up. You'll be mighty hungry before you get back from town."

"I'm not going to town."

"Why not?" Philip asked; he sounded surprised.

"Randy can't g-g-go. It wouldn't be very n-n-nice to go off and leave him."

She seldom stuttered any more except in moments of great stress. It annoyed her excessively that she should do so now; she said, "I s-s-simply don't care anything about going."

Philip stared at her. He reached for a piece of toast and buttered it. He said, "Oh nonsense. Of course you want to go; you've been talking about it for a week. Why do you make such a thing out of everything?"

"I d-d-don't."

"You can drive in with me if you like and then come back with the others in one of the carriages."

Cathy wanted to be invited less off-handedly. She appeared to hesitate: "I'm not sure that I should."

"You could turn into a horrible little prig one of these days, you know," Philip said. He pushed back his chair; Cathy said hurriedly, "Well, if you really want me I'll go."

Philip said absently, "Don't be so silly. Eat your breakfast and stop biting your nails."

"Sometimes I hate you."

"No, you don't. I'm only teasing you."

"I don't like being teased."

"It's good for you," he said. "So don't get above yourself." He grinned at her affectionately and she gave him a weak smile in return. She could never stay angry with Philip very long, not half long enough; it was humiliating to give in so easily.

She glanced at him as she ate. Philip was very handsome; his fair hair and skin and slender build gave him a boyish look though he was quite old, twenty-seven at least. Cathy herself was seventeen and the protuberances were recent. Philip's eyes were as blue as her father's and as intense; he was the only man she had ever seen who did not somehow pale by comparison with her father.

Cathy ventured, "It will be very gay when Aunt Helena and Lisa get here, won't it?" Gay was a word which Lisa used a great deal, gay and amusing. Life in Paris was gay and amusing always, according to Lisa.

Philip snorted, and then, suddenly and unaccountably, he blushed. Cathy remembered that he had acted much the same way all last summer while Aunt Helena was here. Cathy and Lisa had sat on the stairway and laughed and whispered together at the silly way Philip had devoted himself to Aunt Helena, hanging over her chair, picking up her handkerchief, just looking at her. Last year it had seemed very funny; Cathy discovered that this year it did not seem funny at all.

She chewed thoughtfully on a small piece of meat, making it last a long time, studying Philip now and then from the corners of her eyes. Secretly she regarded Philip as her own special property. On the day when he first had appeared at Keepsake with a letter of introduction to her father, looking pale and a little dazed by the unexpected turn in his fortunes which had brought him there, and pushing back his thick fair hair with the nervous restless gesture which was habitual to him, he had appealed to Cathy's twelve-year-old imagination as a hero straight out of one of her books.

She was his special pet too in his adopted family; everyone in the household recognized that, even though he bullied and criticized her sometimes. He let her attach herself to his heels like a puppy; he confided in her; he went out of his way to provide treats for her; he allowed her to adore him, and he made her the repository of his moods, good and bad. She, in her turn, had an intuitive understanding that his occasional displays of nervous temperament were caused by dissatisfaction with his life rather than a personal grievance. He was her dear dear Philip no matter how he behaved; recently, however, she had grown more susceptible to criticism and readier to take offense. She occasionally flared into temper or burst into tears; Philip met these outbursts with a blank look of surprise. "For heaven's sake, you always used to be a cheerful reasonable little thing," he said once. "What's happened to you?" Cathy herself could not account for these variances in her behavior; her feeling for Philip was the same as before, but she herself in the bewildering process of growing up must be different. At any rate she found herself bristling now and then with barbed defenses. She looked back wistfully to the days when she had taken Philip's perfection for granted.

Cathy finished her breakfast and went upstairs. Randy was sitting up in bed. Theresa sat beside him; both of them looked up and smiled at Cathy as she came in.

"You look very nice," Cathy's mother said; she could make one feel one looked nice just by saying so, perhaps just because she herself was so beautiful. She adjusted the watered silk sash about Cathy's waist with quick deft fingers and asked, "Are you going in with Philip to meet the train?"

"I don't know. He asked me. Shall I?"

"Don't you want to?" Randy asked, going directly to the heart of the matter.

"Not particularly. I mean, I don't mind staying if you would

15

like me to read to you or something."

"Read to me?" Randy looked astounded, since he had long been reading books with words which Cathy could not pronounce, much less understand. He said hastily, "It's very kind of you to offer."

"Randy won't be lonely," Theresa said. "He is feeling much better and he is going to be allowed to get up later in the day."

"Well, then . . ."

Suddenly Cathy was crying without knowing why. The tears simply surged to the surface and brimmed over, and she was making a silly childish face and sobbing against Randy's pillow that nothing was wrong, she was just worried about Randy and a little upset, they weren't to pay any attention to her. The two of them, quiet, alike, their emotions more deeply submerged, were loving and sympathetic; they put protective arms about her and told her they loved her, and teased and cajoled her a little, ever so gently. She was given to occasional outbursts of this kind so nobody was shocked or wounded; they knew that presently she would be laughing. And presently she was, not able to imagine what had come over her. "Everything has seemed wrong side up all morning, I don't know why. It isn't the morning, it's me."

Her mother kissed her as she was leaving and said, "Try not to give way to your feelings, dear. Or else what will happen to you when something really big comes along?"

Randy, so much younger, gave her a sympathetic look. Randy understood, perhaps because he was sick so much, that when nothing really big ever happened to you it was difficult to be indifferent to the small things which did.

Cathy tied her hat, a large leghorn with black velvet streamers, under her chin, and sat in the hall waiting for Philip. The hall, called the Great Hall, was one which visitors always exclaimed over; it was enormous, rectangular in shape, and with a vast expanse of shining marble floor. There was a great branching stairway at the back; the wall behind the wide landing was of stained glass, the other walls hung with tapestry; the light filtering through had a soft subdued radiance, like a church. The hall ceiling was painted with fat cherubim and angels in a blue sky with white clouds, and there were five crystal and gold chandeliers hanging along its length. Between the rows of arched doorways leading to the formal downstairs rooms the walls were of raised plaster picked out with gold; all the double doors were closed this morning as they usually were when Michael Brett was away from home, for during his absence the large formal rooms were seldom used.

It worried Cathy because her father, who liked beauty and elegance so well, must surely have expected something a little more elegant in the way of a daughter. He did not say so; he assured her often that she suited him exactly as she was and most of the time she passionately believed him.

She sat up very straight on one of the great carved chairs ranged along the wall. She thought: a great man's daughter, like Caesar's wife, must be above reproach.

She felt tall and rather stately. She walked up and down the length of the hall several times, trying to swish her skirts, which were neither long enough nor stiff enough to swish. She abandoned the attempt and instead ran and slid, as she had done since she was a child, along the delightfully shining slippery surface.

Sam, coming to fetch her, was watching her with a strange expression on his ugly wrinkled brown face when she turned her head and saw him. He said, "Look at that. What kind of behavior for a young lady is that, I'd like to know?"

Sam, like Stacey, believed in keeping up appearances even when there was no one to see. He said, "People in the Capitol going to shake their heads, going to be mighty disappointed, that's what they're going to be."

"People in what Capitol?"

"King and Queen of England, what they going to think? Never had anything sashshaying up to them like that!"

Sam, Stacey, Hester, Rachel; all of them seemed to envision a purple future for Cathy, with the practical intent, she suspected, of teaching her manners.

Cathy asked, "Sam, do you think I'll ever be pretty?"

"No, I don't imagine so. I imagine you'll just look like a picked chicken all the rest of your life. Least you can do is learn to act pretty."

Cathy made a face at him. "Anyhow, I'm not fat, like Lisa."

"Miss Lisa is going to be pretty enough one of these days, mighty pretty."

Everybody said that. Everybody, so long as Cathy could remember, had said that Lisa was going to be a regular beauty one of these days. Cathy couldn't understand it.

"What makes you say that?"

Sam pursed his lips. "You can always tell," he said.

"Well, I can't."

"Must be that you don't want to see, then." Sam gazed at her wisely, obliquely, and then added, relenting: "She isn't going to be as pretty as Miss Helena was, though. And nobody in the whole world could be as pretty as Miss Theresa was."

Sam had known Cathy's mother and Aunt Helena when they were girls; he had been a houseman in their father's house. He could be coaxed sometimes to tell of their parties and beaux, things which still existed for Cathy only in her imagination. He would never tell of the quarrel which had taken place when Michael Brett had come for Theresa, pushing past the man at the door who had been told to turn him away, and Theresa, leaving all her clothes and her mother's jewels and her old life, had descended the stairway from her room and put her arm in Michael's and had gone away with him.

Cathy thrilled to this story. Aunt Helena, who had been sobbing on her bed the whole time with a pillow over her ears to keep out the sound of angry voices, was the only one who would tell it to her.

Chapter 2

THERE WAS THE usual knot of onlookers on the station platform. Cathy, clutching her hat, did her best to make a dignified descent from the light buggy in which Philip had driven them. She knew that the interest displayed was for her father and that she was only a substitute. Nevertheless, flustered, she did the wrong thing as usual; she jumped out of the buggy before it had stopped moving and tripped and nearly fell. Philip, furious, was shouting commands at her; the horses reared and plunged; a number of hands reached out to help her. Cathy righted herself, clutched her hat, smiled, and prayed for divine help so that she would not disgrace Philip, her father, and the whole world by being sick at her stomach on the station platform.

The divine help must have been vouchsafed her, for she began to feel better. A number of people were coming forward to speak to her and shake her hand: "Howdy, Miss Brett." She had regained her confidence and was even beginning to hold a small court when Philip, still shouting instructions to several boys tying the horses, jumped down beside her and put an end to the illusion of dignity. He said, "Never do a thing like that again, Cathy Brett, unless you want to break your fool neck. You might have been killed."

She rallied her forces enough to say haughtily, "It would have been your fault if I had. Father says you drive like a Judas."

"Like a Jehu, I presume you mean."

She was deflated, but only momentarily, for Philip laughed, his good humor restored. Also the people around them were pushing forward again, and because it seemed so kind of them to appear

19

eager to see her and shake hands she put her mind to remembering everyone's name as her father did. Her father said this was one of the penalties for being a celebrity, but Cathy did not think of it as a penalty; she could not help feeling flattered and pleased. Philip stood beside her, his hands in his pockets; she looked up to see him staring down at her with a little smile on his face. She asked, "What's the matter?" and he said, "Nothing. I was just thinking how well you do it."

Cathy's moment of glory was brief enough, for down the track a train whistled, which meant that Michael Brett's private car was arriving, and the attention of the small crowd turned in the direction of the sound.

The train steamed up to the platform, steps were put down, and the conductor and a porter in a white coat stood on either side of the steps with arms extended upward. There was a little pause, during which the onlookers stood immobile, as if they were watching a play. Cathy stepped forward; she was trembling now from nerves and excitement.

The first person to alight from the train was Nola, Aunt Helena's maid. Then came Helena Minard herself, young-looking and beautiful as ever in her Paris suit with huge leg-o-mutton sleeves and her tiny hat trimmed with bird wings on either side and a spotted veil drawn tightly over her face, under her chin, and fastened to her hat with jeweled pins. Several of the onlookers became so overwhelmed by this vision that they turned and spat fervently on the ground. Helena both ignored and included her audience; she smiled graciously at everybody while going straight to Cathy and hugging her, at the same time holding out a hand to Philip, saying in her warm exciting voice how good it was to see them, how adorable it was of them to have made the tiresome drive from Keepsake to meet the train.

Then came Lisa, poised on the bottom step in order to draw attention to herself before she allowed the porter to assist her to the platform. It could only be Lisa, but it was a Lisa who had changed so much during the intervening year that Cathy stared at her in amazement and dismay.

Lisa had taken complete advantage of Cathy by becoming a young lady. Lisa was dressed in a faille traveling suit, fitted tightly at the waist and flaring out in a dashing little peplum. The skirt was long instead of shoe-top length like Cathy's childish linen dress, so long in fact that it touched the ground in front and actually trailed a little in back where a fullness was gathered. Lisa's hair no longer was clubbed in the back under a big bow; it was drawn into a huge chignon on her neck with a fringe of soft ringlets covering her forehead. Her tiny silk hat was no bigger than a saucer; it had two wired velvet bows which stood up like pointed rabbit ears. And, final insult, she was wearing a veil, only a small veil it was true, the suggestion of a veil really, but still a veil.

Nola opened a ruffled silk parasol and handed it to her mistress. Helena Minard exclaimed Heavens yes, this sun was absolutely devastating to the complexion; Lisa must put up her parasol instantly too. "Cathy, dear love, you should have brought one even though your hat is so nice and wide."

Nobody was wearing wide hats in Paris this spring, Lisa said. She kissed Cathy's cheek and glanced out of the side of her eyes at Philip. Philip stared at her coldly; he and Lisa always quarreled, so that there was nothing unusual in his aloofness, but Lisa pouted a little, almost as if she had expected a different type of greeting this year, possibly in recognition of the fact that she had put up her hair and wore a long skirt. She kept glancing at Philip, and when Philip paid no attention to her she whispered to Cathy in a loud affected undertone that Philip's manners became worse each year and that she for one found him impossible.

Philip heard and glared at her. It was soothing to Cathy to have Lisa bear the brunt of Philip's displeasure; Cathy nearly laughed aloud until she saw that Lisa had intended Philip to hear.

Cathy reverted to childhood and made a face of derision at Lisa. Philip caught her at it; he asked irritably: "What in the world are you doing?"

"I h-h-have something in my eye."

Lisa laughed aloud. Philip scowled; Helena Minard came to Cathy's rescue by gracefully gathering her skirts in one gloved hand and saying that they must get started for Keepsake at once.

The carriages which were to take them and the luggage had arrived and were lined beside the dusty courthouse square opposite. Helena was assisted into the one which contained her special driver; she refused gayly but firmly Philip's low-voiced but urgent invitation that she accompany him. "In that little doctor's gig? Never! Carlos understands me, that I'm an old woman and nervous; besides when he goes too fast I can prod him in the back."

"You can prod me in the back if you like."

Lisa laughed aloud again and Philip, stung, stepped backward. Nola took the coveted place beside Helena Minard; she was already opening the bottle of cologne to be used when the road got too dusty or the sun too hot. Aunt Helena's quick voice volleyed instructions even as the carriage drew away: "You have the jewel-case? Yes, good . . . some cologne on my handkerchief if you please . . . *mon dieu*, this sun. Goodbye, my darlings, for a little while; Philip will look after you; don't drive too fast, Philip, but they will be safe with you, I know."

Philip looked a little foolish; he obviously had not intended to drive anyone if he could not drive Aunt Helena. "Well, get in," he said, when his buggy was brought up. Lisa managed to get in first, which placed her beside Philip, with Cathy on the outside. It was a tight squeeze; Lisa made it even tighter by spreading out her skirt and moaning that her dress would be ruined.

"Maybe you had better go in one of the carriages, then," Philip suggested. "Yes, why don't you, Cathy?" Lisa said, as if the suggestion had been made exclusively to Cathy. "It isn't my dress that's taking up so much room," Cathy said.

Philip glanced from one to the other impatiently; he said caustically that if they were quite ready they would get started. Lisa tried to create a little flurry in imitation of Aunt Helena by dropping her handkerchief, rummaging in her purse for cologne which she could not find, and complaining about the dust. Philip interrupted these proceedings by starting off with a jerk and the horses trotted briskly down the street.

The day was very warm now; the sky a hard blue and the sun fiercely glaring. Once outside of town they drove across flat dry country for several miles before entering a canyon. There was a wide shallow stream on the left, its pebbled bottom clearly seen through the pure water. There were more trees here, live oak and scrubby pine, with here and there cottonwoods and elms.

Lisa asked for a drink of water.

"I can see you are going to be a nuisance!" Philip exclaimed, but he halted the horses and took the tin cup from its place on the dashboard.

When the drive was resumed Lisa began a recital of the marvelous time they had just had in New York. "Uncle Michael met us at the boat and had the house filled with flowers for us though it isn't properly open. He took us everywhere, to the theatre, driving, shopping; it was terribly exciting." Lisa glanced at Cathy and said what a pity it was that Cathy hadn't been there.

Cathy stated falsely that she had no desire to be anywhere other than just where she was.

"I don't suppose you even remember living in New York."

"I remember it perfectly." This was not strictly true. There had been a time when they had spent winters in the New York house, coming to Keepsake only in summer, but then there had been the terrible winter when Randy had been kidnapped and though he had been returned unharmed, not even frightened, they had set off immediately in the middle of the night for Keepsake, something in the manner, Cathy romantically thought looking back, of Joseph's and Mary's flight into Egypt. She could remember that it had been dark except for moving lights; she could remember her mother's white still face, her father's strong arms carrying her because she was still very young. There had been a carriage ride and then a train ride—the last Cathy had ever taken—days and days on the train because that was how long it took to get to Keepsake. They had not intended to stay at Keepsake all winter, because it was regarded as remote and isolated and lonely, and there were often severe winter storms which cut it off from the rest of the world. But somehow they had stayed; each year the return to New York had been postponed though always for a different reason. When they got a little older they would go, Cathy's mother said, or when Randy's health was better. Michael, of course, had to be there a great deal of the time and Cathy at first had worried for fear someone might kidnap him in their absence. Her father had laughed loudly enough at this idea to dispel her fears, and indeed he was so big and powerful that the thought seemed ridiculous.

Little by little, though Sam and Stacey had told her to be good and not ask questions, Cathy had learned that it had been enemies of her father who had kidnapped Randy. It was hard for Cathy to believe that there could be people in the world who were his enemies when everybody in her own small world loved him so deeply: her mother, she and Randy, the servants, the people in the countryside; guests, even the most splendid ones, hung on his every word and gesture. He was so splendid himself, so vital, so kind; no, she could not help thinking that the whole thing must have been a hideous mistake.

"Of course you may be going there soon," Lisa said. Cathy roused herself from her thoughts and said, "What?"

"Don't say what in that blunt way. Say pardon, or something of the sort."

Philip inexcusably laughed.

"I'll say what I choose."

23

"You get careless living way out here. You'll have to begin to think of your manners one of these days."

Cathy protested hotly, "My manners are as good as yours." She intercepted a look between Philip and Lisa which startled her; Philip was accepting Lisa almost as an adult. Cathy asked, "Why will I?"

"Well, you won't be here forever."

"Where will I be, pray, Miss?"

"Well, somewhere. Uncle Michael is a very important man. Even more important now that he's going to be Vice President or whatever it is."

"It isn't Vice President!"

"Well, something in the government. Everybody is talking about it."

Philip slapped the horses with the reins, urging them on. He became very interested suddenly in their progress and he no longer glanced sideways at Lisa as he had been doing. Lisa of course was ignorant; she always got things wrong. Cathy's father had been appointed by the President to an important post in the government but something had gone wrong with the appointment; Cathy stared off into space coldly, having no desire to discuss the subject with Lisa.

Lisa chatted on. She was unconscious of nuances in the feelings of others: Cathy's coldness and Philip's sudden absorption in his driving were lost on her. They passed the lodge house where the lodge keeper came out and waved to them. Even at Keepsake, because of the long ago kidnapping and the vague mysterious enemies, there were men watching over the great square piece of land, colored purple on the map, belonging to Michael Brett. Cathy knew what Lisa did not know, however, that Michael Brett, so successful in everything else, was unsuccessful in politics. It infuriated him: he could not bear to be thwarted in any of his ambitions. In Cathy's presence he had called himself the maker of kings who could not himself be king.

"There's the lake," Lisa called excitedly, as if a lake could be lost. "Oh, it's wonderful to be here. It's a terrifically exciting place, really, no matter what people say."

"What do people say?"

"Oh you know, that it's so far away, all that."

Philip laughed again. He said that Lisa had the advantage over all of them by having a one-track mind; he stopped looking at the horses and looked at Lisa again and there was a funny little smile on his face. Cathy did not try to decipher his meaning or the meaning of the smile; she supposed he found Lisa amusing now that she pretended to be grown up.

Government appointments, even those made by the President, had to be approved by the body of men called the Senate. This particular Senate appeared to be in no hurry to approve Cathy's father's appointment; since March there had been various delays and postponements. The Senate must be a brave body of men to risk Michael Brett's impatience and wrath; they would end by doing what he wanted, Cathy was sure. When she tried to picture the Senators, she saw them all sitting in a box, rather like the foolish jurors in *Alice in Wonderland*.

They were nearing the plateau. There was always a thrilling quality to Cathy in the first view of her home after one of her rare absences from it. She felt then as if she were sharing her father's feelings on the day when he first had envisioned it.

She knew the story so well, how he had been exploring the country on horseback, lonely for Theresa who was in New York because he never permitted her to accompany him on his mining expeditions. He himself had enjoyed intervals of the rough life in the mining expeditions and still did occasionally, but Theresa must be surrounded by beauty and elegance; he would not have it otherwise. But he was lonely for her because he had to spend a great deal of his time in the West where his mines were located—as now he had to spend time in the East where other interests were located—and he knew that Theresa even then disliked New York, and thinking of her he had ridden out on the plateau. The plateau was like a natural amphitheatre: at its back were the low hillsides forming a background like the setting on a stage. It faced a wide sunny valley, rimmed in by the distant cone-shaped and purple-shadowed spires of the Cresta Blancas. Michael Brett had seen his house right on that spot like a vision and there he had built it.

That was how Keepsake had come into being. The house appeared now, a great structure of white stone with stately fluted columns. With a true flair for the spectacular Michael Brett had placed his house so that the first view of it was all-encompassing: the ground sloped imperceptibly toward the hills in back and the house stood on its crest.

The effect of the formal stately façade, glittering white in the sun with its graceful side wings following the contour of the dark mountains behind it, was startlingly beautiful. Later, with the meandering of the carriage lane through the trees, the first complete picture was cut off, to reappear at intervals in different perspective and more solid structure. Gradually the details came into focus; the smooth slender pillars, the stone balustrades, the figures carved in bas-relief over the long arched windows.

"I can't imagine what I'll do with myself all summer," Lisa sighed, thus breaking the spell. She ignored the fact that she had spent every summer at Keepsake as long as she could remember.

"You needn't have come, you know, if you find it so dull," Cathy said fiercely. Lisa said, "Ooh, la, la," and Philip chuckled.

Later in the day Lisa was in her bedroom, which this year was the one adjoining Cathy's, with a dressing-room between.

Lisa was running about the room in camisole and petticoats, admiring everything. She called to Cathy to come in. "Won't we have a sizzling time off here by ourselves after everyone thinks we're asleep?"

"A what?"

"A sizzling time. It's what everybody says this year."

"A sizzling time doing what?" Cathy inquired bluntly.

"Oh, all kinds of sizzling things. At school we play cards under a table with a blanket draped over it to hide the light. Or we talk."

"About what?"

"Oh, all kinds of things," Lisa repeated herself airily. She went to a window, pointing out the view as if it belonged to her and Cathy never had seen it before. "Look, I can see the Santa Marias from here. I've always liked them better than the Cresta Blancas. And the little summer house."

"What kind of things would we talk about?"

"All kinds," Lisa said carelessly.

Cathy asked, "Could you teach me to play cards?"

"Well, two-handed, I don't know. It has to be for money to be any fun. Do you have any money?"

"A little."

"Oh well, I'll loan you some." There was this to be said for Lisa; she was generous. She said, "I usually lose; I imagine you are the type who will win."

"I wouldn't want to do that if it was your money," Cathy said conscientiously.

Lisa shrugged; it made little difference to her whose money it was. She bragged: "One night I lost five hundred francs. I would have killed myself then and there except that was the night the candle set fire to the blanket."

"What happened then?"

"It was terrible; you should have seen the excitement!" Lisa dramatically launched into a story which Cathy only half believed. Nevertheless she was drawn into it; she listened as if she completely believed it. She transferred the story from the Academy in France to Keepsake and shuddered with horror; in the new story it went without saying that Cathy and not Lisa was the heroine. It was Cathy's quick thinking which saved Keepsake from the flames which sprang up vividly and wickedly, licking with forked tongues at the window hangings, racing from one room to another. Cathy, bold and desperate, refused to leave the burning house; she coolly, in the face of disaster, organized the kind of fire brigade she had read about. The servants lined up at her instruction, passing buckets of water from one to another until the last flame was quenched while Lisa stood by weeping and wringing her hands, helpless.

"Do you still bite your nails?" Lisa asked, interrupting this agreeable fantasy.

Cathy was forced to admit in all honesty that she did.

"Not quite so bad, though," Lisa said, inspecting them. Yes, truth compelled one to admit that Lisa was generous and amiable always, which Cathy certainly was not. Lisa made careless bequests of all her possessions when the impulse moved her, while Cathy's attachment to anything which was hers was so strong that sometimes as self-punishment she forced herself to give something away.

"How do you like my La Pliante?" Lisa asked.

"What's that?"

Lisa stood up and turned around to show how she went out in the back; she sat down again and described La Pliante for Cathy's benefit. It was an undergarment made of six pieces of steel attached to one's underskirt, almost like a hoopskirt except that the fullness was all in one place. "Isn't it sizzling?" Lisa asked; before Cathy could gather her resistance to meet this attack Lisa said she had another one in a trunk and would give it to Cathy. That ended Cathy's opposition to La Pliante and even to Lisa for the present; Cathy became the grateful recipient of favors.

Lisa's superior beauty one could endure. Cathy did not mind that so much as she did Lisa's ability to get what she wanted; or to want what she had, which was perhaps even better. When Lisa grew old enough she was going to have dozens of young men fall hopelessly in love with her just as they now did with Aunt Helena. Only instead of being kind to them and sending them away to love someone else as Aunt Helena did, Lisa was going to laugh at them and drive them mad.

"Philip just left," Lisa said. "You should have stayed on the terrace with us. We had a very gay time, talking and laughing. Philip isn't so bad; he can be quite charming when he wants to be."

"I suppose he was hoping to see Aunt Helena. Don't you remember how he looked at her last year?"

"That was last year," Lisa said; she smiled.

Chapter 3

HELENA MINARD SAT at her dressing-table, several days after her arrival at Keepsake. The frames of the mirrors and doors in this room, as in the sitting-room next to it, were decorated with tiny exquisite replicas of a feminine toilette, hand mirrors and high jeweled combs; there was a frieze of cupids holding garlands along the walls. The extravagant décor of this suite, reserved always for her, had the effect of making Helena feel pampered and lazy, an ideal way in her opinion for a pretty woman to feel.

She looked up to see Theresa's reflection in the mirror. "Tessa! I didn't see you come in."

Theresa, laughing, said, "No wonder, your eyes were half closed."

"I was wallowing in luxury, as always, when I come to Keepsake."

"Will you have coffee or do you wish to continue to wallow?"

"I'll have coffee." Helena, rising, followed Theresa into the sitting-room.

She smiled a moment later; discontent, like other emotions, made lines in one's face; the only thing to do was to achieve as nearly as possible the blank look of complete idiocy. Helena Minard chuckled; she was far from an idiot, though it was the role which life apparently had chosen for her if she was to be happy, and she was determined to be happy. She drew in the smoke from her cigarette with sensuous enjoyment; she smoked incessantly in private as a sop to that rebellious part of herself which never would quite be stilled though smoking for women was still regarded as somewhat *déclassée*, particularly in America.

Helena Minard was a conventional woman, to her own amusement: "But red-headed women, *surtout*, must avoid being conspicuous," she excused herself when she was seized, in spite of herself, with fears that she was growing vain and shallow. She knew her moments of panic, and because these resulted in wakeful nights and threats to a youthful appearance she leaned more and more on the diversion of small pleasures: long narrow black Russian cigarettes smoked through a holder so that slender white fingers were not stained, a glass of sherry before lunch and dinner, several glasses in fact, but nothing stronger, because Helena well knew that that particular refuge from the boredom of growing middle-aged could be most harmful of all to the looks. She carried on light flirtations, very light, because falling in love was a luxury which she had long since ceased to permit herself.

"You seem very gay this morning," Theresa said; she placed Helena's coffee cup on a small table and held her own, stirring it lightly.

"It's good to be here," Helena exclaimed in contentment; she and Theresa exchanged looks of the deep tenderness and affection which they had for each other. "It's good to have you," Theresa said. "Very very good."

The two sisters smiled at each other. There was a resemblance between them in spite of the differences in their temperament and coloring; they both had the same finely bred look of race, the same delicately chiseled features and long slender hands and feet, the same erect carriages. Theresa's hair was deep mole-brown; it was drawn back into a great loose knot low on her neck while Helena's bright hair was done in elaborate puffs and swirls.

"I think I only really breathe when I am here," Helena said. "Life everywhere else is so hectic; you have no idea, Theresa."

"I think I can imagine."

"Still . . ."

"Yes, still . . ." Theresa said; she smiled.

"Well, it can be exciting. We had, for example, a most exciting time in New York. Michael took us everywhere; between times I shopped and shopped and shopped. Heaven, but it is marvelous to have a brother-in-law with an inexhaustible supply of money."

Theresa laughed outright.

"Going about with Michael is just like going about with a brass band," Helena said. "He always attracts attention and everybody knows him and wants to be noticed by him. Tessa?"

"Yes, dearest?"

Helena raised herself on one elbow; she asked, "What do you think of it? I've waited for you to say something but you haven't and I really can't keep quiet any longer."

"The appointment? I consider it a great honor, of course."

"Ah, don't tease me."

"I don't mean to tease you. What is there to think or say until it is confirmed?"

"But a presidential appointment! Even with this delay it is a *fait accompli* surely?"

"One would think so, but still . . . What does Michael say?"

"He's furious, I'm sure, though he treats the whole thing as a joke, on the surface."

"A joke?"

"He's concerned mostly for you, I think. He knows how you hate the kind of notoriety a thing like this is bound to stir up." Helena scanned Theresa's face anxiously; it was a beautiful face, a little too withdrawn in repose; though delicately modeled it was strong-featured, with high cheekbones and a nose which sloped directly from forehead to tip without indentation at its bridge. People likened it to a Greek cameo.

Theresa was smiling and Helena, relieved, lay back and blew smoke rings at the ceiling. Theresa said, "He need not worry about me, by now I should have become accustomed to the brass band."

Helena, laughing, agreed: "One would think so. But with Michael the band has a tendency always to become bigger and more splendid."

"And now it is going to take us to Washington."

"You'll like that, Theresa. Washington has a great deal more *ton* than New York and you'll be First Lady without difficulty."

"We must reserve that honor for the wife of the President, surely?"

"No, Michael will see to it, I'm sure, that you will be."

"You have Cathy's faith that Michael can work miracles."

"Yes, so I have. And besides, nobody can hold a candle to you. . . ."

"We will hope then that the President's wife is prepared to take a back seat."

Helena, animated now, was excitedly planning: "You will have to find a house."

"I believe Michael has already bought one."

"Good; it will be much the best place for Cathy to come out.

Perhaps Lisa could have a second party there too; it would be an excellent thing for her to make connections in diplomatic circles. Cathy is the one though who will really have her head turned with attention."

"Yes, poor Cathy."

"Why poor Cathy? Everybody else will be dying of envy when she makes her appearance."

"Simply for that reason, I suppose."

"Nonsense, Theresa; she will enjoy every minute of it."

"Enjoy being fawned on and flattered and envied, hated even, just because she is Michael Brett's daughter?"

Helena said uneasily, "Yes, well, a little of that is inevitable for her, Theresa."

"If one could be sure it would be only a little. It seems almost wicked to plunge her into a life which will demand so much character of her before she has had a chance to form her own."

"She already has a great deal more character than Lisa. She's better educated and Keepsake has provided a somewhat more sophisticated background for her than most girls have—no, that's true, Theresa, though I know you have fought against it, and actually I think it's a good thing. Still, a year in school uniform looking like dozens of other girls might make the transition easier."

"She is rather old to be thrust into school, and as you say, used to a different way of life."

"Not so different as it soon will be."

"I'll speak to her about it."

"She will do whatever you suggest, Tessa."

"I know, but she must learn to make her own judgments."

Helena shrugged; she regarded the judgments of young girls as valueless.

There was a little silence which Helena broke: "How furious it would have made Papa if he had foreseen Michael's success and Raymond's lack of it."

Theresa, startled, said, "It would not have made any difference to him."

"Papa? My dear Tessa, Papa did not disdain wordly success, far from it."

"Randy is like him, don't you think?"

"A little. Not so arrogant, though."

"I was arrogant too."

"I wish I had been. It required arrogance to stand up to Papa."
"Ah well. That's all over and done with, long ago."
"Is anything?"
"What do you mean?"
"This happens and therefore that. One thing leads to another." Helena shrugged apologetically: "I found a new wrinkle this morning; that always makes me philosophical. And I touch up my hair now; had you noticed?"
"Your beautiful hair, must you?"
"You never change. Except that you've lost weight, haven't you, Tessa?"
"I thought that was to be desired."
"Troubled about anything?"
"A number of things, naturally."
"In a way it's a great tragedy that Michael could not have been only moderately successful."
"Being moderately successful would be failure to Michael."
"You are thinner, though. Much too thin now that I really look at you." Helena hesitated; she asked, "You haven't let yourself be upset by some stray foolish piece of gossip about Michael, have you?"
"We are spared stray gossip at Keepsake; it's one of the nice things about it."

Helena glanced sharply at Theresa; there was no irony on Theresa's face. Long ago Theresa had chosen to withdraw from life rather than be disillusioned by it. She had acquired at that time a face which betrayed no emotion when she did not choose for it to do so.

Naturally passionate, aggressive, a little arrogant, she had deliberately repressed these traits in her character. Now, faced with Michael's new desire to enter public life and its possible effect on her life and her children's, she needed the support of some of these characteristics.

She was worldly enough so that she was seldom shocked by human behavior; she was human enough to safeguard herself by avoiding certain aspects of it in the person she loved most.

If Michael had allowed her to do so she would have accompanied him into those first mining camps; she would have endured discomfort and dreary boarding houses; she would have gloried in meeting disappointment and real hardships. Instead she had been left behind while Michael had gone off to get rich. He became richer and richer, until their riches sometimes seemed to her like a great octopus with tentacles groping ceaselessly for something new to draw into them.

Theresa Brett had no reason to like great wealth and she had every reason to fear it. She had loathed New York, whose society seemed to her crude and rootless and founded entirely upon money. As Michael's wealth grew Theresa withdrew into herself more and more. She was still in love; she was a person who loved once and without qualification. Though she looked proud and serene, she was as turbulent and passionate in her way as Michael was in his, and it was this violent emotional capacity which had brought them together and which sustained their love through everything. Michael's love was active, throbbing, vital, and Theresa was aware that it was his touch which had brought her to life, that without it she would have grown more elegant and imperious and haughty through the years, like so many Durand spinsters in which the family once had abounded.

She did not flinch from his many but light infidelities; she had been brought up in a tradition which accepted certain male weaknesses for what they were. She did flinch from the sharpness and ruthlessness which began to accompany his business dealings.

They had climbed up, up, up, to fantastic heights. Theresa's sense of guilt seldom left her. She had been afraid most of all in those first days for the children. The tall iron fences behind which they must play, the bodyguards hired to watch over them day and night, seemed to her barbarous. The threats from anonymous letters haunted her; she was never really free from fear.

Michael had laughed at her and reassured her. It was an era when the few fabulously wealthy families in New York accepted bodyguards for their children rather as a badge of success. Michael said, "Never mind; it won't hurt them. We'll take them out West where they can learn to be democratic between times."

The climax had come in the winter when Randy was kidnapped. The family had fled to Keepsake after the kidnapping, and since then, whether consciously or unconsciously, she had found reasons for remaining there. It was the environment in which her talents found most scope, and Michael did not object to the arrangement since she did not; it was like the early days of the mining camps except that positions were reversed. He rather liked the idea of keeping home and family inviolate from his other affairs, shielded from the blare of publicity which accompanied most of his actions.

He brought only honored guests to Keepsake, including now and then one who needed to be influenced by cajolery into accepting the truth that there was another side to Michael Brett than the rapacious beast of industry which it sometimes pleased newspapers to call him.

At Keepsake Michael was the gentleman farmer, the lover, the husband and father, the compassionate and kindly squire. He was completely happy always, for a short space of time.

Later, Cathy consulted with Randy about the exact status of her father's future position in the government. Randy knew everything, and what he did not know he knew how to look up in the *Encyclopaedia Britannica*. The *Encyclopaedia*, like the dictionary, was seldom used by Cathy for informative purposes, though now and then she perused both simply for pleasure. They offered up delightful and unexpected gifts of information: what a yak was, for instance. Cathy had invented an imaginary yak which she once had kept for a pet; she concealed this kind of foolishness from everyone but Randy.

Now she asked, "Is it important? The appointment?"

"Of course. Very important."

"I don't suppose it has a title or anything like that."

"What kind of title?"

"Well, the Honorable, or something like that."

Randy laughed and Cathy reluctantly laughed too. Randy was a slight handsome boy whose delicate features bore signs of frailty in the hollow of his temples and the dark smudges of shadow under his deep-set eyes. He had a high intelligent forehead; the strong noble bone structure of his head seemed indeed almost too heavy a burden for his slender neck to carry. His face was stamped with the look of sweetness of a patient nature which had known a great deal of suffering and learned to surmount it. At the same time there was a quirk of humor in the corner of his mouth.

He was the acknowledged student of the family; though it was summer and vacation time he spent as many hours as he was permitted, because of his health, in the schoolroom. Cathy, less industrious, was present less often and then usually because she was in search of companionship rather than knowledge. Philip, who was tutoring Randy in science and mathematics, was quite often to be found there; perhaps for that reason Lisa had begun to drift in and out of the room with suspicious frequency too.

"No, I don't think so," Randy said.

"It would be nice, though. I'd like to be called the Honorable; the Honorable Catherine. You can laugh if you want to."

"I thought it was Father who was to have the title."

"We would have to have one too, if he did. It will be exciting though, even without the title, won't it? In Washington?"

"Yes, very," Randy agreed, but he looked slightly troubled, as Theresa always did, at the mention of leaving Keepsake.

Chapter 4

THE SUMMER WAS not without its responsibilities; this year Cathy was being initiated into household management and accounts.

Today things had not gone well; Cathy, failing to concentrate, made a mistake in figures and came out with three thousand napkins lost between laundry and linen closets.

"At any rate you do things on a large scale, like your father," Theresa said; she threw back her head and laughed.

"Why, exactly, do we bother with it?" Cathy asked. "We could buy more if they were lost; we have all the money in the world, haven't we?"

"Is that what Lisa says?"

"Well, she says we have a great deal."

"So we have. The thing one has to learn is that money is a great responsibility as well as a great privilege."

"I suppose so," Cathy said.

"I want you to be so strong," Teresa said—strangely, for what possible reason could there be for Cathy, who was never ill, to be any stronger? "So that you'll be prepared for whatever happens to you." Theresa smiled reassuringly.

"What is likely to happen to me?" Very little had happened so far, and counting napkins did not seem adequate preparation for the romance which Cathy hoped was lurking in her future.

"That we don't know. But something is bound to."

Cathy went back to the accounts. Theresa inspired one to try to be strong and good because she was so strong and good herself. Her courage and poise were unshakeable; Cathy once had seen her dress a frightful wound in a man's shoulder when his gun had gone off and there was no one else there to attend to it; another time she had loaded a gun herself and had shot a mountain lion which somehow had gained access to one of the patios and resisted, snarling and spitting, all efforts to get him out again. That had been an exciting day; Cathy wished that days like that happened more often. Theresa was never lazy or vain; she could do anything she wanted to do, even to keeping strict control of her quick temper and imperious manner. Everyone said that Theresa was wonderful; Cathy had a strange feeling now and then that perhaps her mother grew tired sometimes of being wonderful and would like to be something less exacting for a change.

"Will we go to Washington soon, do you think?" Cathy asked.

Her mother gave her a quick amused glance. "How our mind wanders. I thought we were still buried in napkins."

"That's what made me think of it, in a way. Wondering who would look after things while we were gone."

"I daresay that can be taken care of."

"Then we are going?"

"Perhaps. Are you so eager to go?"

"I'm not sure. Sometimes I am and sometimes I'm not." Cathy glanced at her mother, knowing this divided point of view to be lamentable.

"Your aunt suggests that you return to France with them for a year at the Academy first. We've always planned for you to go but things have conspired to keep you from going. You are getting older and this might be your last opportunity; what do you think?"

"With the rest of you going to Washington?"

"Well, that may be later. And in any case a year at school might give you more social confidence."

"Will I need that in Washington?" Cathy's pleasure in the idea began to fade. She saw herself gauche, passed over, a pathetic figure. She exclaimed tragically: "I'll be a wallflower; I know I will."

"My dearest! Believe me, you'll be nothing of the kind."

"I'll be much better off staying here counting napkins."

Theresa laughed merrily; her laugh made Cathy feel better. Theresa said, "Come now, little Cinderella, things aren't quite so bad as that."

"Do you really think I'll be a success?"

"I think you must stop worrying about whether you are to be

a success or not for a time and learn to be yourself, without affectation."

"But myself isn't always the same. Sometimes I feel like one person and sometimes another; I can't count on which person I'm going to be."

"Let us try to improve all of them, then."

"It sounds like quite an undertaking, doesn't it?"

"Yes, I agree, it does."

"I wish one of them could go to school and one to Washington and one stay here."

"I wish all of them would pay attention to getting these accounts straight," Theresa said a little ruefully; she asked, "What am I going to do with you?" She looked troubled, as she sometimes did over these vagaries in Cathy's nature. "There seems to be so little time, suddenly, and we've gone about it all wrong, I'm afraid," she said, to Cathy's discomfiture. "Do you mean that I'm hopeless," she asked and Theresa answered firmly, "No, of course I mean nothing of the kind."

The accounts, once Cathy put her mind on them, came out quite easily, and the day was very bright when Cathy, released, sauntered out into it; and as a reward of virtue Philip, dropping by, invited her to accompany him to Angleton, a little mining camp a few miles away, where he had a patient.

The drive to Angleton with Philip was not an unmitigated success, though Cathy, joining Randy and Lisa in the schoolroom where they still had tea together from custom, and because Lisa could eat more away from the watchful eyes of her mother, would have died rather than admit it. Philip had been lofty and critical and Cathy had been tempted to tell him that she had heard Aunt Helena call him a charming boy. He and Cathy nearly quarreled seriously, but when she had asked him if he thought Lisa was pretty he had exclaimed: "That cow? No!" so vehemently that Cathy was mollified. She wanted Philip to remain in love with Aunt Helena as he had been last year; things were changing too fast as it was, and Aunt Helena was kind and gentle and gay; so long as he remained in love with her Philip would not be so likely to threaten to go away as he sometimes did. But when she had ventured, on the way home: "Philip, Aunt Helena isn't so awfully old you know, not even forty," he had turned his head and favored her with a blank stare and the question whether or not she had an idea in the world what she was talking about; if she had not, kindly to keep quiet.

No, the trip had not been a success, and Cathy, leaving Philip downstairs to have tea with her mother and Aunt Helena, was inclined to hope that Aunt Helena would snub Philip, if such a feat could be accomplished.

Randy was resting in a big chair surrounded by pillows; he had had an attack of asthma the night before. Young as he was, Randy had an exquisite sensitivity for other people's feelings; at the moment, however, he hurt Cathy's without realizing it by staring in guileless admiration at Lisa, who was parading up and down the room practising her newly acquired fascinations upon him for want of a better audience.

He glanced at Cathy as she came in, smiling, "Our cousin Lisa has grown very ravishing, hasn't she?" he remarked.

Cathy went to sit on the window seat of the bay window overlooking a side garden which was a wide expanse of lawn leading to a mirrorlike pool surrounded by willows. Cathy tucked her feet under her and stared into the willows; she announced casually, presently, "Aunt Helena says that Lisa will be fat one of these days if she isn't careful."

Randy looked startled at this display of bad manners, but Lisa only laughed and said she had to be careful now, for that matter. "I have to starve myself every minute," she lied dramatically. "But it's worth it, isn't it?" She turned around in the center of the room to show her dress with its fitted waist and full skirt and sleeves showed off her figure. Randy blushed but his eyes continued to hold admiration. Cathy looked off into the distance where jagged peaks were beginning to turn purple against the sky; her chin was propped pensively on her doubled fists.

"Cathy is jealous," Lisa taunted.

Randy's dark grave eyes which were so like his mother's moved to Cathy's face. He asked, belatedly, "Did you have a nice trip to Angleton?"

"Imagine calling a drive to Angleton a trip," Lisa said.

"Well, I certainly don't," Cathy said fiercely. "I only went because Philip begged me and he would have been so disappointed if I hadn't."

Randy's eyes opened very wide at this. Before he could say anything Lisa interrupted: "Cathy has a terrible crush on Philip."

"I haven't. I have not."

"All the girls at school have crushes on older men. It's nothing to get upset about."

"I'm not in the least upset. And all the girls in your school are probably just a bunch of silly idiots, if the truth be known."

"Yes, they are," Lisa agreed. She appeared to like Cathy's phrase for she repeated, "If the truth be known."

Cathy pressed her advantage. "I wouldn't go to that silly school for anything in the world."

"Well, everyone has to go to school somewhere."

"*I* don't!"

"How will you come out?"

Cathy hesitated; she said, "My father will arrange it."

Even Lisa believed that Michael Brett could arrange anything. She said, "If you were older we could come out together this winter."

"No, thank you."

"I don't believe they would take you at the Academy anyhow," Lisa said. "You think so much of yourself and I doubt if you even know how to play games."

"What kind of games?"

"All kinds. Hockey and volley ball. All American and English girls wear bloomers and play games; it's part of their national tradition."

"Well, I'd like to see you playing games," Cathy said. "You're too lazy even to ride most of the time."

Lisa shrugged and laughed; she was never insulted. She said, "I'm only half American; French girls take walks. Actually I could be very good at games if I wanted to be, though of course I'm too old for them now."

"So would I be, then."

"Well, but you've never had them. Everybody has to have them to graduate."

"I don't," Cathy said; she was close to tears. She protested violently: "I wouldn't play their silly games for anything in the world; nobody could make me."

"You'll see," Lisa said. "It's better than taking walks two by two behind a mademoiselle, that I can tell you."

When Philip came into the room, to look after Randy, his entrance made Cathy self-conscious; but Lisa hummed and smiled, she might almost have been expecting him.

Philip picked up Randy's wrist and held it. "You'll do," he said, returning Randy's hand to his lap.

He asked, a little condescendingly: "What is everyone doing?"

"Dancing, as you see," Lisa answered.

Philip laughed and sat down; he suggested a game of chess to Randy.

Lisa moved a chair to sit beside them, watching the chess game. She grew bored presently and began humming again.

"Must you?" Philip asked.

"Must I what?"

"Make that noise."

"I'll stop if it bothers you. What's the piece that hops about in that funny way?"

"Knight."

Lisa dropped her handkerchief and waited for Philip to pick it up. He did so, noticing the perfume: "That's nice, what is it?"

"'April Showers'; it's Mamma's. I'm only supposed to use cologne until next year."

"So you steal your mother's."

"Well, I don't exactly steal it."

"What do you call it?"

"Besides, you admitted it was nice and it suits me."

Philip said, "Oh hush"; he had just lost a bishop. "You make it very difficult for one to keep one's mind on the game."

"Do I really?"

"'April Showers'; yours is more like a downpour."

Randy captured another piece; this time a knight.

"You won't have anything left if you keep on at that rate," Lisa said.

"Very true, so be quiet for at least a minute," Philip said; he hunched his shoulders over the chessboard.

Cathy slipped away; nobody was including her in the group about the chessboard and she could not push herself forward, like Lisa. Also Lisa's taunts about school had found their mark; it was true that Cathy did not know how to play games as Lisa probably did in spite of her laziness, and perhaps now Cathy was too old to begin. She was not even sure that she wanted to begin now that there seemed a possibility of so many other things happening.

Tears were pressing upon Cathy from that fathomless well which lay behind her eyes; she hurried off to give way to them in private. Lisa always had this effect upon her; Lisa spoiled everything, and yet each year Cathy looked forward to Lisa's arrival.

Cathy went out a side door and through a gate to a small garden. The lilacs were in bloom; Cathy pressed her hot cheeks against the cool moist leaves.

She was still there half an hour later when Lisa came through the gate, leaving it unlatched. She pretended as always that nothing was wrong. She asked, "Why did you run away? We were having fun."

"Why did you leave, then?"

"Philip had to go," Lisa said. "He said Randy was to rest, so I came out to find you."

"Thank you."

"Don't be so touchy. I didn't mean to hurt your feelings about the games."

"You didn't hurt my feelings, don't flatter yourself."

"I'm terribly fond of you, actually," Lisa said. "I only tell you certain things for your own good."

Everyone hurt Cathy's feelings for her own good. "Thank you so much," she said with elaborate politeness.

"I'd tell you more if I was sure you wouldn't gab," Lisa said.

"What is there to gab about?"

Lisa glanced at Cathy and then away; she began to laugh. "A man tried to kiss me on the boat coming over."

"Did you let him?"

"Of course not; what do you think I am?"

"What would there be for me to gab, then; I don't see that anything so much happened."

"It was terribly amusing, just the same," Lisa said. She put both hands over her mouth and laughed harder than ever.

"What was so amusing about it?"

"Well, he had a mole right beside his nose and it twitched when he grew impassioned. He was terribly impassioned of course, or at least he would have been if Nola hadn't interrupted us to say Mamma wanted me, and all the rest of the distractions. Toward the end he grew rather quiet but he took my hand and held it and he sort of choked. It was tragic, in a way."

Cathy, whose mouth had been hanging open during this recital, closed it. "It doesn't sound tragic to me. Or amusing either."

"Well, you'll see when the time comes," Lisa said. "One of these days men are going to try to kiss you and then you'll be grateful for my advice."

"Well, if I feel like it, I'll let them," Cathy said. "So you can keep your kind and gracious advice to yourself."

Lisa looked taken aback, which was unusual for her. "You couldn't, possibly."

"Why couldn't I?"

"It just isn't done."

43

"Well, I'm going to do it," Cathy said. "I'm going to let them all kiss me if I like them, every one of them. If I like them I'm even going to kiss them back."

Lisa looked impressed, and slightly envious. Recovering, she brought out a crumpled package of cigarettes; she too smoked in private but in her case it had to be even more private than with Aunt Helena. She offered Cathy one which Cathy refused. "Oh go on, take one," Lisa urged.

Cathy took one; she lighted it on the third try and blew out the smoke in great gusts, wondering what people found to enjoy in the experience. Lisa smoked expertly, drawing in the smoke like a sigh and exhaling it in a thin blue vapor; nobody could possibly expect to be anything at the Academy, she said, unless they knew how to smoke.

"In your case it will be different," she said finally. "I mean Uncle Michael has so much money it won't really matter whether you can do anything or not."

"What does that have to do with it?"

"A great deal, as you'll discover. You have nothing to worry about; it doesn't even particularly matter if you are going to be beautiful or if you aren't."

"Oh," Cathy said. She found this a doubtful compliment.

"It matters terrifically with me, of course. So thank heavens I am."

"Am what?"

"Are what. Beautiful."

"Who says so?"

"Men, mostly," Lisa said. She smirked, objectionably.

"I don't see that you're so beautiful," Cathy said.

"You don't need to," Lisa said. She coaxed, "Don't be mean to me. All you need is self-confidence; a year at the Academy will do wonders for you."

"I don't see that it's done such wonders for you."

"You really should go. I heard Mamma and Aunt Theresa talking about it."

So had Cathy, but she decided not to divulge that. "They talk about it every year."

"Yes, but this year it's different. You are getting older for one thing and soon you'll have to come out. How will you know how to act?"

"I'll act as I please," Cathy said, not very confidently.

"That's all very well but you don't want to be thought strange.

You always say you want to go, but you back out at the last minute."

Cathy began to get excited. Perhaps she did want to go, had wanted to go all along. She protested feebly, "Only because of Randy. It isn't fair for me to go when he has to stay here."

"That's what you say. I, for one, think you're afraid."

"Afraid of what?"

"Well, you wouldn't be the high muck-a-muck you are here. Nobody would pay much attention to you."

"I wouldn't care if they did or not."

"Naturally it will be a come-down. But you'll soon be too old if you don't hurry and make up your mind."

That was true. Indecisiveness could last only so long; Cathy was getting quite old and soon it would be too late.

She asked breathlessly, "Do you think I could learn to play the games?"

"Oh, you won't have to. They'll be afraid of offending Uncle Michael and so actually you'll be able to do as you please. And besides, you can always pretend to have a pain in your side; that's what I always do."

Cathy was disgusted at this deceitfulness. "I thought you were so good."

"Well, that was good, wasn't it?"

"You're such a liar, I don't even believe you had a beau on the ship."

"Don't you?" Lisa laughed, a secret maddening laugh. "I'll tell you something that will really surprise you."

"What is that, pray?"

"I think Philip is beginning to have a crush on me."

"Philip! What gave you that idea?"

"Haven't you noticed the way he looks at me whenever he's here?"

"No, I haven't. He hasn't paid the slightest attention to you so far as I can see, except when he has to."

"He avoids me," Lisa said. "That's always a sign."

"A sign of what?"

"That he's beginning to get a crush on me. He's afraid of me, that's why."

Cathy, dumbfounded, asked, "What is there to be afraid about?"

"Oh, lots of things," Lisa said. She began to hum, airily.

"I thought you said he was so impossible."

"That was only to make him notice me."

"Well, he hasn't."

"He's noticed me, all right," Lisa said. "Don't worry, I can always tell when it's beginning."

"You're crazy! Philip doesn't even like you; he's said so a hundred times."

"He thinks he doesn't, the more fool he," Lisa said. She threw herself down on the grass, leaning backward on her arms and looking upward at the sky. She was smiling, as if at some secret memory.

"You're crazy!"

"You'll see," Lisa said. "I don't see what you're getting so excited about anyhow. You said you didn't have a crush on Philip yourself."

"I haven't!"

"Then what do you care?"

"I don't care! I just think you're crazy, that's all!"

"The more fool you, then," Lisa said.

Cathy tried to imitate Lisa's secret little laugh but it did not sound convincing even to her own ears.

Chapter 5

THE BIG FORMAL rooms were being opened for Michael Brett's homecoming, now only a few days away. Dust covers were removed from the furniture; brocade window hangings and crystal chandeliers had emerged from their muslin bags. Polished surfaces gleamed; the French windows stood open and there were great bowls of flowers everywhere.

Sam and Hester as well as Cathy accompanied Theresa on today's tour of inspection; Helena, saying that all this cleaning frightened her, had escaped to a shaded terrace with a book. Cathy would have liked to join her but she did not want to be suspected of being lazy.

The long paneled mirrors, rising from floor to ceiling in the drawing-rooms and terminating in cornices of carved gold, reflected Cathy over and over. The wall mirrors alternated with painted panels, centering in medallions of fat painted cherubs, with similar medallions repeated in ceiling cornices.

Cathy stared at her reflections. When she stood in the doorway so that she could see the length of both rooms, over a hundred feet, there were dozens of Cathys repeated over and over staring back at her and imitating everything she did. She put out a foot and the Cathys lining the rooms each put out a foot too. She bowed and they bowed. She smiled, showing all her teeth in a rather terrifying grin, and the mirrored Cathys showed their teeth back at her.

They were rather uninteresting in looks too, now that she regarded them critically. They were too short and their Peter Thompsons dipped rather badly in the back, and the big hair-bows, which held back their clubbed hair in what was inelegantly known as a horse's tail, were crooked. Cathy snatched off the bow; suddenly the sight of all those horses' tails was more than she could bear.

Her hair, loosened, fell about her shoulders; it refused to grow very long. It was curly and thick, and Stacey's vigorous brushings kept it glossy. All her life Cathy had suffered under those brushings, but Stacey, one hand pulling up her hair into a topknot as if she were going to scalp her and slapping with the brush with the other, ignored protests and wails alike. "You want to have hair that looks like something, don't you? Hair is woman's crowning glory."

Hair done up in a horse's tail was a long way from being a crowning glory. But loosened it did not look too badly, though it was not long enough to make a chignon like Lisa's. Cathy drew it up to the top of her head; she studied this effect, from different angles, until her arm grew tired holding it.

Theresa, crossing the room, took note of her plight and came intuitively to her assistance. "How about this?" She took pins from her own hair and skilfully fastened Cathy's to the top of her head with little curls escaping here and there. Cathy, enchanted, studied it from every angle; she looked different, proud; she would hardly have recognized herself if it had not been for the Peter Thompson; she stared down at it.

Theresa, following her eyes, said, "Yes, we must have some new clothes for you, perhaps your father will bring you some. And you are to have a corset; Helena is horrified that you have no corset."

Theresa laughed; Cathy, though she regarded corsets with deadly earnestness, laughed too. "Will you like being all bound up, do you think?"

Cathy said, "I don't think I'll mind; I'll get used to it." She wanted a figure at this moment more than she wanted comfort and it grieved her that she was too short ever to have a really elegant figure. But she wasn't fat, that was one thing in her favor.

"Good, then we will see to it."

"Stacey says your waist measures exactly what it did when you were a girl."

"Other things change, however," Theresa said. Her smooth dark hair, done in the great knot in the back, had become slightly loosened from lack of the pins which she had given to Cathy, so that she looked both younger and somehow more uncertain. "Values change, you see," she said; she seemed to be speaking to herself rather than to Cathy.

"Do you think Father would be disappointed in me for wanting a corset?"

Theresa glanced at Cathy; she smiled: "No, I'm sure he would consider it a natural desire, though he has something of an obsession about people being free."

Cathy glanced back at her reflection: "It would give me a sizzling figure."

"Sizzling?"

"That's what the girls say at the Academy."

"Oh? We still haven't solved that problem, have we?"

"Could I have a little more time to think it over?"

"Yes, certainly, though if you are worrying about leaving Randy you need not. You have been a good sister to him and he will be happy having you do whatever makes you happy."

"It isn't only Randy," honesty forced Cathy to admit.

"What then in particular?"

"Lisa says nobody will pay any attention to me."

Theresa raised her eyebrows; she could look surprisingly arrogant when she chose.

"Why not?"

"She says I can't expect to be a high muck-a-muck as I am here."

"And do you want so much to be a high muck-a-muck?"

"Well, I wouldn't like just to be ignored. Could Father take me over if I do go, do you think, and tell them just who I am?"

There was a queer silence; Cathy squirmed inwardly.

Theresa asked very quietly, "And just who are you?"

"Well, even Lisa admits that Father is known everywhere. And if he gets to be important in the government he will be even more well known, won't he?"

"Yes, he will. And you will be bathed in reflected glory; is that what you want?"

Cathy squirmed still more; it was, actually, just what she wanted. "Of course I want to be good and all that too."

"Being good and all that is sometimes difficult under certain circumstances."

"I suppose so. Do you mean I'd be tempted to be vain and selfish?"

"It's possible, isn't it?"

"I suppose so, if all the girls were as mean as Lisa."

Theresa sat down; she patted a place beside her on the sofa. "Shall we talk for a little?"

Cathy sat beside her; the thought of exposing herself to the critical regard of fifty girls exactly like Lisa was appealing less and less to Cathy. She said, "I don't want to go in any case. I'd hate it; I'd hate all the girls."

"But you make friends very easily. And you don't really hate Lisa."

"It's more exciting when she's here," Cathy admitted.

"And you have wanted life to be more exciting for a long time, haven't you?"

"I thought I did, but now I don't know. Things happen that aren't always so pleasant and maybe it's better when everything isn't so exciting."

"But you'll want to come out, as Lisa is going to do. A year at school would pave the way."

"But I don't need the way paved," Cathy put forth excitedly. "Lisa says I'll be the season's most prominent debutante no matter what."

"Lisa says a great many things, it would appear."

"But it's true, isn't it?"

Theresa said calmly, "Yes, I think it may be true."

"Well, then, I needn't worry, need I?"

"It depends on what you want."

Cathy scarcely heard the question. She was entering a ballroom clad in a shimmering gown cut very low. She was graciously promenading about the room, cutting a wide swathe to the accompaniment of gasps of admiration and astonishment, while Lisa watched enviously.

She said, "I only want to be a great success and have everybody wish they were me."

"So that is all, is it?"

"It would be fun, though, putting it over on Lisa."

"It isn't Lisa we're concerned about, but you."

"She's so stuck up; it would do her good."

"But would it do you good?"

Cathy said, "Well"; she acknowledged that Lisa quite often remarked that Cathy thought too highly of herself. "Anyhow Father will see to it that I'm not ignored, won't he?"

"You won't be ignored. But I can't promise that you'll like not being, always."

50

One of the men brought in the mail, which had just arrived in the wagon from town. There was none for Cathy as usual; she had few correspondents. She occupied herself, while Theresa glanced through her letters, by opening a bundle of newspapers and leafing through them.

On the front page of one of the newspapers there was a funny picture of the kind called cartoon; there was a recognizable portrait of Cathy's father, dressed in baby clothes even to a bonnet and hanging in a wooden cradle from the branch of a tree. He was an angry baby; he had his mouth open as if he were howling lustily; he was far too big for the cradle of course, so that the tree was bent close to the ground. There was more to the picture but Cathy's attention was on the baby; she laughed aloud, thinking how it would amuse her father. Theresa came to look too; she put out one hand and said, "I wouldn't look at that," and then she withdrew the hand.

Cathy glanced up questioningly. "Isn't it funny?"

"Not very," Theresa said. She hesitated; she said, "But of course it is funny in a way and there's no reason why you shouldn't look at it."

The picture, on closer inspection, was not really funny. Somebody was making fun of Cathy's father or trying to hurt him.

"You see what I mean, that it isn't always pleasant not to be ignored," Theresa said.

"Will Father be upset?"

"No, I don't think so," Theresa said. "One has to get used to these things in public life. He'll laugh at it, probably, as you did."

The tree in the picture grew money instead of leaves; it was covered with money which was falling from it on top of the baby. Behind the tree was an ocean with the sail of a ship disappearing; the ship was labeled "Ship of State." A number of people were bending over the baby trying to console him by showing him the money but the baby was crying after the ship. A woman was picking up some of the money and keeping it.

Cathy crumpled up the paper and threw it away; she was filled suddenly with a great emotion which gathered inside her like a windstorm over the mountains.

Theresa said, "Yes, it's vulgar and vicious, but we mustn't dignify it by paying too much attention to it."

"Why doesn't Father stop them!"

"I suppose he would if he could."

"He could! He could!"

"We forget, way out here, that there are battles which he has to fight every day."

"Why does he? I wouldn't have anything to do with people like that."

Theresa reminded her: "But you like the feeling of importance."

"Yes."

"It's hardly fair to complain, then, when things go wrong."

"Have they gone wrong now?"

"Yes, somewhat."

"Very wrong?"

Theresa hesitated: "That's a little difficult to say. The opposition to your Father's appointment seems very bitter; nothing which concerns him is ever small, as we know." She smiled but Cathy could not bring herself to smile back. "They will use everything against him that they can," Theresa said. "His success, and those enemies which have been made by it, anything at all in his past which can be made into scandal or used to belittle him. You must be prepared to hear stories about him."

"But you don't believe them!"

"No, of course we will not believe them," Theresa said. Cathy glanced at her to see if Theresa noticed that she had said she would not believe the stories rather than she did not believe them, but Theresa evidently did not notice for she was rising calmly, picking up the discarded newspaper but carrying it with her instead of leaving it with the others to be put in den or library. "We had better get back to work if we wish to see to it that Keepsake creates an especially good impression to offset our bad publicity," she said; she smiled at Cathy to show that she only meant that it was better to keep busy and useful than to brood over what one could not help.

Cathy longed to display her love and loyalty in a more violent way. People loved in different ways, she had noted: there was her father's love for her mother, so tempestuous and dramatic when he was at home, but then there were his long absences too. And then there was Theresa's love, dramatic too in its way but deeper and quieter, more dependable, Cathy was sure, though she could not help admiring her father's way more. She exclaimed, ashamed of a momentary coldness and doubt which had been taking place in her thoughts of her father: "I wish I could do something for him! If I could even go to New York and just be with him. I could look after him and keep him company and I could take care of myself when he was busy; he wouldn't have to bother about me."

"That's a very nice thought; perhaps you may do that one of these days."

"He used to say he would take me with him, but he hasn't said that for a long time."

"He's waiting for you to grow up a little more."

"I'm grown up enough," Cathy said. "He forgets, though; he was going to take me to France with him one summer, do you remember? But then he forgot; and another time he was going to take me to England when he had to be there for a month, and he forgot that too. If I were taller or prettier or a boy or something I don't think he'd forget so much."

"Your father thinks of you a great deal; he does many things for you."

"Yes," Cathy said. "I wish I were very very tall and dignified so he would be proud of me."

"He is very proud of you, dearest, believe me."

"Yes, but I wish there was something I could do," Cathy repeated. She extended her arms to show how great was her desire: "Something big! Really big!"

"You will find your niche, dearest, and soon," Theresa said. "Perhaps sooner than we think," she added; she went on more lightly, meeting Cathy's inquiring glance: "And since you are your father's daughter a great deal is bound to be expected of you."

"I won't mind that."

"I'm sure you won't, and I'm sure you'll have a chance to do something big.

"We must plan what you are to wear to the dinner party." There was to be a dinner party on the first night of Michael's arrival with his guests.

"Am I to be there?" Cathy's irrepressible spirits soared; the thought of attending the formal dinner held for her father and the party accompanying him made her situation seem much less desperate. Last year she and Lisa still had had their meals upstairs with Randy when there had been guests at Keepsake.

"Yes, I think you may be there this year."

"Lisa, too?"

"Lisa of course."

"Has she a dinner gown? A real one, I mean?"

"I believe so, and so we must find one for you."

"With a train?"

Theresa smiled: "Hardly with a train. But we will concoct something very *soignée*, with Helena's assistance." She kissed Cathy.

Certain wheels having been put into motion, Cathy spent the rest of the afternoon being fitted into a gown by Nola and Stacey, with Aunt Helena supervising. The gown belonged to Lisa but it had never been worn by her, which was one consolation. Another consolation was that it had to be taken in a full two inches at the waist.

Chapter 6

CATHY, RIDING HORSEBACK alone the following afternoon, was nearly to Magoon before she admitted to herself that she had had that goal in mind all the time. Having come so far there did not seem much sense in turning back, though she seldom came into the little town by herself; there were unspoken restrictions at Keepsake in spite of its remoteness.

Philip was in his office, but he was not particularly pleased to see Cathy. His office was the front room of a little clapboard house on the outskirts of Magoon, with his living quarters behind it. If it had not been for the servant sent by Theresa once or twice a week to cook and clean for him, the place would have looked even shabbier and more neglected than it did.

Cathy often accompanied whatever person was sent and so she had a proprietary feeling. She ran a finger over a table and blew off the dust.

"Dear me," Philip said. "What am I supposed to do now, serve tea?"

Cathy, ignoring his tone, said brightly, "That would be nice; I'll make some for us, shall I?" and went to the kitchen.

She liked the dark little kitchen with the pump at the sink and the kerosene stove which threatened to blow up whenever one lighted it. Bustling about she felt important and competent. She lighted the stove and put the teakettle on it.

"Who came in with you?" Philip asked.

"I came in by myself."

"Oh? For what reason?"

"To see you."

55

Cathy ate toast and drank several cups of tea because she was hungry and thirsty and glad to be with Philip.

Tea and toast improved Philip's mood, for when he had finished he did not seem in a hurry to have her go. He let Cathy wash the dishes and even dried them for her. He threw cups into the air and juggled them; there had been a day, he said, when he could do three cups. He tried three saucers, which were easier, but one of them fell on the floor and smashed. They both laughed, and while Cathy was picking up the broken pieces she cut herself slightly. Philip glanced at it casually; the bleeding would wash it out, he said. "Just suck it a little," he advised.

Cathy sucked at her finger, followed Philip into his little sitting-room. He stood in the center of the room with his hands in his pockets. From here they could hear the little ping of the bell on the office door if patients arrived; when there was more than one patient they used this sitting-room as a waiting-room. Philip straightened a few magazines in preparation and asked, "What is everybody doing?"

"Where?"

"At Keepsake, where do you imagine? And for goodness' sake take your finger out of your mouth, you look like an idiot."

"You told me to suck it!"

"Not all day. It's only a scratch; don't be such a baby."

Cathy examined her finger hoping it might show symptoms of blood poisoning but it looked normal and the scratch was barely discernible. She said, "Well, Aunt Helena is having her siesta; she nearly always does at this time of day, you know."

"No, I wouldn't know." Philip glared at Cathy as if she were deliberately trying to irritate him and then turned his back. She hurried on, wondering why it was so difficult these days to please him: "Randy is resting too, of course. Well, I don't necessarily mean of course but anyhow he is. I don't know what Lisa is doing."

This was not quite true; Lisa from her own room, where she was reading a French novel smuggled to her by Nola and eating chocolates smuggled by herself, had called to Cathy while she was changing into riding clothes, but Cathy had pretended not to hear.

"Why, have you quarreled?"

"I, for one, find her impossible," Cathy said.

Philip turned around; he gave a short reluctant laugh. "No more impossible than anyone of her age and sex."

"What do those things have to do with it?"

"A great deal, I should think," Philip said. He looked more cheerful, though Cathy could not imagine why. He suggested, "I'd better go back with you; you can wait until office hours are over."

"Oh, good. It's nice of you to offer to take me back."

"It was nice of you to come," Philip said generously. He grinned at her; everything he did meant so much to her that she always spoiled it by acting foolishly.

Now she said, with some malicious intent: "I'm glad you are going back with me. Aunt Helena was asking for you only this morning; she said we aren't seeing as much of you as we usually do. As last summer, for instance."

Philip swung about, angrily; he demanded with narrowed eyes, "What does that mean, if anything?"

"I'm not a baby."

"Oh? That's nice to know; what are you?"

"If you are still infatuated with Aunt Helena I don't see any reason why you should be ashamed of it."

"There are a number of reasons, but as it so happens I am not at all infatuated with Helena, whatever you may mean by the word."

"I know exactly what it means to be infatuated."

"I doubt that, but in any event it's a silly thing to say."

"You mean you are, but chivalry forbids you to say it."

"I mean nothing of the kind and, for heaven's sake, mind your own business."

"Well, you were last year," Cathy defended herself feebly.

"May I ask how you came by that interesting though somewhat improbable idea?"

"We sat on the stairs and watched you," Cathy said. "Lisa and I. You used to stare at Aunt Helena and get red whenever she looked at you, and drop things. Lisa said people acted that way when they were infatuated."

With Philip's furious eyes on her Cathy did not mind in the least sacrificing Lisa. She faltered, after an uncomfortable little pause: "It was Lisa's idea in the first place. To sit there, I mean."

"That's no excuse. You knew better."

"Well, but Philip, I was much younger then."

"So was I!" Philip's face was grim but he seemed less angry with her than with himself. Nevertheless Cathy was reluctant to relinquish the idea that he was still infatuated with Aunt Helena; she tried to believe that he was denying it because it was hopeless.

"Never mind, there's nothing to cry about," Philip said, somewhat destroying the illusion.

"I'm n-n-not crying."

"You have to learn to think for yourself," he said. "Not just imitate everything Lisa does." He was pacing up and down again.

"I kn-kn-know."

"I'm a good one to tell other people how to live their lives," he said; he looked abjectly miserable. A few years earlier Cathy could have thrown herself into his arms, clutching her hands about his neck, trying to comfort him without knowing what it was which made him so miserable. At this strange age in which she found herself she had to sit with a silly smile on her face while Philip lectured her; a great chasm suddenly had opened before them.

"You don't mean harm, but you let Lisa dominate you," Philip lectured. "That's foolish, and very bad for both of you besides."

"Well, but Lisa has advantages that I haven't."

"Such as?"

"She t-t-travels and meets people. She's coming out next year."

"What of it? Hundreds of girls come out every year; what difference does that make to you?"

"N-n-none at all, I suppose."

"Of course it doesn't. Stop stuttering and stop biting your nails."

"I c-c-can't."

"Of course you can if you try."

He came to stand in front of her. Tears were running down her face though she tried to control them. Philip could never remain indifferent to tears; they either irritated him or made him sympathetic. Today he was sympathetic, which only made Cathy cry harder.

"You silly baby," Philip said. He put his arms about her and let her cry against his shoulder. He said, "Don't you know that all these things are going to happen to you in due course of time?"

"I shan't have the slightest notion of how to act when they do," Cathy sniffed disconsolately.

"It does seem darned unfair to spring the whole thing on you," Philip said absently. When Cathy lifted her head to ask what was to be sprung on her he diverted the conversation as people almost always did: "Nothing. You think too much about yourself; you'll have a good time, don't worry. There will be people breaking their necks to see that you do."

All this was ambiguous; Cathy had a literal picture of people breaking their necks. "Why should they do that?"

"Do what? Don't mumble, and do, for heaven's sake, stop trying to dramatize everything."

"Will you be there to help me?"

Philip had lived in New York, but he seemed to despise it in much the same way that Theresa did.

"In what role? The kindly penniless avuncular friend? Helping to launch the new heiress?" He kicked at a little stool without seeing it, and he made a funny sound which was half like swearing and half like groaning. He evidently was due for one of his moods of furious dissatisfaction with himself. Cathy's father said that Philip never would return to the life he had left and never would be content with his present life, and so he was a young man doomed to self-torment. It sounded romantic but it might be uncomfortable.

The little bell jangled. Philip hurled himself out of the room. While Cathy waited, she entertained herself by examining everything in the room, though she was as familiar with it as she was with her own.

There was a faded photograph of Philip's dead mother which she picked up and looked at long and earnestly. Philip's mother, in the photograph, smiled at Cathy with an eternally wistful smile. She was dainty and pretty: her hair was carefully and beautifully curled back from her face, and she wore a dog-collar of pearls.

The photograph of Philip's father, which Cathy preferred, had been thrust out of sight into a desk drawer. Cathy took it out; she herself was responsible for its exile there. She had admired it a month or so before, when she had accompanied a servant sent to clean Philip's house for him; Philip's father had stood on a chest of drawers then and Cathy had picked him up and smiled at him because the man in the photograph, taken at a much younger age than the photograph of Philip's mother, seemed to be smiling at her. Philip's father was a dashing and jaunty version of Philip; there was a roguish twinkle in his eyes and a devil-may-care lift to his huge walrus mustache. "Oh, how nice and kind and jolly he looks," Cathy had said; it was then that Philip had snatched the photograph from her and thrown it, face down, into a drawer. "I was nice and jolly myself once," he had said. "It's easy enough to be jolly when you don't stay behind to face the music."

Philip's father had not stayed behind to face the music. He had lost all his money, of which there had been a great deal, and then he had borrowed and gone into debt as long as he could; when he had come to the end of his rope he had simply shot himself.

All this had taken place while Philip was a medical student in Paris. Philip, quite naturally, had failed to appreciate the dramatic finality of his father's gesture in taking himself off at a time when he would only have complicated matters by staying. Philip, shocked and dazed, had rushed home, blaming himself because his student years preceding this disaster had been extravagant and carefree and a little wild. He had been quite clever in his studies of course, even brilliant some of his instructors had said, but he had not learned yet to take anything too seriously, not even his career.

Following his father's funeral there had been a consultation with lawyers, because Philip's mother was too ill to see anyone, even Philip. All her life Philip's mother had refused to see anyone except when she was perfectly turned out, not only as to hair and dress but in her mind. Now, prostrate from shock, she sent messages begging that her handsome beloved son not come to see her until she was able to present a cheerful face to life once more.

Evidently she had not been able to present that cheerful face, for while Philip was pacing up and down the floor of his bedroom day and night trying to decide what to do next, his mother had solved part of his problems by herself dying without ever leaving the bed to which she had retreated when the first news was broken to her. Her death had been the final blow to Philip's carefree existence. She had killed herself just as surely as her husband had done though her death was attributed more directly to failure of a heart weakened by grief and shock. So far as Philip was concerned his mother had willed to die and she had died: "She always said she would die rather than do this or that," Philip had told Cathy years ago when he had been in the first stages of his grief and she had been young enough so that he had not minded pouring out all his bewilderment and sorrow before her.

Philip had accepted help from friends of his father and had entered Johns Hopkins medical school. His life, of course, had been very different after that. He had joined the earnest students instead of those intent on enjoying themselves along the way. He had worked between classes, mornings and evenings; he had waited on tables and scrubbed out laboratories; he had gone without clothes and sleep and even adequate food. Many other students, it appeared, were doing the same thing, but Philip never before had noticed them. He began to notice them now; he described them to Cathy and she saw them vividly: quiet fellow creatures with tastes and desires similar to Philip's own but not knowing how to gratify them. And earnest. "How earnest they were!" Philip said. "We were," he remembered, correcting himself. "We ate and drank and breathed and thought nothing but medicine for four years. Four years! It seemed like a million!"

Philip had graduated with high honors. Following his interneship he had been offered a position as assistant to a brilliant diagnostician and surgeon. Life once more had become, if not the joyous thing it once had been, at least tenable, assured; Philip could even be grateful that he was no longer a fool living in a fool's paradise.

He was always careful to explain to Cathy, perhaps as an object lesson, that he had been self-righteous and pompous during that phase of his development. He had been full of admiration for his own fortitude in pulling himself together and finishing school under so much less felicitous circumstances than he had begun it. He had been full of ambition in those days too; he had dreamed of alleviating the suffering of all mankind now that he himself knew what it was to suffer. He dreamed of becoming rich and famous also, but not selfishly so; no, fame must be incidental. He had worked like a crazy person; he was so obsessed with the desire to work that it had been with the greatest reluctance that he ever tore himself away from the hospital or the laboratories or his desk to go to bed. He disdained all social life; he ate irregularly when at all; he became a creature deaf and blind to everything except the constricted space which was his present world.

Fate had struck at him a second time. It had begun with a cold which Philip had ignored. He could not ignore the cough which persisted in spite of all his lofty efforts to do so. "You ought to do something about that cough," his contemporaries in the hospital advised carelessly; Philip shrugged off their casual but well-meaning solicitude until one day the Great Surgeon himself, following a consultation, had inquired of Philip rather irritably: "What on earth are you doing about that cough?"

There had been examinations and laboratory tests; the news had been gently broken to Philip that there were tubercular bacilli present in his lungs. Everyone had commiserated with him but nobody had succeeded in hiding from him the belief that his career was over.

After six months in a sanatorium Philip had been advised to live in a high dry climate for at least a year or so. There had been an opening in the territory of Arizona, then a wide area of scattered mining settlements and homesteaders which needed a doctor.

This had been the chain of circumstances which had led to Philip's coming to Keepsake with a letter to Michael from an old friend of Philip's father. Cathy quite often tortured herself by trying to imagine what her life would have been like if none of it had happened.

She was thinking of that when Philip came back; she stood in the center of the room, gnawing absently on her nails.

Philip, glancing toward her impatiently, said, "Stop that."

"Stop what?"

"Biting your nails. Your hands look terrible."

She spread them out; they did look terrible. She said, "I wish you weren't always lecturing me."

The bell jangled again and Philip dashed off. He stuck his head in the door a minute or so later to ask her if she minded blood.

"Whose blood?"

"Anybody's. Do you faint or anything?"

"I don't really know."

"There's a man out here with a bad cut on one arm. If you can hold the edges together while I take a few stitches it will make it easier."

"I think I can do it."

Philip's instruments were boiling in a little pan on his stove. He told Cathy just what to do and she did it without the slightest inclination to faint. The man whose arm was being sewed might have been expected to faint, but he looked out the window as if he weren't even interested.

"That's fine," Philip said. "Thanks, Cathy." And except for a warm feeling of accomplishment inside Cathy that was all there was to it.

The next patient was a fat jolly woman with a baby. The woman jiggled the baby up and down on her hip as she talked to Philip, describing her pains. She had a great many pains in a great many places; she put her hand on her back and her shoulder and her neck to show. Philip listened, frowning with concentration. He asked a few questions to which the woman responded eagerly. Her broadening smile included Cathy, as if to say that Doctor Langley was a good doctor, wasn't he?

Philip was a good doctor, Cathy thought with a thrill of pride. His white coat, his scrubbed hands, his efficient sympathetic manner, all gave his patients confidence. Philip was indifferent to disorder in the rest of his house, but he himself supervised the scrubbing of his office and instruments which required a certain chemical solution in the water to kill germs. Philip had an obsession about germs; he studied them at every opportunity in his own laboratory or in the laboratory at Keepsake equipped for Randy's studies where Philip worked with Randy and taught him. Philip read books about germs; he had even written about germs, certain things he believed and had found out about them. He had sent away some of his ideas to a magazine in the East; the magazine, thanking him politely, had sent them back. These unwanted articles were neatly stacked in a desk drawer, and one day Philip was going to put them into a book and then the world would take notice. In the meantime he persisted in his warfare against germs; germs, it seemed, were everywhere, in the air, in water, in milk. It was an unpleasant thought; Cathy would have preferred to ignore it, except for her loyalty to Philip.

Philip was asking the woman now where she got her water. Philip used the word polluted which he used often; he said far too many of the wells in the valley were polluted because of careless hygienic measures.

The woman shook her head; this was a good well, the water was clear and pure.

"Try boiling it for a while."

"I boil the baby's milk just like you told me. My husband thinks I'm crazy."

"Yes, well, let him."

The baby began to cry and Philip asked Cathy if she would mind taking him in the next room while he examined Mrs. Crossley. Cathy did as she was told, this time with misgivings; she was not very accustomed to holding babies. This one had a wet dirty face and it wasn't what one could call an appealing baby, but it had strength and determination. It pulled Cathy's hair and kicked her in the stomach; it reminded her, because it seemed to have so many legs jutting out, of the pig baby in *Alice in Wonderland*. She was just beginning to feel a little at home with it when Philip came and took it away.

When he returned he said, "There'll be a raging typhoid epidemic here one of these days," while he took off his white coat, signifying that office hours were over.

"C-c-could I be a nurse, do you think?"

"Why not? Better than your ambition to be an opera singer, since you can't carry a tune."

Cathy sighed; the temptation was to want to be something, full-blown, without taking into consideration the necessary steps toward one's goal. She said, "I don't seem to get anywhere."

"You will. You leap around so. Sometimes you are too old for your age, as if you understand quite well what you are in for. Other times you act about three."

"What do you mean, what I am in for?"

"You transcend your limitations, I'll say that for you."

"What does that mean?"

"It means you'll be a great success," Philip said laughing; she did not mind, for this laughter was not the kind that hurt. He stretched, yawned; he put both arms about her in a sudden burst of affection and hugged her tight. "You'll be a great success, and I hope I may be there to see it, Miss Brett." He went on to say a number of things about it being sincerity which counted and belief in oneself no matter what the circumstances, but Cathy had stopped listening. She was experiencing, for the second time that day, a warm feeling of accomplishment, and the texture of Philip's tweed coat against her cheek was extraordinarily pleasant.

They left the drab little office and stepped into the blazing midafternoon sunshine. Philip, as if he had locked care behind him in the dispensary, began to whistle; he took her elbow gallantly and escorted her down the high step.

He suggested, "Let's have a picnic tomorrow. Anything to get away from this heat." He would spend the night then at Keepsake; he would not need to return to Magoon tomorrow unless called; he had office hours only three times a week.

"Oh yes, let's," Cathy said, and then remembered: "Lisa will have to go and she's so tiresome on picnics; she's afraid of everything and she always turns her ankle."

"You worry far too much about Lisa."

Philip's face was red from the sun and perhaps other emotions which Cathy preferred not to analyze.

Chapter 7

LISA, THE FOLLOWING morning, received the suggestion of a picnic with blasé indifference. She had risen earlier than usual and was reclining on a long chair on the east terrace with a book in her hand.

She said, "You went off and left me yesterday; don't pretend that you didn't."

"I don't have to entertain you every minute of the day and night."

"Who suggested the picnic?"

"Philip, if you must know."

Lisa considered; just as Cathy's hopes were rising Lisa said she might as well go since she had nothing else to do. "What shall I wear?"

"What difference does it make what one wears on a picnic?"

"If Philip is going it makes a difference."

"He won't notice."

Lisa smiled; she arose from the chaise longue with unusual vigor. She left the terrace as if she were swimming instead of walking, trailing over her shoulder as she went the information that it would take her at least an hour and a half to get ready and it would be useless to count on her before that.

Randy, reading late in bed, responded to the suggestion of a picnic with enthusiasm. He liked outings and he could dig specimens for his microscope along the bank of the river. He invited Cathy to sit down and talk. "What have you been doing? You look distraught."

Randy used words like distraught without ostentation; Cathy

filed that one away and perched on the side of Randy's bed. "Who wouldn't be distraught with Lisa?"

"What's she been doing?"

"She never thinks of anything except what to wear. She tells lies too."

"Oh? Are you sure?"

"Well, white lies. I do too, of course, only not so often."

"Well, you're both girls, so I suppose that makes a difference," Randy said.

Stacey and Amanda were looking after the picnic hampers and there was now nothing for Cathy to do until it was time to go. She wandered into Helena Minard's dressing-room.

Helena was stretched out on her chaise longue being given a facial massage by Nola. She said, "Hello, little one. So you are having a picnic?"

"Wouldn't you go too, just this once?"

Helena said that when one got to be her age it was folly to expose oneself to sunburn, ants, poison ivy, or other rigors of nature.

"Philip will be disappointed," Cathy said; she clung to this idea with desperate hope.

Helena opened one eye and looked at Cathy. She closed it again and said Philip would have quite enough on his hands with two girls to look after when they went into hysterics over the sight of a cow or a spider.

"Lisa must be sure to keep her arms covered," Helena said. "They freckle. You will all have a very good time, I'm sure, dearest, and I long to join you, but one must know and accept one's limitations."

Cathy looked at her own arms. They were darkly tanned but there were no freckles on them.

"You will have to be bleached out too one of these days, little Indian," Helena said. "Where is Lisa now?"

"Dressing. It's going to take her an hour and a half, she says."

Both Helena and Nola smiled indulgently. "She will arrive, that one," Nola said, and Helena said, "Yes, no doubt. She's pushing me aside already."

"No, that's impossible; Madame could be her sister."

"You know I couldn't, but I haven't given up yet," and Helena rolled over on her stomach so that Nola could do the back of her neck and shoulders.

66

There was peaceful silence in the room while Nola massaged and Aunt Helena relaxed. Cathy fell easily into her habit of daydreaming.

Her dreams centered at this moment on the two beautiful Durand sisters who had been so inseparable until Theresa had gone away with Michael Brett. Sometimes Cathy in her dreams took the part of Teresa and sometimes Helena; now and then she even managed both parts at once.

Though the role of Theresa was more exciting, Cathy usually found it easier to fit herself into the role of the inconsolable Helena, left behind. The flaw in this picture was Uncle Raymond, whom Aunt Helena had married with the full permission of everybody less than a year later; Uncle Raymond was small and nervous and shiningly brushed and creased, but not romantic.

Cathy thought of him as dressed always in a morning suit with a boutonniere and eyeglasses on grosgrained ribbon, as he had looked to her on his last visit to Keepsake, when Cathy was only thirteen. He was unbelievably polite; he was the only person in the world who had ever kissed Cathy's hand. Still, he could not be called romantic for he too, as Cathy was beginning to suspect of herself, was the type who was readily overlooked. "Poor Raymond, I must write to him," Helena would say, and Lisa invariably referred to "poor Papa."

Uncle Raymond no longer came to Keepsake because he had a bad digestion and ocean voyages upset him, but he encouraged Helena and Lisa to come.

"After all, it doesn't cost him anything," Lisa said with shocking candor. "He pretends to disapprove of Uncle Michael but he is much too practical to risk offending his rich American relative."

"Why does he disapprove of him?" Cathy demanded, fiercely belligerent.

"Because he is jealous of him, I suppose," Lisa said, thus taking the wind completely out of Cathy's sails.

"Aren't you fond of him?"

"Uncle Michael? I adore him!"

"I mean Uncle Raymond?"

"Oh poor Papa, what a question!" Lisa cried reproachfully.

"Aunt Helena?" Cathy inquired tentatively.

The massage was over and Helena now was seated at her dressing-table applying skin freshener to her face.

67

"Dearest love?"

"How does one know when someone becomes enamored of one?"

"Enamored?" Helena, peering short-sightedly into her mirror—she would not wear glasses—left her reflection for a moment to stare at Cathy.

"They call it that in books. I like enamored better than saying someone has a crush on someone, don't you?"

"Well, yes." Helena went back to the skin freshener. She said a little dryly, "As a rule when this phenomenon occurs the one enamored will declare himself."

"What does that mean?"

"Ask to marry you, little ignoramus."

Cathy blushed scarlet. "It isn't me; I am never going to marry."

"Do you know that I thought exactly the same thing at your age?"

"You did?"

"Yes. Theresa was so beautiful and so far beyond me in everything that I was sure nobody ever would look at me."

"Oh, but one did, didn't he?"

Helena chuckled, her soft gurgling chuckle. "Several, in fact. Your time will come, little big-eyes. You'll be having parties and beaux and all kinds of gay times."

Helena put the top on the bottle of skin freshener and loosened the lid of another jar which contained skin foods. She began to apply the skin food to her face in gentle experienced pats.

"Do you believe in hopeless love?" Cathy asked.

"Hopeless love! What brings on that question at this hour in the morning?"

"I was just thinking. If Philip, for instance, fell in love with someone who couldn't love him . . . ?"

"Philip? Yes, I see." Helena's great blue eyes dwelt for a minute on Cathy's scarlet face and then returned tactfully to her own image; she said, "Don't worry about Philip."

"I'm not worried about him."

"Philip is completely dependable and Lisa is a silly little fool but she knows quite well on which side her bread is buttered."

"Lisa? Did you think I was speaking of Lisa?"

"Weren't you?"

"Oh no. Philip only admires older women really; he's said so a hundred times."

Helena burst out laughing; in spite of the blow to her feelings,

Cathy was relieved to see her amused instead of concerned, as she might have been.

"You think a great deal of Philip, don't you?" Helena asked, talking woman to woman in a manner Cathy found bolstering to her dwindling self-esteem.

"Well, I respect him," Cathy said cautiously; she glanced at Helena to see if she were smiling.

Helena was not. She said briskly, "So you should. Philip is a most estimable young man. We all have his welfare at heart and so we must find a wealthy and beautiful wife for him and marry him off."

"I'm not sure Philip would like that."

"Of course he would; it is exactly what he would like, only at the present moment he is unaware of it."

"Philip is quite unhappy most of the time."

"Ah well, he will recover from that," Helena said; she was drawing eyebrows on her face where there had been no eyebrows before. "We all do."

The picnic did not get under way until late afternoon after some of the fierceness had gone from the midday sun. Lisa wore a dark green riding habit; her red hair in the late afternoon sun seemed blazing red. She rode far more expertly than she had any right to ride, considering how lazy she was.

Randy was being allowed to ride horseback today; they purposely had selected a picnic site a short distance away. He looked very happy and carefree as he jogged along, letting his horse stop to crop whenever it pleased, not in a hurry, not driven by any impatience to go somewhere without knowing where, as Cathy was. He got down from his horse now and then to look at something on the ground; he had a straw specimen-case hanging from his saddle into which he carefully poked his treasures. He was boy enough to make the most of escaping from Stacey's and even perhaps his mother's anxiety over his health; he himself was indifferent to the wet feet and overexertion which invariably brought on attacks of asthma but he tried to be careful because he was aware that these attacks worried others and caused them trouble.

Their way led through drab plains; on the edge of these, where the plains became transformed into colored wastelands, Cathy too reined her horse. Indian country, her father called this. The colors were so bright: the relentless blue of the Arizona sky, the varied tones of clay and sandstone earth, the smooth vivid red of the sand dunes far off to the left. To the right a solitary jagged peak rose from the tableland, Pajonas Timp it was called by the Indians, who once had believed that it pierced the sky and brought rain.

Philip called: "I'll race you to the bend just beyond that pile of red rocks."

Cathy gathered herself to meet the challenge until she saw Lisa was already started; Cathy reined back then to stay beside Randy. Philip won easily; to make up to Lisa for the humiliation of losing he took her hand and swung it the rest of the way.

At the picnic site, on the bank of the Santos River, Marvin, the driver, descended from the wagon which had preceded them to spread blankets and bring out the hampers. Philip pulled two long wide blades of grass and blew dolefully through them.

Soon everybody was whistling through blades of grass placed between thumbs. The whistles were high and low, loud and shrill, or, like Cathy's, scarcely more than a chirp.

Lisa, for some inexplicable reason, could produce a terrific blast. She was so proud of it that she refused to stop even when the others had grown tired and the noise had become somewhat irritating.

"Stop it, Lisa," Philip commanded good-humoredly.

"Make me," Lisa said; she took a deep breath and blew with all her might.

There was a short scuffle while Philip took the blade of grass away from Lisa. She tried to bite Philip and Philip, growing red in the face, growled, "Stop it, you little devil." It was a game but it wasn't quite a game; Cathy had a violent longing to join in, even while part of her sat apart in severe disapprobation. When Philip finally succeeded in prying open Lisa's hands he was still more red in the face, but both he and Lisa were laughing.

Philip did not continue the game, though Lisa tried to prolong it; instead he went to assist Marvin, who was raking and preparing the site for the campfire. Lisa sulked, glancing at Philip now and then to see if he noticed. Randy wandered off to look for specimens; Cathy should have accompanied him but she was rooted to this particular spot.

"Let's go wading," she suggested.

Lisa said they couldn't possibly; they were far too old. Cathy said, "I'm not," and began to draw off her riding boots and stockings. "Mamma would have a fit," Lisa said; she watched Cathy. "Besides, there might be snakes," she said when Cathy showed no signs of weakening.

"I'm not afraid of snakes; I've seen dozens of them."

Lisa shuddered delicately: "Well, for heaven's sake keep it to yourself. The girls at the Academy will either think you are lying or an Indian."

"I don't happen to be going to the damned old Academy!"

"Don't swear except in French," Lisa instructed; then she said, "It wouldn't do you any harm, certainly."

"I'd do them harm. I'd murder them all, the first day."

"Oh, you're so high and mighty sometimes," Lisa said indulgently; she yawned behind one hand.

Philip came to sit beside them. He said, "Going wading? That's a good idea," and began to take off his own shoes and stockings. Lisa hastily began to unfasten her boots; she commanded Philip to turn his back. Philip asked what for, stared at her, and grew even more red than he had been during the skirmish when he had taken the blade of grass from Lisa.

Cathy, disgusted, walked down to the river's edge and waded in. Philip followed her, standing on the bank and calling out an abrupt order not to go out too far. "I don't want to ruin my clothes rescuing you." Cathy, to give vent to her outraged feelings, turned her back and waded toward the center of the river, though there was a certain amount of danger involved in wading in the Santos River, as they all knew, for though it was wide and deceptively shallow it was known to contain swift currents and quicksand.

"Come on back, don't be a fool, Cathy," Philip called peremptorily.

He took her obedience for granted, and left the bank to speak to Marvin. Cathy considered drowning to teach him a lesson but decided that in the long run she would be the one most inconvenienced. She joined Lisa, who, with a great deal of squealing and exposing of white ankle and leg, was entering the water.

"Nobody is looking at you," Cathy said coldly.

"It's damned cold, just the same," Lisa said, forgetting that it was refined to swear only in French.

Cathy left the water; it had been a foolish impulse, she realized now, in the first place. She dried her feet and put on her riding boots again, at the same time watching Lisa who was wading directly toward the center of the river regardless of the danger. Cathy tried to feel indifferent; still, she couldn't really wish harm to Lisa when it came right down to it. Cathy stiffened; she would plunge into the water and rescue Lisa if it became necessary; she would even die rescuing Lisa.

The sun was setting and the vivid colors in the sky just behind Lisa made her hair seem very red. She was selfishly engrossed in enjoying herself, skipping stones, showing off whether anyone was looking at her or not. Silhouetted, she became less Lisa than a figure, quite a lovely figure when regarded in this way, bending, standing straight and graceful, skipping a stone, turning to laugh.

"Come on back," Philip called, but Lisa ignored him. Philip, denouncing the coldness of the water and life in general and fools of all kinds in particular as he went, plunged in after her.

Now there were two silhouettes against the sky. Cathy, feeling suddenly a terrible embarrassment, looked the other way.

Randy returned, and Marvin spread out the picnic supper. Lisa and Philip joined the campfire, both of them exclaiming they were ravenous, glancing at each other and then away.

There was a bottle of champagne in one of the hampers, put there, it was to be assumed, for Philip. Lisa catching sight of it while she was seated drying her feet before the fire, demanded it: "Oh champagne, how perfect! Just what we need so that we won't catch cold."

Philip poured some for her and then for himself. He remembered Cathy and hesitated: "A little won't hurt you, I guess."

"I don't care for any," Cathy said stiffly.

Philip and Lisa drank, looking at each other and laughing as they did so.

After supper Cathy tried to initiate a few of their usual games but it was no use; Lisa and Philip refused to join sensibly. In the game of "I went to see my Aunt," they used senseless words and laughed at each other as if each found the other inordinately clever.

The game trailed off into oblivion. Randy did not care; he was stretched on his stomach on a blanket poring over his specimens. Cathy, fiercely, did not care. Certainly Lisa and Philip, quiet suddenly but creating a strangely tense atmosphere about them by their very silence, did not care either.

A purple haze was descending upon them, enfolding them, until they all looked like ghosts. Lisa roused herself; she complained: "I'm cold." She held out her hands to Philip. "Feel how cold my hands are."

"Can't you think of anything better than that?"

"Why should I?" Lisa pouted, and Philip laughed.

Philip took Lisa's hands and held them between his own. He did not advise her to blow on them as he might have done Cathy, who was hugging her knees against her chin and staring with a blank face at the ground mists which were rising on the opposite bank of the river.

Philip proposed abruptly: "Let's take a little walk before it's time to go home." Lisa agreed immediately, springing up, "Oh yes, let's do get some exercise"—she who never took exercise of any kind if she could help it.

Lisa drifted off, not waiting to see who else was coming. "Oh come on, Cathy," urged Philip; he looked as if he really wanted her but Cathy was hurt and stubborn. "No, thanks, I'll wait here with Randy."

It was a long time before Philip and Lisa returned. The campfire had died down and Marvin, tending it, was drowsy. Randy with his head on his arm was soundly and contentedly asleep.

Cathy was not asleep; she greeted Lisa, still talking with suspicious animation, and Philip, looking aloof but sheepish, with Christian forbearance.

"Where on earth have you been, anyhow?"

"Oh just walking," Lisa said.

Philip began to pack the picnic things into the wagon. Cathy refused even to look at him, much less help him.

Chapter 8

RANDY WAS WORKING by himself in his schoolroom laboratory the following morning when Philip came in. It was not Philip's regular morning for instruction and Randy greeted him with pleased surprise: "Hello. Did you forget something?"

"My head, very likely," Philip said; he ruffled Randy's hair affectionately: "No ill effects from yesterday's picnic? Going to sleep on the ground was rather a foolish thing for you to do."

Randy said doubtfully that he supposed so, but . . . "Father Gonzáles hardened himself when he was a young man by sleeping on the ground. The bare ground, without even a blanket."

Philip said, "Oh?" and drew up a high stool: "We can make some slides from the stagnant water in tanks two and three if you like."

They worked together companionably. Philip glanced toward the door several times; he asked presently, "Where are the girls?"

"The girls? Oh, well, Cathy is having vacation, you know; she only studies for an hour or so most days. Lisa doesn't study at all; she usually sleeps until noon."

"Lazy wretch."

"Well, Lisa admits that she's lazy," Randy said. He added, with a matter-of-factness which brought a suspicious look from Philip: "She's grown quite beautiful, though, don't you think?"

Philip shrugged; she said that he supposed Lisa would do very well. "When she grows up."

"She seems quite grown up to me," Randy said. "The thing that worries me is that perhaps having Lisa grow up so fast has made Cathy unhappy."

"Why should Cathy be so concerned about what Lisa does?"

"Girls don't like to be outdone by each other, you know," Randy said.

Philip stared and then burst out laughing. "Where did you learn so much about girls?"

"From books." Randy grinned; he said, "Not from Father Gonzáles, this time."

"No, I wouldn't have thought so."

"Watching Cathy and Lisa too," Randy said. "I suppose boys don't like to be outdone by each other either, but I haven't known many boys. Lisa is very beautiful and she shows off; you can't blame Cathy for wanting to show off too."

"She'll have plenty of chance to do that."

"I know, but it's hard waiting. Particularly with Cathy's temperament. I often think how fortunate it was that Cathy was the one born with the strong doing sort of temperament while I was the one born with the quiet bookish one."

"Do you?"

"My habits won't have to change much even when we do go to Washington," Randy said; he said in an aside: "Do you notice how the idea of going to Washington seems to have affected us all in some way?"

Philip nodded.

"Poor Cathy; she is dying to be a belle but now she's afraid she won't know how to act when she gets to be one."

"She'll carry things off like a dowager duchess, thanks to your mother's training," Philip assured him, and Randy, delighted, said, "You must tell her that; she will be so pleased."

"She doesn't need me to tell her; there will be enough others."

Randy asked: "What's the matter? Don't you like the idea?"

"Of Cathy's turning into a swan? It's selfish of me but I think she's just about perfect the way she is."

Randy covered his astonishment by saying tactfully that Cathy would be getting her first taste of social gaiety tomorrow night and perhaps she wouldn't like it as well as she thought she would.

"What's taking place tomorrow night?"

"Father is coming home tomorrow with guests. Haven't you noticed all the preparations downstairs?"

"Yes, of course. I'd forgotten it was tomorrow." Philip was depressed. "I suppose now the house will be full of people for weeks."

"Up here we don't change very much," Randy said; his grin could be impish and glancing at Philip now it lighted up his face.

"You can seek sanctuary up here when you need it."

"Thank you. Are you laughing at me, you rascal?"

"It would ill behoove me," Randy said. "Surely you're coming for the dinner party tomorrow night? Cathy is going to be there."

"How about you?"

"No, I'm too young. But I shall watch and observe from afar."

Philip laughed; his spirits were beginning to rise.

"Both of the girls will be present, clad in glorious raiment," Randy said.

"Where did Cathy get hers? I haven't heard of anything new."

"It belonged to Lisa, I think. Cut down to fit Cathy."

"You aren't feeling left out?"

Randy chuckled; he said he would not be left out entirely. "Now and then a stray guest manages to make his way even up here. He pats me on the head and says what a splendid little scholar."

"Good heavens," Philip said.

"It's only fair for the observer to be the observed now and then," Randy said. He had left the experiment for the moment and his hands lay quietly on the counter before him; they were long artistic hands, sensitive, very frail. He said, "I don't mind. It's one of the penalties for having a famous father, and most of the time I have only the advantages."

The experiment was finished and Randy noted the results in his notebook while Philip washed and dried his hands and put on his coat.

"Would you like to drive to the Sarabelle with me?" Philip asked. "I have a patient there and I'm looking for company."

"I'm sorry, but Father Gonzáles is coming at eleven to read Greek with me and then afterward perhaps we'll go to the Mission."

Philip finished drying his hands: "You admire Father Gonzáles very much, don't you?" Philip was not a Catholic but he admired the priest too: Father Gonzáles was as unusual a personality as he was a priest. He had been a missionary priest in this diocese for nearly fifty years; he had snow-white hair, deeply tanned skin, penetrating blue eyes, and a handclasp of iron, though he was a frail old man who had undergone many hardships for his calling.

"More than anyone I've ever known," Randy said.

Philip suppressed a slight disgruntlement; until recently he had been the object of Randy's hero worship. "So long as he doesn't encourage you to sleep on bare ground I give full support to your admiration."

"Father Gonzáles was sickly when he was growing up; did you know? He learned to surmount his handicaps and lead a busy useful life."

"And so shall you."

"Yes, I hope so. Sometimes it worries me because so much is given to me and I give so little in return."

"Your job at present is to get well and strong."

"It isn't much of a job, is it?"

Philip, frowning, said, "You mustn't let yourself get morbid."

"Morbid? I don't believe I am. Doesn't that mean unhappy?"

"Well, yes, in a way."

"But I'm not at all unhappy. I could be perfectly happy as things are, all the rest of my life; just reading, studying, working here in the laboratory. But that wouldn't be very useful, would it?"

"Perhaps it would. Who can say?"

"Father Gonzáles was a poet," Randy said. "He's still a poet, only now in a different way. He thinks that being a scientist is rather like being a poet; it can be ingrown and selfish, or it can be turned outward to help people."

Philip said uneasily, "But see here, Father Gonzáles is a remarkable person, certainly, but he is very old and a priest and you are very young with all kinds of decisions still ahead of you."

"That's the strange thing, when Father Gonzáles and I talk together there don't seem to be those differences between us. I don't mean that I'm wise, as he is; it's more as if he helped me up to stand where he is standing and see a little of what he is seeing."

Philip, still uneasy, protested: "Hero worship isn't the same thing as religious conviction, you know."

Randy answered, "I know; Father Gonzáles tells me that too. But I am studying with him and I have a natural feeling for the Catholic religion, I think; perhaps because so many of my ancestors were Catholic. Father Gonzáles doesn't press me; you mustn't think that."

"No, you couldn't have a better teacher or adviser."

"He says that about you too. He says he admires you almost as much as if you were a good Catholic."

"Does he? I'm grateful to him. Well, just don't sleep on bare ground until I give you the word."

"No, I won't, Philip, really. Thank you for coming."

Downstairs, Philip found Theresa in one of the formal drawing-rooms, arranging flowers. He watched her unnoticed for a few minutes; her hands, long and slender and capable, were the most beautiful Philip had ever seen.

She looked up, smiling. "Are you looking for me?"

"Not particularly. It's nice to find you alone for a minute, though; you've been so busy for the past week or so, I've had only glimpses of you."

She laughed, stepping back to admire her flower arrangements. "Yes, I know; isn't it terrible? Tomorrow things will be even worse." There was a little flush of color against her high cheekbones.

"You aren't tiring yourself out, are you?"

She turned her head quickly, giving him a startled amused glance. "Bless you, no. You've got so in the habit of taking care of us that I'm afraid we worry you a great deal."

"You're my family, after all."

"Philip, it's good to hear you say that."

He went to stand beside her; she was a most comfortable person to be with. She was warm without coquetry, and he could without self-consciousness display his deep affection by taking one of her hands and holding it against his face.

"It seems to me that you are wearing yourself out for nothing," he said, referring to the flowers. "Won't they be wilted by tomorrow?"

"What? Oh these, yes of course they will; I was just trying for effect."

"You were a thousand miles off," he accused her jealously.

"I'm afraid I was. I'll be getting as much of a dreamer as Cathy if I'm not careful."

"Speaking of Cathy, I understand she is to appear tomorrow night clad in glorious raiment."

"Yes."

"She must be beside herself with excitement."

Theresa laughed. She returned to the flowers, pulling out a stem and returning it with gestures unusually aimless, for her.

"Randy is going to the Mission with Father Gonzáles; does he go very often?"

"Quite often. Is there any reason why he shouldn't?"

"None at all, no."

"Philip, what will we do without you?"

"I've just been wondering the same thing."

"It will only be for part of each year in any case."

"Yes, but things will be bound to be different. There's a difference in the air already. Everyone seems unsettled and waiting for something to happen."

"Has it upset Randy, do you think?"

"No, no. I was thinking more of Cathy." Philip continued gloomily, "I feel like running off with Cathy and hiding her somewhere to keep her from growing up."

Theresa said quietly, "Yes, that would be nice, but I'm afraid we will find she is already grown up."

"She'll turn into one of those simpering empty-headed fashionable young monsters, I suppose. She trusts everybody; she hasn't any judgment."

"I'm not so sure of that."

Philip kicked at the carpet; he was a young man who had trained himself to run away from his sensibilities rather than suffer from them. He felt morose and sullen; he was being made to acknowledge that it was possible for even those he loved to be hurt.

He said, "I suppose she will fall in love as soon as possible and get her heart broken."

There was silence; Theresa could not express her fear that Cathy already was in love and that her heart was in imminent danger of being broken. Theresa studied Philip's face; it showed no awareness of Cathy's plight, if that was what it could be called. His blindness, combined with his genuine concern and affection, made matters the more complicated: poor Cathy. A feeling of helplessness assailed Theresa; she too had been very blind. There was much to be said for Helena's worldly attitude that it was her duty to guide her daughter into an advantageous marriage; such a procedure seemed at the moment much more satisfactory than abandoning Cathy to the uncertainties of her emotions.

Theresa said lightly, "There's no remedy for that, I'm afraid. Except the one you suggest, running off with her in your pocket." She kept her head turned; surely she had spoken too frankly. Philip would become self-conscious, and she, Theresa, already self-accused of selfishness in failing to understand her daughter, would have contributed to her difficulties.

"It might be a good idea, at that," Philip said, and Theresa drew a deep breath. "I have a feeling of inadequacy all of a sudden where Cathy is concerned," she confessed; Philip stared at her in astonishment; he would as soon have thought of the stars and moon as inadequate.

"I have forgotten all the things that are entailed in launching a daughter in society," Theresa explained.

"Oh, that. I wish she didn't have to go through it."

"I wish she didn't, too."

They fell silent again; they were stalemated, though Philip did not know it. Philip, the one person who could have spared Cathy the suffering he dreaded for her in the next few years, was staring out of the window, as Theresa excused herself to attend to household duties.

He asked, "Is that Cathy, on the terrace?"

"No, Lisa, I think."

Philip, left behind, regretted Theresa's going. If he crossed the terrace at this moment with Lisa on it he would have to speak to Lisa and he was not in the mood to do so. Telling himself how little he was in the mood to respond to Lisa's particular brand of foolishness, he crossed the terrace, pretending not to see her.

She called, "Philip!" in a plaintive voice. She was dressed in a long linen duster with her head swathed in yards of green veiling.

"Hello. Did you call me?"

"Of course I did. I've been waiting for hours, simply hours."

He halted. "For what?"

"To see you."

"I thought you never got up before noon."

"I don't, very often. I knew you were going to one of the mines and I thought I'd go with you."

"How did you know that?"

"I heard you order your horse," Lisa said. She said, "I changed the order, by the way, to a buggy with a top. Mamma wouldn't have let me go otherwise."

"What sort of costume is that?"

"It's what they wear for motoring, other places. It keeps off the dust."

The green veiling was very becoming to Lisa's bright hair.

"May I go with you?" Lisa asked. She sounded meek; to offset the meekness she gave him one of her bright direct glances and laughed and he found himself obliged to laugh with her.

She said, "I'll be very quiet."

"I'll bet you will."

"If you don't want me of course I won't go."

"Come along," he said with an indifference which would have deceived nobody, least of all Lisa.

Chapter 9

"I'M HUNGRY," LISA complained four hours later.

Philip, watering the horses at a stream, looked up in irritation. "You didn't have to come, you know."

"Are you sorry I did?"

"My dear sweet foolish Lisa, your presence does not matter to me one way or another."

"Really? I was positive I annoyed you."

"Did you get yourself up in green veils before noon purposely to annoy me?"

"It's quite possible."

"Well, you haven't succeeded."

He climbed back into the buggy. She leaned toward him and he grew rigid with protest against this proximity of auburn hair and white skin so similar to Helena's. The similarity ended there. Lisa's eyes were not blue like Helena's; they were, in fact, almost yellow. And the curves of her body were full and vital; she had none of Helena's delicate etherealness.

In spite of her silly posturings, her manner held a languid voluptuousness which startled and excited him. His emotions were at a highly inflammable pitch, and if she had not been Helena's daughter he would have been delighted to make love to her as she obviously desired. As it was he could only set his jaw and curse the day he was born.

She said, "Almost everything annoys you, doesn't it? Or you like to pretend that it does."

"What do you mean by that?"

"Nothing. Nothing at all."

81

She glanced sideways at him again. Her figure under the tight bodice of her dress was feminine.

"You do have a terrible disposition, you know," she said. "Everybody says so."

"Oh? Who, for instance?"

"Everybody. Mamma defends you; she says you can't help it."

"And you can't help being a liar, I suppose, so I shall defend you the next time anybody calls you that."

She turned her head and smiled at him; there was a lazy mischievous glint in her eyes. "Well, you do have a terrible disposition."

"Remind me not to inflict it on you again."

"I like it when you get that fierce proud look."

Feeling extremely foolish Philip nevertheless managed to maintain the fierce proud look.

"You are terribly handsome," Lisa said. "Shall I tell you something? You are a million times more attractive than any of the young men I know at home."

"I suppose you know a great many attractive young men."

"Not many," she confessed ruefully. "Mamma is very strict when we are at home where we have to care what people do and say. And of course I haven't come out yet; when I do it will be different."

Philip said that he didn't doubt it and that there would be scores of young men, each more attractive than the last, for her to choose from.

"Just the same, even though I'm not out, I've had men fall in love with me. Several of them have wanted to marry me. But of course I don't intend to marry for ages and ages."

"Why not?"

Lisa said, in a reasonable voice, that she wanted a little time to enjoy herself.

"Can't one enjoy oneself after one marries?"

"Not the same way. Look at Mamma."

Philip, startled, inquired, "What do you mean; what is there to look at?"

"She has to put up with all sorts of things. Papa has nervous indigestion, you know. And he despises Mamma's afternoons, where people read poetry and discuss intellectual things."

Philip said uneasily that he doubted if he would care for them himself.

"They're quite famous, though," Lisa said. "Women have to

do tiresome things like that after they are married; it's expected of them. Papa expects it, though he won't come. Of course in a way Papa is more devoted than most husbands; he doesn't even have a mistress."

"A what? What are you prattling about?"

"I don't care, most men do," Lisa said. She continued, ignoring Philip's outrage: "Perhaps Papa would too except for his digestion; he never goes anywhere except to the bank and then straight home. He stays off by himself reading; he almost never interferes with Mamma's arrangements. He isn't dictatorial or demanding; he only asks to be let alone; he hardly ever accompanies Mamma anywhere. Quite often I bring him his slippers and try to make him comfortable when he returns home after a difficult business day."

Lisa said this in a tone of unbearable virtue.

Philip, staggered by these revelations which he suspected were half true and half false, said feebly, "Good heavens!"

"Oh, I don't mind."

"I wasn't thinking of you."

"Mamma? Well, perhaps she minds sometimes; she has headaches. I've never had a headache in my entire life, though I've lied about it quite often, of course."

"Why, of course?"

"Well, people have to, or else other people make them do dull tiresome things. Women, at least. I suppose it's different with men."

Philip pulled himself together enough to say quite different; there was a certain honor among men.

Lisa laughed softly; she said that even so she wouldn't choose to be a man. It was far more exciting and more fun, she said, waving her handkerchief gently before both their faces as if it were a fan, to be a woman.

"If you can call yourself a woman."

"I soon shall be if I'm not now. Actually I have been for quite a long time."

Philip glanced at her. Her lashes were long and gold-tipped; her eyes glinted at him under them. Her skin was less white than he had thought; it had a soft glowing duskiness, something like the bloom of an apricot, and her hair was the color of copper. Her forehead was deceptively wide and candid; her mouth was full and luscious, inviting. He could see the swell of her young figure above the square neckline of her dress. Everything about her was desirable; he was dismayed to discover that he was trembling all over.

"Do you like me?" Lisa asked; her eyes brimmed with amusement at having caught him staring at her.

"I think you are a silly little fool, if you must know."

"Why do you? I'm not silly at all. I have to be practical but that isn't my fault. I had far rather not be." Lisa sighed, a strangely sincere-sounding sigh. "Sometimes I think nobody really understands me. Everybody takes for granted that I'm frivolous and silly just because I'm pretty. Sometimes I wish I had a bad complexion and had to wear glasses."

"I'll bet you do," Philip said; he laughed.

"Well, I don't, really, of course," Lisa said; she laughed too. "Just the same I do have serious thoughts."

"Such as what?"

"Such as wishing I were rich. So I wouldn't have to worry about marrying."

"I thought all girls wanted to marry."

"I suppose they do if they can marry anyone they want. In my case it will be different. I shall probably have to marry some rich fat monster."

"Especially rich," Philip said savagely; he was offended and hurt.

She replied, unabashed, "Well, why not? I detest being poor. It isn't the same at home as at Keepsake; at home we have to economize all the time because Papa is French and thrifty and can't bear extravagance even when it isn't his money that's being wasted. But he can't risk offending Uncle Michael and it's Mamma that Uncle Michael gives the money to, and so Papa can do nothing except raise a great fuss now and then. Mamma can do as she pleases because of the money; you see what I mean?"

Philip, by way of answer, started up the horses.

"If it weren't for Uncle Michael we would have to do without all sorts of things," Lisa said as calmly as if she were not at this moment being rocketed around dangerous curves in a light buggy by a madman who had just discovered himself in love with her and was not pleased by the discovery.

"That would be a great pity, wouldn't it?"

"Yes, it would. It would be silly, besides. That would really be silly, to be poor when there was no need to be poor. And I don't need to be poor and I don't intend to be, so don't glare at me. People stare at me wherever I go; I'm just beginning to realize it. And I like it. It's like finding out you can sing, and it would be foolish to waste it."

"Very foolish," Philip said evenly. He pulled up the horses; he said, without excitement, "Well, I wish you luck with your rich fat monster."

"All rich men aren't monsters. Look at Uncle Michael."

"Many of them are. In one way or another."

"I believe you are jealous."

"Don't be an idiot."

"I wish you were jealous."

"Do you? Well, I'm not."

"I like you so much. I'm glad I came with you today; are you glad I came?"

"Not particularly."

"At home I wouldn't be allowed to spend a day like this with a young man, off by ourselves."

"Well, you are quite safe with me. I'm old enough to be your uncle."

"But you aren't, are you?" Lisa asked. She laughed.

"No, and it's a good thing for you I'm not."

"Why? Do you hate me?"

"Of course I don't hate you."

"You don't like me. You don't even like to be with me; you just said so. And you think I'm spoiled and selfish."

"So you are."

"Well, but it isn't altogether my fault. And I'm fond of you, Philip. Really fond. I've thought and thought about you ever since we got here this time."

"Have you?" he asked. He cleared his throat.

"Don't you believe me?"

"I'm not rich or fat. You are wasting your time thinking about me."

She turned her head and smiled into his eyes. "No, I'm not. I like thinking about you."

"You'll forget me as soon as you leave."

Her eyes did not waver. There was an expression of wistfulness on her face. She said, "No, I won't."

"Are you practising on me?"

"Practising what?"

"Practising charming your rich fat monster!"

She abandoned the wistful expression for one of intense merri-

85

ment. His spirits fell, proportionately.

She said, "You aren't at all susceptible, are you?"

"I hope I am old enough to recognize childish pranks when I see them."

"You could be mistaken, however," she said. She was not looking at him now; she was staring ahead. He glanced at her a number of times, his face exposing his longing to trust her even a little bit.

She said presently, "It's wonderful here at Keepsake, isn't it? I wish I could live here all the time."

"Yes, it should be rich enough even for your blood."

She ignored his sarcasm and admitted frankly, "Yes, it is." Her complete self-interest was as magnificent in its way as her hair, her eyes, or her figure. She said, "And besides, it's so important and famous. Everyone has heard of Keepsake, even in France. Everyone has heard of Uncle Michael too."

"And I suppose that makes you feel important."

"Certainly it does. Everybody envies me when I tell them about it, all the gold, you know, and silk sheets, and so many servants. Some of the girls even pretend not to believe it because they are so mad with jealousy, except that all of them have heard enough about American millionaires so they have to believe it whether they want to or not. One of the girls said it sounded like a fairy story and do you know that's exactly how I feel when I am at Keepsake, like a princess in a fairy story."

Philip said roughly, "Cathy is the real princess." He glanced at Lisa to see how she was taking that.

She stared at him coolly. "Cathy is not the real princess."

"Why isn't she?"

"Because nobody has kissed her yet," Lisa said. "Everybody has to have a kiss to be the real princess."

"Have you?"

"Not yet."

She leaned closer to him, lifting her face. He stared down at her soft uplifted mouth; her eyes mocked him. "You little devil," he said. He kissed her, a brief tantalizing kiss.

Instantly she sat up straight and began to laugh. It was a gay laugh of pure high spirits, and after a startled pause he laughed too. They laughed together uproariously. It had been a long time since Philip had laughed with anyone in just this way. It swept him back, with violent nostalgia, to his youth, to the gay carefree days when he had been an undergraduate in Paris and had strolled along calm wide boulevards and wasted hours in the dim coolness of basement cafés drinking wine and holding long intellectual discussions and singing and dancing and making love to girls as beautiful and seductive and soulless as Lisa. Lisa's appeal was frankly to the senses; Philip had grown a little weary of worshipping a distant star.

"Now I'm the real princess," Lisa gloated.

"You are a spoiled conceited silly young girl."

"And you are a spoiled conceited silly young man."

"So I am. We're a pretty pair."

"But we have a good time together. We like each other too; at least I like you, Philip. Very, very much."

They were following a narrow dusty ravine. The buggy jolted and rocked even at this pace; Lisa was thrown frequently against him. With each contact his nerves were on fire. A sudden tenseness of his grip on the reins betrayed his desire to kiss her, to shake her, to make love to her. Lisa was enjoying herself very much.

When they came into sight of the house Philip's grasp on the reins suddenly slackened. He was a poor country doctor hanging about on the outskirts of a life to which he could never aspire; he would be a fool to let himself be drawn into even the mildest of flirtations with Lisa. Lisa's youth and vitality were dangerous to him since they threatened the hard-won acceptance of his fate behind which he had barricaded himself.

"Here we are," Lisa said.

"Yes," Philip said. "Here we are."

A stableman came to take the horses. Philip held a side door open for Lisa and they stepped inside. The great rooms inside the house were cool and quiet in midafternoon lethargy.

Sam brought them a tray of food and a cool drink in a frosted silver pitcher. He said, "Miss Theresa asks for you to look at one of the men, Doctor Philip."

"Which one?"

"John Mendos. He fell from a ladder and hurt his arm. He has been praying and groaning like a banshee ever since."

Philip excused himself to go look after John Mendos. He encountered Cathy in the outer courtyard; she was sitting on a low wall skipping stones in a small pool.

"Did you have a nice ride?"

"So so." He glanced at her suspiciously. "What's it to you? Are you minding other people's business again?"

"Certainly not." Cathy drew herself up. Philip took one of her arms and hustled her along beside him. "How did you happen to be sitting right here at this particular moment?"

"I knew you had to see John Mendos and so I waited to help you."

Philip grunted, but he said, "All right, if you want to."

John Mendos' arm was broken, as Philip ascertained by expert pinching and probing, despite John's heart-rending groans. Philip then proceeded to set the broken bones, whistling dolefully at the same time between his teeth, an indication that he was in good spirits. John groaned and moaned, so loudly that he disturbed even Philip. Cathy long ago would have been melted down into tears except that her newly discovered professional pride forbade it. She took her cue from Philip, even managing a slight whistle, which became unexpectedly a hiss like a boiling teakettle. Everyone glanced at her, and Cathy managed an apologetic smile.

"You look a little green," Philip said. "Are you going to faint?"

"I . . . don't think so."

"Sit down and lean your head over."

She obeyed and felt better. Mrs. Mendos, who was going to have her fifth baby soon, brought Cathy a glass of water. Mrs. Mendos was very small and the coming baby was very much in evidence; Cathy tried to take it for granted as the others did but she could not help feeling awed by the whole procedure. "You should be the one sitting down, not me," she said, springing to her feet; Mrs. Mendos continued to press the water until Cathy took it and drank it.

"Look at your wife," Philip was admonishing John. "She goes through childbirth every year without half as much fuss as you are making over a simple fracture."

John Mendos rolled his eyes, divided between fright and embarrassment at the frankness of this remark before the young daughter of the man whom he regarded as his patron. "Is that what I have, Doctor?"

Philip laughed. "You'll recover. But it's a mighty good thing it was your arm that was broken instead of your leg or we would have had to shoot you."

John looked still more terrified.

"That's supposed to be a joke, John. You'll be as good as new in a few days."

Philip turned his attention to Mrs. Mendos. "How are you feeling?"

Mrs. Mendos smiled and nodded, too embarrassed by this attention to answer.

"Are you taking your medicine?"

More smiles and nods. "Let me see the bottle," Philip said; he was very strict with patients when he was worried about them. It exasperated him when they failed, through ignorance or neglect, to carry out his instructions. Cathy wished now that his manner were not quite so brusque, since it often defeated his purpose. He could be endlessly patient caring for a sick person, but he sometimes seemed impatient simply because his concern was so great for each one; many of his patients, like Mrs. Mendos, shrinking back as Philip pointed accusingly at the full bottle of medicine, were a little afraid of him. The scene ended with Mrs. Mendos promising with agitated headshakings to take the medicine and Mr. Mendos requesting medicine of his own to take for his arm which was beginning to ache, and all the children adding distressed voices to the confusion.

"That's what I have to put up with," Philip said as he and Cathy came out of the little house together, walking across the courtyard with the sun beating on their heads and the whitewashed buildings about them. Philip walked so fast that Cathy had to run to keep up with him.

"You upset them shouting at them like that," Cathy panted.

"I did, did I? They need something to upset them. Mrs. Mendos is far too frail for so much difficult childbearing; I've thought the last two times I was going to lose her."

Cathy stopped short on the path; the bright vivid colors seemed to be fading about her. She said, "I don't believe I could bear it if she died."

Philip glanced about impatiently; he returned. He said, "You have to bear it. You have to learn to bear things that happen to you."

"I know, but it seems so awful."

"Death isn't really awful. Sometimes it's quite the opposite."

Cathy shuddered. Philip said gently, "Don't take it so hard. We'll do our best to see that she's all right."

"When is the baby coming?"

"Not for several months and she's already exhausted, that's why I'm worried about her."

"I'm sorry I criticized you for not being tactful."

Philip gave a surprised laugh; he said, "You're quite right, I'm not. I'm more of a scientist than I am a doctor."

"Could I be there when the baby comes?"

"Do you want to be?"

"I'm not sure. But I wouldn't faint; I'm sure of that now."

"We'll ask Theresa."

"I'm sorry that I hung around watching for you and Lisa."

"All right, don't be such a little muttonhead. You always have to go to one extreme or the other."

"Muttonhead!" Cathy cried in a strangled voice: "The truth of the matter is that you aren't at all tactful, even polite."

"I admitted I wasn't."

"You simply trample over people quite often and hurt their feelings!"

"What's the matter with you?" Philip cried in amazement. He took Cathy's wrists and held them; Cathy became limp and quiet. Both of them waited for the rush of tears which did not come.

"I'm upset, I guess," Cathy said.

"Upset. That's putting it mildly."

"I'm sorry."

"Don't start that again."

"Life is difficult, isn't it?"

"Yes, it is, quite difficult."

"So much seems to be happening all of a sudden. Father coming home tomorrow and waiting to see if we are going to Washington and Mrs. Mendos having her baby and . . . other things."

"Things have been happening right along only you've just begun to be aware of them."

There was a little silence and then Cathy agreed, "Yes, I expect that's it."

Chapter 10

CATHY ADORED HER father's homecomings. He always arrived, riding bareheaded, on the stallion which had been sent to the station for him, ahead of the rest of his party which would follow in carriages.

He arrived with a great clatter of hooves and a shout like a rebel war-whoop. Members of the household and the servants were on balconies and terraces and in the courtyard, infected by his enthusiasm and love of drama, and there was a great commotion. Stablemen ran forward to hold the plunging black stallion; Cathy, along with others, waved a white handkerchief frantically.

Even after he had swung himself to the ground Michael Brett towered over the men who were hurrying forward to serve him. His graying hair was fierce and upspringing; his face was burned deep mahogany, which did not disappear during his city interludes, and it was etched with deep lines from sun and wind. His vanity and belief in himself were a power which emanated from him as tangibly as those lines.

His eyes were eternally young, bright and alive; they burned with intense blue against the darkness of his skin. His nose was strong, curved like a beak. His mouth was full and sensuous, his lips beautifully modeled. People fought him or succumbed to him; sometimes they did both.

Theresa today had put a little rouge on her face because everyone said she was pale. She asked, "Does it show?" and there was a funny little smile on her face which caused Cathy to catch her breath with excitement. Theresa today was an elegant stranger, dressed in silk and with her hair, shining like satin, drawn back into its great knot on her neck.

Michael Brett's body was magnificent even in middle age, his shoulders massive, his head carried thrust forward on his broad strong neck. He said, "Tessa, my dearest Tessa," holding her for a long moment before he would look at anyone else. Then he was greeting everyone, hugging Cathy to him in a huge and careless embrace, teasing Lisa by pretending to be awestruck by her beauty, bending down to kiss Helena's cheek. With Randy he was tender and diffident.

In the library he distributed gifts. He loved giving and receiving gifts as much as Cathy did; he always returned home laden with them.

There was a diamond and sapphire pendant for Theresa which he must fasten with his own hands. Theresa had many cases of jewels; she brought them out and wore them when he was at home. She was wearing pearls now, at her ears and about the neck of her gown of stiff changeable taffeta with its stiff fluted collar against which her dark sleek head was poised like the center of a flower. She removed the pearl necklace, laughing, and let Michael put on the new one. "Yes, it suits you," he said, standing off to look at her intently with his head on one side.

There was a gold watch for Randy with the inscription: "To Durand Michael Brett from his father, Michael Brett, 1897." There was a little watch of gold and blue enamel on black grosgrained ribbon for Cathy, to be worn about her neck, and another for Lisa. There was a fleur-de-lis brooch for Helena.

There would be gifts for all the servants too when his trunks arrived; Michael never forgot anyone. There might even be a little fur mantle for Cathy; she had coveted one for a long time and had given several hints in letters about it.

Michael's blue gaze, swinging about the room from one person to another, was like a searchlight. He talked to everyone at once, questioning them with a rapid volley as if he must learn without delay everything which had happened during his absence. He held Theresa's hand as he talked and his eyes swung constantly back to her while he was asking if they were all well, what they had been doing, what had occurred; making it sound as if life at Keepsake whether he was there or not was a constant adventure. And where was Philip, he demanded? He missed Philip; he was always a little hurt if someone among those he loved here at home was prevented from being present to welcome him on his arrival. On being assured that Philip would be here for dinner he said good, good, sounding still a little hurt; he returned the small jeweler's box containing his gift to Philip to his pocket.

Oh, but it was good to be home, Cathy's father said then. He sat down, stretching out his legs and giving enormous sighs of contentment and delight at finding himself unharassed by city life and business and meetings and great decisions; this made them all laugh as it was supposed to do. In a minute, he said, he must see the rest of the house, the stables; he must see any changes which had taken place during his absence, though there were none so far as Cathy knew. He was the one who caused changes; others maintained things as he left them. He must see everything, but just now he couldn't move. One of these days he was going to retire; he was coming home to Keepsake and nothing ever would tempt him away from it again.

He was always promising that. He laughed even as he said it; even Cathy no longer believed it.

"Where are you, Theresa? I can't see you."

Theresa was consulting with Sam in the doorway about the trays of food and frosted drinks being arranged for the guests who would be arriving in a few minutes, hot and dusty. She moved back to Michael. If he cares so much about us all, Cathy thought more coldly than she ever before had thought of her father, why does he leave us so often?

"Let me look at you. Really look at you."

Theresa stood still before him; the odd little smile was still on her face. "How beautiful you are! Isn't she?" Michael asked the others without looking at them. "The most beautiful woman in the world."

"I spent hours making myself so."

"Did you? For me? You would have been beautiful in any case, but did you?"

"I did."

"You wore the gown too that I sent."

"Of course."

"The pearls were wrong for you, too unsophisticated. You are really a sophisticated person, Tessa."

"Am I?"

"Very. And wise. How do women get so wise? And beautiful. How beautiful!"

Theresa shook her head; she was embarrassed by too much praise, as was Randy. Cathy, who expanded under almost any form of flattery, wondered what it would be like to have too much of it.

Theresa and Michael looked at each other; the other persons in the room might just as well not have been there. They were neither welcome nor unwelcome; they did not exist for the moment. It had been exactly the same way, as in Helena Minard's stories, when Theresa and Michael first had met in the ballroom. They had met and come together, and so far as they were concerned, though they could not agree, though they quarreled and caused each other great sorrow and consternation, everyone else in the room and the world had fallen away. There was an excitement about them when they spoke to each other or even when they looked at each other which reminded Cathy of thunder and lightning.

None of the others except Cathy seemed to mind being left out.

Cathy, fingering her watch which hung over a heavy heart, stood a little apart, watching her father and mother and wishing she could take some place in the tableau they performed so dramatically.

Michael was talking about the appointment, though Theresa had signaled to him that this was neither the time nor the place. It was evident that Michael's pride was hurt; he was angry; and he wanted Theresa's sympathy.

He said, striding up and down the room with a fierce impatience which threatened its walls: "I don't know why I started the whole thing; I'm sorry I did. But since I did I'll have to see it through."

"I understand that, of course."

"I'm way out of my natural habitat, of course. You advised me against it; why don't you remind me of that now?"

"Come," Theresa said; she never let people be sorry for themselves.

"I know; I'm a fool," Michael said. "You believe in me?"

"Need you ask?"

"It may get ugly. It's already ugly enough. They're dragging out everything they can lay their hands on."

"That was to be expected, wasn't it?"

Michael laughed; it was evident he had not expected it. "I could break every one of them with my bare hands and I'd like to."

"That would scarcely help."

"If I thought any of this would hurt you," Michael said.

"I shan't be hurt."

Michael took several turns up and down the room; he had something he still wanted to say. Theresa waited; the odd little smile was gone from her face.

Michael said, "They're trying to use everything against me, even that old story."

"I know."

He gave her a quick examining glance: "You've been seeing the papers?"

"Yes, of course."

"Not very pretty, are they?"

"No," Theresa agreed calmly.

"They've even got hold of the woman," Michael said. "McDaniels—what was her name?"

"MacDonald."

"Ah. You do remember. She's to tell her story on the stand again. Do me a favor and stop reading the papers for a few weeks."

Theresa said, "If I didn't believe the story in the beginning then I shan't believe it now."

"I often wonder why you didn't."

"It wasn't even a very clever story as I remember."

"No, it wasn't!" Michael's lowering mood veered suddenly; he laughed uproariously. "Was that the reason you didn't?"

"Perhaps. We've talked enough for the present."

"It convinced quite a few people. And may again. I often wonder why they don't use that poor devil who tried to hold us up that night in New York against me."

Theresa said, "Michael!" her voice for the first time was sharp with protest. "That was self- . . . that was something quite different!"

"Even so his face has haunted me more than the face of a vicious perjuring woman on the witness stand ever did."

"That's because you have a good heart," Theresa said softly. "A really good heart, Michael, when you let yourself use it."

Cathy could not prevent herself from glancing toward them. They were looking at each other in a way she knew she would never forget.

Almost immediately that tableau broke and another was formed. Events became for Cathy, as they so often did these days, a series of tableaus which she stood outside of, watching but taking no part. Sam stood in the doorway saying that the guests had not yet arrived and the ice was melting; Michael stood at Randy's shoulder watching him do a puzzle; Helena Minard stared into the bottom of her glass as if she saw something unusual there; Lisa hung her watch a new way and looked at its effect in a mirror. There never

95

seemed to be a place for Cathy in any tableau. Either she was too old or too young, too eager or too diffident.

Today she was shy in a way she could not remember ever having been with this magnificent father of hers. Usually she was closest to him, pushing against him, heavy and straining with her love. Sometimes she had leaned against him so heavily that he had had to say: "Gently, gently, or I'll be all over black and blue marks; I am a great deal more easily bruised than most people think."

That had been a joke, for of course Cathy could not bruise him, but she knew that he had meant she must be considerate and share him with everybody. His eyes always went first to Theresa and then to Randy; even when he teased Cathy he often continued to look at Theresa, or sometimes, his eyes puzzled and a little wistful, at Randy. Randy never pushed forward; Randy was never tiresome about love. He never needed to be assured over and over that somebody loved him.

Cathy often was tiresome; she wanted to be noticed so much that she had to hold herself perfectly still with her hands clenched at her sides. A short time before she would have bitten her nails but she was determined to conquer that habit and she had succeeded well enough in the past few days so that she could congratulate herself on her progress. She had so many flaws in her character that eradicating them seemed almost hopeless. For instance: she had no business minding that Lisa had been brought a watch exactly like her own, but her heart had gone down and down in spite of everything she could do.

She was about to slip from the room when her father said, "Well, well, here's something I've overlooked; I wonder what this can be?" He brought out a tiny box, looking at it in pretended astonishment, and Cathy knew that it was something just for her. Then she was so ashamed of herself that she had difficulty in keeping from bursting into tears.

Her father put his arm about her and drew her against him while she buried her head against his shoulder. "What's this?" he asked. "Is our Prima Donna becoming bashful all of a sudden?" Being called a prima donna by him made everything suddenly seem natural and good. Her mother smiled reassuringly at her. In the box which Cathy opened was a ring, made of a cluster of pearls twisted together; it was the most beautiful ring Cathy had ever seen. Her father put it on her finger for her and she determined that never, so long as she lived, was it to come off.

She was in her room only a second or so it seemed until suddenly it was time to dress for dinner. One minute she was lying quietly on the bed in the dark, at peace with herself as she had not been for a long time; the next, lamps were being lighted and Cathy was being told sternly to get herself up and start moving if she expected to be ready when the rest of them were.

"Where's Lisa?" Cathy asked, blinking in the light.

"With her mother, so that French maid can look after both of them."

"Stop pushing me. What are you making such a fuss about?"

Stacey snorted; she said Cathy had been making enough fuss in the last few days the good Lord knew. "So come on now."

Amanda stood beside Stacey and even Hester stood in the doorway. "You're making me nervous," Cathy complained. Stripped, she let herself be scrubbed in the tub though she had had one bath that day. She was powdered, her finger and toe nails were attended to, and then the process of dressing was begun.

"Who's going to see my toe nails?"

"Never mind. Ladies look after everything."

"You cut them just day before yesterday."

"Never mind."

She was laced into a corset. There were layers and layers of petticoats, topped by a ruffled silk one Cathy never had seen before.

Her dress was put over her head and settled on her shoulders. Her hair, seized and nearly removed from her head, came through the ordeal in surpising soft deep waves. Stacey pinned it to the top of her head: "Miss Theresa told me just how to do it." She fastened a white flower in it.

They all stood back to survey their handiwork and Cathy, awed, gazed at her own image; she was beautiful. Or almost.

When she hurried down the stairway the guests were aleady assembled in the drawing-rooms before dinner. Cathy paused in the doorway; she had to stand there for several minutes steeling herself before she could enter. When she did nobody noticed her.

It was the first time she had seen this room in just this way, with the candles lighted in the chandeliers and reflected in crystal pendants, filled with people and sound and glittering splendor.

Everything was so transformed that Cathy, moving forward automatically to seek shelter beside Lisa, felt as though she were in some kind of dream. Even Lisa was a little subdued, though she refused to admit it; Lisa accepted a glass of champagne from the tray held before her and Cathy hastily did the same. "You'd better not drink that or you might be sick," Lisa advised; she said then that they had better not sit together or they would look like two children allowed to remain downstairs five minutes before being sent back to the nursery. Lisa had her skirt spread out in a full circle and she was posed before a tapestry with a welcome expectant look on her face.

"Mona Lisa, I suppose that's who you think you look like," Cathy said scathingly, but the smile on Lisa's face did not fade.

Cathy indignantly moved away, still holding the champagne in her hands; she wondered whether to drink it or whether Lisa was right and it would only add to her troubles. Her mother rescued her drawing her arm through hers and taking her from group to group to be introduced. Cathy grew taller and more poised; she was, after all, the daughter of the family; she had a place. Theresa's hand on hers, bringing her forward, made Cathy feel full of potentialities, rather like an ugly duckling turning into a swan.

"You look very nice, dearest."

"Do I really? Stacey nearly killed me, getting me ready."

"Here is Lord Dufton. Lord Dufton, my daughter, Catherine."

Cathy would have curtseyed except that the restraining hand on her arm told her that she was no longer expected to curtsey to guests. Lord Dufton did not look at all as a lord should look, in Cathy's opinion; he had a long somber face and he was not very large. Nobody, meeting him, could possibly have recognized him as a lord.

"Mrs. Rhodes, my daughter Catherine. Senator Rhodes."

Cathy's father was in this group. He winked at Cathy, and she began to feel as if she were enjoying herself.

Senator Rhodes, who was small, was standing beside Michael and teetering up on his toes to peer into the other's face. He broke off what he was saying to seize Cathy's hand and bow over it. He jerked upright and finished his sentence as if there had been no interruption: ". . . of course the entire trend of the country is westward."

Theresa said, "I'll leave you here for the moment, dearest," and Cathy settled herself at her father's side. She sipped her champagne; the Senator sounded as if he were going to make a speech and Cathy resigned herself to listen.

Her father ignored the Senator to smile down at her. "Having a good time, Duchess?"

He called her something different whenever he spoke to her. Sometimes Sweetie, sometimes Little Half Chick because she was inclined to turn as the wind blew, sometimes Duchess. Cathy liked Duchess best. "Oh very, thank you."

"The company is a little old for you, I'm afraid."

"I don't mind."

"And a little dull. All high society is dull, you may as well learn."

Cathy laughed apprehensively; she was afraid that the Senator's wife, beside her, had overheard. Mrs. Rhodes had a long raddled face and she wore a black velvet ribbon tied about her throat. She was staring at Cathy as if Cathy were some kind of curiosity. "But since we are all here for a purpose it doesn't matter so much," Michael said a little more loudly.

Mrs. Rhodes blinked and began to wave her fan; she smiled. It was impossible not to notice how people moved as Michael Brett wanted them to move, rather like puppets on strings. But perhaps only those who did so were invited to Keepsake. Cathy took a larger sip of champagne; she could not bear thoughts like these; the horrid picture in the paper had started them and since then she had been besieged by them. She moved closer to her father; she must be a terrible and disloyal person to countenance them for a moment.

"Taxes are becoming ruinous in the East!" the Senator said.

"Still, everybody can't be expected to live way out here," Mrs. Rhodes said fretfully. Cathy's father winked at her again and Cathy winked back; she was at home on this ground. The Senator's wife, with her husband's eyes on her, let her voice trail away: "I mean, without a great deal of money to provide luxuries. . . ."

The Senator thundered: "We must look to the West, from which cometh our strength. . . ."

Lady Dufton said, "The British have learned to adjust themselves to living in all the tag ends of civilization."

Michael Brett laughed aloud at that, a great shout of laughter which made everything seem natural and good again. Cathy laughed too, somewhat impertinently it was to be feared. She received retribution immediately: Lady Dufton stared at this display of bad manners—her attitude seemed to say that the British had also been forced to adjust themselves to bad manners in all parts of the world, particularly in America. She asked Cathy in a rigidly polite voice how old she was.

"Seventeen, Lady Dufton."

"Ah yes, an interesting age. In England of course you still would be in the nursery."

Cathy hastily put down her empty champagne glass. She felt her father's amused eyes on her and she flushed.

Senator Rhodes was continuing: "Soon there will not be any really large estates left in the East. Everything will have to be cut up and sold in small lots. Taxes are making it impossible for people to live decently in congested areas." Cathy admired his ability to concentrate on his subject.

"I should miss the stores and the theatre so dreadfully," Mrs. Rhodes was murmuring.

"Stores? Ah yes, the shops."

The Senator said in a voice which Cathy found unpleasantly loud: "A little of this gold would soon compensate for other lacks."

"Yes, I suppose so." Lady Dufton glanced at Michael; she looked less haughty. "Ah yes, quite." She inquired of Cathy, almost warmly: "You are still in the schoolroom, I suppose?"

"Yes, Lady Dufton."

"History, languages, all that?"

"Yes, Lady Dufton."

"And I suppose you ride?"

"Yes, Lady Dufton."

"Splendid!" Lady Dufton said in a relieved voice. "My own children were brought up in just the same way." She leaned back; a few minutes later she bent forward to ask: "What is Arizona, a colony?"

"A territory, Lady Dufton."

"Ah well, I suppose it amounts to the same thing."

Sam stood in the doorway announcing to Theresa that dinner was served. Cathy had a great longing to go with him instead of this resplendent company rising to enter the dining room.

Chapter 11

THE LONG TABLE was laid with a banquet cloth of gold lace and the famous gold plate. It was lighted by the soft glowing light of tapers set along its length and in sconces against the wall. The wall was paneled in mahogany rubbed to satin; against it the shimmering gowns and jewels of the women and the white shirt fronts of the men stood out in sharp relief.

Cathy, seated at the table, was still shivering with nerves and excitement. Everything looked so beautiful and even she, in a white mousseline gown with enormous puffed sleeves and a ruffled hem which trailed in a full curve in the back could feel, by exerting her imagination, like a heroine in a book.

She found herself next to an elderly man with kind twinkling eyes; she tried to read his name on his card.

He helped her by saying, "Hello there. I'm James Talbot."

"How do you do, Mr. Talbot? I'm Catherine Brett."

"I thought you must be. You or the other young lady." Mr. Talbot indicated Lisa across the table.

Cathy, startled, said, "Oh no, that's only Lisa. My cousin."

"Only Lisa, eh?" Mr. Talbot chuckled; his twinkling eyes studying Cathy put her at ease immediately. Now that she knew his name she knew who he was; he was the head of the banking firm of Talbot and Company.

He took a bite of his shrimp cocktail and said, "I've been looking forward to this; I remember this sauce from the last time I was here. Your mother serves the best food in the world, I think."

Cathy, delighted, said: "It's a New Orleans recipe; it's called remoulade."

"Well, it's fine, fine." Mr. Talbot quickly finished his shrimp and looked ruefully at the empty plate. Cathy offered: "You may have mine if you like." She was not sure if that was the right thing to do at a dinner party but Mr. Talbot accepted the offer: "Are you sure you don't mind?"

"Oh no. I'm not very hungry and besides we have it quite often."

"Well, in that case . . ." Beaming, Mr. Talbot allowed Cathy to switch plates. He finished Cathy's shrimp as fast as the other but he refused her offer to obtain another serving for him. "It wouldn't do for this distinguished company to get the impression that I'm greedy," he said.

He settled back in his chair and continued to beam on Cathy, looking more like a merry little gnome than an international banker. People, she was beginning to discover, were almost never as impressive as their names sounded.

Mr. Talbot said, "I have a granddaughter about your age; you must prevail on your father to bring you to New York so that you can get acquainted."

"Oh yes, I would like that. But I think we are going to Washington instead."

"Washington isn't very far from New York."

"I've never been there. To Washington, I mean."

"Many people haven't who would like to get there," Mr. Talbot said.

"Still, if you say it isn't very far."

Mr. Talbot played with his soup which he did not seem to care for as much as he did his shrimp. "Don't you like it?" Cathy asked anxiously.

"Like it? Oh, the soup. Yes, very much, so long as we don't all land in it." He wiped his mouth with his napkin; he evidently enjoyed talking in riddles for he became merry and twinkling again. He asked, "Where do you go to school?"

"We study at home. My brother and I."

"Your brother?" Mr. Talbot's eyes traveled along the table until Cathy explained: "Randy is only fourteen. He doesn't come to dinner parties yet."

"And how old are you?"

"Seventeen. This is my first real dinner party."

"Good for you. Are you enjoying it?"

"Oh yes. Do you know all the people here? I hardly know any of them."

"Most of them, I'm afraid. It's something in the nature of a convention."

"I beg your pardon."

"I beg yours. I haven't met the young lady across from us, your cousin Lisa I think you said?"

Lisa's gown was of yellow chiffon, the color of her eyes, and her hair was drawn to the top of her head in a psyche knot and tied with a velvet ribbon sprinkled with rosebuds. She was talking and laughing so excitedly that Cathy thought it quite likely the champagne had gone to her head.

"Yes, my cousin Lisa."

"The young man beside her is looking completely bewitched and I can't say that I blame him."

"Philip? Oh no."

The Senator was speaking across the entire length of the table as if he were giving a lecture. Lady Dufton sat on one side of him and Helena on the other; Lady Dufton looked affronted while Helena, fingering her wine glass, looked amused. As the Senator's voice grew stronger and more mellifluous others at the table stopped their private conversations to turn their heads and listen. "We may as well concede the floor to the Senator," Mr. Talbot said to Cathy, "since he seems to be taking it anyhow."

Cathy tried to give the impression that she was listening to the Senator though inside she was being beset by a number of violent emotions. She sent a stricken glance toward Sam, standing behind Theresa; Sam hastened to her aid.

"A little more champagne," Cathy whispered in his ear; she did not feel sure enough of herself to give a formal order.

"Do you think you should?"

"Of course I think I should."

Cathy smiled at Mr. Talbot who was watching this passage at arms with amusement. She asked, "Will you have champagne?"

"If you please."

Sam filled Mr. Talbot's glass; he poured a little, grudgingly, into Cathy's. He changed his mind, suddenly, and filled Cathy's glass. Cathy, puzzled, wondered: Now why did he do that?

She sat up straight and sipped her champagne; there was no denying that it made her more confident. She was, after all, Michael Brett's daughter; she quite often heard herself called that and it had a distinguished sound. Even Lisa had no claim on that particular title and Cathy was just beginning to realize that Lisa quite likely coveted it. Lisa, had she been Michael Brett's daughter, would have found numberless ways to make a great splash; it was up to Cathy to discover some of those ways for herself.

The Senator was booming the length of the table: "I tell you that this stirring up of class hatred is no laughing matter."

Lady Dufton inquired: "Are there clawsses in America?"

"Naturally."

The Senator's eyes, as he talked, continually strayed toward Michael, somewhat undermining his effect. He reminded Cathy a little of a hound she once had owned; it seemed disrespectful to compare a Senator to a hound but she could see that he was almost too friendly and eager to please.

"We have our aristocracy. No titles, of course." The Senator, his voice restored once again to power, made a little bow toward Lady Dufton. "No curtseying. Americans hate to bend their knees."

"Even in prayer." Nice Mr. Talbot next to Cathy put in unexpectedly.

The Senator looked taken aback; Michael Brett roared with laughter and the Senator then, as if given a signal, laughed heartily too. He repeated, "As Mr. Talbot says, even in prayer, I fear."

Lady Dufton made a jerking motion of her head, rather like a horse held by too tight a check rein. She was not amused. "What constitutes your aristocracy?"

"Blood. Breeding. Background."

"And money," Michael Brett said. One of his great hands lay on the table; he drummed with it restlessly. He looked irritated; Cathy began to feel a little nervous and she could see that others, including the Senator who took out his handkerchief and wiped his face with it, were nervous too.

"Ah," Lady Dufton said, as if her worst fears were confirmed. Her gooseberry eyes, shielded by her lorgnette, studied her host, the dining-room walls, and finally her own plate.

"Our host is being facetious," the Senator protested with heavy tact.

Michael said indifferently, "Our Senator is being coy."

"The golden calf." Mr. Talbot, still beaming and twinkling, entered the conversation again. Cathy noticed that everyone listened when he spoke, even Michael, though Michael did not turn his head. "We bend our knees to that, all right," Mr. Talbot said.

"And why not?" Michael asked; he still did not turn his head but his voice was quieter and more reasonable. "Gold has made us one of the world's leaders."

Lord Dufton spoke up after a nervous glance at his wife: "If you are driven to war with Spain . . ."

Cathy felt alarm; it sounded as if her father, single-handed, was to be expected to fight Spain. She had a vision of David and Goliath. Her father said, staring at Lord Dufton with cold impersonal eyes: "We do not want war with Spain."

"The time will come when you will be more and more involved in world affairs whether you want it or not."

"Possibly. Britain would like us to fight Spain, wouldn't she?"

Lord Dufton, looking small and gray, said, "The British Empire has her own problems."

Theresa engaged Lady Dufton in conversation; she had been presented at Court before her marriage and knew many of the persons in Lady Dufton's circle. Lady Dufton first exhibited incredulity that a member of so remote a colony had been presented at Court, but gradually she relaxed. Theresa could be gracious and proud at the same time; she was both unbending and flexible in a way which Cathy humbly determined to study. Lady Dufton's wandering lorgnette now seemed to take in the gold plate, the perfect food perfectly served, for the first time.

"We aren't interested in colonization like the British," Mr. Talbot was saying. Each time he spoke Cathy felt a surge of pride, as if she herself were taking part in the discussion. He was her dinner partner and he had spoken, until now, almost exclusively to her. He said, patting her hand absently but affectionately, "We would have no use for Cuba if we did free her."

But what a pity not to free her if she needed freeing, Cathy thought; she had a vivid picture of a lovely maiden in chains.

The Senator said, somewhat breaking the romantic spell: "With the end of our own free land we may be driven to some kind of expansion."

"Exactly." Lord Dufton nodded; he said, "Already the world is affecting you. Look at what the failure of crops in India has done to your silver."

"Oh, silver. It's our gold we depend on."

"Yes, it's our gold we depend on."

Everybody looked toward Michael Brett, even Lady Dufton; his face, with its strong jutting nose, turned here and there as if seeking release from his restlessness, while his fingers drummed on the table.

Mr. Talbot began to trace on the tablecloth with one forefinger, making little whorls and hooks. He said to Cathy, "First in any country come the adventurers, like your father. The strong men, the ruthless courageous men, to wrest gold and silver and other resources from the earth. They create a new age, whether for bad or good. Never underestimate the value of persons like your father."

"Oh, I don't." Cathy was grateful to Mr. Talbot, passionately grateful, for expressing himself in that way, because so many doubts had crept into her feelings recently and she could not help noticing that many of the people were not here because they liked her father. They even disapproved of him, like Lady Dufton, but still they were here.

"Then of course come the reformers to tell the people that they and the earth have been exploited and robbed," Mr. Talbot's dry voice went on.

She asked, "Are you a reformer?"

"Quite the contrary. I talk a great deal, don't I? You won't forget, will you, that you and I have a date in New York one of these days. Or in Washington."

Mr. Talbot was a strange dinner partner but he was a kindly considerate one. "I couldn't possibly forget," Cathy said gratefully.

Philip and Lisa must have quarreled for they were not looking at each other.

Cathy sat back in her chair; the dinner party was beginning to turn out well. People were talking, laughing, eating; Theresa at the head of the table was in full command of the situation.

Lady Dufton asked her host with deadly earnestness: "How many acres of land have you?"

"Over a million."

"Incredible!"

Michael Brett grinned; he liked being told that something he possessed or did was incredible. He said, "Not at all. There is still plenty of free land in this country."

"Tillable?"

"Not all of it, of course. Most of it range land."

Lisa and Philip were speaking again, their heads close together, and Cathy's head was beginning to be heavy, perhaps from too much champagne. She held herself straight and glanced about her, wondering if history was being made without her knowing it.

Her father was explaining a mining procedure for extracting gold, called the cyanide process, to Lord Dufton whose long humorless face was so intent that Cathy listened too, though she had heard the process explained many times.

Michael said, "The crushed ores are placed in solution which precipitates gold, cutting down waste which previously existed because of the difficulties of extraction. By 1898 the gold output will be double what it was in 1890."

"What is the exact process?"

"The finely crushed ores are bleached in vats with a dilute of potassium cyanide and allowed to remain for a period of from twelve to twenty-four hours to dissolve the gold."

"And with this process on a waste product alone you expect to double your output?"

"Easily."

"Incredible!" Lord Dufton said, as Lady Dufton had said of the million acres.

Michael Brett grinned. It was at times like this that Cathy loved him most; his face was youthful, genuinely though cynically amused, washed clean of the restless urge toward something new and greater which drove him so much of the time.

The Senator had started to speak again as if he felt he had been silent long enough. He announced: "The attempt to force an income tax on us shows all too well how the wind is blowing."

Michael Brett said, good-naturedly, "Come, Senator, the wind has blown on us before."

"Just the same there is a growing tendency in this country to penalize the enterprising and thrifty for the benefit of the shiftless and the sluggard."

Cathy, more and more confused, turned her head from one speaker to another. James Talbot was next; he said, "There is little use in worrying about a law which has been declared unconstitutional," and another man said angrily, "Senator, are we to be frightened by a tendency?"

"If Bryan is elected . . ."

"He will not be elected."

Theresa stood up; the other women at the table followed her move, Lisa among them, and Cathy's first dinner party was over.

In the drawing-room Lisa sought Cathy, though Cathy purposely had sat in a window recess by herself to have coffee and sort out her impressions. Lisa asked, "What time is it?"

"Where is your watch?"

"I couldn't wear it with a dinner gown, naturally."

"What makes you think I could, then."

Lisa yawned and fidgeted through coffee. Presently she said she had a headache and had better get some fresh air. "If Mamma asks for me tell her I've gone for a bromide, will you?"

"Why should I say that?"

"Don't be mean. You look very nice in my gown, as a matter of fact."

"It had to be taken in two inches at the waist."

Lisa laughed; she stood up. "Nobody can say I haven't plenty of figure."

"I might as well go with you. Nobody particularly wants to talk to us and I haven't anything else to do."

Lisa said quickly, "No, it would look odd if both of us went. I'll be right back."

"Well, I won't lie for you."

Lisa said, "'Tattle tale tit, your tongue shall be split,'" and sauntered off as if she had the world at her disposal.

Cathy sat for a long time by herself, but her impressions would not sort out very well. Her father was David first, and then Goliath. She was sorry she had taken so much champagne. A man named William Jennings Bryan was a reformer; nice Mr. Talbot was not a reformer. The finely crushed ores were bleached in vats with a dilute of something or other to dissolve the gold; with this process alone we expect to double our output. Double our output. Theresa had not been nervous as were the others at the table; she had glanced at Michael and he had changed, softened: a woman's influence is to be treasured above rubies, Cathy thought sentimentally, though she knew she had garbled a number of quotations.

Helena Minard, crossing the room, paused beside Cathy. "Well, little one. Are you all right?" If she noted Lisa's absence she did not comment on it.

The men were entering; Philip was not among them. Theresa went to the music room to play and many of the guests went with her. Senator Rhodes came up to Cathy and said, "Well, well, we can't have this, can we? A pretty girl sitting here by herself?" Cathy fixed a smile on her face and made room for the Senator, who reminded her more of a hound than ever. "There are plenty of young men who would give their eyeteeth to be in my place right this minute," the Senator said, sitting down.

"Do you think so?"

"Do I think so?" the Senator repeated; he shook with laughter at a secret joke.

Lisa and Philip did not come back. A few more guests straggled into the music room, Lady Dufton among them. Cathy excused herself from the Senator shortly afterward when Sam signaled to her that it was long past her bedtime. She was ready to go to bed, otherwise she would have ignored him.

She went to say goodnight to her father and Aunt Helena. "I'm Cinderella leaving the ball," Cathy said; they smiled sympathetically at her and her father embraced her in a warm hug.

"We'll ride tomorrow early, shall we?" Michael asked.

"Oh yes."

"Later we are visiting some of the mines. The Keepsake, mainly."

"May I go with you?"

"Of course; why not?"

Helena said, shuddering, "Nothing could persuade me to jounce over those horrid mountain roads again. The last time I was nearly shaken to pieces."

"We've improved them," Michael said, grinning. "And in any case, from thence cometh our strength." He put a hand over Helena's.

Helena said, "It scares me to death, even so," lightly. She glanced down at the hand over hers and just for a second there was a strange look on her face as if she were going to cry. But that could not have been possible, for immediately afterward she was talking and laughing brightly, making Michael laugh, as she always could. The moment became the gayest of the evening, and Cathy stood leaning against her father, prolonging it.

Helena presently began to tease Michael on his choice of the present company and Michael, taking a drink of brandy and making a face, said it had been no choice at all but a political necessity.

"Ah? That accounts for it."

"A diplomatic plum or so carries weight, and besides there are a number of people who need to be persuaded of my eminent respectability in spite of my being an industrialist."

"You're incorrigible."

"Better than being incredible."

"I never knew you to worry about either before."

"Don't rub it in," Michael said. "I'll make it up to Theresa; believe me, if it weren't for her, of course, I wouldn't have a chance."

"I'm glad you admit it. I would have thought you simply had to wave your hand."

"That's what a lot of people would have thought, including myself," Michael said; he grinned at Cathy to show that the conversation was not so solemn as it sounded.

Cathy was lying in bed, wide awake and thinking, when Lisa stormed in half an hour or so later.

"Mamma sent me to bed," Lisa raged. "Exactly as if I were a child!"

Cathy was lying with her arms behind her head, looking at the ceiling. "What do you care? The party was dull, anyhow."

"I didn't find it so dull."

"Oh?" Cathy asked. She did not turn her head.

"I was out on the terrace with Philip most of the time."

"Were you?" Cathy yawned.

"Don't you want to hear about it?"

"Not particularly."

"Very well, if you wish to take that attitude."

"I know where you were. I saw you go, if you remember."

"I suppose you told Mamma."

Cathy turned her head. "You know perfectly well I didn't!"

"Don't shout. Ladies don't shout."

"I'm not a lady yet."

"You'll have to be one of these days. Somebody told her; she sent Sam to look for me."

"Well I didn't, you horrible monster of a girl, you!"

"Oh, all right," Lisa said. "Don't get so upset; you act like a crazy person sometimes. People just don't talk and act however they happen to feel, and no matter what you think you'll have to start acting like other people sooner or later. I simply thought you might have told her because you have this obsession about Philip, as if he hadn't any right to go anywhere with anyone but you."

"I have not!"

"You act as if you have," Lisa said. "You act as if you owned Philip and nobody else had the slightest right even to look at him."

"I notice you look at him just the same."

"He looks at me too," Lisa said. She unhooked her dress and let it drop to the floor.

"Why don't you undress in your own room?"

"Simply because I happen to want to talk to you, if you'll behave like a civilized person for a change," Lisa replied.

"Well, I simply don't happen to want my room all cluttered up," Cathy said fiercely. She sprang out of bed and kicked Lisa's dress along the floor and into the dressing-room.

Lisa looked startled and then she burst out laughing. "I knew you were jealous."

"I am not."

"Yes, you are."

"Well, if I am it's no concern of yours," Cathy said. She jumped back into bed and lay with her back turned toward Lisa.

Lisa sat on the bed. She could not bear to have anyone angry with her for long. She wanted everything she did to be admired and life to be arranged so that she could have what she wanted without anyone's being hurt. Like someone else whom Cathy knew but would not permit herself at this moment to think about.

"Cathy."

"Shut up and go away."

"You're very rude."

"What if I am?"

"Are you crying?"

"No, I'm not."

Lisa said pleadingly, "Don't spoil everything. I'm just having a little fun and so is Philip. It isn't going to hurt anything if I flirt with your precious Philip a little bit while I'm here."

There was silence. Cathy asked presently in a tight voice from which all childish anger had been drained: "Is Philip in love with you?"

"How should I know?"

"You said you always knew."

"Maybe, a little bit. It isn't anything serious even if he thinks he is."

"It would be serious with Philip."

"He'll forget all about me after I've gone."

Cathy ignored this consolation. She asked, "Are you in love with him?"

"Just a little. No, terribly."

"Do you want to marry him?"

"Of course not."

"Why not?"

"How could I? He hasn't any money."

"What difference does that make?"

"Don't be so childish. It makes all the difference."

"Does Philip know that?"

"Of course he does."

"I don't believe it."

"Well, he does. Don't worry about Philip; he understands those things even better than I do. That's why he hasn't wanted to fall in love with me, only he couldn't help himself. I couldn't help myself either. Please believe me, Cathy, I only intended to flirt with him a little bit. But then tonight . . ."

"What happened tonight?"

"He kissed me," Lisa said. "Really kissed me." Instead of looking pleased with herself she looked a little shaken; she said, "Cathy . . ."

"Be quiet. I don't want to hear about it."

"It was different than I thought it would be. Wonderful, but frightening too."

"Be quiet. You aren't supposed to talk about things like that."

"Oh, why not? I've got to tell somebody. Cathy, he kissed me and kissed me. He said I looked like somebody or other rising from the water in that dress. Aphrodite, I think. He said . . . well, I can't tell you everything, of course. I thought he never would get around to kissing me but when he did I thought he never would stop. And then he said he had been thinking about kissing me and wanting to kiss me all evening."

"Will you be quiet!"

"You would have to let him kiss somebody eventually," Lisa said reasonably. "He'd be bound to fall in love with somebody some time, so why shouldn't it be me?"

"He hasn't fallen in love with you! I don't believe it!"

"He said he has. He said it about a million times, so what do you think of that?"

Cathy sat up in bed. "I hate and despise you, that's what I think!"

"It isn't my fault if Philip likes me better than he does you," Lisa said. She went through the dressing-room, picking up the despised dress and closing the door behind her with exaggerated gentleness.

Chapter 12

CATHY AWOKE TOO late the next morning for the early morning ride she was accustomed to take with her father when he was home. The day was hot and still, not very pleasant for the proposed trip to display the Keepsake Mine to the visitors. Cathy listlessly ate breakfast in her room; her emotions were much too overwhelming for her to take an interest in the excursion, but she knew that attention would be called to her if she did not go. So she dressed in riding clothes and went downstairs, wondering wretchedly how long an aching heart could continue to ache before it either broke or recovered.

Theresa sat in the breakfast room behind a coffee urn dispensing breakfast to those who wished to eat downstairs. It was late, and except for Theresa and Sam going back and forth the room was empty.

"Have a cup of coffee with me," Theresa coaxed. "Did you sleep well?"

"Quite well, thank you," Cathy said; she sighed still more deeply.

"Your father missed you this morning but we thought it better to let you sleep since you were up so late."

"Are you going with us to the mine?"

"Yes, your father has asked me to go this morning and it's such a beautiful day I'm looking forward to it."

Theresa seldom went on expeditions of this kind; Cathy knew that she regarded them as a sort of showing off. Cathy did not mind this aspect of it and this morning Theresa did not seem to mind it either. She was smiling; her gaze, which so often went right through one, was soft and luminous.

Cathy asked in surprise, "Is it a beautiful day? I was thinking it was sticky."

"Late hours don't agree with you, perhaps."

Theresa seldom teased; Cathy enjoyed it when she did. It made the world more light-hearted than it had been before.

Theresa said, "We should have called you to go for a ride with your father. That would have blown the cobwebs away."

"Yes." Cathy had a sudden desire to be riding somewhere, anywhere, as fast as she could go, with the wind blowing against her face.

She asked, "What shall I wear, today?"

"Wear?" Theresa looked puzzled.

"Lisa says nobody wears breeches."

"Lisa, again?" Theresa's face grew serious; she said, "You must not allow yourself to be jealous of Lisa; jealousy is a poison that can make you sick."

Cathy was aware of that; she was already sick.

Theresa said, "You have an English riding habit, haven't you? You can wear that."

"Then I'll have to ride sidesaddle. People . . . Philip . . . might think I was showing off." Cathy brightened, however; she considered the English riding habit very elegant. "I guess I will wear it."

Left to herself Cathy wandered out on the terrace where her father and a number of other men were having after-breakfast cigars. She sat on the parapet beside her father who greeted her by putting an arm about her and calling her Sleepy-Head.

"Nobody woke me," Cathy excused herself; she settled beside him in contentment.

The Senator came to sit beside them. The Senator spoke of the beauty of the view, of the joy of a good cigar after a superb breakfast; he broke off to ask if there were any way to get hold of a morning paper.

"No, mercifully," Michael said; he was looking at the Cresta Blancas. They were his favorites; their purple spires, he always said, reminded him of cathedrals and Theresa's music. He continued indifferently to the Senator: "There will be a bundle of them brought in from the morning train but they will be several days late of course."

"Opposition papers as well as our own?"

Michael laughed shortly; he said, "All kinds." He continued

to look at the Cresta Blancas.

"Can we talk for a minute?"

"Why not?"

The Senator glanced a little nervously at Cathy but he went on: "My point is that the opposition papers show the trend which we have to combat."

"Very well, then, let us combat it."

"There has been a great working up of public opinion against all leaders of industry. Bryan is responsible, of course. The people are being made to believe that they are being exploited."

"I know all that."

"And of course enduring a slander attack is an ordeal."

"The only person who concerns me so far as that is concerned is my wife, and she assures me she is willing to face it."

"Oh, ah. Yes, well in that case, when the Senate re-convenes . . ."

"When the Senate re-convenes we will be ready for it."

Mr. Talbot and two other men, Mr. Kirk and Mr. Gray, had drawn up chairs to make a semicircle. Cathy felt uncomfortable; she had no place in this group except that her father's arm continued to hold her. She was both proud of him and apprehensive; the others deferred to him but they exchanged glances between themselves now and then, rather anxious glances.

"Leaving politics for a minute," Mr. Talbot said, "and speaking of something much more important in my old eyes, is it possible to obtain enough gold ourselves to buy this entire bond issue which you propose?"

Michael said arrogantly, "Certainly."

"At what price is it being offered to us?"

"One hundred and four. I believe it will bring at least one hundred and ten in the open market."

The Senator said eagerly, "In the matter of these particular government grants the committee will defer to your judgment."

"Very kind of it, for two thousand shares of stock per committeeman."

Mr. Talbot chuckled and the Senator cleared his throat. James Talbot exclaimed: "Why the devil you should be so determined to have this political bee in your bonnet I can't understand."

"A man has his vanities."

"Well, it does no harm, I suppose."

Mr. Kirk was saying thoughtfully, "Of course the entire picture will be somewhat changed if we have war with Spain."

Michael said, "It will come; we might as well make up our minds about that."

"I thought you didn't want it."

"I don't want it, but I believe in not deceiving ourselves."

Mr. Talbot said, "I like to see a man who refuses to deceive himself." Michael looked at him sharply; Mr. Talbot twinkled back, his blue eyes as keen in their way as Michael's.

Michael asked, "Are you with me or against me?"

"With you, of course, since my interests are in your direction."

"Otherwise?"

"I like the view from here too. There are times when it is wise to lie low."

Mr. Talbot was speaking in riddles again, but somehow his riddles sounded wise.

"Now?"

"I don't say so. You know what past history can yield to the opposition better than I do."

They all kept their eyes on Michael as if they needed his approval to sustain their convictions, Cathy noted with a thrill of pride. When Michael shrugged, the Senator said nervously: "The important thing is to move slowly, not to commit ourselves until we see how the wind blows."

"A very statesmanlike attitude."

Mr. Kirk said, "We can't afford to be accused of imperialistic ambitions in Cuba."

Mr. Talbot agreed, bending forward: "Particularly since we couldn't make it pay, like the British. We haven't an important mercantile and shipping class."

Michael said stubbornly, "Gentlemen, I didn't say that I favored war; I simply said it would come."

"That would upset things."

"It usually does."

"You take it very calmly."

"There's no use getting excited. And besides we have the gold; with gold we can do anything."

"Ah," Mr. Talbot said; he nodded, looking at the glowing end of his cigar. The others nodded too. Michael stood up, keeping his arm around Cathy.

"And now, if you'll excuse me," Michael said. "The carriages taking those who wish to see this gold at its original source will be ready to leave in half an hour."

He went into the house, taking Cathy with him. Without slackening his pace he looked down at her: "Now you know how business is carried on and empires are won and lost."

"I didn't understand very much."

"You only need to have something someone else wants so that you can trade it for something they have that you want. Have you any idea where I can find your mother?"

"I think she might be dressing to go to the mine."

"She's going, then." He looked pleased and eager, no longer formidable and sullen as he had been looking in business discussion with these men. He looked the way Cathy wished he always could look; as his arm fell away, releasing her, Cathy babbled a little wildly: "Father. You've always liked it here; you've always said you were going to retire and stay here."

"Hello, what's this?"

"We like it here best. Mother and Randy and I. We don't care about your getting the appointment or going to Washington or anything."

He took time to pause and tilt up her chin; he asked, "Is this imagination working overtime again?"

"No, but I only thought if you realized . . ."

"Did you think for a moment I would take a step of any kind without consulting your mother?"

"No, no I'm sure you wouldn't . . ."

"Am I such an ogre?"

"No." He was overwhelming; Cathy paused, out of breath, she might have been running. Her heart was pounding, but she managed to smile.

"We'll have a few years in Washington just to show them how it's done," Michael said; "After that we'll retire."

Cathy went to her own room, sat on a chair, and stared at a little point on the wall which resembled a star. She wondered wretchedly what was the matter with her. She had looked forward so long to being grown up, to making an entrance into the world and taking part in all sorts of exciting events, but now that she was faced with the possibility of doing some of these things she was not enjoying herself at all. She had an impulse to hide until the riding party had gone to the mine without her; but before she could put this thought into action there was the familiar tap on the door, which Cathy had forgotten to lock, and Lisa came in.

Lisa said, "I have something for you," and held out her hand, proffering a little silver powder box as a gift for Cathy. It was a sweet little powder box; when one lifted the lid it played a tinkling Mozart minuet; Cathy had longed for it the minute she had seen it among Lisa's things on Lisa's dressing-table.

"It's a peace offering," Lisa said. "I'll be friends if you will."

Cathy stood looking down at the music box in her hands while it tinkled its little tune.

"I suppose you're still sulking," Lisa said presently. "Though about what I haven't the slightest idea."

"I'm not sulking."

"I apologize for saying you told Mamma about my being out last night," Lisa said. "It was Nola—she told Mamma I had been out in the night air for hours without a wrap—that was what worried her. What a dolt! We had the most terrific scene and I called her a liar and Mamma was too upset by the noise to care what it was about. She just begged both of us to keep quiet and leave her in peace!" Lisa laughed, relishing the memory. She said, "It isn't very good manners to sulk."

Lisa herself had no manners of course except when it suited her. But it did not matter for, whatever mood she was in or however outrageously she behaved, Lisa was beautiful.

Lisa wheedled: "Cathy, you aren't really angry with me, are you? I'll be going away soon."

The music box tinkled gayly. Cathy continued to look down at it. She had an impulse to let it drop to the floor and there had been a time when she would have done so, but now she could not quite bring herself to do it.

"When I'm gone you can have Philip to yourself, you know."

"Thank you."

"So nothing will really be changed. If we quarrel everybody will begin to ask what's the matter."

"Oh, be quiet, can't you?"

"Do you want Philip to think you're so jealous of him that you can't bear to have him like anyone else?"

"No, I don't. Besides, it isn't true."

"Then you'll have to be friends with me whether you want to or not."

It was true that she would; Lisa had a way of dragging out the truth and presenting one with it. Either Cathy was jealous of Philip's affections or she wasn't, and if she was not then she had no real reason to dislike Lisa.

Lisa persisted, "We've always been fond of each other; I'm still fond of you. There's no reason for you not to be fond of me unless you're angry about Philip. And after all Philip has a right to decide for himself if he wants to like somebody or not, hasn't he?"

"Just stop talking, that's all I ask! If Philip likes you it has nothing to do with me; just stop talking!"

"Cathy, just say it's all right."

"Oh, go away and leave me alone. I'm not angry with you; I'm not angry at anybody."

"I'm glad," Lisa said. She threw her arms around Cathy; the strange thing was that Cathy knew that Lisa was glad. Lisa left the room then, satisfied that she had put everything right.

The music box ran down, finally. Cathy did not rewind it, but she placed it on the top of a table where she could see it.

She was standing at a window watching the carriages and horses being assembled in the courtyard when she saw Philip. She leaned forward to call to him, and then she saw Lisa running down the steps of the terrace toward him. Philip swung about as if his name had been called; his face from this distance looked set and far from happy, even though he strode forward to meet Lisa.

Lisa soon would be gone. Good riddance to bad rubbish, Cathy thought; she left the window to put on the English riding habit and occupy herself adjusting and readjusting the stock until somebody should come to call her and tell her it was time to go.

Chapter 13

LISA WAS SAYING, "Philip! I was so afraid I had missed you."

Philip regarded her somberly. In the clear light of morning he was inclined to regard his visions and behavior of the night before as sheerest folly. He said, "No fear. I've been waiting for a chance to see you."

"But then why didn't you send somebody to call me?"

"Possibly because I didn't want to advertise the fact that I was looking for you."

"Is anything the matter?"

"I want to talk to you. Where can we be alone?"

Lisa glanced about her; there was nobody close to them; the party gathering at the carriages and horses was at a little distance. She said, "We're alone here; nobody can hear us if you're quick. What is it, tell me."

"I want to talk to you," Philip repeated.

"Talk to me then; I'm right here." Lisa put a hand on his sleeve; she said softly, "What is it, Philip . . . Philip darling?"

"Stop that," Philip said; he jerked away his arm.

Lisa shrugged delicately; she reminded him, "You called me that last night."

"I know I did. I must have been crazy."

"Why? Didn't you mean it?"

"Of course I meant it, and that's why I must have been crazy!"

Lisa said, coming close to him, "I don't understand. Are you angry at me? Has something happened since last night to make you angry? Philip, I've been thinking about you ever since last night; haven't you thought about me at all?"

"I haven't thought of anything else."

She smiled. She said wistfully, "After all there's no harm in our liking each other, is there?"

"Yes there is, a great deal of harm."

"I don't see why."

"You have an enviable ability to see what you want to see."

"Philip, are you afraid to like me?"

"Hang it, yes!"

"But why?"

"Stop using the word like! Supposing I fell in love with you. Supposing we fell in love with each other. What would happen then? Would you marry me?"

"How can I possibly tell until it happens?"

"Until what happens?"

"Until we fall in love with each other." Lisa smiled upward into his eyes.

"Oh blast! Can't you see that I have to know?"

No, she could not see, and she was a little impatient with him for spoiling the present by projecting them into so nebulous a thing as the future. She asked, "Are you sorry you kissed me?"

"Of course not, only . . ."

"Because I'm not," she said softly. "I thought it was wonderful, the most wonderful thing that ever has happened to me. Philip. Philip darling."

"Lisa, Lisa!"

Their interlude of privacy was nearly over. Several of the guests were being assisted into the carriages; others were being mounted on horseback. Lisa had chosen to ride horseback; as she and Philip walked toward the horse being held for her she tried to coax Philip into changing his mind and coming with them. "Please do."

"I'm a workingman."

"It won't be fun without you. I almost wish I weren't going myself, except that it will be fun to see where the gold comes from. Cathy brags about it all the time and I've never been there."

"You know she doesn't."

"Doesn't what?"

"Brag about the gold."

Lisa said, "Well, she does; she isn't half as perfect as you and Mamma thinks she is. She kicked my new gown all along the floor; what do you think of that?"

"I think she was probably provoked."

Lisa laughed; she admitted that Cathy had been. She forgot Cathy to plead: "Can't you come, Philip?"

"Sorry, not possibly."

"But I'll see you tonight?"

He hesitated, then said shortly, "Yes."

"Don't come to the house. I'll meet you on the terrace."

"No. No, Lisa, that's no good."

"I'll be there. At nine o'clock." She smiled and turned away quickly, ignoring his protest; a stableboy mounted her before Philip could spring forward to do so; she waved and left Philip without looking back.

Michael, in high spirits now that the expedition was about to set off, rode up and down the line of carriages. Cathy had reined her horse beside her mother's; together they sat waiting until everybody was ready to start. Randy and Helena Minard waved from one of the balconies.

"You see, it is going to be a beautiful day," Theresa said. Some of the oppressive atmosphere had lifted; the morning was turning clear and golden.

"Yes," Cathy agreed; she was conscious of the exact moment when Lisa left Philip and mounted her horse and some of the oppressive atmosphere about Cathy's heart had lifted accordingly.

The carriages rolled away one by one. Lady Dufton, her hat tied on by yards of veiling, was in the first one. The Senator's wife in the second carriage had a scarf tied across the lower half of her face so that she looked like a bandit; Cathy laughed aloud at that and even Theresa smiled. Mrs. Jonas Kirk's pale prissy face looked out of the next carriage. It was, all in all, a strange procession. The Eastern visitors were quite obviously out of their element and in extreme doubt as to their possible enjoyment of the adventure, but more fearful of missing something than they were of the hardships to be endured. Not one of them had remained behind, which was in its way a tribute to the compelling personality of their host.

Michael made up in high spirits for any lack of it in his guests, riding up and down, talking and laughing with everybody. He had a particular attachment for the Keepsake Mine; it had been the turning point in his fortunes. He was fond of displaying not only the mine but his country, and he was indifferent to lack of response or nervousness on the part of his audience; people were either impressed in spite of themselves or too stupid to be impressed. He had been known to take violent dislikes to persons making disparaging remarks about the crudeness and wildness of the countryside.

Yes, he bullied people sometimes, quite often in fact, Cathy confessed to herself, but he did not bully those he loved. Cathy trailed at the rear of the caravan; she wanted to be by herself. It was wrong to bully people; but then, did not the people also do wrong who allowed themselves to be bullied?

The way to the Keepsake Mine led directly up into the mountains; the road almost immediately became steep and narrow; there were times when it was a mere ledge cut into the side of the mountain with a sheer drop on one side and a great wall on the other. Lisa was nervous; she insisted on dropping back to ride beside Cathy, as close as possible. She asked, "Aren't you afraid?"

"Of course not."

"You're so smart. What if you fell off?"

"I'm not going to."

"I wish I hadn't come."

"Why did you?"

"I wish I hadn't," Lisa repeated; she looked about her apprehensively and she continued to dog Cathy's footsteps.

"Can't you see how beautiful it is?" Cathy did not wish to converse with Lisa but she was goaded into defending this wild beautiful country whose enchantment was already weaving a spell on her and filling some of the aching void in her heart. It's beautiful and it's mine! She thought suddenly, lifting her head and taking a quick sharp breath. She wanted to say this aloud to Lisa but she could not; it wasn't strictly true in the way which Lisa could understand and Lisa would be quick to point out the discrepancy. "It isn't yours, it's your father's," Lisa would say.

"It's mine because I love it," Cathy said, this time aloud.

"What?" Lisa asked fretfully. She was staring upward to the top of the canyon wall on their right; she said, "It's better when you don't look down."

"I don't mind looking down."

"Well, don't; it makes me nervous just to see you. If this is where you have to go to get the old gold I'd just as soon let it stay there."

"Somebody has to bring it down."

"Well, not me; I'm never coming again. It's getting worse and worse, too."

As they went higher the country was growing harsher and

123

more rugged, the lines straight and uncompromising. There were the straight up-and-down lines of the canyons and tall pines; there were horizontal lines of sky and rock strata, sharply defined in layers, with the line of the horizon far below. Theresa and Michael were riding together at the head of the line now and when the road widened enough to permit it Cathy, with Lisa close behind her, joined them.

Michael hailed them absently; the country was weaving its spell on him too. He looked less arrogant, less restless than he had looked since his arrival. His eyes moved intently, studying every aspect of the physical structure of the land; now and then he glanced at Theresa and smiled.

Theresa rode side saddle, superbly and confidently, speaking now and then in a low calming voice to her mare, who was young and high-spirited.

"I'm not sure that was a good choice of mount for you," Michael said.

"Sarita? She's young; she does very well."

Michael rode a white gelding. He rode closer to Theresa and Sarita made a playful dancing movement to one side.

"Be careful," Michael said sharply. He grasped Sarita's bridle and wrenched it. It was the cruelest thing Cathy ever had seen him do to an animal; concern for Theresa made him do it, Cathy knew, but her heart skipped a sickening beat. Perhaps Theresa's had too for she said, "Michael?" in a puzzled voice, staring at him while patting Sarita's neck with one gloved hand: "Poor Sarita," she said then, her voice reassuringly her own again: "Exposed to mountain roads and then criticized."

"She's skittish, Tessa; don't take chances," Michael said. He was ashamed of his momentary anger against Sarita; he put an apologetic but restraining hand on Sarita's bridle and held it there. He said to Theresa, "I didn't hurt her."

"I know you didn't."

"Just the same, we'll get rid of her if she's skittish."

"I really don't think she is. I've been training her a little myself."

"Have you really? I thought you seldom rode any more."

"I've started again. By myself, mornings." Cathy was surprised to hear of this; she had not known it.

Michael said, "Ah"; he was jealous of the things which Theresa did alone. He was jealous most of all of her music; there was an intent withdrawn look on Theresa's face when she was playing which he could not endure. When she stopped playing there was always a little silence, as if Theresa was returning from a journey, and during that silence Michael stared at her as if he were willing her to come back to him.

She had that look on her face now. She said, "I'll ride with you tomorrow if you want me."

"I want you."

They laughed together; perhaps the thing which had kept them so close together in spite of differences of temperament and ambitions and desires was the fact that they could always laugh.

The skittish Sarita was walking docilely now; everything became docile under Michael's hand. Theresa, half turned from him, was looking out over the valley which lay far below them. She was lost for the moment in reflective thought: "Come back," Michael urged her half comically and half in earnest, and Theresa, turning her head quickly, said, "I'm sorry. I do seem to be getting very vague these days."

"Vague? That isn't a word that fits you, Theresa."

"It is beautiful down there though, isn't it?"

"Yes, but I can't bear it when you go off and leave me."

He went off and left her, of course, but Theresa did not remind him of it. It did not seem to matter, somehow, perhaps because Theresa was too complete in herself to be deprived. Cathy stared at these two people whom she loved so much, with newly sharpened perceptions: there were different ways of loving, as different as the persons who loved, it would seem. Her father's was violent, demanding, like a mountain stream; while her mother's was more like the deep pool which lay at the bottom.

Theresa said, "I don't, really."

"I know you don't. Though Heaven knows why."

"I'm not even tempted to do so."

"How I love you."

"I know. Bless you."

"What's that for?"

"I don't want to get lost. Sometimes I nearly do."

"Theresa!"

Theresa laughed; she patted Sarita's neck. "You encourage me to dramatize myself. I like it far too well, really."

"What a fool I am to let anything separate us, ever."

"Nothing does separate us."

"No. And it won't; it won't, believe me, whatever happens."

"Nothing is going to happen."

"Everything is going to happen. Everything!"

Theresa laughed again, still patting Sarita's neck. She agreed, "Yes, perhaps that will be better." She turned to smile at Cathy, including her, and Cathy, passionately grateful for the inclusion, smiled back to both of them.

They arrived at the basin which held the buildings belonging to the mine. A chasm separated the basin from the great face of the mountain opposite, containing the opening of the Keepsake mine shaft: the chasm was bridged by a steel cable from which was suspended a tiny cage.

Everybody alighted from the carriages and horses; they were stretching, laughing, chattering. The superintendent of the mine and several engineers came out to greet them, shaking hands formally with Theresa first, then Michael; then perfunctorily, with everyone else. Theresa and Michael were treated as royalty.

"It is rather exciting, after all," Lisa said; she glanced at the impressive number of buildings surrounding them; the mill and strong rooms and offices.

Visitors were being organized into parties: those who wished could cross the chasm in the iron cage to visit the mine shaft, others could go to the strong room or any of various other buildings or simply wait in the shade until lunchtime as the Senator's wife, fanning herself now with her scarf, was doing. Theresa and Michael of course were going to visit the mine shaft.

Lisa clung tightly to Cathy; she said, "Isn't it thrilling? What are you going to do?"

"I'm going to the mine, of course." An engineer, second in command, had given orders that Cathy was to make the next trip in the cage if she so desired. "You don't have to go with me."

The engineer was young and susceptible; he glanced at Lisa who continued to cling, pale but determined, to Cathy. It gave Cathy an odd feeling to have Lisa's leadership transferred for the moment to Cathy. Lisa said, "I might as well do whatever you do."

The trip across the chasm was made without misadventure, though Lisa moaned and clutched, first at Cathy and then at the engineer, as the tiny steel structure swung over the depths below. "What are you afraid of?" Cathy asked swaggeringly; she leaned out and looked down. Her showing off did her no good; the engineer was staring at Lisa rather than admiring Cathy's superior courage. Lisa closed her eyes and moaned louder. The cage arrived at the other side and Cathy sprang out, unassisted, while Lisa tottered out on the arm of the young man manipulating it.

They paid their visit to the strong room. Lisa stared at the long yellow bars lying in iron chests and she grew quiet and strangely meek for a while. She asked in a voice of wonder: "Do you mean all that's real gold? Like money?"

"It is money," Cathy said.

One of the chests of gold was closed and locked and carried from the strong room. They followed it outside where it was lifted to the floor of a wagon and bolted into place. The driver climbed into his seat; four men with rifles held across their chests took various positions about him. The wagon started down the mountainside.

"Why do they have all those guns?" Lisa asked.

"So they won't be held up and robbed."

"Held up and robbed? Does that happen very often?"

"Of course it does. It would all the time if it weren't for the guards. Even so somebody gets killed every now and then."

Lisa shuddered; her eyes grew big and bright.

After that, in anticlimax, they all went into the commissary for lunch.

They were late getting started back down the mountain. Michael was in no hurry; he held consultations with the superintendent and engineers and foremen about various aspects of the mine: improvements, problems. Nobody else could start until he was ready; most of the company stood about, restless or bored or nervous about the return trip, eager to return to comfortable rooms and tea and cocktails and the prospect of dinner. A wind had sprung up; it rushed through the canyons with an eerie sound, increasing the general tension. Theresa stood talking to one of the foremen about his wife and family whom he had brought from the East; she discussed schools and the general development of the country with an interest which made the man talking with her flush with pleasure.

Michael gave the signal and everyone climbed into carriages; the caravan started on its return trip. Cathy jogged contentedly along in her role of observer. She was momentarily at peace and acutely aware of the beauty about her. The sun was setting; color filled the great basin below her. She knew suddenly, without reason, a moment of perfect happiness, as if she were suspended in a little period of time which had neither memory nor future to harass her.

For a long time afterward she was often to think: If we had only started back a little earlier. Or: Why was I so happy; if I hadn't been daydreaming, would it have been different? Or, worst of all: Was Theresa daydreaming, too; vague, as she had said; gone off on that journey of hers which she had to make; was that why it had happened?

The freakish wind, as if possessed by a mind of its own, darted at them, played pranks, like some mischievous spirit of evil. It blew dried weeds down the steep embankments into their path; it whined and sighed; it blew some of the color from the day. In a final furious gust it blew the scarf, which the Senator's wife had been tying and retying since the beginning of the trip, from her fingers. The scarf sailed from the open window of the carriage and flung itself directly into the face of Theresa's horse; Sarita, young, frightened, skittish, reared and plunged; she lost her footing on the steep descent and fell over the embankment, disappearing, as in a nightmare, completely from sight.

Cathy put both hands over her mouth and screamed. She could hear her own voice screaming even when she had no idea who was screaming or why.

The voice, thin and weak as a kitten's now, was still screaming when gentle hands lifted Cathy from her saddle, placing her in a carriage, and took her away, back to Keepsake. It was still screaming inside her when she let Stacey and Sam, warned beforehand by some mysterious messenger, lift her from the carriage and take her to the safety of her own room and bed.

It was still screaming long after Cathy knew that there was no longer any use to scream.

Chapter 14

THERE IS ONE blessed thing about great grief, Cathy learned. When it is too great, so that one cannot bear it, it brings with it a feeling of unreality.

All the rest of that long strange summer she seemed to be living in a dream. She ate, slept, did the things she was accustomed to doing, but it was as if somebody else were doing them for her. She did not feel like herself; when she looked at herself in a mirror she saw a person in a long plain black dress of mourning which Aunt Helena had ordered from New York, but it was a person whom she barely knew. She heard herself talking, even laughing, but all the time she herself was standing off and watching and wondering about this person who seemed to be inhabiting her body.

She thought sometimes that her father must have much the same feeling. For when he returned from taking Theresa's body to New Orleans where he had thought she would like to be buried, he looked about him when he first entered the house as if he were not sure exactly where he was. And though he visited the mines and rode about the range land as he usually did when he was at home, and though he sometimes joined them for dinner and for an hour or so afterward, he had a lost look, and he stared intently at anyone who spoke to him and hesitated before answering.

He was drinking heavily, all the household knew that. He sat alone in his den or office, night after night, drinking; often he did not go to bed at all. Once Cathy, waking in the night, heard him singing. She stood outside his closed door, shivering in her nightgown, while he sang song after song, lusty ribald mining songs; she felt as if her heart were breaking but she did not dare knock on the door or try to go to him.

Helena too was shut away in a darkened room most of the time. When she roused herself it was to sit with Randy; they must all be brave for Randy's sake, she said over and over.

Cathy tried to be brave for Randy's sake, though actually it was Randy who comforted her rather than the other way round. Randy, after the first shock of grief had passed, went about his daily routine exactly as he would have done if his mother had been there. He seemed to be upheld by some inner strength which Cathy could only dumbly strive to acquire.

Philip, to whom Cathy instinctively would have turned at this time, was also lost to her. Grief and loss had heightened rather than dissipated Philip's other emotions, she could see; his infatuation for Lisa passed perceptibly into the higher plane of love. Cathy was left behind; she could not even take refuge in the world of her imagination because that world had vanished and stark reality had taken its place. Philip would have done anything rather than hurt her, she knew, yet just saying his name hurt her, so much so that she avoided using it. The loss of a name was a small enough loss compared to others, but there were times when Cathy, half sleeping and half waking, felt that loss more deeply than the greater ones. Something was gone; there was a hole in the fabric of her life. Philip, Philip. When she closed her eyes tightly little shooting stars appeared in the blackness; concentrating on them she was sometimes able to return to sleep.

Philip, himself, realized as Cathy did that his feeling for Lisa had undergone subtle and ennobling alteration; in a way this made his situation easier and in another way more difficult. Certainly Lisa in black, frightened and clinging and distressed, was far more trustworthy a repository for love than she could have been in any other circumstances. Feeling guilty, Philip continued to meet her on the terrace at night, reassuring himself that it was right because their love at this time was gentle and without demands.

Nevertheless the remainder of the summer was as unreal to Philip as it was to Cathy. He was both grief-stricken and elated. Lisa clung to him; she promised unspoken volumes, but he could not pin her down to the spoken avowals for which he hungered. She was young, he told himself; she was still dependent upon the pattern of life laid out for her, and until he could offer her more than dreams he would have to accept separation, evasions, withdrawals.

"Do you love me?" he asked over and over, against his judgment.

"Oh Philip! I love you so much."

"Then you do want to marry me, don't you? As much as I want to marry you?"

On the subject of marriage she became frightened. "We can't talk about that now. I'll be in mourning for at least a year."

"What does that have to do with it!"

But when she cried and said he was heartless he felt like killing himself; perhaps he was heartless to be thinking of nothing but love so soon after Theresa's death.

He saw that for this summer at least he must be content for their hands to touch and their eyes to meet. Lisa was, after all, very young, and he needed more than dreams before he could honorably ask for her hand in marriage.

Once that decision was made he was able to give some time and attention to the other people who occupied his affections. He felt estranged from Cathy and guilty about the estrangement; he had done very little to help her. He watched over Randy's physical needs and encouraged the work in the laboratory.

It was Michael whose need was greatest, and it was Michael whom he could not help, either as a physician or as a friend. Michael, hollow-eyed and gaunt from days and nights with no sleep at all, simply looked amused when Philip finally summoned the courage to suggest something to make him sleep. "Why should I sleep, man?" Michael demanded.

"You've got to pull yourself together," Philip said desperately.

"Have I?" Michael said; he laughed, loud and long.

Michael was more than a little crazy during those first months, Philip realized; perhaps they were all a little crazy. But Michael refused absolutely to adjust himself and to accept the inevitable.

He abandoned his affairs. He pushed telegrams in the wastebasket; he let unattended business pile up on his desk. He refused to see the lawyers, the fellow directors of his companies, the bankers, the politicians, who made the long and anxious trip to Keepsake without benefit of private cars or luxurious surroundings. He got drunk and pounded his impotent fists against the walls of his room until his knuckles bled. And then, unregenerate, he continued to drink until he was unconscious.

It was a state of affairs which could not continue. It was too intense and too feverish; eventually the summer came to an end, and with it came an end to a phase in all their lives, whether they realized it or not.

Aunt Helena and Lisa must return to France. There was now, of course, no thought of Cathy's going with them; they all knew that she would not have left Keepsake for any reason.

Aunt Helena, whose beautiful face was ravaged from endless hours of weeping, wept again at leaving. She embraced Cathy and Randy over and over: "How can I leave you, my darlings?" But she had to go; there was Uncle Raymond waiting for her; she had her own obligations. She would be back next spring, and in the meantime they were to write, they were to take care of themselves and not grieve, and presently they would all find a way to be happy somehow, once more.

Lisa wept too. Cathy, who all her life had wept over everything: a sad story, a song, hurt feelings, a disappointment, could not cry. All the liquid in her seemed to have dried up. She could barely swallow, and her tongue felt too large and too dry for her mouth so that it was difficult to speak.

Michael had returned to the land of the living with an abrupt decision to accompany Helena and Lisa as far as New York. There he would see to the business which was clamoring for his attention, and he would return in November. He suddenly wanted to go, Cathy saw, to escape from this house which had become a house of sadness for him, though he asked Cathy at the last minute if she needed him or wanted him to stay. When she assured him that they would be all right without him he said, "Good girl," as if he had been anticipating her answer, and even as if it would have made no difference in any case.

On the morning when he was to leave he showed her the combination of the big safe in his office where cash was kept, and how to enter in the ledger whatever cash was taken out. Mr. Cross, the ranch manager, and Sam were the only other persons who knew the combination; Theresa, of course, had known it. Cathy was the mistress of the house now, her father said; he put an arm about her and praised her courage. He avoided her eyes as if he knew that she was thinking: It isn't any of this I want; it's just you; it's selfish of you to run off and leave us like this. He was aware of his selfishness; he had always been selfish, perhaps it was his selfishness which was haunting him most. "Philip will look after you," he said. "I'll be back and we'll start over . . . but not yet."

Cathy wanted to tell him that she understood his feelings because she too was a selfish person, but when she tried to speak, her tongue would not form the words properly. And it was just as well because he showed that he did not want her to do so; any attempt to share his emotions with him was an intrusion. He gave Cathy explicit instructions in just what to do if anything went wrong or she needed him; she was to send somebody into town with a telegraph message. But only if it was important was she to send for him, otherwise she was to make all decisions for herself. "I realize that I'm placing a great responsibility on your shoulders," he said. "But you're a strong little thing, and I can't help you right now. The best thing I can do for you now is to take myself off for a time, so look after Randy and God bless you both." Since I can't, he seemed to be saying; it was his haste to get away which hurt.

When he was leaving, mounted on his horse, he looked about the courtyard again and with that strange angry look as if he wondered where he was and what he was doing here. He could not bear to witness the farewells being said by Aunt Helena and Lisa; he wheeled his horse and galloped away.

Helena, concerned with her own leave-taking, did not notice the quality of intensity creeping into the goodbyes of Philip and Lisa. Cathy noticed and despised herself for doing so; under the circumstances it was the worst kind of spying. She threw her arms about Helena Minard in a desperation which brought the whole ordeal to a climax; Helena Minard broke down completely, Nola hurried forward with smelling salts and urged her mistress into the carriage with Lisa following; the carriages started forward and disappeared from sight.

"They're gone," Cathy said blankly. Philip turned; he had been staring after the white square of Lisa's handkerchief waving outside the carriage, which now too had disappeared.

He said, "Yes, they're gone."

They went into the house. Randy was to go to bed immediately; Philip instructed Stacey in the medicine to be given him. Randy went willingly; he looked pale and tired.

Philip asked Cathy if she would like something to help her sleep. She was wandering about the large drawing-rooms which she was thinking would be better closed; perhaps tomorrow; she was not sure if she knew exactly how to go about it. Hester and Sam would know. She said, "No, thank you."

"It wouldn't hurt you."

"I don't need it, thank you just the same."

"It's foolish to be stubborn and refuse help when it's possible to get it."

133

He was thinking, she was sure, of Michael. Michael's refusal to accept help had hurt Philip as it had hurt her. She said, "I'm not being stubborn, really, Philip."

"All right." He was looking down at her and his face softened. He said, "I guess you aren't. Are you sleeping?"

"Yes, quite well."

"Eating?"

The questions were routine; he scarcely waited for the answer. But she assured him, yes, yes, and he nodded, satisfied.

He put his arms around her. He said, "You're a brave little thing; you'll be all right," in almost exactly the same tones which her father had used. Everything in her clamored to protest that she wasn't all right, not by any manner of means, but she had a terrible feeling that nobody would hear her. Everybody was closed off; that was the worst burden which recent experience had thrust upon her.

Philip dropped his arms, releasing her, though the last thing she desired or needed was to be released. She was expected to be a strong little thing and so far as she could see she had no other choice. Therefore she waited to see what was to happen next.

In the days that followed it was Philip who somehow managed to make life seem not only endurable, but almost normal. He went whistling through the rooms, and he would not permit any of them to be closed. He was busy and active, and he inspired the rest of them, even during his absences, to be busy and active too.

Cathy made fumbling efforts to live up to the trust which her father and her mother's training had imposed upn her. The four oldest house servants, Sam and Hester and Rachel and Stacey, could have run the house exactly as Theresa had taught them to run it without help, but they pretended to need Cathy's guidance. There was a conspiracy, she recognized, to make her feel that she was indeed mistress of the house and there was no time for sadness.

One morning when Randy and Philip were in the laboratory Cathy found herself wandering aimlessly downstairs. She wished for her own sake that she had some of the many resources which Randy had. In the music room she stood beside her mother's piano and let her fingers press down the keys. Her mother had tried to teach her music, but Cathy had no talent. She had tried very hard, but the sounds which came forth from her efforts were never the same as she had intended them to be. Theresa, always patient, had tried to instil some of her own feeling: "Like this, you see. Like this. You hear it and your fingers are only the medium for bringing what you hear into being."

But Cathy's fingers stumbled and blurred, and Theresa, laughing one day, said, "Don't look so desperate. The piano is not your instrument; we will find something else for you."

And as a result of all those hours of work Cathy could remember now only one little tune: "The Happy Farmer." She sat down and played it, slowly and inaccurately at first, and then briskly and with a certain dash. Continuing to play it, with little touches of her own to give variety, she thought wistfully that it would be good to have a talent, something within oneself upon which to draw. She wondered if she might find a heretofore undiscovered talent inside her if she were to try, and she determined to try.

Leaving the music room she went across the flagstoned courtyard to her father's office. She worked the combination of the big safe just for the satisfaction of seeing it open. She had no need for money nor anywhere to spend it, but she took a five dollar bill from the box which her father had called petty cash and sat at a roll-top desk entering it in a ledger. There were several stacks of these ledgers; Cathy took one entire stack in her arms, staggering a little under its weight, and placed it on the desk. Each ledger stood for a year it seemed: all household items of expenditure, food, linen, salaries, were carefully tabulated in Theresa's clear hand. Cathy closed the last book; she did not try to put the ledgers back in the safe all at once; two by two they were not so heavy. Little by little, she thought, that was the way; she remembered the nursery poem, "Little drops of water, little grains of sand." You could stand anything a little at a time. There were other things in the safe beside the ledgers and she studied them with feigned interest: there was the gold plate for one thing, and boxes of Theresa's jewelry. Cathy slammed shut the door of the safe suddenly, leaning against it; she straightened and jiggled the door of the safe, making sure it was locked.

She went back to the house through the side terrace which led to the family wing, and into the quiet little morning-room which held Theresa's fruitwood desk and her low chair with its basket of delicate embroidery, just as Theresa had left them. Cathy sat on the floor and put her head on the seat of the chair.

Philip found her there. He said, standing in the doorway: "May I come in?"

She sat up, dry-eyed, and smiled: "Of course; why so formal? I'm resting; I've been working on the books."

Their relationship, though strange, was without strain these days. Philip was as gentle in his attitude toward her as he was to Randy; he no longer bullied or criticized her. And she never flared up now; she was never demanding or touchy. Her love for him had matured so suddenly and so helplessly that she had not the least idea what to do with it. And so she simply accepted it, as she accepted the other tragedy which had come into her life. The burden of it was always with her, but she was learning how to live with it.

Philip said, "I've just come from Mrs. Mendos. Her baby was born."

"Oh! What is it?"

"Boy. She had a hard time; I warned her husband that she can't survive another pregnancy." Philip looked at Cathy and a surprised expression came into his face as if he had just realized that it was to her he was speaking. He said, "I'm sorry, Cathy. I was thinking aloud; I haven't any business talking to you about this."

"Philip, I know all about babies."

"Oh, you do, do you?"

"Yes, of course I do. I know what makes them and how they are born and everything. I've seen animals being born and it's wonderful; I've never seen a baby being born but that must be the most exciting of all."

"Yes," Philip said. "It is." He continued to stare at her, as if in some way she had changed for him. He was, in fact, wondering what was going to become of her; she meant a great deal to him and he could not bear to think of life hurting her. She was so trusting; sooner or later she must be hurt as everyone was hurt. She was growing lovelier by the moment too, in that treacherous way by which women acquired loveliness; she had dark widely spaced soft brown eyes, a tilted nose, a full mobile mouth, and she was learning to hold her head in a proud new way which reminded him of Theresa. She was completely without false modesty or subterfuge; Theresa had done her work well there, perhaps too well.

Cathy asked, "Will you let me help you sometimes when you take care of people who have babies or are ill; really help you? I know Mamma did, and even Stacey says I have quite good hands for that kind of thing."

She held out her hands. He said, surprised: "You've stopped biting your nails." Her hands looked longer, more slender now instead of stubby and childish as he remembered them.

"Yes."

"And I didn't even notice." He smiled at her; he said, "Yes, you may help me if you like; I can use help once in a while."

"Perhaps that may turn out to be my talent."

He wasn't listening; he asked, "What?" absently.

"I need a talent."

"What kind of talent?"

"I don't know. Something that's mine, something that I can work with, something to fall back on . . . when I need it."

"Oh," he said. He was listening now, frowning slightly in thought. He said, "Yes, I see what you mean. We'll see what we can do. To begin with you can take the Mendos children off their mother's hands once in a while if you wish."

"Oh Philip, I would like that."

She went to the Mendos house later that day. She was shy, but the Mendos children were still shier. They hid their faces; they laughed and cavorted wildly, peering through their fingers at her with soft bright eyes.

She coaxed them out of doors with bribes of cookies. They played games and she told them stories, and when it was time for them to go indoors she fed them their supper. A number of women came and went during the afternoon to bring food and take care of the new baby; they treated Cathy with deference at first, but presently they talked to her and to each other without restraint. They showed her the new baby, clicking their tongues and shaking their heads; it was small and weak, very small and weak, see how its head wobbled. "But it will be all right, won't it?" Cathy asked in alarm. They shrugged their shoulders; who could tell about these things?

When Cathy went home that evening she kept seeing the Mendos baby with its wise sad little face and its round little head not much larger than an orange. She yearned to capture it in some way; she felt inside herself the first stirring of creative need for expression. She got paints from the schoolroom and tried to put down on paper what she had seen and felt, first in oils and then water colors, but the paper was flat and unresponsive.

She had been working on the floor and now she sat back on her heels, disappointed; she had felt it so definitely in her fingers this time; even now her hands curved, as if they were struggling to shape something. Not flat, but round, there must be another dimension; she jumped up, suddenly filled with excitement, and rummaged through the shelves looking for modeling clay which once had been there. She found it; it was stiff but she kneaded it and added liquid until it was malleable; she was quite sure now that she had found what she wanted.

The little head grew under her fingers. When it was finished it was crude but it was there; it was the tired sad little baby who was too small and too weak. She put it on a shelf and sat looking at it for a long time.

She showed it to Philip and Randy the next evening after dinner. Both of them said it was wonderful, which she knew it was not, but she basked in their praise. Philip said that when he went to town the next day he would send a telegram to Michael to send materials for her to work with, and Randy offered to sit for her whenever she needed a model.

They were gay and light-hearted the rest of the evening, as if sorrow did not exist.

Chapter 15

IN TWO WEEKS the modeling clay arrived, and with it books, modeling stands, tools, ovens, and every kind of equipment. Cathy modeled everybody's head who would sit for her: Randy, Philip, Sam, Rachel, Stacey. Philip and Randy began studying the casting of molds with her, firing of ovens, and together they spent hours experimenting and poring over the problems presented.

Her first elation cooled a little when she discovered how little that she did was worth anything. Seldom did any piece of work come to life, like the head of the baby; most of the time it was sheer drudgery. Her fingers were often as awkward and fumbling as when she played the piano; it was very rarely that she recaptured that first sure knowledge in them. Much of the time she was not sure that she had any more talent in this than she had in anything else. Even so, she felt as if she had opened a door to a new world to herself, and she worked hard and long to keep that door open.

She was discovering a new world of books too. She re-read *Wuthering Heights*, attracted by a sympathy for the heroine who had the same name as her own. She re-read *Jane Eyre* and *David Copperfield* and *Vanity Fair* and *The Scarlet Letter* and *Les Miserables* from this different vantage point which made them seem new and exciting discoveries.

She read books of history and biography too, and thus she lived intensely, for the first time, in many places and among many people. She found that she was learning a great deal about herself in the process; she was beginning to form, timidly, certain values which were to be her own and not weak imitations of everyone she loved. She was striving, consciously, to mold her character as she molded the clay.

Her life at this time was full and pleasant in spite of the shadow which sadness cast over it. And still she seemed to be waiting, always waiting, for something to happen. She could feel the yearning toward that unknown something inside her, as she had felt creative desire in her fingers on that first momentous occasion of its birth.

Was she waiting for love? Yes, she thought it must be love. Her love for Philip was a separate thing altogether; it was closed away. But there was a throbbing in her, an urgency which was sometimes so strong that it frightened her.

It brought with it a physical restlessness that made her doubt if she would ever be really good or contented with life as it was. She wanted to give love instead of hiding it away; she wanted to be loved in return. She wanted to live instead of reading about living; she wanted to have babies of her own; her arms ached to hold babies. What was all this waiting for, this hunger, this preparation, if all the love and desire which were growing inside her were to be wasted?

When this mood was on her she went for long walks or rides. She was following the river bed one day; she had walked several miles after leaving her horse in the mouth of the canyon.

The valley widened into a flat field of tall strawlike grass with here and there clumps of powdery sage. The sun beat hot on her head though the air smelled of winter; to her left beyond the river were jagged dark hillsides with cedars and piñon growing out of their creases, while rimming the clearing on the east, four or five miles away, the loftier Kautauk Range was still vivid with red and yellow coloring. There had been no rain to quench the autumnal glory of mountain maple and oak, though the leaves drifted steadily to the ground. But the dry dusty earth and wild grass underfoot had taken on the drab colorlessness of winter; the river was little more than a thin stream in a wide bed of cracked rock-spattered mud. The blue bowl of the sky was closer than it had been; fat white clouds clustered and floated about the crests of the mountains, throwing their shadows in long purple patches.

She was startled when somebody called, "Hello. Hello, there." Beyond a jutting bluff on the bank of the river somebody was standing. Whoever it was waved and came toward her; as he came closer she saw that it was a very young man, not much older than herself, dressed in tailored riding breeches instead of the type usually seen in this country, which meant that he was a stranger.

He was sandy-haired and very thin; his face was bumpy, contradictory; he had merry eyes under thick brows which met on the bridge of his nose, and a rather long, agreeably homely face. He had white teeth and a wide pleasant smile.

He started talking to her from a distance, as if they had known each other all their lives. He said, "Thank heaven, I finally ran into somebody; I seem to have got myself lost and I've been wandering about like a lost soul in the wilderness for hours. You aren't by any chance Cathy Brett, are you?"

"Yes, I am."

"My guardian angel hasn't deserted me after all, then," he said. "I'm William Durwent."

"How do you do?"

He looked bewildered; he said, "The name doesn't seem to mean anything to you?"

"I'm sorry. Should it?"

"I'd like to see my father's face, that's all," he said. He held out his hand: "How do *you* do?"

"Fine, thank you. Are you really lost?"

"Completely and absolutely," William said cheerfully. "My horse is somewhere over there, I think, or perhaps over there. . . ."

"But how did you get here? I mean, where did you come from?"

"New York. Oh, today? Saint Cloud. I'm not trespassing, by the way, your father gave me permission to call on you. Only, as I say, I got lost, and my horse began to stumble, and so I decided to leave him and strike across country on foot. I've been walking forever without getting anywhere, and I was just about to resign my bones to the fates and the elements when you appeared, rescuing me." He said, "My guardian angel!" and looked down at her in a way which would have amused her except that her thoughts were somewhere else.

She asked, "When did you see my father?" inserting the question into this stream of chatter.

"I beg your pardon?" William asked. He had been raising and lowering his eyebrows, twisting his mouth into comical grimaces; it appeared to be a habit with him to make faces while he was talking. It was a way of showing off, Cathy supposed; it was also a rather wistful way of trying to make people like him. Cathy felt herself liking him right away. He sat down; he said pleadingly: "Do you mind if I take off my boots? My feet are killing me."

"Of course not." She sat beside him, while he took off first one boot and then the other, tenderly massaging his feet.

She said, "You haven't told me where you saw my father."

"Where? In Saint Cloud most recently, though I've met him in New York before. My father, though you may not know it, is one of the directors in your father's United Mine Industries and quite an important man, in his own mind at least. . . ."

"But my father isn't in Saint Cloud."

William raised and lowered his eyebrows a number of times. "He was last night," he said finally; he began to pull on his boots again.

"Last night? How could he possibly . . . ?"

"Didn't you know where he was?"

"I thought he was in New York," Cathy said. She stood up. "Shall we go find your horse? And then, since you are calling on us, we'd better go to the house, hadn't we?"

William stood up beside her. He thrust his hands in his pockets; he ceased being a clown and became instead a rather awkward anxious boy. "Look here, if I've spilled anything I shouldn't, I'm sorry. But your father didn't say anything about its being a secret."

"I'm sure it wasn't. He just hasn't had time to get in touch with us, that's all."

"That's it, of course," William said eagerly. Walking along beside her he explained with wide expansive gestures of his hands that the directors of the United Mine Industries were meeting in Saint Cloud for business reasons: "There's some kind of big amalgamation going on, buying up small mines and so forth," William said. "I just graduated from Princeton last year so nobody tells me very much, particularly my father, though he's supposed to be training me for his business. Fathers are pretty terrible, aren't they?"

"I don't know many, except mine."

"I'm a violent partisan in the Michael Brett camp; I can tell you that."

"What do you mean?"

William, waving his hand again, said he meant nothing in particular. "But the way he is buying up more mines, in the middle of an investigation, is making everybody nervous. He isn't at all nervous, and that's why I'm a violent partisan in his camp."

Cathy asked, "Are you talking about the appointment?"

"No, the investigation since then," William turned and looked at her curiously; he asked, "Say, don't you know anything?"

"Lately I haven't thought . . . I just assumed everything was all right." And now that she thought of it, she had seen no newspapers recently; she wondered if Sam or Stacey had hidden them.

"Oh, well, the appointment has been shelved, for the moment at least, pending this other investigation."

"What investigation is that?"

"Well, they've charged your father with violating the antitrust law or something of the kind; it's the only thing, I suppose, they could catch him on." William broke off; he said, belatedly, "Look here, perhaps I shouldn't be telling you all this."

"Who are they?"

"They? Oh, the Senate investigating committee. They have been out to get your father all along, you know."

"Why have they?"

William shrugged; he said he supposed they were afraid of him.

"Why are they?"

"You ask a lot of questions."

"Do I? I'm sorry." She walked ahead, keeping her back stiff and erect. William followed docilely in her wake; he said presently, in a voice which sounded snubbed and miserable: "You were such a jolly little thing a minute ago; what made you turn so haughty?"

"I didn't realize I had."

"I'm always putting my foot in it; my mother keeps telling me I haven't any tact."

He sounded so very abject that Cathy relented and slowed down; she said, "It's all right, I haven't either."

"You aren't upset, or anything?"

"No, I'm not upset."

"I mean, these investigations aren't anything; people are always having them. Nobody believes they'll be able to touch your father; it's just a question of time until he mops up the floor with them, if you know what I mean. Only right now he won't take anyone's advice, and that's what is making everyone so nervous."

"Why should it make other people nervous?"

William said, matter-of-factly: "Oh well, obviously none of them can get along without your father, no matter what they may feel about him."

"What do they feel about him?"

"Now I've put my foot in it again and you're turning haughty."

"No, please. What do they feel about him?"

143

"They can't do without him and they know it darned good and well."

"Why should they have to do without him?"

William burst out: "He acts to me as if he's sick and tired of them and Senate investigating committees and a lot of things. Only they're all hanging on to him."

Cathy asked wistfully: "Did you talk with him?"

"No, I didn't really talk with him but I sat at a table with him one whole evening. He was singing songs, mining songs; he was having a good time and he wouldn't talk business with anybody. The next morning he did, though. The next morning he was up earlier than anybody, telling them all what to do. My father said he had never been so exhausted in his life. He said nobody could keep up this pace; that's why he's going back and leaving me to look after his interests."

"Do you know how to look after them?"

"There isn't much to it except to stick around and attend meetings and things. The West is exciting, though, isn't it? I'm having an exciting time; it's the first time I've been on my own. I've been to Europe of course, but not alone—I mean I had to look after my mother and sister—what I mean is that wherever I've been I've led the same type of life as at home. This is so different; this makes me feel good. What I mean is, it widens my horizons, which have been rather limited, I'm afraid."

"I've been feeling the same way here; do you remember *The House with the Golden Windows?*"

"No, has it something to do with mines?" William was not interested in pursuing the subject; he wanted to talk about his own experiences. He had found Saint Cloud both colorful and thrilling and he began telling Cathy about it: "I've never had so much fun in my life. The whole town is gay and riotous . . . at the same time elegant. The women are so beautiful and the men sort of dashing—except for the ones like my father. Everybody has a good time; it's more like a play than real life. But you know better than I."

"I haven't been there for a long time."

"You haven't? I should think you would go all the time; it's only twenty miles."

"Well, but somebody has to take me and my father is too busy and they have a doctor there so that Philip hasn't any patients to see."

"Who's Philip?"

"A friend of ours; tell me more about Saint Cloud."

"Well, there's the big hotel there, very grand. And the Opera House. The women dress in silk even in the mornings and do nothing all day except ride up and down in carriages, even the nice ones. I mean, the other kind ride up and down too, quite openly, that's one of the things that makes it so sort of mixed up and gay. I mean . . . I don't know if you know what I mean."

"Well, I gather you mean that it's gay."

"Yes, that's just what I mean. Not the town, exactly; it's rather ugly in the daytime but at night the lights come on and the women put on their jewels and everyone goes to the Opera House and everything is as gay as anything."

Like Paris, Cathy thought. Very gay and amusing.

He said, "I expect to be here all winter; I hope you'll let me take you to some of the parties."

"Oh yes, I'd like that!"

"Would your father let you go, do you think?"

She said, "My father? Oh yes, I'm sure it wouldn't matter to him," but her face lost some of its radiance and became solemn again.

They walked on together. He was tall; he had a quick irregular stride; now and then he hopped, changing it. He seemed curious and at the same time sympathetic; sometimes he peered at her from under his ridiculous eyebrows, other times he blushed and stumbled or stumbled and then blushed. Always he talked.

"Do you like it out here?"

"Yes, of course, it's my home."

"It was the best luck in the world to run into you. Do you believe in luck?"

"I think so, a little."

"There's gambling, you know, at Saint Cloud. Roulette and poker; things like that, there's sort of a party every night at the hotel. I never had a chance before to find out if I was lucky or not."

"And were you?"

"I won ten dollars at roulette. I wasn't playing for very high stakes; not as high stakes as the others. I watched most of the time; it was more fun. My father would have killed me if he had known that I was gambling. He doesn't care for roulette or games or anything like that."

William stumbled and blushed; he seemed to feel he was on dangerous ground. "I don't mean that your father does either."

"I imagine he does."

145

"Why shouldn't he? I'm a violent partisan in your father's camp."

"Yes, you said."

"I don't suppose that means anything to you."

Cathy said, "Yes, it does, because I am too."

There were others, she sensed, walking along and feeling oddly old suddenly, who were not such violent partisans. Michael Brett had no doubt, since his arrival in Saint Cloud, submitted his colleagues to arbitrary and erratic domination. Memories crowded upon Cathy, against her will, of similar circumstances at Keepsake. Michael had always been demanding. Now his unhappiness would goad him; he would be more impatient of opposition or stupidity, far less reasonable than before.

Cathy asked, "Does he seem terribly unhappy?"

William, prattling about his father's hatred of the West, of gambling, of anything which disturbed the accepted pattern of his life, inquired in bewilderment: "My father? He's hardly ever happy so it's hard to tell."

"No, my father."

"No, not at all; he's been as gay as anything," William said; he stumbled and blushed.

"I'm glad."

"Yes, well," William said; he stumbled and blushed to such an extent that Cathy took pity on him and asked no more embarrassing questions.

William was noticeably relieved. He took her free hand, swinging it as they went along. He asked, "You don't mind, do you?"

"Mind what?" She followed his glance to their two hands; she said, "No, I don't mind."

"You don't think I'm being too familiar or anything?"

She rather wished he had not asked the question; it put things in a different light. She became self-conscious, but when she would have made an excuse to take her hand away he would not let it go.

He said, "Please don't."

"Very well." She continued to let her hand lie in his; he said, "You don't flirt, do you? Like most girls."

"I haven't learned how."

"It was the thing I liked about you, right away," he said. "You were friendly; you didn't seem at all surprised to see me or upset or anything because a stranger spoke to you."

"Why should I be?"

"Well," he said. "My sister would have. She would have been scared to death to run into a strange man in a lonely place like this."

"It isn't lonely to me."

"I don't suppose so." He looked doubtful, however; he said, rather pompously, "It isn't a good idea to be friendly to everyone, you know. I mean, there are people who might misunderstand."

It was the kind of thing Lisa always was saying. Cathy said, "In that case I would stop being friendly."

"Well, yes, but still, you can't just ignore conventions. I mean, of course, some people do, but it isn't always a good idea. Out here, of course, it's all right."

"This is where we are, isn't it? I know all about conventions; you don't need to worry about me."

He suspected that she was teasing him but with her hand tucked inside his arm and his own hand covering it he felt manly and protective. They found his horse grazing along the side of the river a short distance off; Cathy stood at its head, stroking its nose.

She said, "If you keep to this trail you'll come to Keepsake. I'll fetch my horse and meet you there."

"I'll come with you."

"No, please, it won't be necessary."

He ignored her protests and followed her, leading his horse. Though she insisted that this was their private property and that she had walked and ridden over it alone all her life, he could not believe that she should be allowed to do so. He was a stranger and he had trespassed; other strangers might do the same thing.

She asked, "Did you pass a gatehouse?"

"Gatehouse? I didn't pass anything except a little log cabin about a thousand miles back."

"Did someone come out and talk to you?"

"A man with a rifle—out hunting, I thought. He only wanted to borrow a match."

"That was the gatehouse."

He glanced at her from time to time as they walked along. His gaze flattered her; she began to feel feminine, poised, rather touched.

He said, "I've never known anyone just like you."

"Haven't you?"

"You aren't silly like my sister. You're different; I should have known you would be."

"How would you know?"

"Your father is different; naturally you would be. May I come to see you often while I'm here?"

"Of course. I hope you will. Though twenty miles, that's quite a distance, both ways."

"I could stay all night if you asked me."

"Oh, do."

"Will it be all right?"

"Of course. As often as you like."

They walked in silence for a little while. Presently he blurted out, as if unable to hold back the words any longer: "I liked you terribly the minute I saw you. Did you feel the same way?"

"Yes. Yes, I did."

"You did?" He was delighted, all his youthful egotism brought to the surface. He said, "Golly, I'm certainly glad I came, after all . . ."

"What do you mean, after all?"

He stammered, "I only meant I was almost afraid to come. Visiting Keepsake is almost like visiting Buckingham Palace, and I wasn't even sure your father would remember that he had invited me."

"Why shouldn't he remember?"

"Well, it was the kind of party in the hotel I was telling you about and everybody was gay."

"He was drunk, do you mean?"

William said, half admiringly and half disapprovingly: "You're an outspoken little thing, aren't you?"

"There's no particular reason to pretend that he wasn't, if he was."

"No, I guess not." William stumbled so badly that he nearly fell down.

Cathy said, "I don't mind at all; please don't be upset."

"How can I help being upset? I'm a clumsy fool; my mother is always telling me that I am."

His mother's opinions, though unflattering, seemed to be very important to him. Cathy said gently, "I'm sure she doesn't mean it. You aren't, at all."

William was relieved, though bewildered, because instead of his commiserating with Cathy, suddenly it was the other way around. He asked anxiously, "Are you sure I haven't hurt you?"

"No. I mean, I'm quite sure."

Nevertheless he ventured: "If you need a shoulder to cry on you may have mine."

"Thank you, but I don't need a shoulder to cry on."

"You might. You never can tell. And I'm not good at a lot of things, but I'm pretty good sometimes at cheering up people."

She walked on, and he wondered if his blundering had hurt her unbearably, if she might be going to cry. He was accustomed to feminine tears, both his sister and even his mother cried when the brutalities of the world became too much for them, but he had a feeling that Cathy's tears would be catastrophic. He was just about to beg her not to cry when she disconcerted him completely by laughing.

He asked, "Are you laughing at me?"

"No, of course not."

He was looking at her very intently now; she knew, instinctively and very surely, that he was thinking of what it would be like to kiss her, and she felt a responsive quiver along her nerves.

He said, "You have a face like an angel. Are you an angel?"

"No."

"I'm glad of that. Because I think I could fall in love with you very easily."

"You don't even know me."

He raised one eyebrow higher than the other; after you got used to his face it was sensitive and likeable as well as amusing. He asked, "What difference does that make?"

"None at all, I suppose," she confessed.

Cathy began to understand why girls liked to flirt. It was exciting to have somebody like you and say nice things to you and look at you as if they wanted to kiss you. But it wasn't very fair when you had no desire to give anything in return.

It complicated things too. Because she found herself thinking of what it would be like if William were to kiss her, and she found the idea not unpleasant.

When they came to her horse she mounted swiftly. She rode off and he followed.

Chapter 16

THERE WAS NO denying that it was pleasant to have William ride up to the house for frequent visits. Sometimes he could remain only for an hour or afternoon; often he stayed overnight. He was a responsive guest; he took an interest in all their affairs. Randy liked him, the servants liked him, they all liked him.

He was, in fact, so friendly and pleasant that Cathy thought that if she tried very hard she might learn to love him. Actually, he gave her very little indication that he wished her to do so; after that first afternoon his manner was affectionate but impersonal, except that occasionally she found him watching her with a bright intense look. He sometimes continued that look for so long that there seemed little doubt that he was trying to convey something to her, but then, almost immediately afterward he might make them all laugh by talking nonsense.

His behavior was that of a person discovering a freer and easier way of life than that to which he was accustomed and enjoying it, but at the same time being not quite sure of it. He asked questions sometimes, about her mother and her mother's people and where they had come from, about Helena Minard in France, about the reasons why Cathy had remained here instead of going away to school. Cathy understood that he was trying to provide her with the type of background which he had been brought up to believe was essential, and she answered questions with patient thoroughness.

Together he and Cathy pored over the Durand genealogy; when they closed it William said seriously that his mother could not possibly find fault with that, in the manner of one bestowing an accolade. Cathy, pleased that he was pleased, felt rarefied and honored. She would have liked to go on talking about the Durands all evening but William suddenly dismissed them; he said it was all nonsense, the world was changing, only people like his mother hadn't accepted the changes yet. He said that people like his mother clung to family trees and things like that because they didn't know what it was to be happy. He said that he, William, had never been so happy in his life as he had been since he had come to Keepsake.

He took Cathy's hands and held them. For a second he seemed about to kiss her; when he did, she knew, it would be an open declaration of love. But at the last minute he drew back, postponed whatever his intentions were; he did not seem to know his own mind, she thought, any better than she did hers.

Her father, she learned from William, was still at Saint Cloud. William told her other things too, whether unwittingly or not she could never be quite sure. Her father still was drinking a great deal, but he had pulled himself together several times at crucial moments. He was buying up or annexing all the rival mines which were still independent; he seemed to be obsessed with a desire to acquire everything upon which he could lay his hands. There was a lawsuit against him of some kind; several lawsuits indeed, William thought, though William always turned vague when he was being pinned down. Probably nothing serious, William said, though it was true that Michael Brett's associates, including or particularly William's father, were becoming more and more alarmed, feeling that all their interests were threatened. Others, and this group included William, to Cathy's gratitude, though she could not be at all sure whether or not her father would be impressed by the inclusion, said that Michael Brett was still Michael Brett and that in the long run any persons not realizing this would be the ones to suffer.

Cathy felt heartbroken and furiously defensive at first: how dare anyone question her father's behavior when now, of all times, he had a right to be unreasonable and violent? How dared they believe that love could not be so strong and so beautiful that when it died part of the person who loved must die too . . . ?

Gradually, against all her will, she was forced into the knowledge that it was not because he had loved too much that Michael Brett was now devastated by tragedy, but because he had not loved enough. When she realized that, she was besieged by a sadness almost too great to bear; at the same time an enormous feeling of protective love for her father welled up inside of her.

On her eighteenth birthday, Cathy got out of bed with a strange reluctance to face the day. Usually she was brimful and running over with enthusiasm for each new day; even when sad she felt less sad in the early morning, upon first awakening; it had taken several minutes always for sadness to overtake her and press down upon her. But today she awoke to sadness and the feeling that her life had lasted a long long time behind her and stretched before her interminably.

Stacey and Sam and Hester and Rachel were all waiting for her in Randy's room where they had gifts for her. The gifts were piled high on a table: there were books and handkerchiefs and perfume, and a photograph album and camera which Randy had ordered from New York. There were messages and gifts from Aunt Helena and Lisa too.

Philip came during the afternoon with his gift. It was a thin gold chain, with a pendant in which was a tiny cluster of pearls.

Cathy exclaimed with delight. "Oh Philip, it's beautiful."

"I had it made from one of my grandmother's earrings."

"It's beautiful."

He fastened it around her neck and then bent down and kissed her cheek. She stood very still, with one hand curved over the pendant. She was beset by a terrible temptation to throw herself on his mercy, to tell him how much she loved him. He would be distressed and unbelieving at first; he would try to persuade her that she was still too young to know what she was saying. But he would be kind; he would not want to hurt her. He would believe her finally if she were strong enough to make him believe that she loved him enough for both of them. And she was strong, terribly terribly strong where Philip was concerned.

She knew surely that she could make him turn to her; she could trick him; she could make him sorry for her. If she wept now, just a little bit, and he put his arms about her and she pretended to misunderstand and to believe that he cared for her, Philip would not be cruel enough ever to tell her the truth.

He smiled, and she smiled back at him. Her hand, which had been clenched about the pendant, slowly relaxed.

Philip said, "You look very pretty."

"Thank you."

"Quite old, too."

She felt quite old. Older than he knew.

Philip said, "I expected to see young Durwent here."

"He was here earlier. He brought me candy." She showed him, a huge box of French liqueurs from Sherry's.

"Very proper of him." Philip ate some.

"A very decent young man. Is he falling in love with you?"

She laughed. "Not that I can see. Anyhow, I'm not in love with him."

"I thought women got excited over attentions whether they were in love or not. Aren't you supposed to string them up like scalps, or something?"

He sounded bitter. She said, "I just haven't learned how to go about it yet, that's all."

"I hope you never do. When you're in love you'll know it."

"Yes, I think I will."

He gave her a brisk pat of commendation on the shoulder. Then he stopped being brisk; he took her hand and held it, looking down at it. He said, "Wait for love, Cathy; it will be worth it." He sounded sad too. She nearly weakened then; she glanced up, but he was no longer looking at her. He had to go, he said; he had a very sick patient who could not be left very long; he was sorry he could not stay for the birthday dinner.

When he was gone she stood without moving for a long time.

Presently she went into the music room. When one of the servants came to light the lights Cathy told him to leave them. The room was filled with blue dusk and the heavy scent of flowers.

Cathy sat down at the piano. She picked out the air of "The Happy Farmer" with one finger, and then, gaining confidence, she played with both hands.

Suddenly her father shouted from the doorway: "Stop that. Stop that damned blasted racket, do you hear?"

Cathy sat transfixed, frozen with horror. She continued to sit as her father struck a match and lighted several lamps: "What the devil good do you think it does to sit moping here in the dark?" he was shouting; he continued, violently, to light lamps and candles everywhere until the room was ablaze with light.

He turned then; at the sight of her stricken face he pulled himself together. "I'm sorry, Cathy. Only it doesn't do any good to sit around in the dark and feel sorry for yourself, you know."

She sat still, unable to move. He came across the room and . . . sat down beside her, taking her cold hands and holding them. "Did I startle you? I just arrived from Saint Cloud in honor of the day, but I certainly didn't mean to spoil it by shouting at you, my darling," he said. She could tell by the way his words thickened that he had been drinking all day. He said, "I heard someone playing and I'd forgotten that you used to do it sometimes. Forgive me?"

"For what?"

"For so many things. It would be tedious to enumerate them." He was smiling at her but the smile wasn't real, any more than anything in this nightmarish scene was real. He said, "I count on you, but the next time you decide to play the piano light a few lights, will you? The setting was very effective, almost too effective, and I'm not very dependable these days in my reactions."

She said: "I can't play. I've never been able to play."

"Can't you? Would you like to have lessons? We can have somebody in, if you like."

He thought he could fix everything, always, by having somebody in. Cold unforgiving feelings were ugly to have; they not only spread but they hurt. He could be honest with her, that was what she wanted more than anything; she did not have such romantic notions as everybody thought. She did not care what he did or what people said about him, whether it was wrong or right, so long as he included her; that was the truth, if only there had been some way of imparting it to him. She was tired of being shielded, kept in the dark, treated like a baby.

She said, "No, thank you."

"Come into my office with me."

He stumbled slightly as they went out the door. She followed him; she had a feeling that he might deliberately be disillusioning her; it would be like him. She sat down in the chair which he indicated; she was stubbornly determined not to be disillusioned.

He pushed a pile of papers before her. He said, "I want you to sign a few things; I'm transferring part of my holdings to you."

She was shocked into protest, after having been prepared for a birthday present: "I don't understand."

"You needn't; just sign."

"I can't; you've . . . you've always said never to sign anything without understanding it."

He gave a short laugh; he said, "Wisdom comes home to roost, like misdeeds. Very well, I'll explain. My affairs are somewhat involved at the present, what with Senate investigations and attendant lawsuits; everybody is eager to climb on the bandwagon. Now that you are of age it will be safer to have part of our holdings in your name, for both yours and Randy's sake."

"What are holdings?"

"Money and things that we own. Like Keepsake."

"Keepsake? Could they take that away from us?"

"They could and would, gladly." He put a pen in her hand; he said: "It's only a technicality, dearest; don't look so distressed."

"Why do they keep investigating you for so long?"

He frowned, laughed; he said, "Well, this is something a little special in the way of investigations, I'm afraid; we can be flattered in a way."

"But what is it exactly that they are investigating?"

The pen in her hand must have given her courage to pursue the subject in the face of his displeasure; but he wanted her to do something, and once, in what seemed the long ago, he had said that business was having something somebody else wanted to trade for something you wanted.

Her father straightened, appeared to resign himself to tiresome questions, and poured himself brandy. He said, "The latest investigation involves a current litigation which I am having with the government."

He was deliberately using unfamiliar words, she thought; he said a minute later as if reading her thoughts, "Litigation means legal dispute."

"About what?"

"About my right to own my own railroad to bring gold from my own mines."

"Why should they object to that?"

"They have a label for everything now: conspiracy, for instance; it isn't so simple as just getting the gold out of the ground. May I step down, your honor?"

She blushed violently. "I'm sorry."

"You needn't be." He stood sipping brandy, smiling at her; he looked more like himself than he had looked for a long time. "I'm glad to find you so capable of taking an interest in my affairs."

She wasn't, of course. She confessed: "William says . . ."

"Who is William?"

"Durwent. His father is one of the stockholders in the United Mine Industries so probably he owns part of the railroad too."

"He would like to, but he doesn't."

"William is a violent partisan in your camp."

"Ah. And how about you?"

"I am too, but I keep wishing I could understand more."

155

"Don't you read the newspapers?"

"Sam hides them."

"We'll give orders for him not to do that."

"Yes, but even so. Some of them say one thing and some say another."

"Such as what in particular?"

"Some of them say that it's all right for you to own so many mines and railroads and things and others say that you are robbing the people."

Her father looked at her keenly; he said, "Sam didn't hide so many newspapers from you, did he?"

"I found a few of them."

"And what conclusions did you draw?"

"I don't know that I drew any. Except that . . . so long as they feel so strongly . . ."

"Who?"

"The United States Government, or whoever it is. William says that nobody can be bigger than the United States Government."

"William sounds like as tiresome a fool as his father."

"He is on your board of directors. Not William."

"As well I know. I am beginning to realize that fools for friends are even worse than fools for enemies."

"We have plenty of money so that you could retire, haven't we?"

A flash of bitter humor showed from his blue eyes. Michael Brett said, "I didn't dig gold from the ground with my bare hands just to have the government or anybody else dictate to me what to do with it." He had not quite dug the gold from the ground with his bare hands, as they both knew, but it had become a legend, almost a truth, perhaps in his mind too. "No, I've just begun to fight, as they'll discover, sitting back there in Washington and issuing their blasted injunctions." Injunction was a new word; Cathy was adding them day by day to her vocabulary. "Thinking I'm through no doubt, invoking laws that they chose to ignore when it was profitable to do so, as if they were mandates from heaven; they're used to dealing with children and they act like children." He poured nearly a full glass of brandy and drank it as if to wash the bitter taste from his mouth. Nobody seemed to say anything about who was right or who was wrong; once, long ago, Cathy's father had said to her, laughing: "Never do as I do, just do as I say." He was not even saying that now; he seemed to have forgotten her until he turned abruptly and said: "That's enough of that for the moment," and drew the papers together, pointing with his forefinger. He said, coldly: "Come now, sign, Cathy; you can surely make more than an 'X' by now." Cathy, snubbed and indignant, signed her name, Catherine Theresa Brett, over and over, hundreds of times it seemed to her.

When they were all finished her father made a bundle of the papers and carried them to the safe. "That will do for now," he said. "We'll go into them a little more formally later, with our lawyers." He opened the safe and put the bundle inside. He reached back into the depths of the safe and pulled out, one by one, deep metal boxes which he placed on the table before her.

He said, "These are for your eighteenth birthday." He opened one of the boxes and stood looking down at it; it contained jewels which had belonged to Theresa. He said, "They're yours; you are the only woman in the world I could bear ever to have them."

Cathy said, "No, I . . . no."

He scoffed: "No I no; what does that mean?"

"They couldn't ever belong to me."

"Perhaps not; that's up to you."

"That's not fair. I only meant . . ."

He said, standing up and cutting her off: "You are too young to wear most of them now, of course. But they belong to you from now on; you may take them out or wear them or forget them or do whatever you wish with them."

She said quietly then: "Thank you; it's a lovely present."

The flash of interest was in his glance again: "Have you a sense of humor after all?"

"I don't know. But it is a lovely present and I'm grateful; thank you very much."

"You could ask me where you were to wear them and I would be hard put to it to answer."

"I don't need to wear them. I'll just look at them; thank you just the same."

"Umm. Is young Durwent courting you?"

"Courting me?" Cathy blushed and stumbled; she was as bad as William. "I don't think so."

"Don't you know?"

"I don't think he approves of us. Or he thinks that his mother won't."

"That woman! Is it possible we are subject to her approval?" Cathy laughed; they both laughed. It was something which hadn't happened for a long time.

Michael said presently, breaking the breathless happiness of the moment: "I'm leaving for New York tomorrow, perhaps Europe, did I remember to tell you?"

"No. But it's all right."

"Perfectly all right?"

"Perfectly all right."

"I'm depending on you to look after Randy. If you need anything send for it . . ."

When you needed anything all you had to do was to send for it.

Chapter 17

On February 15, 1898, the *Maine* was blown up.

Cathy tried to picture the scene. She tried to feel sorrow for the suffering and the dead, but they were too far away. They made less impression on Keepsake than Randy's wild duck with the broken wing which they had been nursing all winter and which finally drooped and died, or the birth of a new baby to one of the tenant families, at which Cathy assisted in a minor but soul-satisfying way.

She was troubled, because it seemed wrong to live so apart from the world that its catastrophes did not concern one.

Her father was in France on a prolonged business trip. He was staying at the Hotel Vendôme instead of with the Minards because Raymond Minard was ill. That, at least, was the reason given. Cathy feared an estrangement; she could not help thinking of the changes in her father.

The letters which arrived from both Michael and Helena were reassuring enough, on the surface. They dwelt on Raymond Minard's illness as an excuse for Helena's retirement from all social life, though Cathy was aware that Helena Minard would in any case impose upon herself the conventional period of mourning after Theresa's death, and that she would be both hurt and angered by Michael's refusal to do so. "In the end we all fall back on amenities," Cathy could imagine her Aunt Helena as saying: "They are important, whether we wish to admit it or not." However, no hint of this feeling crept into her letters: "We are very quiet, as is to be expected," she said, "but we wish that you and Randy were with us. Next year we must all pick up the pieces of life and start over: Lisa and I will come to New York where your father consents for you to join us and we will all be ourselves once more."

Cathy knew in her heart this would never happen, as Helena must have known it, though Cathy agreed that falling back on the amenities could be a comforting, indeed a life-saving, device. Cathy at the present time was falling back heavily on the amenities; she was pretending that doubt and disaster were two words which could not exist.

Michael wrote: "If it were not for the certainty of war I would send for you and Randy to come and be here with me, but as it is I am sure you are better off where you are, and we are not very gay, naturally, in any case. I remain at the Vendôme because Raymond is to be kept quiet, and as you know it is never quiet for very long where I am. Helena disapproves of me at the moment, which is quite right and I love her for it. Lisa is the bright spot on our present horizon; she abounds in youth and vitality which refuses to be quenched by anything. I aid and abet her though Helena scolds me; she feels Lisa is selfish enough which of course she is. I want you to be selfish also, my dearest one; you will be happier that way in the long run. I love you both dearly and when I come home in April I shall hope to be a better father to you. . . ."

He, like Cathy, postponed uncomfortable conversion until later; Cathy could no longer feel either in awe of him or coldly angry at him. She simply stood, holding the letter, and this was the true and decisive moment of her maturity. She would have postponed it if she had been able, but it was thrust upon her.

Philip, as a matter of course, read all the letters which came from France. He read the page about Lisa's being selfish without comment.

It consoled him to know what Cathy did not know, that Lisa herself was not having a very happy time.

Her letters to him were less restrained than the others. She wrote: "Everything is terrible, so depressing and sad, you have no idea. Mamma remains in deep mourning even though Uncle Michael himself begs her not to do so, and she insists that I be in mourning also. It is not unbecoming, rather the contrary, but of course it is impossible to be gay when one is in mourning. Don't think that I am heartless. I loved Aunt Theresa too, but I want to dance and laugh just the same; is that wrong? Recently

I was introduced to a young man, Francis Tole his name is; he is interested in me. I am only interested in him because Mamma approves of him and she allows me to be with him so don't be jealous, Philip, darling Philip, darling darling Philip. What good is writing; it is all so hopeless! I am unhappy because I am so far from you; I am unhappy about everything. Everything is different: Mamma; this season which was supposed to be the most important of my life; Uncle Michael and Mamma have almost quarreled, I don't know about what. Perhaps because Uncle Michael refuses to observe mourning, he says it is a senseless formality which does nobody any good. I agree with him, don't you? Sometimes he laughs so loudly that I wish that he wouldn't, but just the same he is very good to us and I notice that Mamma still allows him to give us money. I myself am devoted to him and I do not believe any of the things about him which I read in the papers. He is not a bad man at all, as some people say." Lisa, at this point, became prim and self-righteous, and Philip, reading and re-reading her letters, smiled, although it was a rather twisted smile. She wrote, "I understand exactly how he feels and I do everything I can to help him."

She added, as a postscript: "Poor Papa has been very ill."

Michael Brett had written that he was to be home in April, but April was almost gone and there was still no word from him.

Cathy worried anxiously about the possibility of his being in danger on the return voyage, since other ships besides the *Maine* might be blown up. The newspapers which arrived in bundles at Keepsake were nearly a week late, but they were full of enormous and scarifying headlines of war.

Cathy began to have nightmares in which she saw the disaster of the *Maine* all too vividly. She saw a tiny toy boat, rocking along on a calm sea which seemed to be made of canvas. There was a great tumult and the boat was blown into a cascade of little pieces, rather like a skyrocket, and the ocean which now became a real ocean was filled with struggling people.

One of the people was her father. She could see him plainly; he, alone of all the people was not struggling at all. He was smiling. "It does no good to struggle, Cathy," he said. "We must fall back on the amenities, it does no good to struggle against them, no good at all." She tried to think of some way to help him but she knew that there wasn't any way. He went down, out of sight, and the water became canvas water again, like a stage setting, with rippled painted waves.

She had had one of these dreams before this particular morning and as usual it left its aftermath of depression. She puzzled, on waking, as to whether there was such a thing as fate and if there was no escaping it. Her own fate seemed more clearly defined every day. "It does no good to struggle, Cathy," her father in her dream had been saying to her, "no good at all. We are what we are and nothing can change us."

It was a beautiful rain-washed morning. Everything wore a clean and sparkling look.

Cathy went to find Randy. He was not in his room; he had left the house very early, Stacey informed her, while it was still wet, to look after one of his animals. Randy had a house behind the stables where he kept baby or wounded wild creatures; Cathy found him there feeding an abandoned baby fox from a bottle, something like the Spartan boy, Cathy thought. The fox had bitten him several times the past two days, exhibiting not only unattractive social behavior but complete ignorance of its circumstances, but this morning, nestling, its eyes wild and bright, it was taking the bottle of milk which was held for it.

Cathy waited, not too close, until the bottle was empty and the fox restored to its pen.

"I think it's going to be all right," Randy said.

Cathy, watching him as he finished with the other animals, ached for him; he even wore an old white dispensary coat which had belonged to Philip. When he had finished and was coming toward her she said, "Stacey wants you to be sure to change your shoes."

He nodded, automatically acceding to Stacey her right to look after him in these things; he had none of the rebellion against bonds, even of affection, which assailed Cathy. He walked beside her, absorbed in his own thoughts. He was growing into a tall thin youth, far too tall and too thin, so that always those who loved him were fearful about him. He was unspoiled, though he was fussed over continually. There was always that humorous lift to his mouth, now too large for his face as were all his features at this period of his growth. He was as gangling and awkward as any other boy of the same age but it did not bother him; he was even amused. He said that adolescence was an unlovely period for any animal, particularly for the human one. Nothing unfinished was supposed to be beautiful; the important thing was not to remain too long in the unfinished state.

His dark grave eyes, with their occasional flashes of humor, were the only thing about him which remained unchanged. He was in the chrysalis stage, he said reassuringly; presently he would become a butterfly and then they would see.

Cathy, her heart swelling as always with love for him, put out her hand as they walked, and he held it. He glanced at her, calling attention to the fact that he must now look down as he did so.

"I know," she said. "You're getting so big."

"Let's go sit down and talk for a while," he suggested.

"What about your shoes?"

"They aren't very damp." He examined the sole of first one and then another, solemnly. "Hardly damp at all."

"All right. If you're sure."

They went into a small enclosed garden with whitewashed walls and dark shrubs espaliered against them. There were many such small gardens at Keepsake; the high walls were to keep out the winds.

They sat down side by side on a marble bench and instantly Randy became absorbed in an ant at his feet which was carrying a twig many times its size.

"Poor little thing," Cathy said when her attention was called to it.

"But why? He's doing what he's supposed to do."

"Oh. Well, I suppose it doesn't matter to him whether he wants to do it or not."

Randy smiled at this unscientific explanation and Cathy, soothed and relaxed by the peace which enclosed her, leaned back. The sun was warm and invigorating; she lifted her face to it and closed her eyes. But I'm not an ant, she thought: I'm Cathy Brett. She asked, "Randy, do you believe in fate?"

He turned away from the ant to her, giving her his full attention. "What do you mean by fate?"

"Something that decides our lives whether we like it or not."

"Something?" he repeated. "That's very vague." He grinned; he was teasing her because she was so often disorderly in her thoughts. But presently he said, soberly, "Yes, I suppose I do. Our characters determine our fate, I would think."

"Do you mean that the kind of people we are decides what is going to happen to us?"

"Something like that. Or how we meet what happens to us, at least, and that more or less decides our fate."

"But what decides what kind of people we are?"

He glanced at her. He said, somewhat diffidently, "Well, some of that must be decided before we are born and some of it we have to decide for ourselves."

"Oh dear," Cathy said. "I don't understand it at all."

Randy looked at her sympathetically and then back to the ant. He did not understand it either but, like the ant, he did not find it too difficult to follow out the established pattern of his life.

Stacey was coming across the grass. She had some dry shoes for Randy in one hand and mail in the other. She handed the mail to Cathy and stood by, the dry shoes in her hands, while Randy unlaced his wet ones.

Cathy, eagerly scanning a letter, gave a little cry: "He's in New York."

"Father?"

"He may already be on his way home and he has a surprise for us, he says."

Randy was struggling with a shoelace.

"Oh, I'm so glad," Cathy said. "I had a horrid dream."

"What kind of dream?"

"A horrid dream," Cathy repeated. She gave a little shiver; the dream was still very vivid. "It's all right now." She examined the envelope in her hand and said, "This was sent nearly two weeks ago; it must have been delayed. Father is sure to be on his way home; he may get here in a day or so, even today."

"I wonder what the surprise can be," Randy said. There were times when he ceased being a philosopher and scientist and became a boy.

They speculated, extravagantly, as they had used to do. "A bear?" Randy suggested. "Yes, a dancing bear," Cathy agreed. Released from the oppression of the dream she began to feel very light-hearted.

"I would like a balloon," Randy said. "With a basket."

"Yes, a balloon would be very nice."

"We could go sailing off. Nineteen times as high as the moon."

When it was time for Randy to go into the house for his self-imposed hours of study, Cathy walked with him to the side door. She said, "It's really too nice to go indoors; I think I'll go for a ride." She could have studied too, to advantage, but she turned her back on it; particularly when she saw Philip's horse enter the stable courtyard. She waited for him on the nearest terrace; when he caught sight of her he waved.

Since her birthday they had become closer companions. His

conscious attitude was still that of an affectionate protective older brother, but underneath there was a growing respect for her as a person in her own right. She had grown up, and there was about her an unmistakable dignity. Some of the roundness, the confidingness, had gone out of her face; there was a new look of restraint. She had been burdened with adult emotions too early; he did not dream how much he was responsible for that.

He said, "I have to go to Farrington Camp; will you come with me?"

"Oh yes."

She went to dress. He ordered a fresh horse for himself and another for her.

Chapter 18

SHE RODE IN breeches instead of a divided skirt, looking, with her short curly hair caught in a barrette on her neck, like a colonial boy. For all her gentleness she was very much Michael Brett's daughter. Her upbringing had left her free from the false modesties and affectations of most of the young girls of her day. She was forthright and courageous, reckless too.

Philip wished he could foresee her future now that her safe sheltered little world already was breaking up. As for Michael he knew little philosophy, only emotion and action; he made his own code; he was not called a robber baron for nothing. That part of his life was seeping into Cathy's in various ways. Philip dreaded the thought that Cathy might some day be uprooted, thrust into a strange and restricted life without preparation.

They rode in silence for a time. They were climbing Black Canyon; the face of the rock walls hemming them in rose black and sheer.

They came out on an open ridge and reined in to look out over the valley. The valley held the sunlight like a bowl; it was rimmed by multi-colored mountains. The bright changing colors of this country were a miracle whose fascination never dimmed.

Philip glanced at Cathy, looked away and glanced again; her eyes were filled with tears. He said, "Cathy. Go away from here. Go to Helena. Go to New York. Go anywhere. You could, if you insisted."

"Just because I shed a few tears?"

"Not because of anything. Because you used to be teeming with desire to go everywhere and see everything and now you aren't.

What's happened to you? If it's because of Randy it's the most foolish kind of self-deception; Randy will be taken care of."

"Randy hasn't anything to do with it."

"What, then?"

"You swoop out at me so. I stay here because I always have, because nobody suggests anything different except now and then, like now, when they propose it out of a clear sky without whys or wherefores or ways and means, and because everything I want is here."

Philip acknowledged the validity of her case with an amused surprised grunt; his blue eyes, so much more blue than the sky, probed into hers. His beloved face was very close, so close that she could have reached out and touched it, gently, ever and ever so gently, with fingers of love.

Suddenly she wheeled her horse into action and put it to a gallop up the steep narrow road as if a hundred demons were pursuing her.

Philip caught up with her before very long. He galloped his horse on the outside of the path and forced her to slow down. It was a dangerous thing to do, and though her instinct still was for escape from her emotions, she reined her horse to a stop immediately; she could not expose Philip to danger. She could not halt her runaway feelings quite so immediately; she sat with her heart pounding, unable to meet his eyes, longing to keep on running, anywhere at all so long as she never had to stop. She thought surely that this frantic clamoring inside her must communicate itself somehow to him, but when she looked up he was glaring at her angrily, and the tumult died away, leaving her feeling apologetic and silly.

Philip did not spare her feelings. "What the devil do you think you're doing, careening up the side of the canyon like that?"

She said, lamely, "I thought we might race."

"Up the side of a mountain? Are you crazy?"

"I guess so. I just had an impulse to go as fast as I could, and I didn't stop to think."

"Did I hurt your feelings?"

"Hurt my feelings?"

"You used to go off on a silly tangent like that when your feelings were hurt."

"Oh. No, you didn't hurt my feelings."

"Sure?"

"Yes. Yes, I'm sure."

He grumbled, releasing her horse: "Well, the next time you have an impulse like that let me know in advance, will you?"

He was so far from understanding her real reason for a desire for flight that she was moved to laughter. "Yes. Yes, I will."

"What's so funny?"

"You are. If I could let you know in advance when I was going to have an impulse it wouldn't be an impulse, would it?"

He looked at her closely. Her face was flushed and her eyes were bright and shining. Her behavior struck him as illogical to the extreme but it pleased him; he was impatient with her sometimes because it hurt him when she allowed herself to be subdued, no longer on tiptoes with expectation of life. He wanted her to strike out, demand something for herself, all the more so because his own demands seemed less and less plausible or likely of fulfillment.

He continued to look at her, attracted by a new independence which was showing itself; she had been tearful, reckless, gay, in such rapid succession that he could only tag along, far from assuming the leadership which he had always taken for granted.

He asked, "What in the world has come over you? You're acting as giddy as a peahen."

"I do feel a little giddy."

"For any special reason?"

"No. Suddenly I'm just happy. Haven't you ever felt terribly, terribly happy for no reason?"

"No, I can't say that I have."

"Well, I have. And I am this very minute, whether you think it's silly or not."

Her spirits were infectious. He was easily persuaded to enter into her mood; during the rest of the ride they frolicked lightheartedly, racing on the level stretches with the winner mocking the loser, talking nonsense and laughing at nothing.

It was an old game with a new undercurrent of which both were intensely conscious. Their eyes met frequently, and each time their glances seemed to hold a little longer.

Farrington Camp consisted of a few rickety wooden structures climbing the side of a mountain. Each dwelling had a front porch like a balcony, jutting out over the narrow curved road and reached by a steep stairway. They climbed one of them.

A man seated on the porch with a bandaged leg supported by a kitchen chair greeted them.

"Howdy, Doc. Howdy, Miss Brett." His face looked gray and

drawn behind an untidy beard and an evil smell came from the bandage.

Philip asked, unpacking his bag: "What have you been doing to yourself, Reuter?"

"I stepped on a spike, that was all. It bled good, but a few days ago it began to raise the old Cain."

Mrs. Reuter came to the screen door. Philip asked for boiling water and a clean bandage; he sat down and began to undo the dirty gray dressing on the foot.

Mr. Reuter suggested, "Maybe Mike Brett wouldn't like for his girl to be here; this foot of mine ain't exactly no treat."

"Cathy?"

"No, please. It's all right."

The foot was badly discolored. Philip worked over it, his face set. It angered him because the stolid people of the region were so slow to accept new ideas or call a doctor. It thrilled Cathy always to watch him work; his hands were gentle and clever, quick and sure. She sterilized the instruments and handed them to him as she had been taught; she received as a reward a swift glance of approval which sent the blood singing through her body.

Philip talked, as he probed and cleaned the foot, in a matter-of-fact monotone, attempting to divert the man's attention. "Why haven't you been to see me before with this?"

"Well, hell, Doc, I didn't think it was nothing."

"None of you think it's anything until you lose a leg."

"I ain't going to lose this one, am I?"

"Not if you do as I say."

Philip continued to probe; the infection was very deep. Mr. Reuter's eyes became resentful with pain. When the ordeal was over he wiped his forehead with the tail of his shirt and asked caustically: "What was you looking for in there, a gold nugget?"

"Poison. This must be kept clean and moist."

Philip told Mrs. Reuter how to take care of it. She listened with a doubtful eye on her husband as if she knew beforehand that he was not going to lend himself to this part of the program.

Philip, repacking instruments into his bag, said, "I'll be back in a few days. And take care of yourself."

"What for? If there had been gold in that foot it wouldn't have been mine. That's a fact, ain't it?"

"Another fact is that if you don't take care of that foot you'll lose it."

Mr. Reuter looked surly and unfriendly now. He asked, "How

much do I owe you?"

"We'll settle that later."

"I don't get paid when I don't work, you know," Mr. Reuter said. "And if I lose a foot it ain't likely that I'll ever get paid again."

"You won't lose your foot if you take care of it." Philip took Cathy's arm; he said, "Come on, I'm ready; we'd better start back." He was suddenly in a hurry to get away and she thought: He's afraid Mr. Reuter is going to say something unpleasant about us, about Father. Occasionally a man did, when he was drunk or out of work, and in her heart Cathy could not always blame them. When people were hurt or poor it must be hard to see other people who had so much.

The gay mood was gone as they started homeward.

Cathy asked, "Is Mr. Reuter's foot really bad?"

"Bad enough. He won't take care of it, of course, and so in the end it will have to be amputated."

"But what will he do then?"

Philip said savagely, "Do? He'll do nothing except drink and curse his fate."

A great deal of conversation had centered on fate that day, Cathy thought. They rode in silence for a time, then she said, "There's a lot of sadness in the world, isn't there?"

He glanced at her. Her face was pale and strained. He said, "Don't worry about it. Reuter isn't worth much more with two feet than he will be with one."

"I wasn't thinking of just Mr. Reuter."

"Oh," he said. He wondered if it had occurred to her that Michael Brett also was doing too much drinking and cursing his fate. He said, "Yes, I'm afraid there is, but there's no way that I know of to avoid it."

"That's what makes it so frightening."

He put out his hand and she put hers in it; they rode together hand in hand.

Some time later she said, "Philip?"

"Yes, dear?"

A little shiver ran over her, unnoticed by him.

"Let's go home by Echo Canyon."

"If you like."

"Do you remember the Wishing Rock?"

"Of course I remember."

"I'm going to make a wish."

She stretched upward in the saddle, lifting her face toward the sky above the tops of the tall pines. "Oh Philip, it's a lovely day, even with poor Mr. Reuter."

They turned off the path into a patch of pine woods. They came out on a ledge; at the edge a large rock jutted over the narrow chasm of the canyon. This was the Wishing Rock. Below them the mountain stream tumbled and churned white in its narrow bed. The face of the cliff opposite them was broken and rocky.

Cathy stood on Wishing Rock. "I wish . . ." she began aloud; she closed her eyes and made the rest of the wish silently.

"You used to tell."

"That was because I couldn't wait for it to come true."

"Now you can?"

"Yes. Now I can."

Philip was staring at the canyon wall opposite. "Look over there. I never noticed that before."

"Where?"

"Halfway up. To the right of that big boulder."

She looked where he was pointing and saw a black mark that might be an opening in the face of the cliff. From any other angle it would be hidden by the boulder.

"Do you suppose it's a cave?"

"Possibly."

"Let's go and see."

He glanced about him. "It's too steep to go down here. If we go farther down we may lose it."

"We can mark it by the boulder."

"There are hundreds of boulders."

"This one is an odd shape. Like a pear."

"So it is. Come on, then; we'll try it."

They left the ledge and picked their way cautiously, with many turnings and deviations, to the floor of the canyon.

"Do you still see it?"

"I think I see the boulder. Right up there?"

"Yes, that looks like it."

They had to go downstream for a long way to find a place quiet enough to ford. Even so there was a certain element of danger, for Black Stream was treacherous.

"This is foolishness," Philip said. "We should have waited until another day and approached from the opposite side."

"Oh no, that wouldn't have been fun at all."

"It would be fairly easy that way. It's odd we've never seen it before if it is a cave."

They came upstream and left their horses to graze along the river bank. They climbed on foot up the side of the ravine and along rock ledges, using the Wishing Rock opposite for a guide.

"This is about it, I think."

"Do you see the boulder?"

"They all look alike now."

Philip drew an imaginary line across the ravine. "It should be about here."

"Oh yes, I see it; it's easy to see now."

Eagerly, they scrambled up the remaining ascent to the great pear-shaped boulder.

There was a narrow crevice just behind the boulder. Philip edged in first, his hand on the revolver which he carried in his belt on mountain trips, watchful for wild animals.

The crevice turned at right angles into a low narrow corridor. Philip lighted matches, calling to Cathy to follow. The flame of the matches burned steadily though the air smelled damp and musty.

The corridor inclined downward. It came out in a round natural low-ceilinged chamber. The walls and floors were of smooth rock.

"Yes, here's your cave. And somebody has lived here."

They walked about the room, examining it. There were blackened marks of a fire against one wall.

"Here's something." Cathy picked up an object and made a face. "Only an old rusty can."

"Here's another. Here's a whole pile of them."

"Then it didn't belong to cliff dwellers at all."

"No, I'm afraid not. Whoever was here was a lot more recent than cliff dwellers."

In a corner was a pile of old blankets thrown together as if to make a bed.

Philip said, "Somebody camped here, all right. And not too long ago."

"I wonder who it could have been."

"Tramps, I suppose," Philip said, though he could not imagine how tramps could have made themselves so at home on property which was known to be thoroughly patroled.

Cathy preferred to imagine the inhabitants of the cave as more romantic than tramps. "Do you remember those men who robbed a train a year or so ago and were never caught? They might have been the ones."

"Possibly." Philip went outside again to scout around; Cathy followed him. "They had their nerve if it was," Philip said. "Look, you can see Keepsake quite plainly from here."

"Yes, but even so, Philip, it's a perfect hiding place. Nobody would stumble on it in a hundred years, and being so close to the house makes it just that much safer. The posse didn't spend much time around here, don't you remember?"

Yes, he remembered, and it gave him an uncomfortable feeling to think of armed and dangerous men living so close to the house. From the ledge they could have observed the daily activities of Keepsake; it was possible that they had even made occasional sorties for food.

He went back into the cave and examined it more closely. There had been a minimum of fire evidently, closely sheltered, or it would have attracted attention. But it was a perfect hiding place as Cathy had said; there was water close by, possibilities for fire and food, and but for the merest accident nobody would stumble on the tiny natural opening.

Cathy called to him from the outside; her voice sounded excited. He ducked out so hastily that he bumped his head and stood rubbing it ruefully when he saw that she was safe and sound and nothing had happened to her. She only wanted to show him that someone was driving up the road to their house. "See the dust? And look, now you can see a carriage. Who do you suppose it could be?"

"Good heavens, is that all? I thought somebody was kidnapping you."

"It may be Father; he could travel as fast as his letter, couldn't he?"

"I daresay." Philip decided to postpone further explorations until another day after he had reported his findings to Michael. "Come on, then; we'll see who it is."

On the way down the bank toward the horses she said, "Philip?"

"Yes, dear?"

Each time it happened, that endearing word, a wild sweet hope swept over her. She steadied herself against a projecting rock. "Let's not tell anybody else about the cave. It can be our secret."

"I'll have to tell your father."

"Yes, I suppose so. But nobody else."

In the stable courtyard a stableman was rubbing down two horses which were standing in the shafts of a rented hack from the village.

Cathy asked, "Who is it, Carl? Who drove in here?"

Carl said, grinning, "Meester Brett. He is home again."

They dismounted and hurried toward the house. A figure came running down the steps of the terraces to meet them.

It was Lisa. She called to them: "Hello, hello, both of you. I'm the surprise Uncle Michael wrote about; isn't it wonderful? I wanted to come so badly, but of course I never dreamed I could, and then Papa got much worse, he had a stroke, and so Mamma and Uncle Michael decided that I should come with him. Papa has to go somewhere and rest and Mamma is going to take care of him and I would only be in the way. It's all been so terribly exciting—sad, too, of course—we had a horrible crossing, because of the war, you know, expecting every minute to be blown up. I was so frightened, but it was fun too." She stopped talking and drew a long breath and said, "Oh, I am so happy to be here. Do say you are both glad to see me."

"Lisa!"

Philip was staring at her, a dumbfounded expression on his face as if a dream had just come to life.

Lisa repeated: "You are glad to see me, aren't you?"

"I can't believe that it's you."

"It is. It really and truly is."

She was lovelier than ever. There was a subtle deepening and intensifying of her beauty. Her face was thinner and more sensitive-looking; she had lost the flamboyancy which had come with the first awareness of her charms. Her movements were graceful; her eyes and languid smile hinted at mysteries.

Philip could not tear his eyes away from her. She linked her arm in his. She said, with grave wistfulness: "You haven't really said that you are glad to see me."

Unnoticed, Cathy walked alone toward the house.

Chapter 19

AN ELDERLY WOMAN, Mrs. Ellis, had accompanied Lisa as traveling companion and chaperone. She was to stay on at Keepsake, at Helena Minard's suggestion, to act as companion and adviser to both girls in Helena's absence. Mrs. Ellis was an expatriate from New Orleans who had lived in France twenty years; she belonged to the impoverished gentlewoman class, forced to take employment but losing no social standing by so doing; she could provide a proper background for Cathy during this period when there was no one else to do it.

"Exactly what we need to offset William's mother, don't you see?" Michael Brett said to his daughter, introducing Mrs. Ellis. There was a funny little smile at one side of his mouth and he disappeared into his den leaving Cathy to entertain Mrs. Ellis.

Mrs. Ellis did not require much entertaining. She accepted tea, sitting very straight; she was rigidly encased in black silk. She had piercing but kindly eyes and she had a thin patrician nose with a humorous twitch at the end. Cathy liked her.

"Your aunt sends her love," Mrs. Ellis said, as they drank tea together. Mrs. Ellis did not glance curiously about her as most people did on their first visit to Keepsake; she looked directly at Cathy. "She is well, and she hopes you are well too."

"Yes, I am, thank you."

"Who is William's mother?"

"William comes to call on us quite often and he talks about his mother. His mother is very . . . social-conscious."

Mrs. Ellis coughed: "Oh I see, your father was joking."

Mrs. Ellis allowed herself one glance at her surroundings: "This is a beautiful room. Your aunt described Keepsake to me of course. Even so, I must confess, I wasn't quite prepared for it."

"Most people aren't."

"No." Mrs. Ellis came back to Cathy; she said, "Nor for you, either, if I may be frank; I thought you were younger."

"Well, I was younger, when Aunt Helena left."

Mrs. Ellis smiled; her smile did not soften her face exactly, it was more like the sun lighting up a craggy mountain. "You are still not so very old."

"It was good of you to come."

Cathy had made up her mind during the tea interlude that she liked Mrs. Ellis because she looked competent and sensible.

During the next few days Cathy grew to like and trust Mrs. Ellis more and more. Mrs. Ellis was not only capable but cheerful, full of plans and gossipy detail about the future. There were to be people, the right people, invited soon to the house: everything began to seem quite clear and possible when seen through Mrs. Ellis' eyes. Such things as tragedy and possible disaster faded into the distance; and the future became something to be contemplated not only with equanimity but with pleasure. One need only to behave like the princess in the fairy story; presently, lo and behold, everything straightened out, virtue was rewarded, and one lived happily ever after.

Cathy found that she could gaze upon the future quite happily. She listened to Mrs. Ellis' plans without being quite sure how they were to be put into effect, but reassured by Mrs. Ellis' confidence and her repeated statements that she was there to be of help.

It was a time in her life when Cathy most needed help and she received it gratefully.

Mrs. Ellis approved of William when he appeared at Keepsake on one of his regular visits. She knew all about him, drawing upon some fount of information completely mysterious to Cathy. She said the Durwents were fairly new but well-connected: "Quite wealthy, too, not that that matters to you. However, it eliminates the possibility of a fortune hunter—a dreadful word, I quite agree, but one must think of these things."

Cathy had never thought of them before. "Why must one?"

Mrs. Ellis smiled; she said it was the way things were and she did not make up the rules. "They would be different if I were permitted to do so, I can assure you. However, since this is the only world we know and we have to live in it, we have no choice but to accept it."

That was certainly true. Cathy said, "I suppose so," so resignedly, that Mrs. Ellis who had never permitted herself to love a human being since the death thirty years before of a husband who had spent her inheritance and drunk himself to death before retribution could overtake him, leaving her childless and penniless and loveless, found herself loving Cathy against her will and best judgment.

Cathy also loved someone, Mrs. Ellis' acute powers of observation told her; and that someone was not William.

Lisa, of course, was present in the drawing-room when William, very much at home now, strolled in.

Cathy said, "Lisa, may I present William Durwent? William, my cousin Lisa Minard," and waited to see the usual stricken expression creep over William's face as Lisa's soft radiant gaze turned languidly but fully upon him.

But William said, "How do you do," without giving any indication that he was stricken or even at all impressed by Lisa's charms. Cathy regarded William with new interest; Lisa, too, sat up a little straighter.

William was full of excitement which accounted perhaps for his blindness; he burst out immediately with details of a big ball which was to be given the next week at the hotel in Saint Cloud. After his first polite but perfunctory response to his introduction to Lisa he ignored her completely; his only concern was for Cathy who was to be, he stated rather than invited, his guest for the week-end of festivities which had been planned. There were to be parties and a performance at the Opera House; people from the East were coming, even his mother and sister were to be there.

"You see how important it is, don't you?" he said with an intensity which made clear to Cathy just how important it might be, both to him and to her, if she continued to drift as she was now drifting. She glanced at Lisa, who was smiling now that her first astonishent at being passed over for Cathy was replaced by her usual tolerant good humor: "You may have this young man," Lisa seemed to be saying, generously; acceding to Cathy her right to have some attention. Lisa excused herself from the room somewhat ostentatiously, murmuring her standard vague excuse about a headache. Cathy, angrily watching her go, found it difficult to concentrate on William's urgency: "You will come, won't you, Cathy?"

"Where? Oh, yes, certainly."

He glanced at her doubtfully but he said, "It will be an ideal time for you to meet my mother. She won't even have to know who you are until she gets to know you and by that time she won't be able to help liking you."

"Not know who I am?" Cathy was listening now.

"Well, she's old-fashioned and full of a lot of silly ideas," William said. "She'd like to pick out all my friends if she could."

"She wouldn't pick me, then."

William said, "Well. You know how it is."

"I'm sorry; I don't."

"Don't turn haughty. She won't snub you; you can be sure of that."

"Perhaps I shall snub her."

William said, "Oh for gosh sake," he did not take her seriously. Cathy was quite serious; she determined to snub Mrs. William Durwent Senior at the first opportunity. "What's the matter with you?" William asked uneasily. "You've been acting funny ever since I got here."

"Have I? You didn't say so."

"I just noticed it. Is it your French cousin?"

"Lisa? She isn't French."

"Please, please! This is very important!"

It was, to him; it might prove to be, also, to Cathy. Depending on how the wind blew, she thought frivolously. Nevertheless she was more nervous than she allowed herself to admit when William outlined her course of behavior to her. "Just be natural. My mother will be stiff at first; that's nothing to worry about. She hates your father. Well, I don't mean hate exactly . . ."

"What do you mean?"

"Don't turn haughty. Please, Cathy!" His eyes, when they weren't bright and merry, were pleading. Cathy said, "Very well, I won't."

"Just put up with her; that's what I do. She doesn't mean to be difficult. She can do a great deal to help us . . ."

Cathy did not ask what Mrs. Durwent Senior could do to help her; and William was unaware that he had been either tactless or wounding; his very heedlessness aroused Cathy's protective nature; he could not help it if his mother terrified him. He was holding

Cathy's hand, gazing down at her wistfully: "My mother can't possibly find anything to say against my liking you once she gets to know you," he said.

Accordingly, Cathy found herself committed to a week-end at Saint Cloud as William's guest. She would have been pleasantly excited by the prospect ordinarily; as it was she was far from pleasantly excited, she was terrified.

Pride demanded that she conceal this emotion; she responded to all William's plans with a great airiness which she hoped would pass for enthusiasm. She it was who moved her eyebrows up and down this time; she said, "Oh William, what fun!" clasping her hands together and looking fervent and anticipatory as if she could scarcely bear her own state of bliss.

She thought she was doing it rather well, but in the middle of the scene William's face suddenly crumpled; he sat down on the floor beside her and put his arms gently and carefully around her. He said, "Oh Cathy, it will mean everything to me, everything, if my mother sees how wonderful and sweet you are, the way I do." He looked so vulnerable that she could not bear the thought that she might disappoint him; she drew a deep breath and thought if she must impress Mrs. Durwent Senior then she must, and that was all there was to it.

On the whole, however, the prospect of Cathy's first ball was not very inviting. It did not even help to find that Lisa was mildly envious.

"You'll have all kinds of fun," Lisa said. "Really, Cathy, I can't imagine why you've got to be so dull and stodgy; if I were going I would make a sensation, I can tell you."

Mrs. Ellis was doubtful as to the value of the invitation when she heard that Saint Cloud was what was known as a boom town, and Cathy began to hope she would have a legitimate excuse for not going. Her father, coming into the room in time to hear part of the conversation, put an end to that hope by saying with a short laugh that Saint Cloud might be a boom town but it was a celebrated one and everyone who was anyone from New York or Washington would be there for the occasion.

Her father was no different since he had returned from France; he sat alone by himself for hours, brooding; the only deviation in his behavior was when he became angry over news received by telegram or mail. He drank too much always; he was being attacked by more and more people, Cathy learned by anxious perusal of the newspapers now left for her in the library. She read and tried to understand why it was that things which she had taken for granted about her father now were being made to appear wrong. She hoped he would defend himself but he did not. She believed with all her heart that he would pull himself together and make everything come right; she had to believe that because she did not know what else to believe, just yet. And she loved him so much: it was strange and reassuring how little the doubts which crept into one's mind could affect one's heart.

Cathy wished terribly that he would offer to escort her to Saint Cloud, but he did not, though he asked her if she had the proper clothes for the occasion. Evidently he had forgotten the several trunks of clothes which he had brought back for her from Paris and which she barely had unpacked; when she reminded him, he said, "Yes, good, that's all right then," as if she had no other problems.

Later, when they chanced to be alone for a few minutes, he reminded her without looking at her that her mother's jewels were hers, and that if she wished to wear any of them at any time she was free to do so without consulting him. "You know the combination of the safe," he said. "There are more in a vault in New York in your name, but these will do for now, I imagine."

Cathy never would have thought of wearing the jewels but now it seemed to her as if they might give her courage. She took several of the boxes containing them out of the safe one afternoon and carried them to her room. She took the precaution of locking the door before opening them.

She opened all the boxes and dumped the contents on her bed. She drew out a pearl necklace and fastened it about her neck and looked at herself in a mirror; it did not bring about any transformation. She added a diamond necklace. That was better; she was beginning, in spite of herself, to feel a little excited. She fastened a diamond tiara on her head and turned her head this way and that, proudly and regally. She put rings on her fingers; she clasped bracelets on both arms to her elbows.

Somebody turned the knob of her door and then Lisa called, "Cathy! Are you in there?"

Silence. "Cathy!"

"Yes, I am."

"What are you doing? Why is the door locked? Let me in."

Cathy hesitated, but she could not resist seeing Lisa's face. She opened the door and closed it and locked it again, behind Lisa.

"What on earth are you acting so mysterious about?" Lisa

looked at Cathy; she looked again, staring. "Cathy! Where did you get those?"

"They're mine."

"Yours! Who says so?"

"My father gave them to me."

"Oh! Oh!" Lisa ran over to the bed, plunging both hands in the glittering pile which lay there. "Oh! Look! Oh, how beautiful! What a liar; he wouldn't have given them to you!"

"He did, though. Ask him."

Lisa was convinced. "May I try some of them on?" She became strangely meek. Cathy said grandly, "Certainly, if you wish."

"Oh Cathy! Imagine!" Lisa held a necklace against her cheek, caressing it. "Oh, what beauties! Oh, how I envy you!"

"Envy me?"

"I should say I do. What I'd give! I envy you terribly, terribly!"

It was a strange thought. Cathy began stripping the pieces off, one by one. Lisa picked them up and put them on herself. She crowded them on her arms, at her throat, in her hair. She put on a show for herself before the mirror.

"You don't, really," Cathy said.

Lisa said without turning, "What, envy you? Of course I do; I've always envied you. Can you blame me? You've always had everything and I've never had anything."

Cathy stared, stupidly. "You're the one who has always had everything."

"Nothing, really. Nothing worth while; nothing like this. I'd give the world to have jewels like these, even a few. But of course I never shall unless I marry someone who can give them to me. And you don't even appreciate them; they don't mean anything to you. It's so unfair. You'll put them away; you won't even wear them."

"I haven't any place to wear them."

"You could wear them when you go to Saint Cloud," Lisa said. "I would. I'd wear them all, the night of the ball." She whirled before the mirror, entranced with her own reflection. Her eyes sparkled; the jewels already seemed to be more hers than Cathy's.

"It would be very bad taste to wear all of them," Cathy said.

"Who cares? I'd wear hundreds of them anyway. I'd drip with them, and I'd be so beautiful and so fascinating that nobody would dare to criticize me. I'd set a new style . . . Oh, don't put them away, please. I want to look at them just a little longer."

"You may have them," Cathy said. She pushed the heap of jewels remaining on the bed toward Lisa; it seemed to her that Lisa might as well have them.

"What?"

"You may have them."

"Your mother's jewels? Are you crazy?"

"They're mine. I may do anything I want with them; my father said so."

"Not give them away. They must be worth hundreds of thousands of dollars."

This aspect had not occurred to Cathy. She said stubbornly, "If they're mine I can give them away if I want to."

"I wish you could," Lisa said. "But of course you can't. You're such a baby in some ways, Cathy."

"Am I? All right, then, if you don't want them."

Lisa watched the jewels being packed into their boxes without rancor. She asked, "Aren't you going to take any of them to wear at the ball?"

"I don't know. Do you really think I should?"

"Well, Mamma would say you were too young to wear very many, I suppose. But it seems silly to me; how can people know that you have them unless you wear them? And besides, it will make people realize who you are."

"What do you mean, who I am?"

"Oh Cathy," Lisa said in disgust. She sighed exaggeratedly: "If only I had half your opportunities. Just half."

"What would you do?"

"I'd do something," Lisa said. She looked off into space with narrowed shining eyes. "Don't worry; I'd do something."

Suddenly it seemed desirable to Cathy to do something, no matter what it was, rather than to continue to do nothing the rest of her life.

Chapter 20

It was a new and fascinating idea that Cathy could possess something which Lisa coveted but could not have. When Lisa left the room Cathy tried on a few pieces of the jewelry again; growing braver she tried on a few more. Perhaps Lisa was right, she thought, studying herself, that the thing to do was to wear a lot of them, recklessly, and not care what people thought.

She took with her, therefore, a large selection of jewels when she went to Saint Cloud. She carried them with her in a leather case which Stacey said she was not to let out of her hands except in her own room; Stacey, who was not to go with her, grumbled and objected but she packed the pieces Cathy indicated, giving her advice in the meantime: "Going to look like a Christmas tree, that's what."

"Never mind."

"Wild goings on. Bandits and hold-ups right on the street, most likely. Don't go back on your heritage."

"What do you mean by that?"

"Money isn't everything. I don't mean Mr. Michael; he's always been good to me and to everybody. The Lord alone knows what's going to happen to us," Stacey said, and burst into tears.

Did Stacey too read the newspapers?

Cathy put all this behind her in Saint Cloud; she was having her first glimpse of real life. She and Mrs. Ellis arrived late in the afternoon, and the excitement of arriving in an unfamiliar place even though it was only twenty or so miles away, added to the new and general air of holiday and festivity which pervaded the whole town, swept away all Cathy's nervous misgivings.

183

The narrow winding streets were filled on this occasion with smart broughams and sleek horses. Coachmen in livery sat high in the boxes with footmen riding behind, their arms folded, their eyes staring coldly ahead. There were glimpses of women in silks and furs and plumed hats; it was impossible to tell the nice ones from the ones William had said were not nice, and Cathy rather liked that. The splendor of these equipages was in strange contrast to the ugly little one-story buildings with false fronts and the garish saloons which made up most of the town; the carriages swept past these crude reminders of the origins of Saint Cloud's present fame toward the big gabled hotel called the Mansion House.

The Mansion House was said to resemble, so far as it had been able, the Waldorf in New York. It had a long carpeted corridor with fan-backed chairs and potted palms on each side called Peacock Alley. It had enormous and ornately furnished parlors, richly carpeted and crowded with gilt furniture and delicate tables with carved legs. Three pairs of curtains, the first of Brussels lace, the second and third of silk and brocade, enclosed every window and shut out the ugly crass view of the stark sunlight and bare street outside, giving an illusion of perpetual night and its attendant softening of the stark realities of the day. The gas flames in the crystal chandelier provided, day and night, the artificial light regarded as more desirable than sunlight for the softening of faces grown a little hard and avid with greed, with suspicion, with the possession of too much money or the alternate bitterness of seeing too much money possessed by somebody else.

Gold was the keynote of the Mansion House and the common denominator among its guests. Nobody talked about anything else for very long; they were assembled here for one purpose and that was to have a place in this fraternity which had found the magic open-sesame to wealth.

There were gas fires lighted in the black marble fireplaces, though the air was warm and redolent of perfume and wax flowers. The people wandering through the rooms were a democratic mixture. Standards were simple and direct for the most part, in proportion to how much money one had and what one was able to do with it. Wealthy Easterners and their wives, fashionably but conservatively dressed, mingled with newly made millionaires and their far from conservatively dressed wives or consorts; it was understood that on other grounds they would not trespass on each other's acquaintance but for the present they were intimate friends, gushing but watchful.

Certain little cliques, of course, stood in corners or made up private groups; they were the ones whose positions were too exalted and secure to feel the need of adjustment to any standards other than their own, though their very presence in this alien world was an adjustment which they preferred to ignore. Threaded through these various layers of society and adding their own note of color were the usual hangers-on: the gamblers, the opportunists, the pioneer businessmen, and there were miners in rough clothes and high boots whose little pokes of gold admitted them to this splendor.

Cathy and Mrs. Ellis occupied a suite of rooms which Michael Brett kept reserved for himself at all times. Cathy, in the small sitting-room where they had tea, was drawn constantly, in spite of Mrs. Ellis' tolerantly voiced qualms, to the moon-shaped balcony outside their windows which overlooked the main street and its activity. It was more than ever like a play now that the arc lights had been lighted and a purple twilight obscured the bald treeless street. The Opera House with its brick front and bright posters advertising *La Bohème* was opposite the Mansion House; just the sight of this exterior and its promise of glamor and excitement inside fascinated Cathy. She stared at the Opera House, trying to picture what might be taking place there, the activities of the actors and actresses in their dressing-rooms, the actual stage where scenes were being placed. And presently the footlights would be lighted, the audience would be in their seats, the orchestra would begin to play and the curtain would go up. . . .

The following night, Saturday, she was to see the performance of *La Bohème* at the Opera House. She wondered how she could possibly wait; she had never attended an opera or play.

She wished she could stay out on the balcony under the stars all evening and watch the scene spread before her. But presently she must dress; she and Mrs. Ellis were to have dinner in one of the private dining-rooms before the ball with William and his family and a small party of others.

It was the prospect of that dinner which made Cathy decide to wear the jewels, all of them, or nearly all. She put on a diamond necklace, a number of diamond bracelets, and a pair of diamond earrings. She tried on the diamond tiara but decided against it.

Her dress was quite lovely. It was of white point d'esprit; it had a low square neck and tiny puffed sleeves and a crushed pink satin girdle at the waist. The skirt was very full, caught up here and there over a pink satin underskirt. But the diamonds were undeniably the thing which sparkled up the whole costume. Lisa was right, Cathy thought, the thing to do was to wear them and not care what anyone thought.

Without the diamonds she would not have been outstanding in any way, now she glittered from top to bottom, just as Stacey had said, like a Christmas tree. She had selected only the pieces of jewelry made up exclusively of diamonds; the other stones had no particular appeal for her. She wanted to sparkle; she stood before her mirror and acknowledged that the effect was spectacular if nothing else. It was becoming too; her cheeks were flushed and her eyes were brighter than usual. She looked proud, almost stately; she swayed across the room, keeping her face turned over her shoulder to watch herself in the mirror. The stones in her ears, at her throat, along her arms, caught fire and flashed and blazed with blue lights: why, I'm dazzling, she thought solemnly, simply dazzling.

Mrs. Ellis tapped on the door and followed the tap with her substantial presence. The effect on her of the bejeweled figure which met her eyes was gratifying; she stopped short, peered, swallowed, and gasped: "My dear child!"

"How do I look?" Cathy asked. For the occasion she had caught up her hair to the top of her head; at this moment she was on the brink of reconsidering the tiara, which was, in her heart of hearts, her favorite piece. "What do you think?" she asked Mrs. Ellis, snatching it up from the bed and putting it on. "Is it too much, do you think?"

"My dear child! I had no idea you were planning . . . I mean, these jewels . . . where did they come from?"

"They were my mother's."

"Oh, oh dear me, they are magnificent; I've never seen anything like them," Mrs. Ellis said; she came farther into the room; her face was a study of mixed emotions. "Still, I believe that your mother, if she were here, would advise you . . ."

"I know. I really do know, Mrs. Ellis. But tonight she might tell me to wear them if I wanted to, and I do."

"Well, then," Mrs. Ellis said; she fussed at Cathy's girdle, keeping her eyes averted from the brilliance of the jewels themselves.

"Not the tiara though, I guess," Cathy said regretfully; she removed it. "The tiara is almost too much, isn't it?"

Mrs. Ellis agreed with nervous laughter that the tiara was indeed too much. "And perhaps one or two of the other pieces; not that they aren't all beautiful, very very beautiful indeed."

"No, I want them all, just for tonight. It's a special occasion and I need them; it won't matter here in Saint Cloud, I think, so many women seem to be wearing jewels; oh Mrs. Ellis, do say I look spangly and nice."

Mrs. Ellis took a deep breath: "You look very spangly certainly, and nice too though I can't imagine . . . well. As you say, in Saint Cloud . . . still. Well, just for tonight. And the dress is charming for you, most suitable." Mrs. Ellis was rewarded by soft arms about her neck and a warm hug: "Oh Mrs. Ellis," Cathy said, "you're very kind."

Mrs. Ellis could not help hoping, as she followed Cathy along the corridor and down the broad staircase, that the rest of the world, or this particular piece of it, would be equally kindly in its judgments. The child held herself beautifully and there was something dauntless about her appearance: "Brave with diamonds," was the description which flashed into Mrs. Ellis' mind, like the character of Mrs. Cratchet, brave with ribbons. Mrs. Ellis had an intimation that this display of jewelry was not altogether naïveté and she prepared herself to give battle if necessary on behalf of her protégée. William, waiting at the bottom of the stairway, did not make battle necessary; a few minutes later Cathy was carried away to meet William's mother and Mrs. Ellis was left behind for the moment; she found a chair and sat on it, watching the spectacle before her and separating without difficulty the nice women from those not nice.

Cathy walked beside William across the room. She was presented to William's mother, who did not look so intimidating after all, who seemed, in fact, almost as nervous as Cathy herself. William's sister Deborah hovered in the background; she was very plain and quietly dressed. She too looked frightened, glancing frequently at her mother as if for approval before she spoke.

There was a striking resemblance between William and his mother except for their eyes. William's eyes were bright and gay; his mother's eyes were somewhat colorless and certainly not at all gay.

The diamonds had been a mistake; Cathy knew that in the first moment of their meeting. William's mother's eyes passed over them and grew even more bleak and remote. Nevertheless Cathy was glad she had worn them. They were hers; they represented the side of her which craved excitement and glitter and to stand out rather than remain always in the background. She could not honestly deny that part of her and she had a feeling of pride about not meeting William's mother under false pretenses.

Presently she and William were allowed to escape to the private parlor adjoining the dining-room where this particular dinner party was being held. There were twenty or thirty people already gathered there; some of them, to Cathy's relief, were old friends. There was Mr. James Talbot, who took her hand and held it. Her hands were cold but otherwise she was not at all nervous.

"So you've grown up," Mr. Talbot said.

"Yes," Cathy said.

"And very beautifully so, if I may say so. Very, very beautifully so."

"Thank you." Cathy smiled at Mr. Talbot instead of putting her head on his shoulder and crying.

"Where is your father tonight? I haven't seen him."

"He isn't here."

"Oh, I see. You are taking his place then, are you?"

"I don't think I could do that."

"Are you having a good time? I asked you that once a long time ago, didn't I?"

"Yes. Yes, I'm having a good time, a very good time."

"I see young Durwent looking at you with his heart in his eyes, or his mouth. The young fellows never seem to close their mouths nowadays; still he's a nice enough youngster, so I hear."

"William? Oh yes, William is very nice."

Mr. Talbot peered more closely at her; he said, "I suppose you've met his mother, our hostess?"

"Mrs. Durwent? Oh yes, I just met her. She's very nice too."

"I'm glad to hear somebody say so. Personally I think she's some kind of a ghoul."

"Do you really?"

"She always snubs me. Women like that; there's no excuse for their existing, actually, but the sad fact of the matter is that they do exist so we must make the best of them, somehow."

Cathy put her arm through Mr. Talbot's and hugged it; she actually did, for a moment, put her head on Mr. Talbot's shoulder. "Oh, Mr. Talbot, you are very kind."

"Of course I am. Everyone knows that. Mrs. Durwent is far more afraid of you than you are of her, my beauty, so stiffen up."

"But I don't want her to be afraid of me."

"It's dog eat dog, and things are seldom as we want them," Mr. Talbot said with his old liking for speaking in riddles; he smiled at Cathy and she blotted away the dampness at the corner of one eye and stiffened up.

"I'll look after you," Mr. Talbot said at the dinner table, where he was her partner by the simple means of trading his card with William's. William had succumbed to either persuasion or bullying; he sulked beside his sister far down the table. "I'll look after you. You are the most beautiful young thing I've seen in years and you give me new hope. The country is changing, you know; everything is changing."

"I know."

"But not so much as some people think. Do you really care for young Durwent?"

"I'm fond of him."

"Ummm. He isn't half good enough for you but of course . . . Will you dance with me after dinner?"

"Thank you for asking me. I've been afraid nobody would. Except William."

Mr. Talbot chuckled: "From the looks of it a number of people will ask you. You are the center of attention; haven't you noticed?"

Cathy confessed, "I thought it was because I had on too much jewelry."

"Too much? Who says so? Just right, in my opinion."

"No, I have on too much, but I did it on purpose."

"So? Why was that?"

"It's hard for me to explain, exactly."

"I see I need not have worried about you. I claim the first dance, just the same. Jewels and all, you are making a great hit."

"Not with . . . everybody."

"Nonsense. Nonsense." He protested too much and too loud; Cathy knew that quite well even while she smiled at him; one thing, she had completely lost the desire to weep.

She need not have worried. She had had only one turn about the room with Mr. Talbot when she was claimed by another partner. They waited in line to dance with her; they stampeded her. Dazzled and breathless she went from one partner to another; it could not be altogether the jewels.

There were flaws to her happiness. William sulked; he had not yet even asked her to dance. And when she was returned to her chair by a partner she felt an aura of disapproval from the group of women usually sitting there. One could not have everything, it seemed; if you were liked by some persons you were disliked by others.

Nevertheless it was her first ball and she was determined to enjoy it. She had already risked a great deal on it; she knew by the admiring glances of Mr. Talbot, of her partners, of mirrors along the wall, that she was young, spangly, breath-takingly lovely for this moment at least. Nobody should take this from her.

She sat, flushed and breathless after a dance, on a gold chair against the wall, surrounded by men. She waved her program before her face in lieu of a fan and flirted with all of them; it was exciting to flirt and she liked it. She was drunk on champagne and excitement and life.

She looked across the room and met the dark eyes of a man watching her. She smiled automatically; she turned away and back and smiled again. He did not smile but his eyes continued to be fastened on her.

He came across the room. He said, "May I have this dance?" She stood up and acceded, without consulting her card. Protests rose behind her but she ignored them.

Her partner's name, he introduced himself as they danced, was Dan Cartwright.

"Have I seen you before?"

"I don't know. I've been looking at you all evening."

"You seem familiar."

Dan Cartwright was big, not heavy but big as a man should be, broad-shouldered, well-built and muscular. He was as light on his feet as a panther; dancing within the circle of his arm was effortless and gay, like dancing in one's dreams. He had black hair, black eyes, and an irresistible grin.

"Perhaps you have. I'm a miner."

"My father used to be a miner."

"I know. Romantic, isn't it?"

"Then you know who I am?"

He made a sort of bow; he said, "Believe me, I do."

"Is that why you asked me to dance?"

"That and other things."

"What other things?"

"The diamonds. They hit me in the eye the minute I came in the room and I like things that hit me in the eye."

"Oh. I see."

"You sound disappointed. Didn't you wear them to hit somebody in the eye?"

"I suppose I did."

"Why be ashamed of it, then?"

He interrupted the conversation for a moment by swooping down the length of the ballroom in long graceful glides, masterfully carrying her with him as if she were so much thistledown. She tried to decide if she liked being treated quite so arbitrarily and then gave herself to the enjoyment of motion.

Presently he was laughing down at her again. "Now, where were we?"

"I'm not sure."

"We get along well together, don't we?"

"Dancing?"

"Perhaps other ways too." He grinned and she blushed. He said, "I confess that I asked you to dance to prove to myself that you weren't as lovely as you looked but now I see that you are."

She did not know how to counter that; still blushing, she said: "That wasn't very nice," and looked away.

"Dan Cartwright never knows his own luck," he said solemnly. "That's the Irish in me—you are Irish too."

"Half Irish."

"Half what else?"

"French, I suppose, American."

"Which half is uppermost?"

"I . . . don't know."

They danced once more without talking; Dan seemed to like to concentrate on one thing at a time. When he was enjoying motion he put his whole soul into it. Dancing this way was even more exhilarating than riding very fast, because it was being shared with another person.

"And to think I very nearly didn't leave the mine to come into town tonight," Dan said after a while. "But that wouldn't have been the Dan Cartwright luck, would it?"

"Have you a mine?"

"The Catherine," he said.

"When did you name it the Catherine?"

"One minute ago."

"Oh. What was it before?"

"The Mamie Lou. Camp cook. The Catherine is much nicer."

"Yes."

"Do you mind?"

"No."

He mocked her: "Yes. No. Is that all you can say? Can't you say, 'Thank you, Mr. Dan Cartwright'?"

"I don't know you well enough to know when you're serious."

"Not know me! But we were getting to know each other very well, I thought."

It did indeed seem as if they were.

"You must come to see the Catherine," he said.

"Yes, I would like that."

"Your father has been trying to buy her, by the way."

"But she isn't for sale?"

"Not just for money. She brought me here tonight; we've gone through hard times together. I lived up there alone for a year, digging with a pick and shovel: 'Bide your time, old girl,' I told her, and we bided it."

When he spoke of the mine he became excited; he danced with even more positive enjoyment. Now Cathy knew why he had seemed familiar; he reminded her a great deal, in a troubling way, of her father. Her instinct told her that he was too hard, too showy, like the diamonds. But when he grinned down at her something in her responded and she smiled back.

The music had stopped. They stood in the middle of the floor, looking at each other. "It will start again in a minute," he said, halting her when she would have turned to leave the dance floor.

"But didn't you enjoy it?"

"Enjoy what? The digging? Of course I enjoyed it. Particularly thinking of the dividends it was going to bring me."

"But I mean just for itself."

"Enjoy loneliness and breaking my back? No, I was thinking of the future, when I would be dancing like this on a floor smooth as glass in a room filled with flowers and beautiful women, and I would have the pick of them in my arms."

"What is it she's for sale for, if not just for money?"

"You talk a lot for a pretty little thing."

"Yes, I know."

He laughed; he said, "What I'm after is a position in the company, quite a high position."

"The United Mine Industries?"

"Is there any other in this part of the world? It's gobbling up all the rest of us, but I've put myself in a key position to strike a bargain."

"I should think you would rather keep your own mine and be independent."

He said, "Would you?" and laughed. "And how is my gold to be shipped from the mine?"

"On the railroad?"

"With one set of freight rates for me and another for the big company? No, that doesn't pay."

"Are they allowed to do that?"

"Your father can do anything; didn't you know? This injunction won't stop him for very long, you'll see. That's why I want to run with the hounds instead of the hare."

If he was angry he did not look so; he was smiling. He looked down at her and said, "I confess that I asked you to dance with the idea of having a friend in court, but there are some things an Irishman cannot do," and placed his hand on his heart.

The music stopped again. Cathy said, nervously, "I think I should dance the next dance with William."

"Who is William?"

"Over there. He brought me."

Dan glanced over his shoulder at William sulking against the wall. "Ah yes, William Durwent. Don't waste your time; the Durwents have ceased to be important, or will cease to be so soon."

"Do you know them?"

"My dearest child; I spent the long winter evenings poring over society columns in old magazines and the social registers. I know everything about everybody."

"That was an odd thing to do."

"Was it? I thought it might be useful to me one day; all is grist that comes to the Dan Cartwright mill. No, the Durwents are definitely on the downgrade, believe me."

"But that hasn't anything to do with why I like William."

"Ah, why do you like William?"

The music started again; Cathy was dancing for the third time with Dan. William could have claimed the dance, but he did not. It was humiliating that he had not; it was also a little humiliating that Dan took so much for granted. "I'm a little tired, if you don't mind," Cathy said.

Dan said instantly, "Come then, we'll duck out on a balcony."

"No, thank you."

"No? Why not?"

There wasn't any really good reason. Cathy said, "William wouldn't like it."

Dan raised his eyebrows: "Are you engaged to the worthy William?"

"No."

"Well, then."

She could not let him make fun of William. She said, "But I'm fond of him."

"Oh? How fond?"

"Very very fond."

"But not as fond as you are going to be of me."

"I don't know." She met his eyes directly; she said soberly, "The first time I met William he said I could cry on his shoulder if I wanted to. I don't believe that your shoulder would be very comforting to cry on."

"Well, I'll be ——" he said. He said softly, "So that's what has been going on in that head while I was congratulating myself that I was making a conquest. Ah, Dan Cartwright, you can be a great fool."

Cathy, painfully embarrassed, said, "No, please, I've enjoyed dancing with you so much . . ."

He asked, roughly, "And why should you, of all people, need a shoulder to cry on?"

"I don't, actually. It's just a way of judging if people are kind."

"Kind?"

"Yes, kind. Really kind, you know."

He said, "Well, I'll be ——" again. He bowed and left her as William came up. Dan must have left the ballroom too, because she could not find him among any of the dancers though she searched for him constantly during the next dance. William noticed and asked jealously who it was she was trying to see.

"Nobody."

After that she tried to keep her thoughts centered on William; it wasn't fair not to do so when he had gone to so much trouble for her. William's blunt humorous face looked miserable; now that he was dancing with her he did not seem to be enjoying it. He missed several steps and presently he asked her to go out on a balcony with him.

"Do you think we should?"

"Please, Cathy!"

On the balcony he behaved more and more strangely. He kicked at the balcony rail with one foot; he put his hands in his pockets and hunched his shoulders. She had thought he was going to make love to her and stiffened herself to meet it, but when he did it was not at all as she had expected. He said, "I'm mad for you!" explosively, gazing out into the darkness and without taking his hands out of his pockets. He said, "I'm going crazy, I think!"

"Are . . . aren't you enjoying yourself at all?"

"Enjoying myself! This is the end of everything, for me."

"I don't understand."

He said, "My mother has been having hysterics in her room ever since dinner. Haven't you noticed how often I had to be away?"

Guiltily she realized she had not noticed. She asked, "Because of me, do you mean?"

"Well, not only because of you. Though you do look different tonight. Cathy, don't be hurt, but I wish you hadn't decked yourself out like a . . . I mean, you look beautiful to me, but my mother is very old-fashioned. And everything is strange to her out here, and of course with the papers full of the injunction and hinting at even more scandal than we've already had, she's almost beside herself."

Everybody was talking about an injunction. Cathy asked, "What exactly is an injunction?"

"Cathy, this is no time to ask foolish questions; can't you see what a predicament I'm in?"

"What is it that you want me to do?"

"Just understand, that's all. You can do that, surely; it isn't my fault. My mother hasn't been well; she shouldn't get too excited. She made me promise to go home with her, early tomorrow morning, just for a little while. Just until things blow over; I had to promise, Cathy, please understand. But I'll be able to persuade her easily enough once I get back there that you aren't . . . that you're sweet and good and wonderful . . . and I'll be back, Cathy; I'll come back if only you'll wait for me."

Unbelievably, he was crying. He put his hands over his face; he would never come back; he did not even want to come back and both of them knew it. Cathy watched him with a sick contempt which rose in her like an icy creeping tide. She had thought that he was kind and he wasn't kind at all.

He asked her, "Cathy, what shall we do?"

"Well, just this minute," she said, "suppose we go back inside and finish our dance. Then I'll go upstairs to my room and tomorrow I'll go home."

"Cathy, I know how you must despise me."

The icy tide was receding. She could even wonder, as they finished the dance, why William had taken so much for granted when he had never, in Aunt Helena's phrase, declared himself, when he had never asked her if she cared for him or would be willing to marry him. She could only suppose that people like the Durwents planned these things carefully and well in advance, without taking risks.

"Cathy!" William said, as he escorted her to the stairs.

"Hush," she said. "It's all right. I'm not hurt, you know, only my pride. I'm not in love with you."

"You aren't!" He looked stricken rather than relieved; he said, "I'm in love with you, Cathy. Aren't you with me, even a little?"

"I don't think you have the right to ask that, have you?"

"I could kill myself. Really I could."

"Goodnight, William." She started up the stairs and then, halfway up, after William had disappeared, she changed her mind and came swiftly, holding up her long skirts, down the staircase again.

There was someone she wanted to see and it was not William. She was free now; she made her way through the crowded parlors, searching, ducking under elbows, squeezing through narrow places. She was sure she would find Dan somewhere and she wanted urgently to see him. She felt confident, breathless, excited, almost desperate.

She saw him presently. He was in one of the side gaming rooms where there weren't any women; nevertheless she walked quickly through the doorway and across the room before she should lose her courage.

He looked up as if he had been expecting her. "Are you looking for somebody?"

"You."

He was playing roulette. He asked, "Would you like to sit in for a few minutes?"

"No, thank you. I . . . I haven't any money."

"No money, eh?" Dan closed his eyes; he groaned; he said, "No money. That does it. I can't make up my mind if you are about to revive my romantic faith in fairies and beautiful women or whether you are far more sophisticated than you have any right to be."

"I wanted to see you."

Dan pushed his chips across the table and received money in return which he stuffed carelessly in his pocket. He stood up. He said, looking down at her, "Well, here I am. What is it you want? A shoulder to cry on?"

"Yes. No. I'm not sure."

His eyes narrowed, smoldered. He raked one hand through his

rough black hair, leaving it standing straight up. He said, "Never let it be said that a Cartwright failed a damsel in distress."

He took her hand and made a path for her through the crowded rooms. He led her out on a balcony; she was dismayed at finding herself on the same balcony for the second time that night. She protested, rather ineffectually: "Not here. Somewhere else."

He held her and kissed her before she could speak again. Not once but many times. On the mouth. Being kissed on the mouth, she found, was quite different from being kissed on the cheek or forehead.

Chapter 21

She did not go home the following morning. She went to lunch with Dan; she drove in the afternoon with Dan, unaccompanied by Mrs. Ellis. Mrs. Ellis was troubled at not going, but she found it difficult to insist under the circumstances; Cathy had not been brought up according to any of the rules governing the young women of Mrs. Ellis' acquaintance and it seemed late to begin now. Cathy took it for granted that if she wished to go miles into rough country with a young man even rougher, in Mrs. Ellis' opinion, she was free to do so; she did not have to say in so many words that her father would have permitted it. Other things conspired to keep Mrs. Ellis at home, if these strange circumstances in which she found herself could be called home: the light sulky brought about for the proposed trip would hold only two, and those two with scant comfort. Mrs. Ellis stared sternly at Dan Cartwright: "You will be back before dark, of course?" and he answered, "We will, I promise." He had a straightforward way about him which Mrs. Ellis admired, though she still could not understand how Cathy had met him: he had not been of the party the night before. "A friend of her father's, perhaps?" she interrogated Dan while they waited beside the sulky for Cathy, who was taking an unexpectedly long time to dress. Mrs. Ellis, having inspected sulky and young man as she felt to be her duty, now longed to go back to her room and draw the shades and call for a cup of tea, but her conscience had to be clear first.

Dan said, "Perhaps."

"What does that mean?"

"A friend of Cathy's. Wouldn't that be better?"

"But where did you meet her? Have you known her before?"

"At the moment I feel as if I have always known her."

Mrs. Ellis said, "Oh," just as Cathy came out. She watched Cathy being handed into the sulky. The young man might be rough and the sulky uncomfortable and the country they were about to traverse crude and even dangerous, but Cathy's face showed no misgivings.

"You'll be back before dark."

"Yes, we will, Mrs. Ellis, I promise you. We are all going to the Opera House tonight, you know."

Cathy was looking forward to the Opera House. Though Dan Cartwright, Mrs. Ellis was sure, was accustomed to more sophisticated pleasures, he too seemed to be looking forward to something in the evening's entertainment, perhaps Cathy's enjoyment of it.

He said to Cathy, "We'll make a sensation. You must wear all your diamonds again," thus undermining Mrs. Ellis' sentimental picture.

Cathy said, "No, I won't."

"Why not?"

"People stare at me."

"Let them."

"Oh, I don't mind that. But of course if you deliberately make yourself conspicuous you have to be very discreet, to make up for it."

Dan Cartwright turned to stare at the girl beside him with a look which Mrs. Ellis, as she went back to the hotel, found reassuring.

They were going to the Catherine mine. At every opportunity he stopped the horse and kissed Cathy. Alive, tingling with emotion, she kissed him back.

The Catherine was a beautiful mine. Cathy, brought up with the knowledge of mines since she could remember, loved every inch of her.

"You mustn't dream of selling her."

"Your father wouldn't like to hear you advise that."

"What did you mean when you said you were in a key position?"

"I must be careful of what I say in front of you; I see that. I've been busy organizing other small mine-owners; they will do as I do."

Cathy, not understanding completely, still insisted: "You mustn't dream of selling her."

"Never mind her; look at me," Dan said; he drew Cathy to him and kissed her.

199

She wore the diamonds that night to please him.

They sat in a box, extended almost over the stage; the players and audience took notice of them at first almost as much as the events taking place on the stage. It was exciting but not what Cathy had imagined. She had expected to lose herself in *La Bohème*, instead she was conscious every minute of Dan and of the people in the theatre and of the fact that Mimi's tragedies were only make-believe.

Dan must have noticed her disappointment for he said, coming out of the Opera House: "It wasn't a good production. We'll see a far better one, one of these days."

They went to a gaming room after Mrs. Ellis had been tactfully persuaded to go to bed. This time Cathy had money; she had borrowed it from Mrs. Ellis.

She was lucky. She attracted attention by her luck as well as the diamonds. Strangely, this time it was Dan who minded the crowd around her.

He whispered, "Let's get out of here."

"But I'm winning."

"The wise person quits when he's ahead. He or she. Come on, let's get out of here."

They went back to the same balcony where so much that was climactic in her life seemed fated to take place. Dan said, "I could have killed all of them. Looking at you."

"Why shouldn't they look at me?"

"Now listen. I'm thinking of you, not of myself for once in my life. This isn't any place for you. I want you to go home, tomorrow, do you understand? I'll come to see you quite soon."

Everybody wanted Cathy to go home. Dan kissed her, this time rather differently. It must have been because of that and an excess of feeling that Cathy cried herself to sleep that night.

She could hardly wait to get home the next day. She jumped down from the carriage, looking about her with hungry eyes; she felt as if she had been on a long journey.

The house looked strange. She supposed that was imagination until Sam, coming to meet her, made too much of a fuss, meanwhile avoiding her eyes.

"What's wrong?"

"Did you have a good time?"

"Tell me what's wrong."

Her father had had a stroke. Lisa hysterically described it when

Cathy sought her out as the best source of information in the face of Sam's and Stacey's and Hester's determined refusal to speak of anything which was far better not faced.

It had been the night before. "We were playing backgammon, Philip and I," Lisa wept. "Uncle Michael was watching us, part of the time. He was restless; he said he was going to New York today or tomorrow. He'd been in a bad mood all evening; I think he had had bad news sometime. Anyhow he wasn't like himself at dinner; he went into a rage when somebody, not Sam, spilled something on his coat."

"Was he . . . drinking?"

Lisa had not noticed. "I suppose he had had something to drink. But we were playing backgammon. . . ."

"Yes, you said. Where is Philip now?"

"He stood there, watching us, and then suddenly he slumped forward. I'll never forget it as long as I live."

"Where is Philip now?"

"Philip jumped up; he told me to get his bag. Sam got it; I hadn't the slightest notion. . . . Philip gave him a hypodermic."

"Where is Philip now?"

"I thought he was dying but Philip said it was only a slight stroke. He sent me away. Philip? He's with Uncle Michael, I suppose."

Cathy went there. Philip came to the door; he made light of the event. "Your father is asleep. We weren't expecting you until tomorrow."

"I came home early. Is he all right?"

Philip hesitated, closing the door behind him. He said then, shortly, "No, he's far from all right. He has a bad heart but he refuses to adjust himself to it; he has to be quiet for a time but who knows how that is to be accomplished."

"Is he in danger?"

"Not immediately," Philip said.

Cathy slumped with relief against the wall; anything not immediate was outside her comprehension at the moment.

Philip said grimly, "I've tricked him; I've given him a sedative. He's asleep. I never saw a man fight so against unconsciousness."

"May I see him?"

"When he wakes up."

"Now? I'll be quiet."

Philip let her in the room, standing just behind her. Together they looked down on Michael Brett. No wonder he had fought against unconsciousness, Cathy thought; never before had she seen him look so defenseless. She turned away quickly; she felt disloyal at having insisted upon seeing him.

"There's nothing to worry about for the moment," Philip repeated outside the room. As if to stress his point he asked, "Did you have a good time?"

"A good time?"

"In Saint Cloud."

"Oh." She pondered; it seemed a long time ago. "Yes, I had a very good time."

"Tell me about it."

He was just diverting her attention, of course, but she told him all about it . . . or almost all. He listened, his mind somewhere else.

The next day Philip told Michael that if he wished to avoid similar and more severe attacks he would have to be careful.

Michael, seated in a chair in robe and slippers in defiance of Philip's instructions to remain in bed, received this unpleasant information with bad grace. His magnificent health and strength he had always taken for granted, and the idea of decay and weakness occurring in his own body shocked him far more than the attacks on his character had done.

"You're drinking too much, for one thing," Philip said, as inexorably as he would have spoken to any of his patients.

"Am I now?" Michael said. His eyes met Philip's; his eyes belied the soft tone of his voice. "It's a good joke on me, I suppose," he said. He poured a glass of brandy and drank it; he threw his arm about Philip's shoulder in apologetic camaraderie immediately afterward.

Dan Cartwright came frequently to the house to see Cathy. Because her father was invalided to his rooms the two men did not meet. This troubled Cathy. When she tried to tell her father about Dan's visits, however, Michael brushed them aside; the name of Cartwright either as a mine-owner or as a possible suitor of Cathy's meant less than nothing to him. "Yes, enjoy yourself; yes, excellent, I am glad we are having guests," he said; he was intensely preoccupied. He had sent for his secretary from New York, Mr. Abbot, a thin nervous little man was kept busy writing letters, running in and out of Michael's study with incoming and outgoing messages.

Something momentous seemed to be in the air but Cathy had no idea what it was. Her own affairs were at a standstill. When she was with Dan she felt confident of herself and of him. He kissed her and she responded; she looked forward to being with him and he never failed her expectations. Together they did the things which she had been doing alone; they rode; they walked; they played games with Randy; and life began to take on a certain color to which one had looked forward all one's life. He made love to her and she liked it; he called her endearing little names; his eyes, smiling into hers, held both a challenge and a promise.

And yet, afterward, there was always a sinking feeling of weariness for which she could not account. She could hardly wait, after his visits, to gain the privacy of her own room and throw herself into the forgetfulness of sleep.

She was very much alone when Dan was not there. Randy was absorbed in his studies; Lisa and Philip wandered in the encased and self-centered world of two people in love, unaware that it was possible for anyone besides themselves to exist. And that was exactly how Cathy felt when she was with them, as if she did not exist.

She forced herself to work on her clay portraits. She made dozens of little clay heads of everybody in the household, though all of them fell so far short of her original conception as to be sickening. She destroyed them all, one violent afternoon.

She thought, in the reaction of remorse: that was wrong. She realized that one could not escape from one's mistakes that way. Nor one's dreams nor hopes nor fears.

Later that afternoon, in the library, she began a little clay bust from memory. It was the first attempt she had made to reproduce Dan and she could see him vividly as she worked. The little clay head came to life: it had high cheekbones and a strong jutting nose and full curved lips.

She sat looking at it when it was finished. It was good, almost too good, the best she had done. She thought, why is that? It was a foolish question because she knew the answer.

She looked again at the face of the statue. It might have been smiling at her. It was a strong face but it wasn't a good face. Something was lacking; nevertheless it called to her. She could feel the lips on hers; she could feel her heart pounding. She had responded to his love-making; how could that be when she was not in love with him?

She knew herself better than most young girls of her generation.

She had seen passion in its various forms; it could be strong and beautiful or it could be cheap and furtive.

It was an essential part of life. Because of it life continued, babies were born, and it was nothing of which to be ashamed. It rose up in one as sap rises in a tree; it was a great and natural force.

But it wasn't all of life. It wasn't all of life and it wasn't all of love.

Cathy rested her head on one slender hand, shielding her eyes. The time would come when she would have to make a decision. She would have to decide whether it was better to have part of life than nothing. She knew very surely that the time for that decision was coming, and she did not want to be called upon to make it.

Her father, still in robe and slippers but otherwise seeming as vigorous and as restless as he normally was in an interlude of quiet, came into the library. Before sitting down he poured a glass of brandy and drank it, then he poured another and held it.

He sat down, extending his legs and with his head slumped forward. There were deep circles under his eyes. He was unshaven; his open collar exposed the sagging skin of his jaw line. His mouth compressed itself, jerked; a nervous tic pulled at the corner of his mouth at intervals almost as if he were smiling, until one saw that he was not. It was terrible to notice these things, loving him so much; yet, loving him how could one help noticing them?

He asked, "Where is everyone? I've been wandering through empty rooms in search of a little companionship and the house seemed to be deserted until I found you."

"This is the time when Randy rests, you know. Philip and Lisa have gone for a ride."

"Philip and Lisa?" A muscle twitched in his cheek; he asked, "Is there anything there?"

"I really couldn't say."

"Helena wouldn't like it. I always had an idea you and Philip . . . you could do worse. Have you ever thought of it?"

"No, Father."

"It would have been a good thing. Philip and Lisa, eh?" The muscle twitched; he repeated with cynical humor: "Helena isn't going to like that. We'll have to do something about it to help Philip's case."

Cathy did not answer and he did not seem to expect an answer. He hunched one shoulder as if physically pulling himself out of his thoughts. He poured himself more brandy. He looked at her as if just remembering her presence. He asked, "What have you been doing with yourself?"

She indicated the little statue before her. He studied it, not without interest; he had respect for anybody's work. His gaze sharpened. He held out one hand and she put the clay head into it. He studied it more intently; he looked from it to her and back again. He asked finally: "Where did you meet this young man?"

"In Saint Cloud, Father. I told you about it. He has been here to see me several times while you were ill."

"Has he indeed?" The blue eyes could be very cold, even when looking at her. He said heavily, "Helena is right, I should look after you better. I suppose he has made advances to you?"

Advances? She wasn't quite sure which one had made the advances; certainly she had met anything which could be called advances halfway. She said, "He's been very nice to me, very nice."

"I'm sure he has. He is an ambitious young man."

"You remember him, then. He didn't think you would."

"I have a good memory for people who force themselves into my presence and try to hold me up. Your young man seemed to consider himself in an excellent bargaining position over a mine and he pushed into my office. Before I had him thrown out I told him that if he wanted to approach me he would have to do so through the usual channels."

Cathy said, aghast, "Father."

"Not dreaming he would find a way to scrape up an acquaintance with you. How did that happen?"

"Was he angry?"

"When I had him thrown out? How do I know? No, that kind is seldom angry. He is, as I said, a very ambitious young man."

Cathy looked down at her hands. They lay in her lap motionless; they did not seem to belong to her or the turmoil inside. She was not thinking of Dan, though they were talking of him; she was thinking of her father who little by little, piece by piece, was destroying her belief in him. Destroying it almost deliberately not by the discovery that he was not perfect—she thought she had always known that—nor even by the discovery that he was not always good or honest. She could find excuses for the revelations that his business affairs as well as some of his personal ones were not above reproach; he was beset by unusual temptations and he lived by his own code, which might prove eventually a wrong and dangerous thing to do. But this man opposite her who flew into a rage when a servant spilled something on his coat, who violated his own sense of justice by having a young man thrown out of his office simply because he was young and ambitious, who became moody and petulant at the slightest crossing of his wishes, was a stranger to her.

He was sick; she assured herself desperately that he was sick; soon these troubles would be cleared up and he would be himself again. At the same time she knew with a knowledge she would have given anything to forswear that his sickness was an eroding one and of long standing; she saw in a vivid flash the picture of his hand on Sarita's bridle in a burst of irritation against himself rather than Sarita, yet contributing perhaps to the mare's skittishness and so eventually to disaster.

But that was not fair; Cathy pushed away that thought though she could believe that it must have occurred to him many times and that he took whatever refuge he could find. He had built a barrier about himself, and though they spoke to each other she knew in her heart that neither of them ever would be able to cross the barrier.

Her father was asking, "Do you understand what I mean?"

"Yes, Father. I think so."

"But you don't agree with me?"

"Not altogether."

"Or perhaps you think I haven't the right to judge?"

"No, please." For all the emotion displayed they might have been talking about the weather.

"You haven't the misfortune to consider yourself in love with this . . . whatever his name is?"

"Dan Cartwright. I . . . I don't know."

"Then he has, I take it, made love to you?"

"Yes."

Her father made a wry face; he tossed the figurine on the table; he said, "My best advice to you is to forget all about him."

"I . . . can't do that . . . just without any reason."

"There are reasons enough but I doubt if any of them would make an impression at this moment. Well, you will have to learn life in your own way."

"Would you rather he didn't come here?"

Her father shrugged, retreating into the indifference which was hardest of all to bear because it was so unlike him: "Why not? Keepsake is yours, I deeded it to you some time ago. You may invite whatever riffraff you like; I don't set myself up as your mentor."

"Father."

"Don't look so shocked. If you are old enough to have a lover you are old enough to know that you are an enormously wealthy woman and that you will have to take that into consideration whether you want to or not. I am sure that your lover already has done so."

"He isn't . . . my lover."

"He has made love to you . . . I only use the word in that sense. I spoke roughly, I apologize. I don't want you to be hurt."

If he did not want her to be hurt he was going about preventing it in a strange way.

Her father continued: "I am forced to put certain responsibilities on you, Cathy; I haven't anyone else to depend on. Randy isn't old enough or strong enough; also he hasn't the temperament. He has no desire for money or anything money can buy, so far as I can find out, even Keepsake."

Cathy wanted to cry out that she hadn't either, but she could not because it would not have been true. She loved Keepsake, too much perhaps, and it was possible that she loved money too, for though she had had little experience with it she had not failed to notice that its possession gave one importance in the eyes of others.

Without money, without the name of Brett, she knew well enough that nobody at the hall would have noticed her. That was why she had worn the diamonds and that was why she had gone that evening to look for Dan Cartwright.

Her father said, "I can trust you to look after Randy. I approve of matriarchies; women have more stamina than men for holding on to things once they are established. You'll be trained, little by little, to look after the affairs which will eventually be yours; you may fall in love with whomever you wish but I think in the long run you will find that no man can give you the things which you already possess for yourself."

He summed up the situation thus and dismissed it; whatever she chose to do she must choose for herself. He said, "I'm leaving for New York tomorrow."

"But are you well enough?"

"I have wasted enough time and in any case I have little choice in the matter. I have been summoned to testify as to my rights to continue in the use of certain properties against which the government has seen fit to place an injunction."

"What is an injunction?"

"Don't bother about it, Cathy."

"I would like to know."

He made a restless movement but he answered patiently enough: "An injunction is a restraining order from a court, in this case the Federal Court, taking away the jurisdiction of a piece of property from its stockholders awaiting trial."

"But . . . can they do that?"

"I would not have thought so, but it appears that they have."

"Is there to be a trial, then?"

"Yes, there is to be a trial."

"With you . . . ?"

"Don't look so distressed; I haven't been arrested. It's merely a question of proving that land grants on which the railroad was built and several of the mines are legitimately mine."

She had to ask the next question: "And are they?"

"They were given to me by government officials who are now quaking in their boots, I should imagine. However, they will have to appear for me, for their own self-protection. Don't worry; Keepsake is not involved, nor the Keepsake Mine; I've taken care of that."

"But who did the land really belong to?"

He said, with a flash of grim humor: "It belonged to the Indians, poor devils."

"But now?"

"That remains to be seen. The indefatigable efforts on the part of this thing called reform may make me their scapegoat but they will have their hands full doing it; I can assure you of that."

Cathy cried out: "But isn't there a right and a wrong?" Surely in this case, involving the land which he first had explored, he would be able to assure her that his was the right side; she waited, breathlessly, ready and eager to believe him with all her heart.

He looked at her a long time as if translating what she was saying from a foreign language; he said, "Yes, I suppose there must have been once; the Indians must have thought so. But I doubt if the present case will be decided on those simple values."

His face, bleak and forbidding, turned away from her, making it clear that he too would do whatever he chose to do, alone.

Chapter 22

AFTER HE HAD left the room she sat motionless for a long time. She had understood only about half of what he had been saying, but certain words continued to ring in her ears. Keepsake was hers. She was an enormously wealthy woman.

It was like the possession of the jewels. She did not know what to do with them, but they attracted her with a pulling fascination.

She went upstairs to her own room. She sat down at her dressing-table. She lifted her eyes and looked at herself in the mirror, a long look.

She picked up the music box which Lisa once had given her; she wound it slowly; she lifted the lid. The little tune began to play.

Lisa came in while she was sitting there. "What are you doing?"

"Nothing. Sitting here."

"I can see that. Were you expecting Dan, is that why you are sitting here moping?"

"I wasn't moping." Always she was on the defensive with Lisa. She felt like saying: I am an enormously wealthy woman; instead she said, "Where have you been?"

"Riding, with Philip."

"Did you have a good time?"

"Heavenly," Lisa said.

There was a tap at the door.

"Who is it?" Lisa called.

"Amanda. To see to Miss Catherine's bath."

"Never mind now; she isn't ready for her bath."

Amanda went away from the door, doubtless to report to Stacey who would come soon enough to put a stop to this nonsense.

Cathy carefully rewound the music box.

Lisa said, "Do shut that thing off, for heaven's sake. It gets on my nerves."

Cathy had one weapon against Lisa, irony. She said, "You might let me decide when to take my own baths and play my own music box."

Lisa did not understand irony; she said, "What? Oh. What possible difference can it make whether you take a bath this minute or not."

"Well, let me see. It might make a difference if I happened to be in the mood to take it now."

Lisa looked at her sharply. "I never know when you are joking. You have such a queer way about you sometimes. I don't consider that remark particularly brilliant."

"No?"

"You've been strange ever since you came back from Saint Cloud. Did something happen there?"

"Oh yes. Quite a lot happened there."

"What?"

"William's family didn't approve of me. He had to tell me that he couldn't marry me."

"Oh, what nonsense," Lisa said. She looked skeptical; she said, "You can't have managed it very well; with Uncle Michael's money there isn't anybody in the world you couldn't marry if you wanted to."

"Because of Father's money?"

"There's no need to be touchy about it," Lisa said. "I only wish I had it."

"Sometimes one would like to be liked for oneself."

"Well, it doesn't necessarily follow that you won't be," Lisa said. She studied Cathy with her head on one side. "The trouble with you is that you haven't learned to make use of your particular type. You've grown quite pretty, you know. You aren't beautiful, of course, but you have a flair. I could teach you a lot of things if you'd let me."

"Thank you. I'm grateful."

"Nothing frightens men more than for a woman to be sarcastic," Lisa said. "Or clever. Or even too rich. Except a certain type of man, of course." She continued to study Cathy, her eyes wide and innocent and then she said, melting suddenly: "Let's not quarrel. We've always been like sisters to each other, Cathy, why can't we still?"

The music box was running down. Cathy let it die a slow agonizing death.

"Oh!" Lisa exclaimed in exasperation. She snatched the box from Cathy's hand and threw it across the room. "Now will you listen to me? Will you stop being hateful?"

"You've broken it," Cathy said. She was angry, beyond all reason, because Lisa had broken the music box.

"I'll get you another," Lisa said.

Cathy took a step toward her. Lisa backed hastily; she said, "Cathy, can't we be friends? Why do you keep acting as if you hated me?"

Cathy stood still. She said, her eyes meeting Lisa's, "Because I do hate you, I suppose."

"Because of Philip?"

"Not only that. You've always spoiled things for me."

"Spoiled things for you? How can you say that!" Lisa was deliberately working herself into a tantrum; she walked with quick dramatic steps up and down the room, raising and lowering her eyebrows in a way which reminded Cathy of William, throwing out her hands as if asking heaven to witness her innocence. She said, "You are the one who has always spoiled things for me!"

"In what way?"

"Mamma thinks you are so perfect. She's always telling me about your strength of character. Philip thinks the same thing about you if the truth be known. You have no idea what a perfect torment my life is. No freedom, no money, nothing. You can do exactly as you please whenever you please. And now, when I have the tiniest little time to be happy you begrudge it to me!"

Cathy, floundering in this flood of words, seized upon those which meant most to her. "What do you mean, Philip thinks the same thing about me?"

"He idealizes you. He holds you up to me all the time for a model. Look at Cathy. Cathy is brave, noble, self-sacrificing, and everything else! What a pity he isn't in love with you instead of with me."

"Yes," Cathy said slowly. "What a pity."

Lisa glanced at her. "Life isn't a bed of roses for me, I can tell you that. There are plenty of times when I envy you. If I were in your place I could have anything I wanted, anything! As it is, of course, I am helpless."

Cathy with difficulty dragged her attention from the sudden wayward journey of her thoughts back to Lisa. "What do you mean, you are helpless?"

"You know as well as I do that I'll have to go home soon: And when I do all this will be over, my whole life will be over as far as I'm concerned. I'll have to let them announce my engagement; I was only able to put it off because of being in mourning and then Papa's getting sick was like a miracle, though I felt very badly of course and I cried and cried and made special prayers every day. Still it was like a miracle; everybody was saying that I would have to make up my mind one way or the other. I escaped, for a little while at least, but of course I'll have to go back. I don't think about it, I've put it completely out of my mind, but of course the time will come and I'll be led back and enslaved and everything will be horrible. Now do you see why I want to be as happy as I can while I'm here?"

Lisa looked wistful and melancholy; at the same time it was impossible not to see that part of what she was saying was true. She was unhappy; she was, even, a little frightened.

Cathy said with sudden fierceness: "No, I don't see. Why should you go back if you don't want to go and if Philip doesn't want you to go? Nobody can make you. If you are really in love with Philip you won't go back, you'll stay here with him. And if you aren't in love with Philip, why are you pretending to be?"

"I'm not pretending. I am in love with Philip, terribly terribly in love with Philip!"

Lisa stopped dramatizing herself. She put her hands over her face; she said, "Cathy, please help me. Help both of us."

Cathy closed her eyes and then opened them. No inner protest was of any avail: Philip loved Lisa, and it was a pity, perhaps, as Lisa had said, but that was the way it was. Cathy asked, "How can *I* help you?"

"You can't, I suppose. Nobody can."

"*You* can. There's no reason for you not to marry Philip if you love him. He wants to marry you, doesn't he?"

Lisa sank into a chair. She leaned her head back and closed her eyes. She said, "Of course he wants to marry me."

"Then why don't you do it? Why are you making all this fuss —there isn't anything, really, to stand in your way!"

Lisa opened her eyes. She narrowed them slightly, looking through thick gold-tipped lashes at Cathy. She said, "That's all very well for you to say."

"I'd marry him without money!"

Lisa shrugged and she studied the tip of one slipper. "I daresay you would, you're such a goody-goody."

"I am not."

"Yes, you are. Anyhow I should think you would be glad that I can't marry him."

Cathy's eyes wavered. She looked down; she said desperately: "If you didn't want him why couldn't you let him alone!"

"I don't know. I wish in a way now that I had." After a minute Lisa said, "I certainly didn't mean for this to happen. Do you think I'd put myself to all this suffering on purpose?"

"You can't be suffering so awfully much."

"Naturally you don't believe me. You think you are the only one in the world who can suffer."

Cathy cried indignantly, "What about Philip? Does he have any idea there's another man that you're supposed to be engaged to?"

"Of course he does." Lisa picked at her handkerchief with nervous fingers.

"I don't believe you."

"Well, he does. He knows all about Francis."

Cathy's curiosity allowed her to be temporarily side-tracked: "What's he like, anyhow?"

"Who?"

"Francis, or whatever his name is; the man you are supposed to be engaged to."

Lisa said angrily, "You can stop calling him the man I'm supposed to be engaged to. His name is Francis Tole and the engagement is quite definite; I can tell you that there's no way to get out of it now even if I wanted to. That's why I'm so upset; I can't keep putting it off forever. His letters are getting more and more difficult as it is."

"Are you in love with him?"

"What? I don't know, a little; yes, he's very nice. If it weren't for Philip I'd be in love with him; I was in the beginning, you know. But when I think of giving up Philip I don't know what to do, I feel desperate. . . ."

They faced each other. Lisa's eyes were brilliant with tears; it was strange to know that it was true that Lisa was suffering, in her way. Philip would suffer much more. Cathy said, "Lisa. Would you marry Philip if he went somewhere else, to a city, where he could get a larger practice and more money?"

"I've thought of that. But Philip is so stubborn; he refuses to accept help from anyone, even Uncle Michael."

"You wouldn't starve, even here. Philip has a house and quite a lot of patients."

"A house! In Magoon? What kind of life would you call that?"

"It would be a good life. Philip goes all over the country; he helps all kinds of people."

Lisa closed her eyes and raised both hands in the air in an attitude of prayer. She said, "Oh, give me strength!"

Cathy said, "You can stop acting all over the place for my benefit. Exactly what is it you want me to do?"

Lisa opened her eyes wide, looked blank, and then laughed. "How do you know I want anything?"

"You usually do."

"Well, then, I do; I want you to ask Uncle Michael to use his influence to get Philip established in a practice somewhere else. New York perhaps, or Washington; it doesn't really matter to me." Lisa looked noble and self-sacrificing; she added, "It would have to be done very subtly of course so Philip didn't know about it until it was done."

"Do you mean you want Father to buy him a practice without telling him about it?"

Lisa shrugged her shoulders; she knew nothing of these details.

"Suppose Philip won't accept it?"

"He'd have to, after it was all done. I mean, it would be terribly selfish and ungrateful of him if he didn't, and it would mean that he didn't really love me, besides."

Cathy let the full implication of this sink in, then she said furiously: "Don't count on me in your schemes. I'll have nothing to do with them."

"You would do anything to keep Philip away from me, wouldn't you?"

"No, I wouldn't. On the other hand I refuse to help you trick him just because you are too selfish to marry him without money."

Instead of being angry Lisa was suddenly humble. "Cathy, I'm not like you. I know I'm selfish and greedy, Mamma tells me often enough. I can't help it. I don't want to settle down or be poor or do anything difficult and horrid. I just want to enjoy myself while I can."

"Is Francis Tole wealthy?"

"Oh, certainly; I'd have everything. Mamma thinks I'm mad to risk losing him even for a minute."

"Then why are you, when money means so much to you?"

"I tell you I don't know myself. I tell myself how fortunate I am, and I make up my mind to give in and let Mamma and Francis decide for me. And then I think of Keepsake and Philip, and I can't!"

Cathy realized that she no longer held hard feelings toward Lisa, they had melted away. She tried to summon them; they had been a protection. Lisa was selfish, she admitted it, but this time Lisa for once was acting against her best interests. Lisa was caught in a net of circumstances no less than Cathy and Philip and Cathy's father and all the rest of them.

Lisa said, "Oh Cathy, you don't hate me, do you? I'd undo everything I've done if I could."

"No doubt you would," Cathy said; she halted, she said, "No, I don't hate you."

"I've always loved you, you know. Like a little sister. It was so nice, wasn't it, when we were children? Before any of this happened."

"Well, we had to stop being children some time."

"I've been so worried for fear Mrs. Ellis would write to Mamma. I've seen her looking at me; I'm sure Mamma told her to watch to see that I didn't do anything silly."

"Mrs. Ellis, spying? I don't think she would do that."

"Oh, not spying exactly. But she doesn't approve of me, she makes that plain enough."

"I don't know why you say that. She is very kind."

"Oh, bother, everybody is kind, but what good does that do me? Anyhow your Mrs. Ellis has taken precious good care to find excuses to come out on the terrace when I was saying goodnight to Philip; once she very nearly caught him kissing me."

A paralyzing embarrassment fell between them. After Lisa had gone to her own room Cathy picked up the broken music box.

Chapter 23

When Cathy went downstairs the following morning her father already had left the house to be driven into town to take the early morning train, eastbound.

It was a relief when Philip and Lisa left the house; the atmosphere was less strained, though Cathy seemed unable to settle down to anything. She supposed she was experiencing a reaction from keyed-up emotions: everything happened too fast or not at all. She longed to see Dan and at the same time she was reluctant to see him; she wanted something to happen and dreaded its happening. The Little Half Chick was blown by a north wind at the moment; wandering through the empty spotless downstairs rooms she was assailed suddenly by a trembling so violent that she had to sit down. This would not do; she had to be stronger than this. Even when the trembling stopped she felt numb and cold; she looked back almost with wonder on the feeling of elation and excitement which had swept her through the days in Saint Cloud. Her father would not have made all these arrangements for her and Randy's protection if he were not expecting trouble so drastic that he would be helpless to protect them; he had gone off, sick and tired, and in an ugly mood which forbode catastrophe. There was nothing to do but wait; the whole house seemed to be waiting. She was frightened, that was it, but not because of anything tangible. Her father would do what he chose to do; he would make decisions and carry them out, right or wrong; everybody had to make decisions and abide by them.

Cathy made one; she rang for Sam. "Is there somebody who can ride to Saint Cloud?"

"Yes, certainly; do you want to go there?"

"No. I want somebody to take a note to Mr. Dan Cartwright; he may be in the hotel or he may be at his mine: the Catherine. Somebody can give directions."

She wrote the note, inviting Dan to a little party. Then she was puzzled as to who else was to come to the party; she added, "Bring another couple if you know one; there are only three of us."

One too many, she thought, sealing the note.

Dan arrived at three the following afternoon; he brought with him a Doctor and Mrs. Macomber who had recently arrived at Saint Cloud, he said, introducing them. Doctor and Mrs. Macomber appeared delighted with the prospect of a party at Keepsake; everybody indeed appeared to find Cathy's impulse to have a party quite a normal and natural one except Philip who had been sullen and aloof at the first mention of it and remained sullen and aloof when he arrived late for dinner.

Lisa enchanted, asked, "Why don't we do this more often? I don't think much of the Macombers, though; how did you happen to ask them?"

"I didn't; I just asked Dan to bring somebody."

"Oh well. A party is a party. Dan's horribly in love with you, isn't he? He scarcely looks at me."

Even Mrs. Ellis thought that the idea of a party was a good one, though she excused herself from it to have dinner with Randy. "It will take your mind off things," she said; not saying what it was that Cathy needed her mind to be taken off of.

The Macombers and Dan were to spend the night; they were shown to their rooms. Cathy did not find the Macombers appealing either, and Dan apologized for them when he and Cathy were alone for a few minutes in the drawing-room before dinner; "They were the best I could do on short notice; they're harmless, I imagine. Is this a call for help?"

"In a way, I guess." Perhaps because of the Macombers, Cathy already was regretting her impulse; the evening stretched very long before her. She had never, she realized now, seen Philip and Dan together; the contrast was disastrous to the picture of Dan she had been building up in her mind. Unfair to him too; she tried to smile at him with a confidence she was far from feeling.

He said, "You aren't wearing the diamonds."

"No."

"You look a little washed-out." It was noticeable, then, that she looked washed-out without the diamonds. "Is anything wrong?"

"No, nothing."

He studied her for a minute but he did not pursue the subject. Dan, like Lisa, enjoyed a party, any party. He roamed about the room; he stood before the mantelpiece; he made the room come to life. He toasted her in the champagne: "To The Catherine. The one and only Catherine." He asked, immediately afterward: "Did you know that I've sold her?"

"Oh no. Dan, I'm sorry."

"Don't be sorry; I got an excellent deal out of it. Instructions came yesterday meeting all my terms; was that some of your doing?"

"No. At least I don't think so."

"She belongs to you now, really. I don't begrudge that."

Her father must have sent the instructions; Cathy did not know whether to be glad or sorry.

Doctor Macomber was a young-old man with pale blue eyes; he was hearty and affable; his manner toward Philip was slightly condescending. Mrs. Macomber, who was small and dark, assayed everything with quick flicks of her eyes: the house, the servants, the value of the paintings on the wall, of the china, of the crystal, of the silver in her long nervous fingers.

No, the Macombers were not a success, Cathy was not even sure they were harmless. Cathy was distressed, but since there was nothing to do but endure them, she made what effort she could to instil a gay mood into her party.

Certainly Philip did not help her; he grew colder and more silent as the evening progressed. Still Cathy was not altogether sorry she had given the party; action was better than non-action; emotions were better brought to a climax, some sort of climax, than left lying about unresolved.

Only Lisa and Dan were imperturbably high-spirited during the long, far too drawn-out dinner. Lisa was dazzling, there was no other word for it. She was at the high point of her life; her happiness seemed to be sweeping her upward as if she were carried by a great wave. Philip could not tear his eyes from her and Cathy could not blame him. Lisa's eyes, brilliant with the joy of living, seemed also, as they moved from one person to another, to be sightless except for some secret vision inside herself; she smiled, she seemed to be looking down on them from some peak of exaltation which they could only imagine and envy. Mrs. Macomber, in particular, Cathy noted, appraised Lisa's high mood in somewhat the same manner as she had appraised other things in the house. Mrs. Macomber looked from Lisa to Philip and back again, and there was a little smile in the corner of her mouth which Cathy did not like.

Dan ate and drank with the same enormous zest for food and drink which he displayed toward other things; he talked and laughed and flirted with Lisa just enough but concentrated his attention upon Cathy. Mrs. Macomber studied them too, and her smile became even more knowing. It was a disagreeable smile, but no matter, they would never need to see Mrs. Macomber again.

There was one bad spot when Mrs. Macomber said, "Dan is celebrating because he sold his mine, yesterday, the Catherine," and Philip asked, "The Catherine?"

"Yes, hadn't you heard of it?"

"How would I have heard of it?"

"Don't bite my head off, please. I simply happened to mention it."

"Can you blame me, now that you've seen the original?" Dan asked; he made a second toast to the Catherine.

Mrs. Macomber said, "No, I certainly can't blame you," significantly.

"She's still in good hands," Dan said, and the moment passed. Dan was not insulted by its implications; he was at ease; he dominated the table as Michael Brett himself might have done.

They went into the drawing-room and Cathy sat before a little table, pouring coffee and liqueurs. She chose a crème de menthe for herself, holding it to the light because the color pleased her more than the drink itself.

She heard Lisa say urgently behind her: "Meet me outside, afterward. Please, Philip," and she was sure that Mrs. Macomber heard it too. She felt she should warn Lisa but she feared the warning might be resented and anyhow she thought that it did not matter since Mrs. Macomber was a stranger and could not report Lisa's doings to Aunt Helena or the Toles or anybody actually concerned. Cathy made conversation with the Macombers to cover the minute when Lisa had a headache and went early to her room.

Later in the evening Cathy circumvented the look which she read in Dan's eyes, asking for a private rendezvous, by accompanying Doctor and Mrs. Macomber to their rooms and sending a message back by Sam that she too was retiring. She gained the blessed privacy of her own room, closing the door behind her as if all the hounds of hell were after her.

It was late that night when Lisa softly let herself out of one of the side doors opening on a terrace.

She had slipped through the dark house to a rendezvous with Philip a number of times before; but she was quite sure, with some subtle sureness which she did not try to define, that tonight was different.

There was a mounting excitement inside her. Her heart was racing; her sense of wrongdoing and fear of eventual atonement added to the quickening of her senses. She felt daring and joyous, at one with the white mysterious beauty of the night. She let the moonlight enfold her; she breasted it like the figurehead of a ship.

A current of emotion was sweeping her along; all her instincts urged her forward to some mysterious fulfillment. She felt neither curiosity nor reluctance as to its nature; she was for this space of time wholly a creature of instinct. She sat down for a minute beside a tiny pool, watching the quick flashing in the moonlight of goldfish half hidden by lily pads; she was savoring an interlude of suspense before a definite, if unknown, climax.

She pushed open a second gate. Philip stepped out of the darkness to meet her.

"Lisa, where have you been?"

"Darling, I came as soon as I could."

"I thought something had happened."

"They all stayed downstairs for hours; I thought they'd never go to bed. And then Mrs. Macomber came to my room, to borrow a sleeping powder, she said."

"Did she suspect anything?"

"No, I don't think so."

"For heaven's sake, aren't you sure?"

"Would it matter to you if she did?"

"Yes, it would. I hate sneaking out here to meet you like this, and you know it."

"Why do you do it, then?"

He gripped her shoulders, staring down angrily into her face. "You know why I do it."

"Say it."

"Because I love you, I'm mad about you, and you won't let me come out openly and say so."

"I love you too, Philip."

Her head was back; her eyes were deep and lustrous as they had been all evening. He bent over her, his face darkening, but she held him back.

"Not yet. Not yet."

Her mood of expectation was too glorious to be broken. She moved ahead of him toward a white gate; he followed, sensing something new in her which puzzled him and made violent attack upon his senses. She was always capricious, abandoning herself just so far and then withdrawing swiftly into innocence.

The garden they entered was sheltered by a thick border of fir trees. There was a center expanse of lawn around a fountain; grouped on the lawn were ghostly marble benches.

They stood in the darkness of the fir trees. Lisa turned, raising her face to his. She whispered urgently: "Now kiss me. Kiss me."

Her lips clung to his until, dazed, he himself raised his head from the embrace. He stared down into her face, trying to read it. He could see that she was smiling. He took his arms from around her and walked a little distance away. He sat down on the grass and put his head in his hands.

She came and sat beside him. "Philip, darling, what's the matter?"

He lifted his head. He said, half angrily, half despairingly: "Oh Lisa, didn't that mean anything to you?"

"What do you mean?"

"That. The way you kissed me."

She leaned against him. She traced the outline of his jaw with one finger. "Of course it did. It meant that I love you."

"I wonder."

"Why do you wonder?"

"Lisa, when will you marry me?"

"Do we have to think about that now?"

"Yes." He covered her restless finger with a firm hand and held it.

She said, "I don't know, Philip. We must wait."

"Why must we wait? What will change?"

"If only you would be a little patient."

"I have been patient."

She sighed. "When you act like this I'm not even sure that I want to marry you."

"Lisa, for heaven's sake."

"I'll marry you as soon as I can. Can't you believe me?"

"No, I can't."

"Now you are being hateful."

"We have to straighten this out. If we love each other we must want to marry. If we don't there's no use going on with it."

"I've said over and over that I want to marry you."

"When?"

"When Papa is well."

"You know as well as I do that that's no good. He won't approve; we'll just have to make up our minds to do without that."

"An elopement would break Mamma's heart."

"Oh, this isn't getting us anywhere."

"Everything will turn out as we want it if only we are patient."

"How will it?"

"There are ways. For instance, if you have a big position in a city . . ."

"But I haven't a big position in a city. I've been saving to buy a practice, but even so it will be several years before I can aspire to anything which you could call very big."

"Uncle Michael would help you."

"Don't start that again."

"Why are you so stubborn?"

He struggled for patience. "Darling, even if I did take help from Michael we would be poor for years paying him back."

The idea of repayment surprised her. "Uncle Michael doesn't need the money."

"Darling, darling, couldn't you stand being poor for just a little while?"

"I simply don't see the necessity for it."

He looked at her in desperation. They came to this blind ending each time; he could see no solution to their future together.

He said, "Then we must end this right now."

"No, Philip, wait."

"There's no use in waiting. Things won't be different for a long time, maybe never."

She began to cry.

He looked stern and remote; neither her tears nor her pleadings had produced the effect for which she had hoped. She became frightened. "Philip?"

He did not turn.

"I know I'm a coward. I can't help it. I don't know how to

222

be poor, not the way you mean. I'd hate it and after a while we'd hate each other."

He drew a deep breath. She was right; she belonged to a different life from anything he could hope to offer her; he had been crazy to dream otherwise.

She said, "I love you so terribly. I can't give you up."

"We've got to give each other up."

"But why, Philip? Why?"

"Oh Lisa, can't I make you understand?"

The passion in his voice thrilled her. In the moonlight his face was chiseled by shadows into a look of gaunt desperation.

She said, "I do understand."

He turned his head and stared down at her. She was leaning back on her arms, her body tensed, her face turned upward to the sky.

He said, "Lisa . . ."

"I do understand, Philip."

He took one of her arms and pulled her roughly into a sitting position. He said, "Don't be a fool."

She leaned against him, pliant and yielding. He steeled himself against her; he was conscious always of the need for self-control which her volatile emotions and ignorance imposed upon him.

"Philip?"

He sat turned to stone; his body rigid against hers. She could feel his muscles tense, like the gathering of some force. The force flowed from his body to her, quivering along her nerves; she felt herself swept irresistibly forward, far beyond the safe channels of innocence and unawareness.

"Philip, I do love you so much."

She caressed his cheek with her own with a soft sensuous movement. "Darling, why do you look so unhappy?"

"Unhappy? I'm in hell."

With one hand she turned his face toward her and stared into his eyes. He returned the look savagely, his face haggard from the straining of his passion against its self-imposed limits. A delicious sensation of helplessness and languor began to steal over her.

She whispered, "What would make you happy?"

"Be quiet!"

"Would it be wrong for us to be happy?"

"You don't know what you're saying."

"I do know what I'm saying."

The struggle inside him was so great that he felt it must surely tear him apart. He tried to recall honor, but it was only a word which had no meaning.

"Lisa?"

Her eyes were wide; there was in them an expression of rapt blindness.

"Lisa, I cannot . . . I must not."

They were only words.

The deep shadows of the thick sweet-smelling pine trees enclosed them.

Chapter 24

THE HOUSE SEEMED very dark when they returned. They said goodnight at the side door under the portico, and Philip watched Lisa slip through it alone.

It was there that they were accustomed to parting after their secret nocturnal meetings. Philip, clinging in a futile gesture to the code to which he had always subscribed, seldom spent the night at Keepsake now.

He wished that tonight could have been different. He should have remained with her, protecting her, instead of lurking alone in the darkness like a thief. But Lisa would not hear of it; she said goodnight, kissing him and then breaking away, urging him to be quiet, even laughing when he stumbled over a stone and nearly fell, but at the same time insisting that he must go. "We'll see each other tomorrow. Please, Philip."

Lisa moved languidly through the dark silent house. She realized that it was very late. She heard the ticking of a clock in the hallway through which she passed and it reminded her that she must hurry. She could not seem to hurry. Her movements were very very slow, like those of a person intoxicated.

For some reason that thought amused her so much that she almost gave way to hysterical laughter. It was astonishing that she should have the impulse to laugh after what had occurred. She had expected somehow that some amazing transformation would have taken place. But it had not.

And that was the emotion which people made so much fuss about! That was the mystery, the object of dark hints of a strange and awesome experience which had loomed before her all her life, the subject of endless girlhood speculations and laughter, the ultimate destination, the Thing which lay in wait for her when she was old enough and which she must know in order to achieve what every girl wanted to achieve, marriage, the sacred initiation into wifehood, into the state of being able to do as one pleased. Well, she had experienced it and she had not yet been struck by lightning.

She felt her way carefully up the stairs toward the long dark corridor which led to her bedroom. In the bedroom adjoining hers Cathy would be asleep; it was the thought of Cathy which brought home to Lisa with a sudden sense of shock the realization that she had entered into a new phase of her life. She could not boast of this adventure; a gulf of experience now stretched between her and Cathy, once crossed there was no going back.

The stairs had never seemed so long or so steep. She reached the top; she was standing clutching the banister before she noticed that somebody had just turned the corner and was coming down the hall toward her carrying a lamp.

Her heart gave a leap of fright. She tried to get to her room but she could not make it; she turned to retreat but it was too late, she was seen. The person with the lamp called, "Lisa. Miss Minard; how you frightened me; I can see that I must have frightened you too."

It was Mrs. Macomber. "Dear me," she said, coming closer: "I couldn't imagine who could be creeping about in the dark at this hour of the night. I was just about to call for help; it's fortunate I didn't, isn't it?"

Lisa assumed a haughty pose: "Are you looking for something?"

"Another headache tablet, I'm afraid."

"I gave you the bottle."

"Oh, so you did; I'd forgotten." Mrs. Macomber laughed in a high voice: "I simply couldn't sleep." She held the lamp high, her curious eyes flicking over Lisa, taking in with swift appraisal Lisa's disheveled hair and crumpled dress. She said, "Why, you haven't even undressed, you bad thing you, and you went to bed hours ago."

"I couldn't sleep so I got dressed again and went outside for some air."

It was a mistake to make excuses for herself; Lisa knew that instantly. Mrs. Macomber laughed again, a silly laugh that infuriated

Lisa while it turned her knees to water; she said, "Well, I won't tell on you."

"There is nothing to tell."

"No. Well. The doctor is very attractive, though I can't say I found him very agreeable at dinner. But perhaps, under the circumstances he doesn't feel that he has to be."

"Be quiet."

Mrs. Macomber's eyes narrowed; she said, "Perhaps under the circumstances you would do better to adopt a more polite tone of voice too."

"Goodnight, Mrs. Macomber."

Mrs. Macomber continued to stand in the middle of the corridor, blocking Lisa's progress; she did not move. She said, "Oh, but why? Since neither of us can sleep we may as well entertain each other; I am enjoying this conversation very much."

"I am not."

"Well, but still . . . One hears so much gossip about this place but so few lowly local residents have an opportunity to study it first hand. You mustn't hold it against me if I make the most of my present advantages."

"You will never be invited here again; I can assure you of that."

"I wouldn't be too sure. Your nice little cousin, who owns it, I understand, may find herself in need of a friend."

"You could never be that."

"A true friend," Mrs. Macomber said. "That would be beneficial to me and to my husband too; I have to think of these things because he doesn't."

Panic threatened Lisa but she fought it down. It seemed the most incredible bad luck that a person like Mrs. Macomber should appear on her horizon on this night of all nights; she was superstitious, and she shivered. But it was simply bad luck, nothing more: Mrs. Macomber was only a woman, and an unattractive woman; Lisa could not have believed herself afraid of any woman under the sun. She said, "Stand aside; I am going to my room."

"You seem very nervous. Where is the doctor, gone home? Perhaps we should call your cousin now; she might like to learn what is going on under her roof."

"Stand aside, I tell you."

"Ah, you don't like that idea, do you? I was right then: your cousin does not know of your innocent meetings with the doctor and if she did know she would not approve of them."

"How exactly will you explain your presence, sneaking about in a house where you are supposed to be a guest?"

Mrs. Macomber laughed softly. "I don't think attention will be centered on me, but if I need to make an explanation I will think of one. My appearance, at any rate, is somewhat more conventional than yours."

Lisa hesitated; the truth of this statement was obvious. Mrs. Macomber was in a dressing-gown while Lisa, fully clothed, was not certain as to the extent of her disarray. In her preoccupation with her emotions she had given little thought to it; she made a betraying motion to her dress and hair.

Lisa changed her tactics; she smiled and shrugged. Smiling and shrugging, she listened intently; the silence of the house reassured her. The only persons sleeping on the floor of this wing of the house besides Cathy were Randy and Stacey, and their rooms were far down the corridor. Only Cathy was near by and Cathy slept very soundly. Lisa would be safe if she could get to her room before the sound of voices aroused Sam and Hester on the floor above or Cathy or Stacey or all of them, and so brought the house down upon Lisa's head.

Lisa asked, "What exactly is it you want? If it's money I can give it to you."

"Really?"

"Yes, really. And you had better consider; you won't make such a pretty picture yourself with your revelations, whatever you may think. Cathy won't thank you for them, believe me. You are in a position to embarrass me, but it will do you very little good."

Mrs. Macomber wavered; it was evident that she too was thinking. Lisa made the mistake of pressing her advantage; she stepped forward, and instantly Mrs. Macomber moved too. The lamp swayed; their shadows swayed with it. It went over. For a second they were in darkness and then a tiny flame burned at Lisa's feet; it caught the thin stuff of her dress and shot upward.

Lisa stared down at herself in horror. A consciousness of her danger reached her; terrified, she knew nothing to do but to run, run as fast as she could, to the safety of her room.

Cathy came out in the hall just as Lisa came running toward her. Cathy, utterly confused, reacted to an instinct which came to her from somewhere. She saw nothing at first but a figure enveloped in a mysterious illuminating glow; she saw then that the figure was Lisa and that the glow was fire.

She flung herself against Lisa to hold her; Lisa now seemed to be a blaze of fire. Cathy beat at the flames, frantically. Panic still urged Lisa to run, but fortunately she was too weakened by fright to succeed in pulling herself away; her knees were beginning to buckle. She implored weakly, "Cathy. Cathy, do something."

Cathy commanded, "Lie still," while she continued to beat at the flames. She ordered the second figure in the hall, without knowing or caring who it was: "Get a blanket." Mrs. Macomber, jolted into action, rushed into the nearest bedroom and brought a blanket. She came to Cathy's assistance and together they held Lisa down, wrapping the blanket about her and beating at it desperately.

It seemed years, though it was only a few seconds, before the fire was out. Lisa's voluminous underskirts had protected her from actual disaster, Cathy thought, but it was impossible to be sure. Lisa lay moaning on the floor. She was alive at any rate; the hall was dark. Cathy ordered the person beside her: "Get a lamp and then go for Sam and tell him to send someone for Philip." The lamp revealed Mrs. Macomber, pale and shaking with fright. Cathy had forgotten these strangers, but with Lisa moaning on the floor there was no time to wonder how Mrs. Macomber and Lisa had come to be involved together in this strange scene; she said, "Have them get Philip! No, wait. Your husband is a doctor, isn't he?"

"Yes."

"Bring him, then."

It was the last thing in the world which Mrs. Macomber now wanted to do, but there was no help for it. She hurried off, her hand shaking so violently that she scarcely could hold the lamp.

Cathy waited beside Lisa. Lisa was moaning more loudly now; it was impossible to know how badly she was hurt. Cathy sat beside her, soothing her, reassuring her that help was coming soon. Lisa began screaming in the darkness. She screamed and screamed, a high thin scream of pain and protest against the darkness and the terror.

Doctor Macomber came running down the hall, followed by Sam. Together they lifted Lisa and carried her into her bedroom. Others in the household began to be roused now: Mrs. Ellis, Dan Cartwright, a number of house servants added themselves to the group of people in the corridor.

Doctor Macomber's wife assisted him; she was a nurse, he explained. She was awkward; she dropped first a pair of scissors and then a roll of bandages on the floor. Her husband rebuked her irritably, "What's the matter with you, Mabel?" It seemed inexplicably prosaic that Mrs. Macomber's name should turn out to be

Mabel; Cathy could scarcely believe her own impulse to laugh at the idea, and the small explosive sound which came from Lisa, whimpering now, could surely not have been laughter.

Doctor Macomber's pale blue eyes betrayed his curiosity as he finished dressing Lisa's burns and gave her medicine to alleviate the pain. Lisa stopped whimpering and grew sleepy. She had one hand in Cathy's, clutching it tightly; she whispered once, "Don't go away," and Cathy said, "I won't."

It was amazing what a solid feeling of loyalty existed between her and Lisa against these outsiders. Whatever had happened was no affair of anyone's except theirs; Cathy wished that Aunt Helena had been there so that she could, with her quiet poise, her ultra-civilized manner, simply have swept these curious strangers from the room.

Doctor Macomber said heartily, "She is going to be fine and dandy, fine and dandy. Thanks to the petticoats that you gentle ladies wear and to somebody's quick thinking." He raised pale eyebrows at Cathy and waited for Cathy to tell what had occurred.

Cathy said nothing.

Doctor Macomber said, "If she had been in nightclothes, for instance . . ."

Cathy felt a little surge of color in her face at this open calling of attention to the fact that Lisa was still dressed when she should have been undressed long ago. She stiffened to meet Mrs. Macomber's curious eyes upon them, but Mrs. Macomber did not turn. That was odd, very odd; before Cathy could speculate on its meaning Doctor Macomber was babbling on: "This young lady has been fortunate, very fortunate indeed. I am quite sure that she will suffer few ill effects, though of course we must look after her. My wife will remain here to look after her; quite a happy coincidence, is it not, that both a doctor and nurse should be in the house of this very mysterious accident, ha ha."

Lisa's eyes opened, entreated Cathy, and closed again. Cathy said, "Stacey and I will look after her."

"Well, if you are quite sure. I'll be on call, if I should be needed, and I'll look in the first thing in the morning, of course. Though it's nearly morning now."

Mrs. Macomber, in the background, said nothing, but when she approached the bed Lisa opened her eyes wide and looked at her; she asked, "Have you enough sleeping powders, now, Mrs. Macomber?"

Doctor Macomber fussed: "I still can't understand how you

came to be roaming about a strange house at this hour of the night, Mabel."

"Mrs. Macomber wanted a sleeping powder," Lisa said. "I'm sure she didn't mean to be careless with the lamp, though of course, if Cathy hadn't been there . . ."

Stacey took charge; she ordered, "You go along to bed now, Miss Cathy. There's been enough foolishness for one night. I'll sit right here and see to it that Miss Lisa goes to sleep the way she's supposed to do and that she stays there too."

Lisa's eyes were still wide open; she was watching Cathy. She said to Stacey, "I want to talk to Cathy a minute."

Lisa said to Cathy, "I suppose you are wondering why I got dressed again?"

"Not particularly. I heard you tell Philip you would meet him later."

"Oh," Lisa said.

"Mrs. Macomber heard you too. You weren't very discreet, if it was supposed to be a secret."

"Oh, was that how it happened?" Lisa asked; she said then, "You might have warned me."

"You expect a great deal of me, it seems to me."

"It was nothing; I just wanted to persuade Philip to let Uncle Michael help us; but then we quarreled, it's probably all over between us. And then that horrible Macomber woman was sneaking around spying; she said bad wicked things; she said she had heard gossip about Keepsake and everything. So then she tried to prevent me from passing her, and the lamp got overturned and that was all there was to it."

Cathy was glad enough to accept this rendition, but Stacey was not. Stacey said sternly, sticking out her lower lip: "You know better than to act like that! Sneaking outside when you're supposed to be in bed and meeting young men, even if it was Doctor Philip. What's Miss Helena going to say?"

Lisa moaned softly: "I know it was wrong, Stacey, but don't scold me now. I hurt; I hurt all over."

"You'd better be mighty thankful that you don't hurt worse than you do. You might have been killed, that's what, or burned so bad that you might never have got over it or look the same."

Lisa forgot everything else: "What do you mean, look the same?"

"Just what I say. I saw a woman once burned so bad that there wasn't anything left of her face but scars all over it and two holes where her eyes used to be."

"Stacey! You're just trying to frighten me."

"It happened to her and it could have happened to you just as well as not," Stacey said.

"But it didn't! I'm not going to have any scars."

"If the Lord wills it, you aren't," Stacey said relentlessly. She knew her Lisa, and she had no intention of letting Lisa's wilfulness go unchastened.

"Stacey! The doctor said I would be all right."

"He said you were fortunate; that could mean anything. Besides, doctors don't know everything; a clear conscience is the best thing."

"Please, Stacey, don't frighten me."

Stacey, settling herself imperturbably in her chair, said, "It wouldn't be anybody's fault but your own if you did wind up with your face so scarred that nobody would be able to look at you. You can't expect to dance to the piper and not pay for the tune."

Lisa turned her face into the pillow. Stacey's old-fashioned shock treatment was having its desired effect: Lisa had no wish to pay the piper for this evening's escapade, which already was beginning to seem as far-off and unreal as a nightmare. She craved nothing on earth now but to be safe, to marry a man who would make her feel protected, who was substantial, unromantic, and a little dominating as one expected French husbands to be dominating.

This business of having emotional demands made on one, of being asked to make decisions, was not only frightening but tiresome. Actually, when one came right down to it this was all Philip's fault: at the thought of her own susceptibility and the price she might have to pay for it a sob of self-pity rose in Lisa's throat.

She whimpered, "If there are any scars I'll kill myself; so I warn you, Stacey."

"I reckon there won't be any scars," Stacey said soothingly, relenting now that she had pointed out to Lisa the error of her ways and brought about a penitent mood. "Not this time."

There wasn't going to be any next time. Lisa knew that. Her brief dance to the piper was over.

Stacey said, "You go along to bed, Miss Cathy. You look worse than Miss Lisa does."

Lisa turned her head, glanced at Cathy, and turned away her face again.

"Goodnight," Cathy said. She felt exhausted and strangely light, as if nothing except air were holding her. She put her hand to her forehead and noticed for the first time that her hands were throbbing. She held them out and looked at them by the light of a near-by wall bracket; they were red and swollen.

Dan Cartwright came out of the shadows toward her and said, "I've been waiting for you." He took her hands and examined them. He insisted that she show him the way to the dispensary and allow him to treat them. There was no need to call Doctor Macomber again, he said: "I noticed you disliked having to use his professional services."

"It wasn't that," Cathy protested.

"I know. You don't want outsiders around when your little cousin makes a fool of herself," Dan said; he was bandaging her hands as skilfully and gently as Philip could have.

She said, "That's not true."

"Which? That Lisa is indiscreet or that you don't want outsiders to witness the fact? The truth of the matter is that I'm not sure you want outsiders around at any time."

He finished the bandaging. Her hands stopped throbbing; they had been paining her for a long time far more than she had realized. She said, "Thank you."

"You're welcome." He was smiling down at her; she could feel him gazing into her and reading her thoughts even though she would not look up. He said, "This isn't the last time you are going to be burned if you continue to pull chestnuts from the fire for the beautiful Lisa."

"How can you think you know so much about us when you have met Lisa only a few times?"

"I watched you at dinner. All evening you let Lisa outshine you. You weren't at all my girl with the diamonds."

"The diamonds were only a sort of gesture."

He laughed heartily, disconcerting her. "You do everything as a sort of something, don't you? Weeping on a shoulder is a sort of way of measuring kindness. Wearing diamonds is a sort of gesture. Would you like to weep on my shoulder now?"

"No, thank you."

"Good. I like my girl with the diamonds better."

"But that wasn't really me. I'm not really like that."

He looked at her intently. "Maybe you don't know yourself." He changed the subject so suddenly that she was startled. He asked, "Are you hungry?"

Now that she thought of it she was, a little. "Yes, are you?"

"Starving."

"I'll call somebody."

"Can't we forage for ourselves?"

He whistled as he moved about the kitchens, examining everything. "This is something like in the way of a kitchen." He explored the great ranges and central brick ovens and fireplaces with spits for turning chickens and hams and whole piglets; he opened and closed the doors of cupboards and ice chests, with the open delight of a little boy turned loose in a toy shop. He said, "I'm a good cook; I've been cooking for myself for some time now." He made her sit down and would not permit her to help him. "In just a few minutes you will witness an omelet that is a masterpiece."

They had finished eating the omelet when he said suddenly, "You are disappointed in me because I sold the Catherine, aren't you?"

Startled, she protested: "Not really. Not because of the name I mean."

"There will be more Catherines, many of them."

She was sure there would be, but somehow she could not take much interest in them.

"I'm beginning to wonder myself now if I should have been in such a hurry. What exactly is going on in Washington?"

"I haven't any idea."

"And you wouldn't say if you did have."

She nodded, agreeing that was true.

"I'm not here to try to get inside information," Dan said. She wished he had not said that; it made him seem more the person her father had warned her against and less the person she wanted him to be. He said, "Rumors are flying thick and fast in Saint Cloud that there's a downslide which may be difficult to stop. There may be a cave-in; I don't like to think of you being caught in it."

He was speaking in mining terms; she understood him. But she had no answer for him; fortunately he did not seem to expect one.

He said, "Personally, I'm betting on your father; that's why I've changed sides. Maybe knowing you had something to do with it, too."

"I wish . . . it hadn't."

"It doesn't obligate you," he said; he was smiling, but not with his eyes. He said, "I'm quite responsible for my actions and you can't make an omelet, as I've just demonstrated, without breaking eggs. But I thought it might make you understand better why I sold the Catherine, after naming her the Catherine."

She stood up. He came to stand beside her, looking down; he was very strong and sure of himself.

She became conscious that she wore only a dressing-gown with nightclothes underneath. She held the dressing-gown high on her neck and said, "I must go to bed now, I think."

He said, his eyes intent on her face, "I'm leaving early in the morning. Wear those diamonds and hold up your head. I'll be back one of these days."

Chapter 25

PHILIP WAS STANDING at a window of the morning-room with his back to the room. He said with obstinate fury, for the twentieth time: "Begin again. I can't understand what could possibly have happened. Nothing anybody says makes sense."

Cathy said, "There was some kind of accident. Nobody knows just how it happened but a lamp was overturned and Lisa's dress caught fire. She was burned but not seriously, she isn't in the least danger. She ate breakfast this morning and she's perfectly all right, Philip, believe me, except for being upset and shaken, of course."

"Then why should this fat fool of a Macomber tell me that she doesn't want to see anybody, including me, and that it's better not to get her excited."

Cathy said, "She was terribly frightened. Doctor Macomber was here in the house and it seemed the best thing to let him take care of her for the time being, at least."

"For the time being! He acts like the family physician; he pats me on the shoulder and tells me I know how it is, old boy, and the important thing is not to excite the patient. Heavens, how could I upset her! Even Stacey lied to me; she came outside the door and said Lisa was asleep. She wasn't asleep; I had just heard her talking, but Stacey looked me right in the eye and said it was better to let her sleep and for me to see her later; tomorrow, perhaps."

Philip swung about, wild-eyed. He said, "What is this, a conspiracy? Has everybody gone crazy? What right does Macomber have to regard Lisa as his patient even if he was here? Lisa can't possibly prefer him to me, can she?"

Cathy said, as she had said several times before: "Sometimes it's easier to have a stranger take care of you, Philip."

"Why, in heavens name?"

"Woman's vanity," she pointed out patiently and wearily. She herself had pleaded with Lisa to see Philip, and she was as much at a loss to account for Lisa's right-about-face as Philip was, but to spare him she made up excuses. She added: "I should think a doctor could understand that."

A little mollified, he went back to his original statement that the whole thing did not make any sense. "How could Lisa's dress have caught on fire?"

"I don't know. She and Mrs. Macomber were in the hall when I heard them and came out of the bedroom. The lamp must just have been overturned, anyhow it was dark and then there was a funny light and Lisa ran down the hall toward me with the flames caught on the bottom of her skirt."

"My God!" Philip said. He went pale; he returned to his position at the window, his back rigid, his hands in his pockets. He asked presently with his voice grown suddenly quiet: "Is it true that Lisa refuses to see me or is that fool of a Macomber just trying to be officious?"

Cathy began again: "She's just frightened and upset and you know how she hates to be seen at a disadvantage. . . ."

Philip swung around. "Try again. The truth, this time."

"She says she doesn't want to see you, Philip."

"Just me? Or not anybody?"

"Philip, she's not herself; she's hysterical. . . ."

"Never mind. Just how badly was she burned?"

"Not very badly. Not seriously at all. There are a few places that are a little painful, but she will be perfectly all right in a few days, Doctor Macomber says."

"Good," Philip said. "Fine. And so she wasn't seriously burned and she's sitting up in bed and she ate breakfast and she can see everybody except me."

"Philip . . ."

"I'm sorry, Cathy," Philip said. He came across the room: "I haven't any right to take my feelings out on you. Only I'll be hanged if I can understand what is going on."

He picked up her bandaged hands and looked at them. He asked, "Are you Macomber's patient too?"

"No. Dan Cartwright did them."

"Is he a doctor?"

"No, Philip, of course he isn't. I don't need a doctor."

"We'll see," he said. He sat down beside her and began to unwrap the bandages. She watched him as he worked; his face was set and mutinous. He looked down at her bare hands; he said, still in an ominously quiet voice: "You did a good job. You probably saved Lisa's life." He went for his kit and spread salve on her hands and bandaged them again. He asked, "Just when did all this happen? What time, I mean?"

"I don't know exactly. Quite late."

"Didn't Mrs. Macomber sleep in the guest wing?"

"Yes."

"Then what in the devil was she doing clear over in your wing upsetting lamps?"

"Mrs. Macomber came to Lisa's room to borrow a sleeping tablet. They were talking and somehow the lamp got overturned...."

Philip, ceasing to listen, had gone back to the window. He was beginning to imagine the scene which had taken place the night before; Mrs. Macomber was all too obviously a malicious gossip who would go to any lengths to ferret out scandal. He had a sinking feeling that Lisa had been in need of his protection and he had not been present to protect her; his troubled doubts as to whether it had been he or Lisa who had led the way, which had come to him in the night with maddening persistency, vanished. He was the one responsible; he said presently, his voice thick, "Cathy. You know, I suppose, that I am in love with Lisa."

"Yes."

"I've got to see her. I've got to see her whether she wants to see me or not; or whether it is ethical for me to insist upon seeing another doctor's patient or not. Believe me, I've got to see her, that's all!"

"Why don't you go upstairs and see her, then?" Cathy asked.

She was suddenly sick of all this nonsense, this shilly-shallying. She was angry too, shockingly, childishly angry, that so much should be demanded of her with no choice given as to whether she was capable or willing to meet the demands. She thought, how dare he tell me that he is in love with Lisa! And there was her father, determined to be invincible, no matter what it cost him, no matter what it cost all of them who would so much rather have had him, the person, rather than the conqueror. And Dan, selling the Catherine, intimating that he had done so to help Michael Brett who would have spurned his help, telling her to hold up her head and wear diamonds and he would come back.

Shorn of all this fuss and feathers the truth was obvious enough; they were all doing what they wanted to do. If Philip wanted to see Lisa so badly all he had to do was to walk upstairs and into her room: "After all, nobody can stop you," Cathy said, dropping each word with the cold precision of its own naked uncompromising weight.

Philip gave her a startled look, and then he dashed out of the room and up the nearest staircase.

He hesitated for a minute outside Lisa's door, his burst of confidence ebbing. He had to know where he stood, however; he opened the door without the ceremony of knocking and walked in.

Lisa was propped up in bed. She was lovely in a satin bed-jacket and with her glorious hair hanging softly about her shoulders. She did not look very ill or at a disadvantage. He came closer to the bed; he said, in as stern a voice as he could summon: "Lisa, what are you up to? Why have you refused to see me?"

She looked up, her eyes veiled. She pulled the jacket higher about her shoulders; said plaintively, "Really, Philip. It's terribly inconsiderate of you to come bursting in this way. The doctor doesn't think I should have excitement; I've had a dreadful shock and I must be very quiet."

He looked helplessly down at her. He saw that for her the events of the night before might not have happened. They had been too much for her and she had simply decided to abandon them.

He said, "Lisa!"

She glanced at him out of the side of her eyes. He had become, suddenly, an enemy who threatened her. She said, "You shouldn't have come here. If your feelings are hurt at the idea of another doctor taking your place I'm very sorry, but Doctor Macomber was here and Cathy called him. I had nothing at all to do with it." She looked down at her hands; she said coldly: "After all, you weren't here."

"Lisa, how could I possibly have known?"

"I'm not blaming you," she said. "I'm only saying that your attitude is rather strange, under the circumstances."

For a second she almost succeeded in making him feel as if he deliberately had run off and abandoned her. Common sense asserted itself; he said, as reasonably as he could: "I am here now, and I'm through with all this hypocrisy. Even you must see that we've got to make our position clear; we can't put off telling them any longer."

"Telling them what?"

"That we love each other and are going to be married."

"That's all changed," Lisa said. "You don't realize . . . please don't make it harder for me than it is, Philip."

"Nothing has changed, darling. I love you more than ever, more than I can tell you. Lisa, don't worry; I'll take care of you, believe me . . ."

She put her head back on the pillows. She said, "I feel terrible, my head aches. I can't discuss this now, Philip; don't ask me."

"Lisa, we've got to discuss it."

She turned her face away from him. She said, "Stacey will be back in a minute. She's angry enough with me as it is. She said it would have served me right if I had been burned so badly that I was covered with scars. My whole life could have been ruined!" She put one hand to her throat; she said, in a shaking voice, "Please, Philip, don't torture me any more. Go away and let me alone."

"I'm not trying to torture you. I'm just trying to make you see that now, of all times, you must let me take care of you."

She had closed her eyes. Now she opened them, blazing: "I don't want you to take care of me. When I think of what could have happened I almost hate you!"

"Good heavens, Lisa, you don't mean that."

"I do. I do. Why do you think I haven't wanted to see you? You nearly ruined my life, that's why. And now you haven't even the good taste and the decency to let me alone."

"I love you."

"I don't want you to love me. And I don't want to love you. What good will that do us? And I'm not free, besides."

"What do you mean, you aren't free?"

"There's somebody . . . in France. Mamma has her heart set on it . . . there's nothing else for me to do, please believe me."

He said, aghast, "But Lisa, you can't possibly . . . Lisa, don't you realize . . . didn't what happened last night mean anything to you?"

He accomplished one thing, he succeeded in jolting her out of her make-believe that nothing had happened the night before which she did not choose to remember. She said in a furious whisper, "How dare you bring that up? You must be crazy!"

"I am nearly crazy. Lisa, I love you."

"Then why are you insulting me? Why are you making it sound as if I must marry you if I want to or not? Why did you come here when you knew that I didn't want to see you?"

He took one of her hands. He made a great effort at self-control. "Lisa, I only want to do what's best for you. Don't be afraid of what happened; don't close yourself away from me. I love you; I'll take care of you."

"You can't. You weren't here to take care of me last night. It was horrible. That awful Mrs. Macomber was waiting for me; she knew exactly what had happened. She threatened to tell everybody; think what that would have meant! Mrs. Ellis would have written Mamma; oh, I've been so foolish. I told you from the beginning that I wasn't strong enough to face unpleasant things; you can't say I didn't warn you. Now we must just forget everything that has happened."

Philip said, "Darling, we love each other. What happened was because of that. There's nothing to be ashamed of. We're going to be married; we can't just forget that."

"Yes, we can. We must. We never would have married, we were just pretending all along, you must have known that. Oh, why must you be so stupid! I don't want to marry you; I want to go home. Why did you come here; why do you force me to say these things? I don't want to hurt you. I did love you, Philip. But can't you see that it's all over; can't you see we've been deceiving ourselves?"

"Lisa, for pity's sake. All I can see is that I love you."

"Then go away and let me alone. We're safe; Mrs. Macomber will be afraid now to say anything here, and that's all that matters."

He tried to believe that this was a momentary hysteria because she had been so badly frightened. He said, "Lisa, stop it. Can't you see that unless you love me and intend to marry me what happened last night was absolute madness?"

She began to cry. She cried genuine tears of pity for herself and for Philip because she saw quite clearly that their love had never been meant to be and it was now at an end. The whole thing had been utter madness. But it had been very beautiful and she would remember it as long as she lived.

When Stacey returned with a bowl of soup for Lisa Philip acceded helplessly to her suggestion that Miss Lisa had better rest a little now, Doctor Philip. Stacey was a wise old woman: "I've got to get her safe back to her Mamma," Stacey said. "Otherwise heaven knows what piece of foolishness she'll be committing next."

"Yes, I know, Stacey, I'm going," Philip said. He glanced at Lisa but her lowered eyes refused to meet his. He said, "Goodbye, then," and waited in vain for some sign of weakening in her. But she did not look up, though one hand picked nervously at the coverlet over her.

He dashed downstairs, ordered his horse and rode home. In the little clapboard house on the outskirts of Magoon he walked from room to room, taking in all its bareness and ugliness with a relentless urge to rub salt on his wounds.

He went to the pump in the kitchen and drank glass after glass of water. Then he put his head under the pump and pumped water on it. He had never known so terrific a desire for water.

For days that thirst followed him. When he dreamed at night he dreamed of shining pools, of mountain streams crystal-clear. Otherwise he went about his business, sane, normal, rigidly and determinedly sane and normal.

He did not go near Keepsake. He began to make plans for getting away from his present environment, now grown untenable. The army needed doctors; he heard everywhere of the need for doctors to care for the malaria and yellow fever rampant among the force of men sent to attack Santiago.

He could not leave until he was sure Lisa would not need him. For several weeks he held himself in readiness to answer a summons from her which never came.

Cathy came to see him. She drove in one day with the mail wagon; she asked no questions as to why he was, in effect, hiding himself away. He blurted out without warning his intention to leave, temporarily at least; he could turn over his practice to Doctor Macomber and a Doctor Blake recently arrived in the valley. He was no longer essential here and he needed to get away, to keep up with medical progress. He grew excited just talking about it, pacing up and down, pouring out suddenly all his hunger to lose himself as an individual in a crowded hospital or army camp. He wanted to be surrounded by people, stimulated by contacts with minds engrossed in the same work that he was. He broke off to say, "The worst of it is I'm deserting you. Randy doesn't need me; his care now is more or less circumscribed and Doctor Blake is a good man. But what about you?"

"Why me?"

When he did not answer immediately she asked, "Because of Father?"

"I haven't a doubt in the world that Michael will come out on top, and you mustn't either. I haven't followed the legal ins and outs; I've deliberately not followed them." Cathy thought he glanced toward the drawer where his father's picture had been but that might have been her imagination. Philip said, "None of this will affect you and Randy; Michael told me that. I'm glad you are out here, safely out of it all." It was hard to know how one could be safe anywhere when one's world was crumbling, or crumbled, but it was easy to smile and agree.

"It will all be over soon. I'll keep an eye on things wherever I am. Would you rather I waited until Michael comes back?"

"You'll write to me. And send for me if you need me," Philip stated rather than asked. He needed reassurance; he looked at her and she said, "Yes, of course, Philip. I'm glad you are going; you should go, and you'll be back."

"Yes, I'll be back. Don't worry about Randy's health; he has outgrown a great deal of his trouble. Don't worry about Michael's health either; he's strong as an ox, really." He did not meet her eyes.

"I know. There's no need to go into all this, Philip."

"Well . . ."

On the day he was to go he asked her to marry him. He was leaving for Montauk Point, Long Island, where there was a big government hospital. He wrote the address for her; he said abruptly, while she was storing the address carefully away: "Would you go with me? Marry me?"

"No, thank you, Philip."

"Don't thank me," he said; he laughed so that she could laugh too.

When they parted that afternoon he kissed her. He kissed her cheek and then when she turned her lips he put his mouth against hers, very tenderly.

He said, "Cathy . . ."

"I know. It's all right. Goodbye, Philip."

Chapter 26

It was in the newspapers that Cathy first learned that the United Mine Industries, one of Michael Brett's largest organizations, and many of its subsidiary companies had failed, and that Michael Brett had declared himself bankrupt and gone into receivership.

Cathy read each account, word by word and then folded each newspaper and put it away. There was no one to ask just what the words might mean to her father, or to the rest of them. The word bankruptcy struck terror to her heart because it was the word which had caused Philip's father to seek the solution which once had seemed to her so romantic. She rode all day that day, by herself; she returned home reassured that her father would not seek that solution, that he would face the music. And as if he were seconding this particular belief in him, or need to believe in him, she received a note from him the following day telling her that a ship need not founder because it had lost its captain, and Keepsake was the ship and she was the new captain, and that presently he would return.

Thereafter she faced the day's news reports with far greater courage. Her own name, astoundingly, began to appear in the newspapers, hints that all Michael Brett's fortune had not been lost, that part of it had been saved by the procedure of having it transferred to his daughter, Catherine Brett.

On July 14, 1898, Santiago capitulated, and Michael Brett was cited for contempt of court for ignoring the injunction placed against him by a Federal Court.

He appealed to the Supreme Court, and so began one of the most famous judicial dramas which the country had vicariously enjoyed for a long time; though those most concerned, the residents of Keepsake, could not have been said to enjoy it.

To offset these troublous times, a phrase which came to Cathy's mind from somewhere and stuck there, there were frequent and encouraging letters from Philip. As an adjunct to his hospital work he was being given an opportunity to work in the laboratory where they were testing serums and cultures whose possibilities only recently had been brought to light by the war. It was an exciting research after his long years of routine practice.

Philip was dragging himself out of the deep sense of personal failure which had haunted him so long, by hours and hours of this work. And ironically, a small measure of success came to him now that he no longer needed it so badly. He had written a number of articles on his findings with certain experiments with cultures plus a discovery of his own in the prevention of gangrene in limbs crushed in mining accidents. He received letters of congratulation and several offers for openings in large hospitals.

Cathy responded to the news of this modest but welcome success so excitedly that Philip's letters began to display a mounting excitement too. He forgot reticence and modesty, describing in longer and longer letters just what he was doing, confident of her sympathy, if not her understanding. But she displayed surprising knowledge of what he was saying; he was unaware of the hours she spent poring over books supplied by Randy. Randy was her greatest source of information; he patiently went over and over with her each scientific step in the findings which had received recognition. Randy too was excited; he and Cathy together studied intently the articles which Philip sent to them. They formed a strange little three-way group; they seemed to be clinging to each other's hands; by unspoken agreement they excluded everything from the letters except these detached safe scientific explorations.

To Cathy this contact with Philip was at once a delight and a despair. His letters gave her hope where she had been sure there was no hope. They destroyed the calm which she so carefully had created for herself.

She had not dared let herself think of what had happened between Lisa and Philip that night, but she knew from the tight-lipped misery on Philip's face and the flashes of panic in Lisa's eyes that it had been devastating to them both. Because of it Lisa had sent Philip away; she never spoke of him and she refused to read his letters; he might never have existed so far as Lisa was concerned. Lisa's whole being was concentrated on getting back to Paris and her future marriage as fast as she could go. She was fretful of the delay, caused by her father's continued illness and somewhat mysterious suggestions from Aunt Helena that it would be better to wait until affairs in America were "cleared up"; nervous, irritable in a way Lisa had never been before.

What losing her would mean to Philip, Cathy had no way of knowing. Eventually Cathy forced herself to face what must have happened between Philip and Lisa to have frightened Lisa so terribly. Facing it was like deliberately thrusting a knife into her own heart; she well knew that such a thing could not have happened lightly so far as Philip was concerned.

But once Cathy had faced the terrific onslaught which the truth made upon her she felt relieved. She thought: it could have happened to me. She thought: it did happen to me, in my mind, the night I met Dan.

She thought: it's only because I've loved Philip so much that I've known what love should be.

And she thought: I'll be waiting for Philip, all my life, if he should ever decide to want me.

She had to tell that to Dan. Dan rode up to the house one afternoon after several months' absence. He was unshaven; he looked tired and unlike himself.

He said, "I've come to take you away from all this."

"Away from what?"

"We can start over. I love you, Cathy, diamonds or no diamonds."

"I still have the diamonds."

"You probably won't have much longer. Cathy it's foolish not to face facts; we've all been duped. You, too. When I think of how flattered I was at the idea of trading the Catherine for company stock I could kill myself. I deserve losing her, but I don't want to lose you too."

"I don't understand."

"Don't you? Stock in the United Mine Industries is so much paper, that's all. He must have been laughing like anything when I couldn't wait to show what a brilliant businessman I was."

"My father? I'm sure he wasn't."

Dan became calmer; he said, "No, I suppose he thought he was strong enough to work miracles right up to the end. He gambled

246

and lost; the worst of it is that so many innocent people lost at the same time."

Cathy said, "Weren't they gambling for him to make them rich?"

Dan turned; he asked, "You, too?"

"It doesn't seem fair to me for everyone to turn on him now."

"Turn on him! They've lost everything; where can they turn? You should see Saint Cloud now; it's like a ghost town. It may be a ghost town before long."

"Maybe not. The country is still the same; you said yourself there would be plenty more Catherines. Somebody else will have to take his place, that's all."

"Who?"

"One man can't be responsible for everything. Too many people depended on him, waited for him to do the things for them they should have done for themselves."

"Like me?"

"All of us. All of us."

"Apart from all this, Cathy, do you love me?"

"I . . . I . . . no."

"Did you ever love me?"

"No."

"Someone else?"

"Yes."

Dan simply looked at her.

It was an autumn of violent storms. The war with Spain was over: hostilities had been suspended August twelfth pending peace negotiations in Paris not later than October. The world was at peace, but now suddenly nature itself seemed to be in revolt against the violence of man.

The case in Washington, so remote and still affecting them all so much, dragged on and on. It began to seem as if it always had existed and always would exist.

Men came to Keepsake, messengers from Cathy's father with papers for her to sign, during that fall and winter. Cathy signed whatever was given her to sign: she wrote her name, Catherine Theresa Brett, hundreds and hundreds of times.

Other people came to the house, men and their wives and families from Saint Cloud who had lost positions and homes. Cathy saw all of them; to some who asked for it she gave money until the cash reserve in the safe became low and she had no idea how to go about replenishing it. Mr. Barnes would have known but Mr. Barnes, disapproving of this kind of trouble, had taken his family and moved away. The lawyers who came and went doubtless knew, but they were too engrossed in important affairs to be bothered. Cathy's father would see to it; in the meantime there was nothing in the safe which really belonged to Cathy except the boxes of jewelry. She offered a piece of that to an angry supplicant one day in desperation, diffidently, remembering how she once had tried to give it to Lisa and been told that she couldn't. A pearl necklace, it was true, was a cold substitute for a home and for the cheerful feeling of belonging somewhere; still, it was all she had. She need not have worried about having her offering spurned; she felt a little sick after the first session. Eyes had fastened on the jewels, hands had grasped after them avidly; both had been concerned only for their value and not at all for their beauty. The second time it was easier to bring out one of the boxes. Cathy dipped into them again and again; they were her reserve in a way, at this time, her strength.

In a way they had all become strangers, living separate lives under one roof.

Mrs. Ellis lived in some faraway past. She sat and knitted, hour after hour, as if by keeping her hands busy she would stave off whatever trouble threatened them from the outside world. She ignored the newspapers, though Cathy suspected that she forced herself to keep abreast of events, pleasant or otherwise, by studying them in private.

When they met at mealtimes Mrs. Ellis was the only one who ate as if she knew what she were eating. She would taste a dish, give a definite nod of approval, then proceed to savor it.

Lisa, who always had been so greedy, now had to be coaxed to eat. She crumbled her bread and burst into tears if there had been no letter for her in the morning's mail. Or, if there had been, she was too excited to eat. She either chattered interminably, outlining in detail her plans for the future, or was tragically silent. Between times she tried her hair in new ways, changed her clothes seven or eight times a day, or merely lay, doing absolutely nothing, on her chaise longue. She could lie for hours, completely motionless. Or else she was in a frenzy of activity, demanding something exciting, demanding to know why life was being permitted to pass over her in this manner. "I'll be old soon; I haven't even begun to live. When is this going to end; I think I am going crazy!"

Cathy herself felt as if she were living in a suspension of time. Except for the interlude when she was forced to face people coming to the house either with papers or accusations she was able to close herself away, neither happy nor unhappy, neither restless nor quiet. But she knew this period would not last; they were all moving, slowly but inexorably, toward some climax.

Randy never had cared what he was eating except for the observance of religious fast days. Cathy noticed one day that he was observing these days more frequently and he ate sparingly whatever the day.

She spoke to him of it, hesitantly, one morning when he and she were in the old schoolroom. She was modeling a clay head and he was working in the laboratory.

She was not sure if Randy read the newspapers or if he had any realization of the trouble hovering over them. He never spoke of it, and she hoped he was too absorbed in his scholarly world to know anything about it.

She asked, "Randy, are you eating enough?"

He gave her a quick startled look and a boyish embarrassed color mottled his thin skin. He looked far too frail for his big awkward body and he had a patient resigned look which twisted her heart.

He said, "I think so. Why do you ask?"

She said, "I've noticed . . . it seems to me you are almost too strict. I mean, in your case, when you aren't very strong, aren't there exceptions? I could ask Father Gonzáles about it if you would let me."

"Father Gonzáles hasn't imposed restrictions on me."

"Then you aren't fasting?"

"Yes," he said. "In a way, I'm fasting." He sat down. He stared at his hands; they were big hands now, very white, very clean. It occurred to her that they had never been dirty as a boy's hands were supposed to be dirty. He said, "It's hard to explain to you when you aren't religious, that is when you aren't religious in the sense of belonging to the Church. We fast, you know, when we make special prayers or need special guidance."

"Do you need special guidance?"

"Yes. I'm trying to come to a decision."

She waited and presently he looked up and smiled his singularly sweet smile. "It worries me for fear it may be a selfish decision," he said.

"What is it?"

She knew suddenly, without being told, what it was. She rebelled against it; with all her will she rebelled against it.

He said, "I would like to join a religious order."

"Be a priest, do you mean?"

"Something like that; wherever I can be fitted in."

"Oh Randy!" she said. She almost said, And leave me alone? Haven't I lost enough?

"The only thing that troubles me is leaving you. But in the long run it will leave you more free; you've given up so much for me, too much." When she tried to protest he continued, "But that has nothing to do with my wanting to go. It's because here, I'm nothing, I can't be of service to anybody . . . no, Cathy, let me say it. In a religious order I could be useful, I could feel as if my life had some meaning."

She looked at him in bewilderment. He had seemed so contented in his quiet secluded little world, but now his face was flushed with earnestness and his eyes were shining. He looked very young to possess so much inner resolution.

She asked, more quietly now: "But, Randy, how can you possibly *know?*"

"It's hard to explain." He turned the problem around, studying it; she could have laughed at this typical Randy way of approaching a question except that she was close to tears. He said then, simply and directly, that you knew because all the little pieces of your life which you had been collecting suddenly came together and had meaning.

Her tense nerves became quiet. "If you feel that way of course you must go. Does Father Gonzáles encourage it?"

"Yes. He thinks I may have a vocation, but of course I'll have a number of years first to make sure."

"But are you strong enough?"

"Oh yes, that will be taken into consideration, and when the time comes I won't be allowed to enter any work that I'm not strong enough to do well."

He spoke so matter-of-factly that it seemed as if the coming separation already had taken place. She said, longingly, "I wonder if I'll ever feel that way about anything."

"I'm sure you will."

"It seems so strange for you to be really religious while I have no religion at all."

"You'll find religion of some kind presently."

"Must everyone?"

"It seems to me that to be at peace with oneself one must. But I'm not very orthodox in that sense; it seems to me that religion can take different forms in different people. Perhaps with you, like Abou Ben Adhem, it may come in loving your fellow men."

She saw that he wanted to make her laugh and she tried to smile. "Will I be allowed to visit you?"

"Of course. I'll be in school for several years and I don't hope to enter a strict order; I would like to teach or something like that."

"You won't have to go right away, will you?"

He was silent for a minute and then he said, "Yes. Both Father Gonzáles and I think that if I go it will be best for me to go right away. There's a Franciscan school in California that will take me; that isn't so far away. But it's up to you, Cathy. If you need me I'm not to go; Father Gonzáles himself has said that."

There was a lump in her throat. She bent down and kissed him, rumpling his hair. She said, "I'm very proud of you, and of course you must go."

He left two mornings later, seated beside Father Gonzáles in the priest's high little gig. Father Gonzáles was a frail saintly man; his presence upheld Cathy during the ordeal of parting.

Chapter 27

THE WIND ROSE to new heights of violence. Even through the thick walls of the house they could hear the trees creaking, bending, twisting under the onslaught. The room was flooded with an eerie light.

"Oh mercy," Lisa said. She was standing at Cathy's bedroom window, her back to the room. She said softly and monotonously, over and over, "Oh mercy. Oh mercy."

"Don't, Lisa."

Lisa turned and picked up a coffee cup from the breakfast tray. She was in a white satin dressing-robe, her hair hung loosely about her shoulders. She had brought her tray to Cathy's room for companionship, but since she had entered the room she had stood with her back to it as if she were alone.

The voice of the wind rose to a frenzy. It shrieked, died away, swooped down upon them like an enemy trying to find an entrance into their stronghold. Lisa's hand shook suddenly; her cup clattered against the saucer.

She said, "I'm frightened."

"What is there to be frightened about?"

"How do I know? Something is happening. Cathy! We're so alone here."

"With thirty people on the place?"

"You're so literal and stolid. Actually, we are alone."

"Very well. We're alone."

"All those terrible things that are being printed about Uncle Michael in the newspapers. And why doesn't Mamma send for me? Aren't you concerned, at all?"

"Yes," Cathy said. "I'm a little concerned."

"But you have to be cold and superior and pretend to rise above everything. What is going to happen to all of us?"

"I don't know."

"Oh Cathy!" Lisa said. "You're impossible!"

"Drink your coffee. You'll feel better."

"You're so infernally noble," Lisa said. "Sometimes I wonder why I don't hate you."

"What do you want me to do? Scream? Have hysterics? Don't you suppose that I'm frightened too?"

Lisa pressed her face against the streaming glass, peering into the gloom. She said, "Somebody just ran across the terrace."

"That isn't unusual."

"It wasn't anybody from here. It was a stranger. A man in a long overcoat."

"I'll see him, whoever it is."

"Somebody begging money, probably. What possessed you to start dealing out jewels like so much paper; naturally they all think they can come here now and get something."

"They can't, now," Cathy said. "They're all gone."

"Gone! Your mother's jewels?"

"Or mine. However you like to put it."

"What madness!" Lisa said. She looked out the window again. "I suppose they'll come to rob us now. Or murder us."

"I hardly think so."

"You've gone mad, in my opinion. The whole world has gone mad. I will too, if I don't get out of here." The wind swooped and pounced; Lisa's teeth chattered; she exclaimed, "*Mon dieu, quel pays!*"

"You sound like that French governess we used to have. The one with the big teeth and false front that didn't match the rest of her hair; don't you remember? It seems like a long time ago, doesn't it?"

"Yes, it does," Lisa said. She poured herself a cup of cold coffee and drank it.

"You've never been here in early spring before," Cathy said. "We often have bad storms in the spring."

"It isn't just the storm. There's something else; can't you feel it? What is all this that is happening? If Uncle Michael is in trouble we will all be in trouble. How is it possible for him to be in trouble? He is so rich and powerful; even in France his name is like magic. Why does he allow himself to be attacked in this way?"

"I don't imagine he is enjoying it any more than you are," Cathy said. She added, in a dry flat voice, "You might spare a little of your concern for him."

"Do you imagine that I do not? I'm not as selfish as you seem to believe. It's only because I'm frightened that I think about myself. Mamma doesn't send for me although I've written asking her to let me come home, even begging her—it's because of money arrangements for a dot, I think, that have to be made. Don't be angry, Cathy, I can't help it. And Francis is frightened too by all this publicity—he shows it in his letters. His family is very strict, very proper; they will absolutely wither at the first hint of scandal."

"Then they must have withered long ago," Cathy said.

Lisa gave her a furious glance; her face crumpled and she began to cry.

"I'm sorry," Cathy said. "I really am sorry. Only I haven't the slightest idea of what to do to help you, or my father either."

The room became very still. Even the wind outside paused for a moment, gathering itself for a new attack. The silence was like a weight, pressing upon them with a terrible foreboding.

Lisa said, "All my life I've looked up to Uncle Michael—far more than to Papa. Papa is so insignificant. It must have hurt his feelings because we never really paid any attention to him. It was Uncle Michael who gave us money for nice clothes and trips and even an allowance to Mamma so that she could be as extravagant as she liked. Papa didn't object to Mamma's taking the money but he used to object to her being so extravagant. I used to think that Mamma loved Uncle Michael far more than she did Papa, just as I did."

"Be quiet," Cathy said.

"Why? What difference does it make? You have such a childish conception of love. You have to idealize someone in order to love them."

"No," Cathy said. "I don't. Not any more."

Lisa turned back to the window. She leaned her forehead against one arm which rested against the glass. She had an uncanny ability for exposing weaknesses which one had believed carefully hidden. Having no reticence herself, Lisa assumed that nobody else had any either.

"I wish something would happen," Lisa said. "Anything would be better than this waiting."

"Don't say that, Lisa!"

Lisa half turned. There was real fear on her face now. "You

don't really think that anything terrible could happen to Uncle Michael, do you?"

"I don't know."

"It couldn't," Lisa said. "It's impossible!" She went over to Cathy's dressing-table and began to put cream on her face. She was like Aunt Helena in that way, Cathy thought, in going to her dressing-table whenever she wanted to push away disagreeable thoughts.

Watching Lisa put cream on her face and wipe it away and bend forward to inspect the radiant skin underneath, Cathy was swept back to her childhood.

Her father had once seemed so strong and so wise. And now, when she knew that he was not strong or wise, she saw that he might have been so, that the seeds of these virtues had been in him, but that he had allowed them to be destroyed.

Lisa opened a drawer and took out the little music box tucked away in a corner. She stared at it curiously. "Have you kept this all this time?"

"As you see, by opening my private drawers."

"But why?"

"Because I wanted it, I suppose."

Lisa tried to wind it. She opened the lid; it would not play. She said, "It isn't any good. It's broken."

"You broke it, remember?"

"It's like everything else, it's broken," Lisa said. She sat very still, looking down at the box in her hand. She said, "I wish I hadn't broken it. It must have brought me bad luck."

"It's only a toy."

"Let's go downstairs," Lisa said. "I feel as if I were going crazy up here."

She crammed the box back into the drawer out of sight. "Please, Cathy. Let's go down."

She gave a nervous shriek when there was a tap on the door.

Sam stood in the hall; he was smiling widely. He said, "Doctor Philip is downstairs. Doctor Philip is home."

"I knew I saw somebody," Lisa said. She whirled on Cathy: "Did you know he was coming?"

"No," Cathy said. At Sam's words she had taken several joyful steps forward, hesitated, and now stood still.

"He's changed into dry clothes. He's waiting in the blue parlor," Sam said. He looked from Cathy to Lisa and back. He said, "I'm mighty glad to see him, mighty glad. Somebody should hurry down to make him welcome."

He closed the door.

Lisa said, "I can't see him, Cathy! I can't. Don't ask me."

"I shan't ask you," Cathy said.

Lisa said suddenly, "Maybe he wants to see you, and that's why he's come back. I've always thought Philip cared for you far more than he had any idea. Maybe he'll turn to you now; I'm almost sure he will if you give him the slightest hint of the way you feel about him."

Cathy said, "You've given me a great many things when you were through with them, but you can't give me Philip. Philip will have to do that for himself."

Another time she might have laughed at the dumbfounded expression on Lisa's face.

It wasn't after all much of a victory, Cathy thought, as she walked, instead of running, down the stairs and through the house to meet Philip. Lisa and Cathy, Lisa and Philip, Philip and Cathy: they were all too mixed up now to know what any of their lives would have been without the others.

At the door of the blue parlor she paused, her heart in her throat. Philip did not hear her; he was packing his pipe, his face in the light of the match-flame set and aloof. She had expected somehow that she would find, at the last minute, courage to run forward, to pour out her love for him in one breathless torrent, to tell him that she would be satisfied if he could love her a little bit, only a little bit.

But a paralyzing restraint crept over her. When finally she forced herself to speak it was in a high unnatural voice: "Philip, is it really you? I feel as if I were dreaming. You must have been soaked to the skin; did Sam look after you? Have you everything you need?"

He looked up swiftly, his face eager, and then the eagerness faded. She saw it fade and felt sick, not knowing that he had hoped for a different greeting and that her strangeness infected him. She wondered, almost stupidly, why she had assumed that Philip would necessarily turn to her after losing Lisa. She always underestimated Lisa, refusing to see, because she did not wish to see, that Lisa was more than merely beautiful.

Always, in her heart, Cathy had believed herself superior to Lisa. She had stored away inside herself everything derogatory anybody said about Lisa: Lisa will be fat one of these days. Lisa is selfish. Lisa is careless; Lisa is lazy.

Never, Lisa is truly beautiful. Never, Lisa is joyous and gay and romantic, exactly as Cathy would wish to be if she could.

"Yes, thank you," Philip said. "I have everything I need."

Cathy's face felt pulled into a wide stretched smile. She could not seem to stop smiling. "Did you write us? Were we supposed to know you were coming? It doesn't seem like a very gala homecoming."

She looked about her vaguely. She was not sure what she was looking for but presently she crossed the room and pulled the bellcord. "Sam will bring us coffee. Or brandy. Would you like something to eat? Have you had breakfast?"

"Long ago. It's nearly lunchtime."

"Oh. So it must be."

"I'll have coffee." Philip was staring down at his pipe again, as if he sensed her awkwardness and was sorry for her.

"When did you come? Are you home now to stay?"

"On the morning train. It depends . . . I'm not sure."

"Oh yes, I see," she said. She had not the slightest idea what she saw but it was the easiest thing to say. Sam placed the tray with the coffee urn and cups and saucers on a table before her; he fussed about the room before leaving it, adjusting this and that, delighted that Philip was home. Sam knew her secret, if anything could be called a secret which everyone appeared to know except Philip. She saw that Sam was trying to bring about, by sheer force of will, the happy denouement which to him must seem so simple and inevitable. He did not trust Cathy to bring it about; he kept looking at her over his shoulder, wishing, probably, that she would perk up. She could imagine his scolding: that isn't the way to get a man, looking so droopy and wet-feathered. You have to flash and sparkle, like Miss Theresa, like Miss Helena, like Miss Lisa.

She had to smile, because Sam's wistful anxiety was so ridiculous under the circumstances. For the first time she felt relaxed and natural. She said, "It's good to see you, Philip."

"It's good to be here."

They were both lying, she thought, but it was better, sometimes, to lie.

He said, "I heard about Randy; he wrote me a long letter. Are you alone now?"

"No. Lisa and Mrs. Ellis are still here."

"Oh." His painful embarrassment told her that if he had known that he would not have come. "I hadn't thought of that. I worried about you, thinking you were here by yourself."

"You needn't have worried."

"I suppose not." Silence fell between them. Philip broke it; he said with an effort, "Well, now that I am here let me look at you." He studied her, as he once might have studied her long ago, his hands against her shoulders; he said, "I'm not so sure somebody shouldn't worry about you; you haven't any color, and you're all eyes."

"This weather keeps me indoors."

Silence fell between them again. Once the state of her health had been established there seemed to be nothing more to say.

Philip's hands dropped from her shoulders. He began repacking his pipe. He said presently, as if he were speaking of the weather: "We've all failed you, haven't we?"

"No. Don't think that."

"You look tired to death. Tired to death of all this foolish hurtful behavior."

"I haven't slept very well. You can understand that."

"Yes, I can understand that."

Her soft dark hair was drawn to the top of her head and held in place with combs; the short hairs still escaped in close little curls. She looked very young and lovely, and very sad and weary.

She said, "Everything seems so much better now that you are here."

"Does it? I can't imagine why."

She looked at him directly now, her eyes wide and dark. "Will they put Father in prison? Is that why you've come back?"

"Of course they won't."

"The newspapers said that in one court he had been sentenced for contempt of court and that the penalty for that was six months in prison."

"You shouldn't read them."

"Oh, Philip."

Philip said, "He only had to appeal to a higher court, that was all."

"But now he is in the highest court?"

"The very highest."

"What if the verdict is the same?"

He started to say, "Cathy, don't torture yourself." He took a deep breath and said, "Michael will find a way out, don't worry."

"But what if he doesn't? What if he can't?"

"Don't let yourself think such a thing."

"I must. And the papers say there are other charges against him now, waiting to be brought, charges of bribery and embezzlement." The very words were ugly; they fell like stones; Cathy never had spoken them before.

"Cathy, you can't judge men like Michael by ordinary standards."

She said, "I'm not judging him. Did you think I was? But I can't go on pretending that things can't happen to him that happen to other people. Something has happened to him!"

"It isn't all over. He's still fighting."

"I know," Cathy said. "But now he's in the highest court; there isn't anywhere else to go. That's the thing that tortures me. Philip, he'll never submit to being treated like anyone else if this verdict should go against him. Something terrible will happen to him, I know that it will."

He tried to reassure her, knowing full well his reassurances were useless: "Michael knows what he is doing, never fear."

"Oh no," Cathy said. "Don't you see? He doesn't know what he's doing; he hasn't known for a long time now. That's why I'm so afraid for him. He's destroying himself. I've watched him; he thinks, just as you said, that he should be spared the things that happen to ordinary people. Tragedy and sorrow and unhappiness and disappointment; he hasn't been able to face those. I understand how he feels because I've been the same way. I haven't really cared whether he was right or wrong. I thought he never could do anything really wrong; I thought, you can't judge men like my father by ordinary standards."

She was trembling. Philip said, "And neither can you."

"Yes, you can," she said. "You must. He is being judged right now by ordinary standards. And I don't know what is going to happen to him."

"Cathy."

"I'm sorry. I've been needing to talk to somebody but I didn't mean to unburden myself on you."

"Cathy."

"And we haven't even talked about you."

He was feeling sorry for her and no wonder, she thought; when he would have come closer she moved away.

Mrs. Ellis joined them at lunch and to Philip's consternation Lisa also appeared. Philip experienced several bad moments, though

Lisa greeted him with a casual friendliness which he could only admire.

He tried to match her casual attitude, but he dropped his napkin and nearly overturned his water glass like a schoolboy. His awkwardness had its merits; it set everybody to talking furiously. Also the scene convinced him that Lisa had no claim to make upon him, that she wanted nothing more than to get the whole dismal affair behind her and forgotten as quickly as possible.

After lunch they all sat together in the blue parlor. Mrs. Ellis was knitting. Lisa stood at the window looking for the mail wagon which was delayed because of the storm.

Cathy poured coffee. Nobody wanted coffee but everybody took some. The storm outside bathed them all in a strange light. Each pause was hurried into; two persons spoke at the same time, apologized, and spoke again.

Mrs. Ellis presently folded her knitting and went for her afternoon nap. Lisa yawned, picked up a magazine and put it down, yawned again. The room began to seem very close and warm.

The mail wagon was heard to arrive and Lisa sprang to life. She hurried out of the room without making any excuse for her departure, down the corridor toward the office where the mail was sorted.

Philip said, "Well, as you can see, that romance is quite dead and buried."

Cathy's eyes were fixed on his face.

He said, "I suppose this is neither the time nor the place, but I've got to tell you that I discovered after I went away that I love you. I've always loved you; you've been there all the time deep inside of me, but of course I didn't have enough sense to know it. You've been too close; I didn't realize how close; as close as the beating of my heart."

She did not answer. She sat quietly, staring at him. He had not dreamed that she could be so unapproachable. She had been so receptive, always, so ready to meet his moods whatever they were.

He said, "It's too late now; isn't it?"

"Too late for what?"

"For you to love me."

"I've always loved you," she said. "As long as I can remember. I think I shall always love you."

He dropped down beside her and put his arms around her. She was as still and rigid as one of her little statues. He leaned his face against her. He said, "Cathy, dearest Cathy. My little love. I've been so blind; please forgive me."

"There's nothing to forgive," she said. She tried to feel something but she could not. She told herself that Philip loved her, that he was saying the things she had hungered for long to hear, but it didn't mean anything.

He took his arms away. He stood up and walked across the room and stood with his back to her. He asked, "What is it? If you love me, what is it that's still between us? Is it Lisa?"

"No."

"Because you must see for yourself that Lisa means nothing to me and I mean nothing to Lisa. I've hurt you; I've been a fool, I know. Be angry with me, be anything, only don't just sit there as if you were turned to stone. I can't bear that, believe me, I can't."

She stood up. She might have been weighted with lead except that her knees seemed to have turned to straw.

She said, "I don't know. I don't know what's the matter with me; maybe I'm not used to happiness. I thought you still cared for Lisa; you can't expect me not to find it something of a shock to tell me suddenly, after all these years, that you love me. I was going to tell you that I love you so much that if you could love me just a little bit it would be enough, but then I realized that it wouldn't be enough. So I don't know now what to say or do because I don't know yet what you mean by love. And it may be that I'll have to get used to the idea gradually, because right now I don't seem to feel anything, anything at all. And I am tired, you were right, very very tired."

Far off, down the corridor, there came the thin sound of a scream. It was Lisa screaming; she must be running toward them because the screams became louder. She was screaming words as she ran: "Cathy! Cathy! Something terrible has happened; a man just came from Saint Cloud to tell us."

She stood in the doorway; her words were barely intelligible because she had a hand pressed against her open mouth. She said, "They've taken Uncle Michael to prison; he has had a stroke; he's dying."

Her high voice of fear continued: "He got away from them, the man said; he escaped. They're looking for him; nobody knows where he is. They'll come here to look for him, the man said; we'll all be arrested."

"He's ill?"

"Yes, yes, dying, they thought, but he got away. Oh what shall we do?"

"But he got away."

"But they're looking for him, I tell you; everywhere. When they find him they'll put him in prison."

Philip jerked around and leaped forward just in time to catch Cathy as she pitched forward into his arms.

Chapter 28

WHEN SHE AWOKE the next morning she had no idea how long she had been asleep. She remembered that Philip had given her the pills which he said were to make her sleep, and that she had taken the pills, and that he had sat beside her and held her hand and smiled down at her and she had tried to smile back, and that she had wished, just before she had sunk down and down into unconsciousness, that she need never wake up again.

But now she was awake. She turned her head on her pillow and stared blankly at the wall.

The memory of the afternoon's events flooded over her. There had been Philip, telling her the unbelievable words that he loved her, and then there had been Lisa's screams and the words which announced the final disaster which had been hanging over them for so long. She, Cathy, had fainted. When she came to it was to a scene of confusion: she was lying on a couch with Philip beside her. Lisa, in a chair, was moaning now; Mrs. Ellis, her hair in the kid curlers which accompanied her afternoon nap, was remonstrating with Lisa. Sam and Hester and Rachel and Stacey were lined against the wall, their good kind faces stricken and anxious.

Cathy had said, "I'm all right now." She sat up; it was, more than anything, Sam's and Stacey's faces turned toward her that made her capable of so much effort. She said, "I'm all right, really, Philip."

Mrs. Ellis said, "It isn't as bad as it seems, I'm sure."

The messenger from Saint Cloud was brought to the room, over Philip's protest. He told the story more quietly, without Lisa's hysteria, but it was the same story. The Supreme Court had upheld the decision of the lower courts: Michael Brett had been convicted of contempt of court and sentenced to six months in prison.

The federal marshal and his men, reluctantly carrying this news to the hotel where Michael, out on bail, was awaiting the verdict, found their important prisoner gone. Michael had suffered a severe heart attack, it was learned, only a few minutes earlier, and a public ambulance had been called for him. He had been carried to the ambulance and from then on he had simply vanished. Neither his secretary nor doctor nor even the ambulance interne, through some negligence believed calculated, had ridden beside him. It was believed now that Michael himself had managed this series of coincidences, though it was testified by any number of people that he had been unconscious, believed dying, when he had been taken away. The messenger from Saint Cloud grew a little graphic at this point; he himself was awed by the momentous turn of events and his own position as bearer of news of them. "For heaven's sake, skip all that," Philip commanded, but Cathy said, "No, please, Philip, I want to hear it all."

Whatever had happened—whether bribery or incredible carelessness had brought about the opportunity for Michael's escape— the indisputable fact was that the ambulance had arrived without him and that though everybody was looking for him he still was not to be found.

Word had been received at Saint Cloud first because there was a direct wire service there. "So I thought maybe I should ride over and break it a little gently," the telegraph operator from Saint Cloud said; he glanced at Lisa and swallowed; he said, "I guess it wasn't so gently, the way it turned out."

"It was very kind of you."

"I want to say too that I hope they don't ever find him. There are still plenty of us who are willing to help him if he gets out here."

"Thank you."

When the man had gone Cathy turned a wild look of hope toward Philip. "Could he . . . do you think it's possible . . . ?"

"I don't know, Cathy; I just don't know." But she could see from his face that he believed it hopeless.

She lay back on the cushions of the couch and closed her eyes. And when Philip bending over her, had urged her to take the pills which would make her sleep, she had taken them.

But now she was awake. She was awake and rested and in spite of everything hope surged in her. Her father had done the impossible before, and he was, for the moment at least, free.

There was nothing to do but to wait.

It took several days for more detailed news to reach them by the newspapers. When they came they had little to add to the original story: Michael's final appeal had been denied; he was sentenced to six months in a Federal prison; he had been thought dying; incredibly, he had escaped.

Day after day the announcement was made that he was expected to be found momentarily, that he was too ill to go far, that he could not simply vanish. Yet he had vanished, and now week followed week with no more news of him than the brutal summing up at the end of each newspaper account that he was still "at large."

Cathy was quite sure in her heart that if it were at all possible her father would come to Keepsake eventually. Others were sure of the same thing, because suddenly the countryside and the estate itself were full of strangers. Every train brought more: reporters, government men, the angry desperate people who had lost their money and learned that Michael Brett had saved a great deal of his by having it transferred to his daughter before disaster had overtaken him, the curious, the robbed, the hostile, the people whose business it was to find him, all came to take part in the final chapter.

Two of the government men came directly to the house and asked for rooms in which to stay while they waited. They had a search warrant, and they went over every part of the house and outbuildings and grounds as if Michael Brett were capable of magical transformation into a fly or a piece of paper hiding under a blotter or rug. They went through closets and bureau drawers, solemnly inverting shoes and boxes; they peered inside teapots and kitchen canisters; they turned over mattresses and piles of blankets and even emptied flower vases. Cathy, following them those first unbelievable days, stifled an impulse to give way to hysterical laughter.

They were not rude, but their callous indifference was difficult to endure. They went from room to room whistling, their hats on the backs of their heads, their eyes alert and cold.

Cathy had received them with naive courtesy on the first day of their invasion, before the final truth had been thrust upon her that Keepsake was a fallen country and that these, the conquerors, were in supreme authority. She said, "My father is not here."

The two men, their hats which they did not trouble to remove somehow indicative of what was to come, said affably, "Have you any objection to our taking a look?"

"Would it matter if I did object?"

"Afraid not."

She stood back. One of the men took a piece of paper and showed it to her. "Search warrant. We don't mean to trouble you any more than we have to, Miss Brett."

Hester and Rachel and Stacey supervised the scrubbing-out of the whole house after the men had been through it. They took down curtains, waxed floors and furniture, polished glass. But the stain of having been exposed to prying and alien eyes lingered: a house could be shamed just like a person so that it was never really the same again.

The government men took charge of all mail, scanning each piece with callous indifference before handing it over. Lisa snatched hers from them furiously; she had lost her awe of them now she had discovered they were only men. "How dare you! How dare you!"

"Sorry, miss."

The long-awaited letter arrived for Lisa telling her to come home. There was another for Cathy, pleading with Cathy to come at the same time. "Mrs. Ellis will accompany you. I would come at once except that I feel it will be far better for the present for you to come here." Helena's letter, though concerned and hastily written, with underscoring and exclamation points, showed no real comprehension of the situation; she, like everyone else, found it incredible that Michael would not find a way to turn disaster into success. She assured Cathy that these terrible happenings were only temporary: "Heartbreaking for you, my dearest one, but you must not allow yourself to believe what you hear; stories about Michael are always exaggerated. We will wait for him here; he would prefer that, I am sure."

To Lisa she wrote that the Toles were very upset by the unpleasant publicity, of course; fortunately, however, since it was taking place in America they did not regard it too seriously. They were more upset by the dwindling hopes of a settlement for Lisa. But Francis had taken a firm stand, and they agreed now to a quiet wedding as soon as possible. So Lisa was to hurry home without further delay.

There had to be a slight further delay, however, in Lisa's affairs while money was found for her and Mrs. Ellis's passage home. That in the safe had gone long ago, and Aunt Helena did not mention it in her letters.

Lisa, while they waited for a solution to this problem, threw clothes into trunks, stayed in her rooms most of the time, and occasionally flared out in anger at the casual violence which was being perpetrated upon Keepsake. She stared down the government men when she encountered them, and one of them even removed his hat. She dressed with elaborate care; she addressed herself pointedly to Cathy when now and then they were subjected to questions or interviews; she made it quite clear that for her none of this existed. She was magnificent, but she was frantic to get away and it would have been folly to count on her continued support.

They became deluged with letters from Aunt Helena, to Lisa, to Cathy, to Mrs. Ellis, giving instructions, telling them to hurry, but none of them containing money. Cathy promised Lisa she would find some without borrowing from Mrs. Ellis or Philip as Lisa threatened to do; she was given an interval of time when the government men showed suspicion of this flurry of trunk packing. Cathy explained, "My cousin wishes to return home. Mrs. Ellis is to be her companion."

"A little sudden, isn't it? Is there any particular reason?"

"Her mother has sent for her. Is she free to go?"

"We'll see. In a day or two."

Letters came from Randy too. They were worried, anxious letters, asking what he could do to help her. "I would like to come home if I wouldn't be just one more burden to you. I am so glad Philip's there; please tell me what to do."

Cathy's return letters asked him not to come home, for the present at least. She told him that Aunt Helena had asked her to come to France, and she lied a little bit, intimating that she might soon do so.

With her whole heart she was thankful that Randy was not there to witness what was really happening to them all, to Keepsake: the Federal men strolling over the grounds or lolling with outstretched legs on one of the terraces, the carriages which rolled to the rim of the plateau and paused while those seated inside leaned forward to stare at the house.

Sometimes people descended from the carriages. They trespassed on the gardens and terraces, climbing over walls and even slipping through side doors into the house. They looked at Cathy with eyes of curiosity and resentment, occasionally one of them spat on the ground or the floor.

Cathy came upon one of them in the music room one day. She was frightened at first, then she was shaking with a fury such as she never had known before. Her fury demanded violent expression; she wanted nothing in the world except to throw herself on this intruder and pound at him and smash him.

She turned and ran instead. She descended upon the Federal watch-dogs with all the passion of an avenging angel and demanded rights heretofore unthought of, rights as a citizen, a taxpayer, a human being.

The Federal men, startled into recognition of their duty, drew guns and escorted the sightseer from the house.

Cathy felt white and sick. And her fury was wasted, for without keeping a constant guard posted it was impossible to keep the carriages from climbing to the plateau and the curious and bitter from forcing their way inside the house.

She did not protest again, and gradually the daily visits of these invaders became a fairly common sight.

There was nothing to do about them; there was nothing to do about anything except wait.

Two weeks later she was still waiting, they were all waiting, and the strain of waiting was beginning to show on all their nerves.

Lisa, at any rate, was about to escape; the Federal men, after examining all luggage, had said they had no reason to keep them if they wanted to go. The question of wherewithal had been foolishly simple: Cathy had broached the subject to the accountant from the firm of her father's lawyers who had been closeted daily in the office for several weeks going over ledgers and books. "Could I . . . did my father leave instructions . . . about money for me to use?"

"Money?" The accountant looked flabbergasted, then apologetic: "Oh of course, I should have thought."

He asked in a businesslike way how much she wanted and gave her a paper to sign, and that was all there was to it.

Mrs. Ellis was reluctant to go without Cathy, but Cathy persuaded her, intimating as she had to Randy that she doubtless would follow soon, and that in the meantime she had plenty of people to look after her.

To keep Mrs. Ellis from worrying, as well as all the others who watched over Cathy anxiously, it was necessary to smile, to behave as if she were not living in a nightmare, as if there were no thick filmy cobwebs between Cathy and everything she touched.

Lisa, at the moment of parting, realized she was leaving Keepsake for the last time. She turned white; she clutched Cathy as they stood together on the steps of the terrace where they were saying goodbye.

She said in panic: "Cathy! I have a terrible feeling, really terrible. *Triste!* It will never be the same; I can't bear to leave you this way. You think I haven't any feelings but I have. I'll never be happy again, never, I'm sure of it."

Then Lisa threw both arms around Cathy and cried and Cathy cried too: genuine tears of love and loss, not so much for each other but for the things which they had had in common. Lisa finally entered the carriage, Mrs. Ellis got in beside her and the carriage disappeared, as so many carriages had disappeared so many times carrying people away from Keepsake, over the rim of the plateau.

And still there was nothing to do but to wait.

Philip kept in the background during this period, always there and ready to help when he could but not forcing his love and anxiety upon her. Cathy was grateful for that; cut off as she was by these confused feelings of unreality, she could not possibly know what her true feelings were. She loved Philip; there was no doubt of that in her mind. But what her life was to be, how she was to pick up the scattered pieces and put them together, she had no idea.

She was sure that her father would somehow get in touch with her and give her instructions about the enormous responsibilities which were suffocating her. Keepsake, the servants, the tenant farmers and ranchers: something would have to be done about all of them. She could not burden Philip with them, but neither could she just abandon them.

She had a dream one night. She was walking down a long, long corridor to which there was no end. Philip was following her. "Cathy," he called to her, but she walked faster and faster. Then she was running, running; somewhere the corridor must have an end. She heard his voice, "Cathy, Cathy," but she could not stop. She could not turn around. The end of the corridor must be reached, even though she dreaded whatever lay there.

"Cathy!"

She sat up in bed, wide awake. The room was very dark; it was still night.

"Miss Cathy." It was Sam.

"Yes?"

"Hush. Don't make a sound. Dress and come to the south portico as soon as you can."

"Yes, Sam."

"Wear riding clothes," he said. "Don't show a light. I'll be waiting for you there."

He was gone. She got out of bed and dressed quickly. Her hands were not trembling. Her mind was working very quickly, like something apart from her.

She thought, the south portico, yes, that's right. The government men were sleeping in the other wing. At first they had taken turns keeping guard at night, but lately they had both gone to bed. They believed that the remoteness of Keepsake made their work easier. And they believed too, no doubt, that if they waited long enough Michael Brett, notorious for his impatience, would grow tired of waiting and walk into their trap.

When she was dressed she went silently down the corridors and stairway to the south portico. She could not see anything, but Sam's hand reached out of the darkness and guided her. "This way. I saddled the horses and took them to the foot of the drive so they wouldn't make any noise."

As if she were still in her dream she went with Sam down the winding carriage drive, keeping to the soft ground on the edge so that their footsteps would make no sound, keeping too to the shelter of the trees though it was a black night and she would have lost her way without Sam's hand to lead her.

Once there was a scuttling sound in the underbrush around them which set Cathy's heart racing, but it must have been only a rabbit. At the foot of the plateau two horses were saddled and waiting. Sam held his hands for Cathy to mount; he got on his own horse and led the way. They walked the horses, cautiously.

They went silently across the broken ground and into the ravines. Sam, leading the way, followed the stream bed. When finally he halted and dismounted they were in a narrow canyon with sheer walls rising on either side. Cathy, looking about her in the darkness, recognized the spot; they were in the wishing-rock canyon where she and Philip first had found the cave where somebody long ago had camped.

Sam was unloading saddlebags from his horse. He said, "This way," and guided her. Once more she was climbing up the face of the wall which led to the pear-shaped boulder. It seemed to her that she had been climbing, climbing, toward this moment for as long as she could remember. It was like her dream; she had to keep on until she came to the end of the corridor.

On the final ledge she stopped for a second to rest. She leaned against a rock; her heart was pounding. Sam looked back; he pleaded, "Don't slip now, Miss Cathy," and his voice was heavy with anxiety.

They came to the mouth of the cave. She could hear Sam give a little sigh of relief in the darkness. He lighted a candle, shielding it carefully against the wall of the cave. He called, in a low voice: "It's us, we're here, Mr. Michael," and guided her through the low tunnel into the back of the cave.

Her father was lying on a shake-down in a corner. She scarcely recognized him because his face was deathly white and he wore a scraggly beard which was also white. His blazing blue eyes were the same; he raised himself on one elbow and said, "Hello, Cathy," as if he were meeting her under the most ordinary of circumstances. He turned his head toward Sam. "Hurry up with that, will you? You've been gone for hours." He was breathing heavily, almost fighting for each breath; he kept his eyes fastened on Sam as Sam took a bottle of brandy from the saddlebag and filled a tumbler and handed it to him. Michael drank it; he relaxed then and his breathing grew quieter. He said, "That's better," and stayed motionless for several seconds, waiting for the brandy to take its effect. Then he lay back on his improvised bed with his arms under his head. "Well, Cathy, your eyes are as big as saucers."

Sam said, "No wonder, Mr. Michael. I woke her out of a sound sleep."

"Are you sure that nobody followed you?"

"Yes, sir, Mr. Michael."

"Good," Michael said. He looked again at Cathy. He said, "You'd better sit down, little one. You look as if you were about to faint."

"I'm all right, Father."

"Sit down, anyhow."

Sam put one of the saddlebags, now empty, beside her and Cathy sat on it. Sam was placing the provisions which he had brought in orderly fashion against the wall, as if he were setting up housekeeping. The whole thing was as unreal as the nightmare she just had been having.

"Nobody must know that I'm here, of course," her father was saying. "I'm sorry I had to bring you into it, but it couldn't be helped. There are things that need to be done and I'm not quite ready to grace their prison cells yet."

Cathy faltered, "But, Father . . . so close to the house. The Federal men spend every day just tramping around; surely they'll find you here?"

"I've been here for a week," he said. "They haven't found me yet. No, I'll be able to stay here for as long as I need to stay, I think."

She did not ask where he was planning to go next. He said, "Philip told me about the cave months ago, after you and he found it. He was concerned because somebody evidently had been hiding here for some time without being discovered. I remembered it, and I thought that if it had sheltered some other poor devil it should be able to shelter me."

He stretched out a peremptory hand and Sam, pouring another glass of brandy, placed it in his hand.

"No, don't worry about the Federal men," Michael went on contemptuously. "I sent a note to Sam by a Mexican tramp looking for work and he delivered it right under their noses. Sam has been bringing me supplies right under their noses too."

He drank the brandy. He looked very tired; his eyes had receded into dark hollows in his face. He said, "I haven't time to explain everything; you'll have to be getting back to the house before it gets light. But you remember that I told you I had put Keepsake and a great deal of money in your name?"

"Yes, Father."

Didn't he know, she wondered, that everyone knew that now; that because of it they were saying that Michael Brett had betrayed his friends as well as his enemies? He must have known it, but he would not concede, he still had some plan.

"It's safe. It's all safe, no matter what happens to me. I'm helpless, of course, for the present. I've written a letter for Sam to mail to James Talbot telling him to come here to see you and telling him just what I want done. He'll come; he'll take care of things; he'll tell you exactly what to do. That's why I had Sam bring you here tonight. You'd better not come again, not until I send for you; it's too dangerous. Sam will let you know. Goodbye, Cathy, and God bless you."

272

He closed his eyes. He did not seem to be breathing; he looked, in the flickering candlelight, like a man carved out of stone.

Cathy protested, desperately alarmed: "But you can't . . . you are ill!"

He opened his eyes. He chuckled, a little ghost of a chuckle. He said, "Not too ill to get here. I went down into Mexico and up through the mountains. It wasn't exactly like riding in a private car and I've got soft. But I got here, and if they want me they can find me. A man has a right to pick out his own prison, it seems to me."

He chuckled again. His head had slumped forward; he looked as if he had fallen asleep. But he wasn't asleep, for he stretched out his hand for more brandy.

Cathy said, "I'll bring Philip. You can't stay here, Father; it's damp. I'm sure you're too ill!" She jumped up; she was wild now with fright; she repeated: "I'll bring Philip."

Michael said, "No."

"But you can't stay alone like this, without care!"

"Sam takes care of me. The fewer people who know where I am, the better."

"But we can trust Philip."

He said, with strange patience, "My dear Cathy, do you want to get Philip into trouble?"

"No. No, but . . ."

"Philip can't do anything to help me," he said. "There's no use bringing him into it."

"But . . . if you need medicine . . . ?"

"Sam brings me everything I need for the present," he said. "The only thing I really need, and that you can help me to get, is a little more . . . time." His voice lost its intensity; he repeated the last words several times: "Time . . . time . . . that's the important thing," as if he were speaking to himself rather than to her. Then his eyes met hers and he said, "You go now, Cathy. Act as if nothing has happened and wait until you hear from me."

"But if you get worse you'll let me call Philip?"

"Yes, yes . . . but now you must go and go quickly. Sam will tell you; he'll be in touch with me. Go, Cathy. . . ."

There was nothing to do but to obey. Cathy wanted to kiss him but he had closed his eyes as if he wanted above everything else to be alone. She hesitated, and Sam touched her on the hand, gesturing that they must do as he wanted as they always had done.

She followed Sam through the narrow tunnel once more. She

said, "I can find my way. You must stay here to take care of him."

"It's better if I'm not missing in the morning, Miss Cathy."

He was right, of course. She was not accustomed to thinking in terms of being hunted. She felt a spasm of fear; half way down the side of the canyon she had to stop for a minute because she was trembling so violently she could not go on. She turned blindly to Sam, who was so much wiser and more controlled than she. "Will they be able to find him, Sam? Do you think they'll find him?"

Sam said, with dreadful simplicity, "No, Miss Cathy, I don't think they'll find him before something else does."

She knew what he meant. And she knew that her father also knew, and that he had known all the time.

What was it he had said: that a man had a right to pick his own prison?

There was a light in the east when they got back to the foot of the plateau where they parted. Sam led the horses around the base of the plateau, approaching the stables by the long way where he would be less easily discerned from the house.

Cathy went to her own room. She did not meet anybody, though she could hear some of the servants stirring at the back of the house.

She sat for a long time at her window, leaning with her face in her hands, thinking of nothing.

Chapter 29

ONE OF THE government men, on an indefatigable tour of inspection, discovered a pair of riding boots thrust back in Cathy's closet with soles still slightly damp. He called his fellow; together they studied the boots and each scratch on their polished surface, and drew the accurate conclusion that an excursion had been made with these boots during the night and that the excursion had been partly on foot over rough terrain.

They became quite sure now that Michael Brett was hiding somewhere in the vicinity. They believed their vigil drawing to an end; they had only to find out where the hiding place was, which did not appear too difficult.

Two days later some of their confidence was ebbing. The country was wild and unfamiliar; it resisted their efforts to uncover its secret as Cathy, white, tired, her eyes enormous under the strain, was finding strength to resist them.

Men were beating the countryside. Colonel Snowden, lately sent to Magoon to supervise the entire operation of bringing this case to a close, because the people involved were so important, was pacing up and down one of the large formal drawing-rooms. Colonel Snowden did not keep his hat on his head; his manners were courtly; it was evident that he had a headache and he detested an inquisition of this kind where some innocent by-stander, in this case a young girl with a sweet smile and big sad eyes, had to be questioned as if she were a criminal.

Cathy sat in a straight chair, outwardly calm, though her hands hidden in the folds of her dress were clenched so tightly that her whole body ached. From time to time she became aware of their betraying rigidity; she forced her hands to lie, relaxed and quiet, in her lap, but when she forgot they went back to their former position.

Colonel Snowden's head was down and his hands were clasped behind his back. He was baffled and unhappy. Two of his men sat on fragile gilt chairs; they looked a little ridiculous and were unhappily aware of the fact.

Sheriff Anderson, the local officer, sat in one corner, his blue eyes kind and watchful. Philip stood at a window with his back to them, his whole attitude rigid with protest and anger.

"Miss Brett, we have our duty to perform like anyone else," Colonel Snowden said. "We aren't trying to hurt you; we don't mean to be cruel."

No, they did not mean to be cruel. None of them meant to be cruel, not the man leaning back on a priceless chair and straightening up again as if he were a schoolboy caught at something he should not be doing, nor Colonel Snowden with his soft voice and his quick eyes waiting to pounce on any mistake that she made, nor the sheriff thoughtfully chewing on a toothpick and disapproving of the Colonel's methods but helpless to do anything about them, nor the people who shouted ugly words at her because they had lost their money and were desperate, nor the men hunting with dogs and calling to each other as if they were on the trail of an animal, nor the merely curious who only came and stared, as if the tragedy were a drama being enacted for their entertainment.

"We do not wish to intrude on your personal rights more than necessary."

"I understand."

Personal rights. The Colonel did not wish to intrude upon her personal rights, which was unnecessarily punctilious, for she no longer had any personal rights. The estate, the gardens, even the house, were filled with people. All their personal photographs and photographs of Keepsake with strange titles were in the newspapers. There were fantastic descriptions of Keepsake itself and the life which was supposed to be led there, so that they sounded like people taking part in a bacchanalian orgy.

They were not themselves any more: they were part of a sensational mystery. "The Unsolved Brett Disappearance," it was called, and everywhere, all over the world, people were reading the intimate details of her father's life twisted into lurid distortions.

With her whole soul Cathy longed to shout the truth at them

that, whatever else he had been, Michael Brett once had been, to a child, a knight in shining armor, but that would do no good. He was beyond their reach for a little while, at least. He could not be harmed more than he had harmed himself.

"Miss Brett, we believe that you know where your father is."

She did not answer. Even he, she thought, with his sharp face and his relentless questions, could not imagine that she would betray her father.

"You do know, do you not?"

She still did not answer. Silence was her only weapon; as long as she did not answer they could not trick her into telling what they wanted to know.

Colonel Snowden sighed, a deep sigh. "Miss Brett, don't you realize that you are being very foolish?"

No answer.

"We could arrest you, you know. For withholding information necessary for the apprehending of a criminal."

He watched her closely. She saw that he expected her to deny that her father was a criminal; he was trying to make her angry.

"You must know that your father will be found. And that the charge against him will be far more serious than if he were to give himself up voluntarily?"

No answer.

"Very well, Miss Brett. We will assume that you do not know where your father is, but that you are willing to help us as much as you can. Will you answer a few questions?"

She moistened her lips. "If I can."

"You went for a ride late last Thursday night, did you not?"

"Perhaps. I do quite often ride at night."

"Were you alone?"

"Perhaps. I sometimes ride alone, sometimes not."

"Who saddled your horse for you?"

"I quite often saddle them for myself."

"But on this occasion someone went with you. Two horses left the stables that night, though great care was taken to make it seem as if they had not."

No answer.

"Where did you go that night, Miss Brett?"

"I go various places when I ride, no particular place."

"Such as?"

"Sometimes down into the valley. Sometimes up. It's hard to say."

"Who was riding with you?"
"I don't know."
"Who usually rides with you?"
"My cousin Lisa used to ride with me."
"But she has been gone for some time, has she not?"
"Yes."
"Who else?"
"Anybody. Sometimes one of the stableboys."
"We've questioned them. They all deny knowing anything about it."
"Sometimes a guest."
"You have no guests at present, I believe?"
"No."

Philip made a violent protesting movement. Colonel Snowden's eyes moved reflectively toward him and back again. "Could it have been Doctor Langley who was with you?"

They had already investigated Philip and found that Philip had spent that night with Doctor Blake taking care of an emergency accident; Philip had been called as consultant and had been far away. So Cathy said with confidence, "No."

"Are you sure?"
"Yes, quite sure."
"How can you be so sure when you are so vague as to the actual night in question?"
"I am quite sure because I haven't ridden with Philip for a long time, over a year. At night, that is."
"But you have ridden with him at other times?"
"Yes. Yes, of course."
"Possibly this particular time has slipped your mind. Possibly the moonlight made it seem like day."
"There was no moon." She gripped her dress with her hands; her heart began to pound, sickeningly.

Colonel Snowden said smoothly, "Yes, Miss Brett? There was, as you say, no moon on the night in question . . . ?"

Cathy was very quiet. Philip had jerked around; he was glaring at Colonel Snowden. It was no use, Cathy thought. They were too relentless; they kept pounding at her, and she was no good at half truths. Sooner or later, if she tried to deceive them with evasions, they would trip her up.

Colonel Snowden continued, pressing his advantage: "Then you do remember the ride to which I am referring, Miss Brett?"
"Yes."

"You went out that night?"
"Yes."
"Where did you go?"
"I refuse absolutely to answer any more questions."
"Who went with you?"
"I refuse absolutely to answer any more questions."
"You realize that refusal on your part is tantamount to an admission that you saw your father that night?"
"I refuse absolutely . . ."

Philip was staring at her, dumbfounded. Colonel Snowden drew a deep breath. It was her eyes, so grave, so full of sorrow, that baffled him. He had no idea what to do with her; she looked so gentle to be so obdurate. He tried another line: "Miss Brett, you love your father, don't you?"

She turned her head and looked away from him. The whole proceedings began to seem incredibly foolish. She answered politely, "Yes, I do."

"Wouldn't you like to help him?"

A little smile appeared on her face. Colonel Snowden felt himself convicted of being very naive, and it did not help his temper. He slapped his hat on his head and slammed out of the room, with the others, one by one, following him. The questioning, for the time being, was over; but it would begin again soon; it would go on and on; Cathy did not deceive herself about that.

Cathy was left alone with Philip. He said, "Cathy, for heaven's sake, let me do something. I can't watch you going through this any longer."

"There isn't anything you can do. It won't last much longer."

"It's insane. What is he trying to prove? How could you possibly know where your father is?"

"I do know where he is. That's why we must be so careful."

He stared at her blankly.

She closed her eyes. She rested with her head on the back of the chair. She said, "I'm so afraid, all the time, that I'll say the wrong thing and give it away. . . ."

"Do you mean that he's here, in the house?"

"No."

"Where, then?"

"I can't tell you, Philip. He told me not to; he said it might get you in trouble."

"You've spoken to him?"

"Yes, that night . . . the night they've been talking about. . . ."

She opened her eyes. Philip was still staring at her but his thoughts had moved away; he was thinking intently. She had a great feeling of relief, as if a burden of responsibility had been transferred from her shoulders to his. Philip would take charge; Philip would know what to do.

He said, "Don't be a fool. Where is he?"

"In the cave. That cave that we found and that you told him about where somebody had been hiding."

"The cave? Oh yes." She could see him remembering. He said, "That's a good place. I'll go see him. I'll be careful; I'll go from the opposite side, so don't worry, darling."

She said, "He's ill. He's dying."

"Yes," Philip said. "I thought he must be. I'm glad he made it; I'm glad he got back." And then he said again, "I'll go to him tonight, Cathy. I'll do everything I can."

"You'll be careful?"

"Don't worry."

"I'm glad you know. I'm glad you're going to him; he's so alone, so terribly alone, that's what worries me more than anything. Even Sam daren't go very often now; he has to go on foot when he does. Oh Philip, he always wanted people around him, and now, when he's dying, he's alone."

"Yes," Philip said. "I know."

He did know. "Philip," Cathy said. "They won't find him, will they?"

"No, they won't find him."

He stood looking down at her and then he put both of his arms about her. She felt some of the bands enclosing her heart loosen.

He took her face in his hands. He kissed her hair, her eyes, her lips. He said, "My darling, my sweet sweet love."

"Philip. Philip."

"You do love me, don't you?"

"So much. I've always loved you so much."

"My darling. My darling. I wish I could spare you this."

"Philip, if they do find him they will take him away, won't they? Even though he is so ill."

"I suppose so. Yes, they would have to."

"I can't tell them where he is. I can't."

"No."

"But I had to tell you. I couldn't just let him die there."

"Cathy, dearest, my dearest."

"I hope they won't find him. I don't know if it's right or wrong but I hope they never find him."

"They won't."

"Philip, he has a right to hide, hasn't he, when he's so ill? Even an animal . . ."

She leaned against Philip. Suddenly her whole body was tortured with sobs which she could not control.

Sam came into the room. He stood in the doorway; she became aware of him before she saw or heard him. She lifted her head; she was still torn with violent grief beyond her control and she sensed immediately what he had come to say.

Sam said, "I think Doctor Philip had better try to get there now, if he can make it."

"Sam . . ."

"I've just come from there," Sam said. He repeated heavily, "I think you should go now, Doctor Philip, if you can make it."

"Yes, I'll make it," Philip said.

"You know the way?"

"Yes."

"They'll be watching you. You'll have to be careful. It would be a cruel thing for them to find him . . . now."

"I'll be careful," Philip said. "I'll ride off toward Magoon and then come back by the upper canyon."

Cathy started up wildly, "I must come with you."

Sam's arm came around her, detaining her; he said, "They're watching you in particular, Miss Cathy."

They were three conspirators. Sam, acting old and doddering and half deaf, amazingly had escaped the attention of the enemy, but he too had to remain behind now.

They could not even watch Philip ride off. They waited for his return, going about their separate affairs, meeting only when they would ordinarily have met and then without giving indication of what lay between them: acting, always acting, for the benefit of the hostile audience imposed upon them.

"Lunch, Miss Catherine."

"Thank you."

"Tea, Miss Catherine."

"Thank you."

Happily they were alone together with Sam serving tea and Cathy sipping it when Philip returned. One glance at Philip's face told them both that the need for further acting was over.

But Cathy cried out in vain, as people must cry: "Philip! He isn't . . . he isn't . . . !"

"Yes," Philip said. "He's dead."
"You were with him."
"Yes."
"I'm glad! I'm glad!"
Her voice was rising; it would attract watching men, but that now did not matter. She could not stop herself, "I'm glad! I'm glad!"
"He's safe now," Sam said.
Philip's arms were tight about Cathy. She clung to him, fighting the dark waters which were closing over her head.

Michael Brett was dead. He was safe: rightly or wrongly he had chosen his own prison. Wherever he was now, he was free of his pursuers, of himself, of the fierce driving instincts which never had let him rest.

Those left behind had to pick up the wreckage.

Colonel Snowden threatened furiously to arrest Cathy, to arrest Philip, to arrest every servant in the household. Everywhere he had turned in his inquiry he had met with a blank wall of resistance. And now, as a final humiliation, he learned that his quarry had been living almost within sight of the house where he and his men had been quartered for weeks.

The furor on the grounds became greater than ever. Colonel Snowden made no attempt to keep anybody off; he considered privacy a luxury which Keepsake had forfeited. He decided finally, however, that to arrest everybody on the place on the charge of aiding and abetting a fugitive from justice was a luxury which he himself could not afford; he was in danger of becoming a laughing-stock as it was. He confined himself to shouting orders in a large voice to the men driving a wagon along the narrow stream bed to fetch the mortal remains of Michael Brett from its hiding place.

Cathy kept to the house. She heard the shouts of the men and the sound of wagon wheels as they rolled along the drive and she knew what they signified. But it did not matter what they did to Michael Brett now: everything that anybody could do to Michael Brett now, to help him or hurt him, was over and done with.

But the train of events which is set in motion by each person on the day of his birth, and which goes on after his death, continued.

Mr. Talbot came to Keepsake, accompanied by four lawyers. He explained to Cathy, as her father had done and as she already knew, that though the Brett Mining Industries, or United Mine Industries, and many other companies depending on it, had failed, she was nevertheless an enormously wealthy woman. She was safe and Keepsake was safe.

They all sat in the library, Cathy at one end of the long table where Michael Brett had held so many directors' meetings. Mr. Talbot sat at the other end with the four lawyers in between. The lawyers said very little, but they nodded their heads occasionally in agreement.

Mr. Talbot read off the list of holdings which he said now belonged to Cathy. There were the names of companies, of banks, of real estate which she had never seen. And there was an enormous amount of what Mr. Talbot called liquid holdings: Michael, Mr. Talbot said, had been systematically robbing, that was to say liquidating, his own companies for over a year to transfer them into her name. This money must be reinvested . . .

Mr. Talbot fussed with the papers in his hand for a minute and then he said, "If you'll sign these papers we'll get things in order for you. You've read the instructions from your father so you know that is what he wanted you to do."

"Yes," Cathy said. She lifted the pen to sign, as she had done thousands of times, millions of times it seemed, and put it down on the table again. She asked, "What would have happened to this money if it had not been transferred to my name?"

"I beg your pardon?"

"If it still belonged to my father, what would have happened to it?"

Mr. Talbot moistened his lips. "Believe me, there's no culpability on your part. . . ."

"What would have happened to it?"

"It would have been thrown into the receivership."

"The stockholders would not have lost their money?"

"Perhaps not. Not all of it at least. The company might even have been saved . . . but you aren't responsible for that."

She said, "I want everything to be made over again to my father's name."

"But that's impossible. It will be absorbed by the receivership; you don't realize what you are saying."

"I know what I am saying. All this is his, not mine."

"It's yours, legally and morally. Nobody could contest that, believe me."

"It belonged to my father. I want it put into his name."

"He is dead. It won't help him, and he went to great lengths to safeguard it for you."

"It's his. He might have found a way . . . now he can't. I want it put into his name."

"My dear child. You are distraught, naturally; we are here to look after your interests. Just sign your name on these papers and trust me."

It was odd, she thought, how difficult it was to give something away if it was large enough. People told you that it was yours and then they told you that you could not give it away. Like the jewels, she thought; she remembered Lisa saying, you really are a baby in some ways, Cathy.

Remembering that helped to dispel the panic that was beginning to undermine her resolution. She stopped pleading; she sat up straight. She asked quietly, "Haven't you said that this money belongs to me?"

"Yes, of course, but . . ."

"Then I wish it to be transferred back into my father's name, as part of his estate . . ."

Mr. Talbot glanced at her and then at the table. He asked, "Everything?"

"Almost everything. There are a few people who must be taken care of."

"Keepsake? You'll never be able to keep it under these circumstances."

"I realize that. No, not Keepsake."

"There will be little left, you know. And that little will be tied up for a long time, perhaps always."

"I understand."

"There's your brother Randy, too, to be taken into consideration."

But he had no case there; Randy did not want the money, nor need it.

The lawyers conferred; they were thrown into consternation. They glanced at James Talbot, who refused to meet their eyes. Mr. Crown, junior member of the firm of Kirk and Crown, said, "You are very young, my advice to you is to wait. . . ."

"Thank you. I don't wish to wait, but you are very kind, and thank you."

Nobody could understand that the only purpose for the money

was to be put to the use of clearing the name of the man who had amassed it, wisely or unwisely.

Except Mr. Talbot. Mr. Talbot, still speaking in riddles, said, " 'Go and do thou likewise.' "

Mr. Crown looked as if he believed that Mr. Talbot had lost his mind along with numerous others, and that he was making a mental note to report this decision when he returned to New York.

It had seemed very simple to Cathy in the beginning, but of course it wasn't that simple. When an enormous amount of money was involved, she discovered, human nature being what it was, nothing was simple. It took endless hours, of preparing new papers, of attempts to dissuade her. Only Mr. Talbot did not attempt to dissuade her, and his attitude was more of a man witnessing a miracle than of understanding.

But now that she had taken her affairs into her own hands, Cathy felt calm and sure. She stated exactly what she wanted done with certain money while it was still in her possession: trust funds for the older servants and advance wages for the others, and an opportunity for the tenant farmers and other employees to buy their homes and pieces of land.

"You would have made a good businesswoman," Mr. Talbot stated regretfully.

They all believed, these men gathered about the table, that she was making a noble and sacrificial gesture. They had no idea that above everything else she wanted to be free: free to choose her own life, free from this terrific burden of obligation and guilt.

Philip alone understood and Philip upheld her. She saw that it would be a relief to Philip too when the whole business was over and done with.

But even Philip could not come between her and the shock of realization one morning that, by her own decision, Keepsake was no longer hers.

She came down the great staircase. She came down this particular staircase almost always these days, for a number of reasons, going out of her way to do so, though it was seldom used otherwise. Several men were engaged in taking down paintings and tapestries and examining them.

She asked furiously, "What are you doing?"

"Cataloguing the interior of the house, madam. The contents have to be catalogued before they can be sold."

"Oh, of course."

She went blindly past them and down the corridor to the morning-room. At the fruitwood desk she put her head on her arms and cried until all the soreness in her heart was cried out.

Philip had accepted the offer of an opening in a hospital in Baltimore and when they were married that was where they would live. Philip took the matter of their marriage into his own hands; he brought a minister to the house one day and they were married in the blue parlor with Sam and Stacey and Rachel and Hester for guests.

They had a strange honeymoon. They remained at Keepsake, together watching the final preparations for its abandonment. They packed personal belongings; they said goodbye to Sam and Stacey and Hester and Rachel, who had been persuaded to return to New Orleans for the time being at least, and to others who were scattering everywhere.

She and Philip did all these sad things, but they were not altogether sad, because they were together in doing them. Their fingers touched and their eyes met. They were in love, and Cathy became aware, more and more, that a strong new life was surging up on the ruins of the old one.

She asked Philip one day, "Was I right to break up the lives of so many people? Should I have tried to keep some of it together . . . Keepsake?"

"Do you regret it already?"

"Not for me," she said, though this was not altogether true, and Philip knew it. He said, smiling at her, that Keepsake would not have fitted very well in the life of a poor doctor's wife and that was what she was now.

"Sam and Stacey and Hester . . . their whole lives were here."

"I know. But it had to be everything or nothing, so don't look back."

Don't look back. Look forward; that was the trust in the future to which she had to cling.

She asked Philip another time: "Won't having me for a wife hurt your career?"

"In what way?"

"People watching me, staring at me, taking pictures and asking questions . . . all that?"

He laughed, "My dearest Cathy, as Mrs. Philip Langley you will be a nonentity."

"Oh." A little startled, she said, "I'm not sure I'll like that."
"Yes, you will; I'll see that you like it."
"Oh, Philip."
"My dearest." He held her; with Philip's arms around her she was aware that the pieces of her life were coming together and she was coming into her own.

Nevertheless there were times, even with Philip's arms around her, when she realized that she was about to embark on a strange new adventure; she was about to be thrust into a new way of life, far different from the old one, and that even with Philip's help it was not going to be as easy as she once might have imagined it might be.

It was their next to the last day. All the trunks and valises had been packed into wagons and taken away. In the morning they too would be gone.

They stood on the edge of the plateau. Behind them the house seemed already to be stripped and emptied.

In spite of herself Cathy shivered.

"You're cold," Philip said. "I'll get you a wrap."

"No, I'm not cold. Really, Philip."

"I'll only be a minute."

He went up the driveway to the house and she was left alone.

The sun was setting. Its last slanting rays struck the windows of the house and blinded them, so that the house looked blank and deserted.

Against the spiny background of the long mountain range behind it in the distance, the house had a naked defenseless look. It was easy to imagine it as it would look in a few years. Nobody ever would live in it again: it was too big, too extravagant in conception and demands, too inconvenient and removed. The dazzling white marble façade would be blackened by time and neglect, the curved balustrades of balconies and verandas would be broken and missing. Grounds and terraces and gardens would wither and die for lack of attention, until presently the plateau would have the bare wind-swept look of other mountain plateaus, and the only foliage would be piñons and juniper and mountain oak which were sturdy enough to stand up against blazing sun and savage mountain storms. In the fading light it already had met this fate: it was only the ghost of a house, abandoned, besieged from within and without, the object of curiosity seekers.

Cathy's teeth were chattering uncontrollably; yes, she was cold, very very cold.

And then footsteps sounded coming toward her, walking at first and then running; it was Philip, bringing her a wrap.